The Dog Book

The Dog Book

edited by Jerrold Mundis

ARBOR HOUSE
New York

With love, this is for my sons—
Shep Siegel and Jesse Mundis

Also by Jerrold Mundis
Gerhardt's Children
The Dogs (originally under the pseudonym Robert Calder)
The Guard Dog (nonfiction)

Library of Congress Catalogue Card Number: 83-70481
ISBN: 0-87795-461-5
MANUFACTURED IN THE UNITED STATES OF AMERICA
10 9 8 7 6 5 4 3 2 1

This book is printed on acid free paper. The paper in this book meets the guidelines for
permanence and durability of the Committee on Production Guidelines for Book Longev-
ity of the Council on Library Resources.

Designed by Antler & Baldwin, Inc.

Acknowledgments

"Blue and Some Other Dogs" by John Graves. From *From A Limestone Ledge* by John Graves. Copyright 1977, 1978, 1979, 1980 by John Graves. Reprinted by permission of Alfred A. Knopf, Inc.

"The Dog That Bit People" by James Thurber. Copyright 1933, 1961 by James Thurber. From *My Life and Hard Times,* published by Harper & Row. Reprinted by permission of Helen Thurber.

"Elegy for a Dead Labrador" by Lars Gustafsson. Reprinted by permission; copyright 1981 by Lars Gustafsson. Originally in The New Yorker.

"Kooa's Song" by Farley Mowat. From *Never Cry Wolf* by Farley Mowat. Copyright 1963 by Farley Mowat Ltd. Reprinted by permission of Little, Brown and Company in association with the Atlantic Monthly Press and by permission of the Canadian publishers, McClelland and Stewart Limited, Toronto.

"Poor Tweed" by Ian Niall. Copyright 1975 by Ian Niall -0688- 03031-9. Reprinted by permission of the author.

"A Robust Matter of Some Delicacy" by James Herriot. Copyright 1976, 1977 by James Herriot. Reprinted from *All Things Wise and Wonderful* by James Herriot by permission of St. Martin's Press, Inc., New York, and Harold Ober Associates, Inc.

"Nuptials" by J. R. Ackerley. Copyright 1967 by J. R. Ackerley, Fleet Press Corporation, New York. Reprinted by permission.

"The Origin of the Dog" by Edwin H. Colbert. Copyright the American Museum of Natural History, 1939. Reprinted with permission from Natural History, 1939.

"An Honest Dog" by Donald McCaig. Copyright 1983 by Donald McCaig. Printed by permission of the author.

"Dogs, and the Tug of Life" by Edward Hoagland. Copyright 1975 by Edward Hoagland. Reprinted from *Red Wolves and Black Bears,* by Edward Hoagland, by permission of Random House, Inc.

"A Boston Terrier," pages 68–70 from *One Man's Meat* by E. B. White. Copyright 1939, 1967 by E. B. White. First published in Harper's Magazine, July 1939. Reprinted by permission of Harper & Row, Publishers, Inc.

"Guard and War Dogs in History" by Jerrold Mundis. From *The Guard Dog,* copyright 1969, 1970 by Jerrold Mundis. Reprinted by permission of the author.

"Lurchers" by Leslie Norris. Reprinted by permission; copyright 1978 by The New Yorker Magazine, Inc.

"Rufus" by H. Allen Smith. Copyright 1972 by H. Allen Smith. Reprinted by permission of the Harold Matson Company, Inc.

"Dog-Fighting and Baiting Sports" by Phil Drabble. Copyright 1948 by Phil Drabble. Reprinted by permission of the author.

"On Dogs and Introductions: A Letter" by John Steinbeck. Copyright 1964 by John Steinbeck. Reprinted by permission of McIntosh and Otis, Inc.

"For I Will Consider Your Dog Molly" by David Lehman. Copyright 1980, 1983 by David Lehman, all rights reserved. Reprinted by permission of the author.

"Huskies" by Robert Dovers. From *My Friends, the Huskies* by Robert Dovers. Copyright 1957 by Robert Dovers. Reprinted by permission of Farrar, Straus & Giroux, Inc.

"Dog Days" by Konrad Lorenz. From *Man Meets Dog* by Konrad Lorenz. Copyright 1953 by Konrad Lorenz. Reprinted by permission of Houghton Mifflin Company and of Methuen as the British publisher.

"My Last Five" by Elizabeth of the German Garden. Excerpts from *All the Dogs of My Life* by "Elizabeth." Copyright 1936 by Doubleday & Company, Inc. Reprinted by permission of the publisher.

"Country Matters" by Vance Bourjaily. Copyright 1973 by Vance Bourjaily. Reprinted by permission of Russell & Volkening as agents for the author.

"To the Man Who Killed My Dog" by Richard Joseph. From *A Letter to the Man Who Killed My Dog* by Richard Joseph. Copyright 1956 by Richard Joseph. All rights reserved. Reprinted by permission of Frederick Fell Publishers, Inc., New York.

"The Story of Two Dogs" by Doris Lessing. Copyright 1958, 1962, 1963 by Doris Lessing. Reprinted from *A Man and Two Women* by Doris Lessing, by permission of Simon & Schuster, a Division of Gulf & Western Corporation and Curtis Brown Ltd., London, on behalf of Doris Lessing.

The engravings are from the collection of Kathy Darling, Dog Ink, 46 Cooper Lane, Larchmont, New York 10538, and are reprinted here by her permission and from the editor's collection and are reprinted here by permission.

Contents

Introduction

I like dogs—not as pets in the usual pejorative sense of that word, or as living possessions, but as creatures in their own right, as, literally, Man's Best Friend. A good argument can be made that they're the next best thing that ever happened to us (the first being that *we* happened).

We got together with them, or they got together with us, about fifteen thousand years ago. That's not more than a few eye-blinks in our long march from the shrouded beginning, and even less in the dog's. On the other hand it covers just about all our history you can think of. They were with us long before we set up housekeeping in any but the most temporary way, long before we struggled toward even the first *idea* of the pyramids, long before Troy fell, or Rome rose. We go back a long way. And our relationship is unique. Though we take advantage of the dog and it gains advantage of us (the weight in our favor), there is a mutual and abiding altruism here, loyalty, even love. There simply isn't any comparable bond between two species in all the natural world.

To attempt to formulate the essence of the dog, or even to pin down the basis of the relationship between it and man in an introduction, a long essay, or even an entire book is nearly as futile as attempting to explain man himself or his relationship with his fellows in the same way. We've been working on those latter questions probably since the day we realized that we existed, and certainly from the time we began to keep any sort of record of ourselves. And in that record, we included dogs from the first—they appear in neolithic pictographs, in hieroglyphics, cuneiform; they're seen in Assyrian bas-reliefs, pictured on Greek pottery; addressed by emerging religions and codes of law; found in the meters of song and heroic epic. There's scarcely a moment in anything we can remotely call of our conscious life when the dog hasn't been our companion.

I've lived with several dogs over the years. All were individuals, different from one another even when they belonged to the same breed. They gave me much—comfort, trouble, camaraderie, tribulations. In retrospect, I don't regret a one of them, and each made my life larger and more full, even when they put me through trials that I would decline, trembling and looking for the near exit, to face again.

This isn't the place to go into any of those stories, and there are a number of other dogs just beyond these first pages waiting to take their place on stage. I'll mention only one, the first, and her just briefly. She was a small dog named Friskie, with no spectacular ability or trait, whom I and my brother appropriated when she was about a year and a half old from a neighborhood family whose children abused her badly. She was a mixed breed, a little under twenty pounds, with

9

gentle eyes, a long though wide face, hanging black ears and hair of moderate length that was smooth and soft, mostly russet, with black markings. A fistfight was involved in the appropriation. The parents of her former family were happy enough to see taken out of their home this creature who had innocently drawn forth and revealed to them qualities in their children they did not like, and since my own parents, both of whom had been raised with dogs, had been promising us one for some time, Friskie was ours.

She seemed not to associate her previous abuse with people in general, and within a week or two was buoyant and cheerful, and throughout her life willingly extended the benefit of the doubt to new persons she met. The only lingering trace of her early experience was a sudden nervousness and unwillingness to accompany us whenever, during the course of our play, my brother, my sister or I happened to wander into the vicinity of the house from which we'd taken her.

I remember: summer in Chicago. Night. In bed on the screened-in back porch. Happily tired after a day of play. The night and darkness pleasingly heavy in some way. The smallest of breezes rustling the leaves of the big maple tree just outside the open windows. Fireflies randomly flashing. And Friskie. The sheer joy of her presence, of loving and being loved. There. Then. Immediately. And, one night, when I was seven, eight, maybe even nine, a sudden seizure of shock and horror when I realized—for whatever reason the knowledge had come—that someday she would die and be taken from me.

Many years later in New York when my wife was out walking our dog early one morning, before the onset of rush hour when the streets were still empty, a man jumped from the doorway of a ramshackle building and made a grab for her. Olex, a heavy-boned, quiet, introverted German shepherd of restraint and a dignity that prevented him from being as fully happy as he would have liked, but which he could not overcome, surged from around the fender of a car, where unseen he had been investigating scents. He hit the extension of his leash, went up on his hind legs and roared and clashed his teeth into the face of the attacker, whom my wife had not seen until that instant. The man fled. In New York, during that one crucial moment, my dog had displayed aggression for what was his.

That's already two dogs, and a bit longer than I'd intended.

To this particular book then. The first hope is that the selections will entertain you. The second is that each will illuminate some aspect of the diverse relationship we have with the dog. There isn't any fiction here. While some good work exists in that form, I felt the book could best achieve its purpose if I reserved fiction for some other occasion.

I was unwilling, however, to sacrifice the magic of story-telling, the pleasure of carefully crafted language. I therefore chose contributors for their literary merits, whether they published their works as naturalists, philosophers, scientists, scholars, historians or literary artists. They all share in common, for our purposes, the ability to write well in addition to their knowledge of dogs and close experience with them.

They are mainly contemporary writers, but a few have been drawn from the past and some of the selections concern themselves with history. There are memoirs here, essays, adventures, letters, portraits, pensées and recollections. They depict the dog in a variety of roles, from shepherd, hunter and guard to friend and companion. Some of them are humorous, provocative or sad; some compelling, insightful or tense; others poignant, cheerful or exhilarating.

I have included three poems. Why, in a book of nonfiction? Well, each clearly addresses an actual event. And poets shouldn't be penalized simply for telling their truths in fancy dress. And finally, because I like them.

That is the basis, in the end, on which all the decisions were made.

William Cole, another poet, has stated: "In every writer's past there's a dog or two waiting to be resurrected into print."

He's right, and I feel fortunate for that. I hope this anthology makes you feel the same way.

—Jerrold Mundis

Blue and Some Other Dogs

by JOHN GRAVES

ONE cool still night last March, when the bitterest winter in decades was starting to slack its grip and the first few chuck-will's-widows were whistling tentative claims to nest territories, the best dog I ever owned simply disappeared. Dogs do disappear, of course. But not usually dogs like Blue or under conditions like ours here in the cedar hills.

A crossbred sheep dog, he had spent his whole ten years of life on two North Texas country places and had not left the vicinity of the house at either of them without human company since the age of two or less, when his mother was still alive and we also had an aging and lame and anarchic dachshund who liked to tempt the two of them out roaming after armadillos and feral cats and raccoons and other varmints. This happened usually at night when we'd neglected to bring the dachshund into the house, or he had tricked his way outside by faking a call of nature or pushing open an unlatched screen door. The dachshund, named Watty (it started as Cacahuate or Peanut), had a very good nose and the two sheep dogs didn't, and having located quarry for them he would scream loud sycophantic applause as they pursued it and attacked, sometimes mustering the courage to run in and bite an exposed hind leg while the deadly mother and son kept the front part occupied.

It was fairly gory at times, and I'm not all that much at war with varmints except periodically with individual specimens that have developed a taste for chickens or kid goats or garden corn. In fact, I rather like having them around. But the main problem was the roaming itself, which sometimes took the dogs a mile or so from home and onto other property. In the country wandering dogs are an abomination, usually in time shifting their attention from wild prey to poultry and sheep and goats and calves, and nearly always dying sooner or later from a rifle bullet or buckshot or poison bait, well enough deserved. Few people have lived functionally on the land without having to worry sooner or later about such raiders, and the experience makes them jumpy about their own dogs' habits. Thus they find much irony in city visitors' standard observation that country dogs are very lucky to have so much space for roving and playing.

To cope, you can chain or pen your dogs when they aren't with you, or you can teach them to stay at home. While I favor the latter approach, with three dogs on hand and one of them a perverse and uncontrollable old house pet too entwined with my own past and with the family to get rid of, it was often hard to make training stick. At least it was until the dachshund perished under the wheels of a pickup truck, his presence beneath it unsuspected by the driver and his cranky senile arrogance too great to let him

11

scuttle out of the way when the engine started.

Blue's mother was a brindle-and-white Basque sheep dog from Idaho, of a breed said to be called Pannish, though you can't prove that by me since I've never seen another specimen. Taut and compact and aggressive, she was quick to learn but also quick to spot ways to nudge rules aside or to get out of work she didn't savor. She came to us mature and a bit overdisciplined, and if you tried to teach her a task too roughly she would refuse permanently to have anything to do with it. I ruined her for cow work by whipping her for running a heifer through a net fence for the hell of it, and ever afterward if I started dealing with cattle when she was with me, she would go to heel or disappear. Once while chousing a neighbor's Herefords out of an oat patch toward the spate-ripped fence watergap through which they had invaded it, I looked around for Pan and glimpsed her peeking at me slyly from a shin oak thicket just beyond the field's fringe, hiding there till the risk of being called on for help was past.

Not that she feared cows or anything else that walked—or crawled or flew or swam or for that matter rolled on wheels. She attacked strange dogs like a male and had a contemptuous hatred of snakes that made her bore straight in to grab them and shake them dead, even after she had been bitten twice by rattlers, once badly. After such a bout I've seen her with drops of amber venom rolling down her shoulder where fangs had struck the thick fine hair but had failed to reach her skin. Occasionally she bit people too, always men, though she was nervous enough around unfamiliar children that we never trusted her alone with them. Women, for her own secret reasons, she liked more or less indiscriminately.

She was a sort of loaded weapon, Pan, and in town there would have been no sense in keeping such a dog around, except maybe to patrol fenced grounds at night. But we were living then on a leased place just beyond the western honky-tonk fringe of Fort Worth, where drunken irrationals roved the byways after midnight, and I was often away. There, what might otherwise have been her worst traits were reassuring. She worshiped my wife and slept beside the bed when I was gone, and would I am certain have died in defense of the household with the same driven ferocity she showed in combat with wild things.

A big boar coon nearly got her one January night, before she had Blue to help her out. The old dachshund sicked her on it by the barn, where it had come for a bantam supper, and by the time I had waked to the noise and pulled on pants and located a flashlight, the fight had rolled down to the creek and Pan's chopping yap had suddenly stilled, though Watty was still squalling hard. When I got there and shone the light on a commotion in the water, all that showed was the coon's solemn face and his shoulders. Astraddle Pan's neck with an ear clutched in each hand, he was quite competently holding her down despite her mightiest struggles; big bubbles rolled up as I watched with dachshund Watty dancing yet uproarious beside me on good firm land. Grabbing up a stick I waded into the frigid chest-deep pool, whacked the coon out of his saddle, declined his offer to climb me in retaliation and sent him swimming somewhat groggily for the other bank. But by then Pan was unconscious, and on shore I shook and pumped the better part of a gallon of water out of her before she started to wheeze and cough. Which didn't keep her from tearing into the very next coon her brave, small, black friend sniffed out, though I don't recall her ever following another one into water. She was not too rash to learn what an impossibility was.

We had a plague of feral housecats at that place, strayed outward from the city or dumped along the roads by the kind of people who do that sort of thing, and a huge tom one time gave the dachshund his comeuppance. After a notable scrap with Pan the tom decided to leave as I arrived, but she grabbed him by the tail as he went. At this point old Watty, thinking in dim light that the customary face-to-face encounter was still in progress and gaining from my arrival the courage the cat had lost, dashed in for a furtive chomp and was received in a loving, tight, clawed embrace with sharp teeth in its middle. His dismay was piercingly loud and he bore those scars for life. . . . The tomcat got away, wiser too I suspect.

If my less than objective interest in these violent matters is evident, I have the grace to be a bit ashamed of it, but not much. I have friends among the hound-dog men whose main pleasure in life lies in fomenting such pursuits and brawls, and some of them are very gentle people—i.e., I am not of the school that believes hunting per se makes worse brutes of men than they already are, or ever did or ever will. Though I still hunt a little myself, I don't hunt in that way, and these home-ground uproars I seldom encouraged except occasionally much later, when Blue had become our only dog and had constituted himself our Protector of Garden and Poultry. The toll of wildlife actually killed over the years was light, reaching a mild peak during the brief period after Blue was full grown and before Pan died, when they hunted and fought as a skillful team. Most chases would end with a treeing and I would go and call the dogs home with no blood spilled on either side. But Man the Hunter's association with dogs is very very longstanding, and anyone who can watch a slashing battle between his own dogs and something wild and tough, when it does occur, without feeling a flow of the old visceral reckless joy, is either quite skilled at suppressing his emotions or more different from me than I think most men are.

There being of course the additional, more primary and cogent fact that in the country varmints around the house and barn and chicken yard are bad news, and the best help in keeping them away, if you dislike poison and traps and such things, is aggressive dogs. They can give you a bad turn on occasion, though, as Pan did one evening when she assailed something in a tight V-mesh fence corner and, hearing high shrill yipes, I thought she was murdering a friend and neighbor's treasured tiny poodle, a wide wanderer named Pierre. I ran out and yanked her away, and out came not Pierre but a quite rumpled little gray fox, who did not give his name but streaked off to safety.

Unable to find any males of Pan's breed in this region, we mated her with one of those more numerous sheep dogs, similar in build and coat but colored white and black-speckled gray, known as Queensland Blue Heelers or more commonly just as Australians. Three of the resultant pups had her hue and the fourth was Blue, marked like his sire but with less speckling and no trace of the blue "glass" or "china" tinge that many, perhaps most Australians have in one or both eyes, sometimes as only a queer pale blaze on an iris. When the time came to choose, we picked him to keep, and as a result he turned out to be a far different sort of grown dog than he would have if we had given him away.

For Pan was an impossibly capricious, domineering mother, neurotic in her protectiveness but punitive toward the pups to the point of drawing blood when they annoyed her, which was often. The others got out from under at six or eight weeks of age, but Blue had to stay and take it, and kept on taking it until Pan died—run over too, while nudging at the rule against chasing cars. Even after he had reached full size, at seventy-five pounds half again bigger than either Pan or his sire, he had to be always on the watch for her unforeseeable snarling fits of displeasure.

I used to wish he would round on her and whip her hard once and for all, but he never did. Instead he developed the knack of turning clownish at a moment's notice, reverting to ingratiating puppy tricks to deflect the edge of her wrath. He would run around in senseless circles yapping, would roll on his back with his feet wiggling in the air, and above all would grin—crinkle his eyes and turn up the corners of his mouth and loll his tongue out over genially bared teeth. It was a travesty of all mashed-down human beings who have had to clown to survive, like certain black barbershop shoeshine "boys," some of them sixty years old, whom I remember from my youth.

These antics worked well enough with Pan that they became a permanent part of the way Blue was, and he brought them to his relationship with people, mainly me, where they worked also. It was quite hard to stay angry at a large strong dog, no matter what he had just done, who had his bobtailed butt in the air and his head along his forelegs on the ground and his eyes skewed sidewise at you as he smiled a wide, mad, minstrel-show smile. If I did manage to stay angry despite all, he would most often panic and flee to his hideout beneath the pickup's greasy differential, which may have been another effect of Pan's gentle motherliness or may just have been Australian; they are sensitive dogs, easily cowed, and require light handling. For the most part, all that Blue did require was light handling, for he wanted immensely to please and was the easiest dog to train in standard matters of behavior that I have ever had to deal with. Hating cats, for instance, he listened to one short lecture concerning a kitten just purchased by my small daughters for twenty-five cents at a church benefit sale, and not only let her alone thereafter but became her staunchest friend, except perhaps in the matter of tomcats she might have favored, which he kept on chasing off. And he learned things like heeling in two hours of casual coaching.

Which harks back to my description of him as the best dog I ever owned. He was. But it is needful at this point to confess that that is not really saying much. Nearly all the dogs I owned before Blue and Pan and Watty were pets I had as a boy in Fort Worth, a succession of fox terriers and curs and whatnot that I babied, teased, cajoled, overfed and generally spoiled in the anthropomorphic manner of kids everywhere. Most perished young, crushed by cars, and were mourned with tears and replaced quite soon by others very much like them in undisciplined worthlessness. In those years I consumed with enthusiasm Jack London's dog books and other less sinewy stuff like the works of Albert Payson Terhune, with their tales of noble and useful canines, but somehow I was never vouchsafed the ownership of anything that faintly resembled Lad or Buck or White Fang.

The best of the lot was a brown-and-white mongrel stray that showed up already old and gray-chopped, with beautiful manners and training, but he liked grownups better than children and stayed with my father when he could. The worst but most beloved was an oversized Scotty named Roderick Dhu, or Roddy, who when I was twelve or thirteen or so used to accompany me and a friend on cumbersome hunting and camping expeditions to the Trinity West Fork bottom beyond the edge of town, our wilderness. He had huge negative will power and when tired or hot would often sit down and refuse to move another inch. Hence from more than one of those forays I came hiking back out of the valley burdened not only with a Confederate bedroll, a canteen, a twenty-two rifle, a bowie knife, an ax, a frying pan and other such impedimenta, but with thirty-five deadweight pounds of warm dog as well.

The friend's dog in contrast was a quick bright feist called Buckshot, destined to survive not only our childhood but our college years and the period when we were away at the war and nearly a decade longer, dying ultimately, my friend swears, at the age of twenty-two. A canine wraith, nearly blind and grayed all over and shrunken, he would lie in corners and dream twitching of old possums and rabbits he had harried through the ferns and poison ivy, thumping his tail on the floor when human movement was near if he chanced to be awake.

With this background, even though I knew about useful dogs from having had uncles and friends who kept them for hunting and from having seen good herd dogs at work during country work in adolescence, as well as from reading, I arrived at my adult years with a fairly intact urban, middle-class, sentimental ideal of the Nice Dog, a cleancut fellow who obeyed a few selected commands, was loyal and gentle with his masters, and refrained conscientiously from "bad" behavior as delineated by the same said masters. I had never had one and knew it, and the first dog I owned after years of unsettled existence was the dachshund Watty, who was emphatically not one either.

He started out all right, intelligent and affectionate and as willing to learn as dachshunds ever are, and with the nose he had he made a fair retriever, albeit hardmouthed with shot birds and inclined to mangle them a bit before reluctantly giving them up. He was fine company too, afield or in a boat or a car, and we had some good times together, even collaborating on a book about a float trip we made down the Brazos River. But his temper started souring when I married, and grew vile when children came, and the job was finished by a paralyzing back injury with a long painful recovery, never complete, and by much sympathetic spoiling along the way. As an old lame creature, a stage that lasted at least five years, he snarled, bit, disobeyed, stank more or less constantly and from time to time broke wind to compound it, yowled and barked for his supper in the kitchen for two hours before feeding time, subverted the good sheep dogs' training and was in general the horrid though small-scale antithesis of a Nice Dog. And yet in replication of my childhood self I loved him, and buried him wrapped in a feed sack beneath a flat piece of limestone with his name scratched deep upon it.

(While for Blue, than whom I will never have a Nicer Dog even if perhaps one more useful, there is no marker at all because there is no grave on which to put one . . .)

I do think Watty knocked out of me most of my residual kid sentimentality about dogs in general—he along with living in the country where realism is forced on you by things like having to cope with goat-killing packs of sterling canines, and the experience of having the sheep dogs with their strong thrust and potential, never fully attained—to the point that I'm certain I will never put up with an unmanageable dog again. I remember one time of sharp realization during the second summer after we had bought this cedar-hill place, long before we lived here any part of the year or even used it for grazing. That spring after the dachshund had been thrown from the pickup's seat when I jammed on the brakes in traffic, I had carried him partly paralyzed to the vet, a friend, who advised me frankly that the smart thing would be a lethal painless shot of pentothal. But he added that he had always wanted to try to cure one of those tricky dachshund spines, and that if I would go along with him he'd charge me only his actual costs. Though by that time Watty was already grumpy and snappish and very little pleasure to have around, sentimentality of course triumphed over smart. The trouble was that with intensive therapy still going strong after several weeks, "actual costs" were mounting absurdly, to the point that even now in far costlier times I can grunt when I think of them.

Engaged that summer in some of the endless construction that has marked our ownership of the place, I was in and out every day or so with loads of lumber and cement and things, and paused sometimes to talk with a pleasant man who lived on the road I used. He had a heterogeneous troop of dogs around the yard, some useful and some just there, their ringleader a small white cur with pricked ears and red-rimmed eyes who ran cars and was very noisy, but was prized by the man's children and had the redeeming trait of being, quote, hell at finding rattlesnakes.

One morning as I drove in, this dog was sitting upright under a live oak fifty yards short of the house, with his head oddly high and askew. He had found one snake too many. His eyes were nearly shut and on the side of his neck was a lump about the size of his head. Nor did he acknowledge my passage with as much as a stifled yip. Thinking perhaps they didn't know, I stopped by the house.

"Yes," said my friend. "He run onto a big one up by the tank yesterday evening and by the time I got there with a hoe it had done popped him good."

"Did you do anything for him?"

"Well, we put some coal oil on it," he said. "I was going to cut it open but there's all those veins and things. You know they say if a snake hits a dog in the body he's a goner, but if it's the head he'll get all right. You reckon the neck's the head?"

I said I hoped so, and for days as I passed in and out I watched the little dog under his oak, from which he did not stir, and checked with the family about him. They were not at all indifferent; he was a main focus of interest and they kept fresh food and water by him. The neck swelled up still fatter and broke open, purging terrible fluids. After this happened he seemed to feel better and even ate a little, but then one morning he was dead. Everyone including me was sad that he had lost his fight to live, and the children held a funeral for him, with bouquets of wild prairie pinks.

And such was my changing view that it seemed somehow to make more healthy sense than all that cash I was ramming into a spoiled irascible dachshund's problematic cure. . . .

"Good" country dogs are something else, and are often treated like members of the family and worried over as much when sick. This is not sentimentality but hard realism, because they're worth worrying over in pragmatic terms. There aren't very many of them. As good dogs always have, they come mainly from ruthless culling of promising litters and from close careful training, and most belong to genuine stockmen with lots of herding work to do. These owners routinely turn down offers of a thousand or more dollars for them, if you believe the stories, as you well may after watching a pair of scroungy border collies, in response to a low whistle or a word, run a half-mile up a brush-thick pasture and bring back seventy-nine Angora wethers and pack them into a fence corner or a pen for shearing, doctoring or loading into a trailer, all while their master whittles a mesquite twig to a point and picks his teeth with it.

Blue wasn't that kind of dog or anywhere near it, nor was there much chance to develop such talent on a place like ours, where the resident cows and goats are fairly placid and few problems in handling them emerge that can't be solved with a little patience and a rattling bucket of feed. For that matter, I don't know nearly enough about the training of such dogs to have helped him get to be one, though a livestock buyer I know, who has superb dogs himself and handles thousands of sheep and goats each year on their way from one owner to another, did tell me after watching Blue try to help us one morning that if I'd let him have him for six months, he might be able to "make a dog out of him." I was grateful and thought it over but in the end declined, partly because I mistrusted what six months of training by a stranger might do to that queer, one-man, nervous Australian streak in Blue, but mainly because I didn't know what I'd do with such a dog if I had him, in these rather miniature and unstrenuous livestock operations. His skills would rust unused, and the fact I had to face was that I didn't deserve a dog like that.

What Blue amounted to, I guess, was a country Nice Dog, which in terms of utility is a notable cut above the same thing in the city. These dogs stay strictly at home without being tied or penned, announce visitors, keep varmints and marauding dogs and unidentified nocturnal boogers away, cope with snakes (Blue, after one bad fanging that nearly killed him, abandoned his dam's tactics of headlong assault and would circle a snake, raising hell till I came to kill it, or to call him off if it was harmless), watch over one's younger children and are middling to good help at shoving stock through a loading chute or from one pen to another, though less help in pastures where the aiming point may be a single gate in a long stretch of fence and judgment is required. Some learn simple daily herding tasks like bringing in milk cows at evening, though I've observed that much of the time these tasks involve an illusion on the part of the dog and perhaps his owner that he is making cows or goats or sheep do something, when actually they have full intention of doing it on their own, unforced. Or the whole thing may be for fun, as it was with one old cowman I knew, who had an ancient collie named Babe. When visitors came to sit with the old man on his porch, he would at some point level a puzzled blue glare across the pasture and say in conversational tones, "I declare, Babe, it looks like that old mare has busted out of the corral again. Maybe you better bring her in." And Babe would rise and go do as he had been bidden and the visitors would be much impressed, unless they happened to be aware that it was the one sole thing he could do and that the mare was in on it too.

On the whole, to be honest, Blue was pretty poor at herding even by such lax standards—too eager and exuberant and only occasionally certain of what it was we were trying to do. But he was controllable by single words and gestures and like his mother unafraid, and in his later years when I knew his every tendency, such as nipping goats, I could correct mistakes before he made them, so that he was often of some help. He was even more often comic relief, as when a chuted cow turned fighty and loaded him into the trailer instead of he her, or when a young bull, too closely pressed, kicked him into a thick clump of scrub elm, where he landed upside down and lay stuck with his legs still running in the air. When I went over and saw that he wasn't hurt and started laughing at the way he looked, he started laughing too, at least in his own way.

For a sense of humor and of joy was the other side of that puppyish clowning streak which he always retained but which turned less defensive with time. The nervousness that went with it never left him either, but grew separate from the clowning, ritualizing itself most often in a weird habit he had of grinning and slobbering and clicking his teeth together when frustrated or perplexed. He regularly did this, for instance, when friends showed up for visits and brought their own dogs along. Knowing he wasn't supposed to attack these dogs as he did strays, Blue was uncertain what else to do with them. So he would circle them stiff-legged, wagging his stub and usually trying to mount them, male or female, small or large, and after being indignantly rebuffed would walk about popping his jaws and dribbling copious saliva. I expect some of those visiting friends thought him a very strange dog, and maybe in truth he was.

He was a bouncing, bristling, loudmouthed watchdog, bulkily impressive enough that arriving strangers would most often stay in their cars until I came out to call him off. Unlike Pan, he bore them no real hostility and never bit anyone, though I believe that if any person or thing had threatened one of us those big white teeth would have been put to good use. Mainly, unfamiliar people disconcerted him and he wanted nothing to do with them unless I was around and showed myself receptive, at which point he was wont to start nuzzling their legs and hands like a great overgrown pup, demanding caresses. Once when the pickup was ailing I left it at a garage in town and mooched a ride home with a friend whose car Blue did not know. No one in the family was there, and when we drove up to the house there was no sign of Blue, but then I saw him peering furtively around a corner of the porch, much as his mother had eyed me from those shin oak bushes long before.

With his size, clean markings, silky thick coat, broad head, alert eyes, and usual mien of grave dignity, he was quite a noble-looking fellow. Having him along was often a social asset with strangers, even if it could turn out to be the opposite if something disturbed him and he went

into his jaw-popping, drooling phase. One day when he was young and we were still living outside Fort Worth, I was apprehended in that city for running a red light, though I had thought I'd seen no light on at all when I drove through the intersection. I explained this to the arresting officer, a decent type, and together we went back and watched the damned thing run through six or eight perfectly sequenced changes from red to yellow to green and back again. Blue watched with us and, attuned to the situation, accepted a pat from the cop with an austere but friendly smile. Against pregnant silence I said with embarrassment that I guessed my eyes were failing faster than I'd thought, accepted the appropriate summons, and went my disgruntled way.

When I got home that afternoon my wife said the officer had telephoned. More decent even than I'd known, he had watched the light for a while longer by himself and had finally caught it malfunctioning, and he told Jane I could get the ticket canceled.

She thought me off in the cedar hills and believed there was some mistake. "Did he have a sheep dog in the back of the pickup?" she asked.

"No, ma'am," said Blue's till-then secret admirer. "That great big beautiful animal was sitting right up on the front seat with him."

We spent a tremendous lot of time together over the years, Blue and I—around the house and barn and pens, wandering on the place, batting about in a pickup (his pickup more than mine, for he spent much of each day inside it or beneath, even when it was parked by the house), or at farm work in the fields. When young he would follow the tractor around and around as I plowed or harrowed or sowed, but later he learned to sit under a tree and watch the work's progress in comfort, certain I was not escaping from him, though sometimes when he got bored he would bounce out to meet the tractor as it neared him and would try to lead it home. Fond of the whole family and loved by all, he would go along with the girls to swim at the creek or when they went horseback across the hills, good protection for them and good company. But he needed a single main focus and I was it, so

completely that at times I felt myself under surveillance. No imperfectly latched door missed his
notice if I was indoors and he was out, and he
could open one either by shoving or by pulling
it with his teeth, as permanent marks on some of
them still testify. Failing to get in, he would ascertain as best he could, by peering in windows
or otherwise, just where I was located inside and
then would lie down by the exterior wall closest
to that spot, even if it put him in the full blast of
a January norther.

At one friend's house in town that he and I
used to visit often, he would if left outside go
through the attached garage to a kitchen door at
odds with its jamb and seldom completely shut.
Easing through it, he would traverse the breakfast room and a hall, putting one foot before
another in tense slow motion, would slink behind a sofa into the living room, and using con-
cealment as craftily as any old infantryman,
would sometimes be lying beside my chair before
I even knew he was in. More usually we would
watch his creeping progress while pretending
not to notice, and after he got where he was
headed I would give him a loud mock scolding
and he would roll on his back and clown, knowing he was home free and wouldn't be booted
back out, as sometimes happened when he was
shedding fat ticks or stinking from a recent battle
with some polecat.

But there were places he wouldn't go with
me, most notable among them the bee yard, his
first apicultural experience having been his definite last. It happened one early spring day when
I was helping a friend check through a neglected
hive someone had given him and Blue had
tagged along with us. The hive body and supers
were badly gummed up with the tree-sap propo-
lis bees use for glue and chinking, the combs in
the frames were crooked and connected by
bridge wax and tore when we took them out, and
on that cool day all thirty or forty thousand work-
ers were at home and ready to fight. They got
under our veils and into all cracks in our attire,
and those that didn't achieve entry just rammed
their stings home through two or three layers of
cloth. They also found Blue, a prime target for
apian rage since they hate all hairy things, probably out of ancestral memory of hive-raiding
bears. With maybe a hundred of them hung
whining in his coat and stinging when they found
skin, he tried to squeeze between my legs for
protection and caused me to drop a frame covered with bees, which augmented the assault.
Shortly thereafter, torn between mirth and pain,
we gave up and slapped the hive back together
and lit out at a hard run, with Blue thirty yards
in front and clouds of bees flying escort. And
after that whenever he saw me donning the veil
and firing up my smoker, he would head in the
other direction.

He did work out a method of revenge,
though, which he used for the rest of his life
despite scoldings and other discouragements.
Finding a place where small numbers of bees
were coming for some reason—a spot on the
lawn where something sweet had been spilled,
perhaps, or a lime-crusted dripping faucet whose
flavor in their queer way they liked—he would
stalk it with his special tiptoeing slink and then
loudly snap bees from the air one by one as they
flew, apparently not much minding the occasional stings he got on his lips and tongue. I
suppose my scoldings were less severe than they
ought to have been; it was a comical thing to
watch and for that matter he got few bees in
relation to their huge numbers, unlike another
beekeeper friend's Dalmatian, afflicted with similar feelings, who used to sit all day directly in
front of a hive chomping everything that flew
out, and had to be given away.

Maybe Blue considered bees varmints. He
took his guardianship of the home premises dead
seriously and missed few creatures that came
around; along with clowning, I guess this was the
thing he did best. Except for the unfortunate
armadillos, which he had learned to crunch, the
mortality inflicted was low after Pan's death, as
I've said, for most could escape through the net
yard fence that momentarily blocked Blue's pursuit and few of them cared to stay and dispute
matters except an occasional big squalling coon.
With these we did have some rousing fine midnight fights, though I'd better not further sully
my humanitarian aura, if any remains, by going
into details. During the time when cantaloupes

and roasting ears were coming ripe and most attractive to coons, I would leave the garden gate open at dark and Blue would go down during the night on patrol. There was sometimes a question as to whether a goodly squad of coons given full license could have done half as much damage to garden crops as the ensuing battles did, but there was no question at all about whether the procedure worked. After only two or three brawls each year, word would spread around canny coondom that large hairy danger lurked in the Graves corn patch and they would come no more, much to Blue's disappointment.

I talked to him quite a bit, for the most part childishly or joshingly as one does talk to beasts, and while I'm not idiot enough to think he "understood" any of it beyond a few key words and phrases, he knew my voice's inflections and tones, and by listening took meaning from them if meaning was there to be had, responding with a grin, a sober stare, melting affection or some communicative panting, according to what seemed to be right. Like most dogs that converse with humans he was a thorough yes type, honoring my every point with agreement. Nice Dogs are ego boosters, and have been so since the dim red dawn of things.

I could leave him alone and untethered at the place for three or more days at a time, with dry food in a bucket under shelter and water to be had at the cattle troughs. Neighbors half a mile away have told me that sometimes when the wind was right they could hear him crooning softly wolflike, lonely, but he never left. When I came back he would be at the yard gate waiting, and as I walked toward the house he would go beside me leaping five and six feet straight up in the air in pure and utter celebration, whining and grunting maybe but seldom more; he saved loud barks for strangers and snakes and threatening varmints and such.

Last winter I slept inside the house instead of on the screen porch we shared as night quarters during much of each year unless, as often, he wanted to be outside on guard, and I hadn't moved back out by that March night when he

disappeared. He had been sleeping on a horse-blanket on a small open side porch facing south, and I'd begun to notice that sometimes he would be still abed and pleasantly groggy when I came out at daybreak. He was fattening a bit also, and those eyes were dimmer that once had been able to pick me out of a jostling sidewalk crowd in town and track me as I came toward the car. Because, like mine, his years were piling up. It was a sort of further bond between us.

He ate a full supper that evening and barked with authority at some coyotes singing across the creek, and in the morning was gone. I had to drive two counties north that day to pick up some grapevines and had planned to take him along. When he didn't answer my calling I decided he must have a squirrel in the elms and cedars across the house branch, where he would often sit silent and taut for hours staring up at a chattering treed rodent, oblivious to summonings and to everything else. It was a small sin that I permitted him at his age; if I wanted him I could go and search him out and bring him in, for he was never far. But that morning it didn't seem to matter and I took off without him, certain he'd be at the yard gate when I drove in after lunch, as he had invariably been over the years that had mounted so swiftly for both of us.

Except that he wasn't. Nor did a tour of his usual squirrel grounds yield any trace, or careful trudges up and down the branch, or a widening week-long search by myself and my wife and kids (whose spring vacation it used up and thoroughly ruined) that involved every brush pile and crevice we could find within half a mile or more of home, where he might have followed some coon or ringtail and then gotten stuck or been bitten in a vein by a rattler just out of its long winter's doze and full of rage and venom. Or watching for the tight downspiral of feeding buzzards. Or driving every road in the county twice or more and talking with people who, no, had not seen any dogs like that or even any bitches in heat that might have passed through recruiting. Or ads run in the paper and notices taped to the doors of groceries and feed mills, though these did produce some false hopes that led me up to thirty miles away in vain.

Mastiff and Hound *by Howitt*

Even his friend the two-bit cat, at intervals for weeks, would sit and meow toward the woods in queer and futile lament. . . .

I ended fairly certain of what I'd surmised from the start, that Blue lay dead, from whatever cause, beneath some thick heap of bulldozed brush or in one of those deep holes, sometimes almost caves, that groundwater eats out under the limestone ledges of our hills. For in country as brushy and wrinkled and secret as this we can't have found all of such places roundabout, even fairly close.

Or maybe I want to believe this because it has finality.

And maybe he will still turn up, like those long-lost animals you read about in children's books and sometimes in newspaper stories.

He won't.

And dogs are nothing but dogs and I know it better than most, and all this was for a queer and nervous old crossbreed that couldn't even herd stock right. Nor was there anything humanly unique about the loss, or about the emptiness that came in the searching's wake, which comes sooner or later to all people foolish enough to give an animal space in their lives. But if you are built to be such a fool, you are, and if the animal is to you what Blue was to me the space he leaves empty is big.

It is partly filled for us now by a successor, an Old English pup with much promise—sharp and alert, wildly vigorous but responsive and honest, puppy-absurd but with an underlying gravity that will in time I think prevail. There is nothing nervous about him; he has a sensitivity that could warp in that direction if mishandled, but won't if I can help it. Nor does he show any fear beyond healthy puppy caution, and in the way he looks at cows and goats and listens to people's words I see clearly that he may make a hell of a dog, quite possibly better than Blue. Which is not, as I said, saying much . . .

But he isn't Blue. In the domed shape of his head under my hand as I sit reading in the evenings I can still feel that broader, silkier head, and through his half-boisterous, half-bashful, glad morning hello I still glimpse Blue's clown grin and crazy leaps. I expect such intimate remembrance will last a good long while, for I waited the better part of a lifetime to own a decent dog, and finally had him, and now don't have him any more. And I resolve that when this new one is grown and more or less shaped in his ways, I am going to get another pup to raise beside him, and later maybe a third. Because I don't believe I want to face so big a dose of that sort of emptiness again.

The Dog That Bit People

by JAMES THURBER

PROBABLY no one man should have as many dogs in his life as I have had, but there was more pleasure than distress in them for me except in the case of an Airedale named Muggs. He gave me more trouble than all the other fifty-four or -five put together, although my moment of keenest embarrassment was the time a Scotch terrier named Jeannie, who had just had six puppies in the clothes closet of a fourth-floor apartment in New York, had the unexpected seventh and last at the corner of Eleventh Street and Fifth Avenue during a walk she had insisted on taking. Then, too, there was the prize-winning French poodle, a great big black poodle—none of your little, untroublesome white miniatures—who got sick riding in the rumble seat of a car with me on her way to the Greenwich Dog Show. She had a red rubber bib tucked around her throat and, since a rain storm came up when we were halfway through the Bronx, I had to hold over her a small green umbrella, really more of a parasol. The rain beat down fearfully and suddenly the driver of the car drove into a big garage, filled with mechanics. It happened so quickly that I forgot to put the umbrella down and I will always remember, with sickening distress, the look of incredulity mixed with hatred that came over the face of the particular hardened garage man that came over to see what we wanted, when he took

a look at me and the poodle. All garage men, and people of that intolerant stripe, hate poodles with their curious haircut, especially the pom-poms that you got to leave on their hips if you expect the dogs to win a prize.

But the Airedale, as I have said, was the worst of all my dogs. He really wasn't my dog, as a matter of fact: I came home from a vacation one summer to find that my brother Roy had bought him while I was away. A big, burly, choleric dog, he always acted as if he thought I wasn't one of the family. There was a slight advantage in being one of the family, for he didn't bite the family as often as he bit strangers. Still, in the years that we had him he bit everybody but mother, and he made a pass at her once but missed. That was during the month when we suddenly had mice, and Muggs refused to do anything about them. Nobody ever had mice exactly like the mice we had that month. They acted like pet mice, almost like mice somebody had trained. They were so friendly that one night when mother entertained at dinner the Friraliras, a club she and my father had belonged to for twenty years, she put down a lot of little dishes with food in them on the pantry floor so that the mice would be satisfied with that and wouldn't come into the dining room. Muggs stayed out in the pantry with the mice, lying on the floor, growling to himself—not at the mice, but about all the people in the

23

next room that he would have liked to get at. Mother slipped out into the pantry once to see how everything was going. Everything was going fine. It made her so mad to see Muggs lying there, oblivious of the mice—they came running up to her—that she slapped him and he slashed at her, but didn't make it. He was sorry immediately, mother said. He was always sorry, she said, after he bit someone, but we could not understand how she figured this out. He didn't act sorry.

Mother used to send a box of candy every Christmas to the people the Airedale bit. The list finally contained forty or more names. Nobody could understand why we didn't get rid of the dog. I didn't understand it very well myself, but we didn't get rid of him. I think that one or two people tried to poison Muggs—he acted poisoned once in a while—and old Major Moberly fired at him once with his service revolver near the Seneca Hotel in East Broad Street—but Muggs lived to be almost eleven years old and even when he could hardly get around he bit a congressman who had called to see my father on business. My mother had never liked the congressman—she said the signs of his horoscope showed he couldn't be trusted (he was Saturn with the moon in Virgo)—but she sent him a box of candy that Christmas. He sent it right back, probably because he suspected it was trick candy. Mother persuaded herself it was all for the best that the dog had bitten him, even though father lost an important business association because of it. "I wouldn't be associated with such a man," mother said, "Muggs could read him like a book."

We used to take turns feeding Muggs to be on his good side, but that didn't always work. He was never in a very good humor, even after a meal. Nobody knew exactly what was the matter with him, but whatever it was it made him irascible, especially in the mornings. Roy never felt very well in the morning, either, especially before breakfast, and once when he came downstairs and found that Muggs had moodily chewed up the morning paper he hit him in the face with a grapefruit and then jumped up on the dining room table, scattering dishes and silverware and spilling the coffee. Muggs' first free leap carried him all the way across the table and into a brass fire screen in front of the gas grate but he was back on his feet in a moment and in the end he got Roy and gave him a pretty vicious bite in the leg. Then he was all over it; he never bit anyone more than once at a time. Mother always mentioned that as an argument in his favor; she said he had a quick temper but that he didn't hold a grudge. She was forever defending him. I think she liked him because he wasn't well. "He's not strong," she would say, pityingly, but that was inaccurate; he may not have been well but he was terribly strong.

One time my mother went to the Chittenden Hotel to call on a woman mental healer who was lecturing in Columbus on the subject of "Harmonious Vibrations." She wanted to find out if it was possible to get harmonious vibrations into a dog. "He's a large tan-colored Airedale," mother explained. The woman said that she had never treated a dog but she advised my mother to hold the thought that he did not bite and would not bite. Mother was holding the thought the very next morning when Muggs got the iceman but she blamed that slip-up on the iceman. "If you didn't think he would bite you, he wouldn't," mother told him. He stomped out of the house in a terrible jangle of vibrations.

One morning when Muggs bit me slightly, more or less in passing, I reached down and grabbed his short stumpy tail and hoisted him into the air. It was a foolhardy thing to do and the last time I saw my mother, about six months ago, she said she didn't know what possessed me. I don't either, except that I was pretty mad. As long as I held the dog off the floor by his tail he couldn't get at me, but he twisted and jerked so, snarling all the time, that I realized I couldn't hold him that way very long. I carried him to the kitchen and flung him onto the floor and shut the door on him just as he crashed against it. But I forgot about the backstairs. Muggs went up the backstairs and down the frontstairs and had me cornered in the living room. I managed to get up onto the mantelpiece above the fireplace, but it gave way and came down with a tremendous crash throwing a large marble clock, several vases, and myself heavily to the floor. Muggs was so alarmed by the racket that when I picked myself up he had disappeared. We couldn't find him anywhere, although we whistled and shouted, until old Mrs. Detweiler called after dinner that night. Muggs had bitten her once, in the leg, and she came into the living room only after we assured her that Muggs had run away. She had just seated herself when, with a great growling and scratching of claws, Muggs emerged from under a davenport where he had been quietly hiding all the time, and bit her again. Mother examined the bite and put arnica on it and told Mrs. Detweiler that it was only a bruise. "He just bumped you," she said. But Mrs. Detweiler left the house in a nasty state of mind.

Lots of people reported our Airedale to the police but my father held a municipal office at the time and was on friendly terms with the police. Even so, the cops had been out a couple of times —once when Muggs bit Mrs. Rufus Sturtevant and again when he bit Lieutenant-Governor Malloy—but mother told them that it hadn't been Muggs' fault but the fault of the people who were bitten. "When he starts for them, they scream," she explained, "and that excites him." The cops suggested that it might be a good idea to tie the dog up, but mother said that it mortified him to be tied up and that he wouldn't eat when he was tied up.

Muggs at his meals was an unusual sight. Because of the fact that if you reached toward the floor he would bite you, we usually put his food plate on top of an old kitchen table with a bench alongside the table. Muggs would stand on the bench and eat. I remember that my mother's Uncle Horatio, who boasted that he was the third man up Missionary Ridge, was splutteringly indignant when he found out that we fed the dog on a table because we were afraid to put his plate on the floor. He said he wasn't afraid of any dog that ever lived and that he would put the dog's plate on the floor if we would give it to him. Roy said that if Uncle Horatio had fed Muggs on the ground just before the battle he would have been the first man up Missionary Ridge. Uncle Horatio was furious. "Bring him in! Bring him in now!" he shouted. "I'll feed the———on the

floor!" Roy was all for giving him a chance, but my father wouldn't hear of it. He said that Muggs had already been fed. "I'll feed him again!" bawled Uncle Horatio. We had quite a time quieting him.

In his last year Muggs used to spend practically all of his time outdoors. He didn't like to stay in the house for some reason or other— perhaps it held too many unpleasant memories for him. Anyway, it was hard to get him to come in and as a result the garbage man, the iceman and the laundryman wouldn't come near the house. We had to haul the garbage down to the corner, take the laundry out and bring it back, and meet the iceman a block from home. After this had gone on for some time we hit on an ingenious arrangement for getting the dog in the house so that we could lock him up while the gas meter was read, and so on. Muggs was afraid of only one thing, an electrical storm. Thunder and lightning frightened him out of his senses (I think he thought a storm had broken the day the mantelpiece fell). He would rush into the house and hide under a bed or in a clothes closet. So we fixed up a thunder machine out of a long narrow piece of sheet iron with a wooden handle on one end. Mother would shake this vigorously when she wanted to get Muggs into the house. It made an excellent imitation of thunder, but I suppose it was the most roundabout system for running a household that was ever devised. It took a lot out of mother.

A few months before Muggs died, he got to "seeing things." He would rise slowly from the floor, growling low, and stalk stiff-legged and menacing toward nothing at all. Sometimes the Thing would be just a little to the right or left of a visitor. Once a Fuller Brush salesman got hysterics. Muggs came wandering into the room like Hamlet following his father's ghost. His eyes were fixed on a spot just to the left of the Fuller Brush man, who stood it until Muggs was about three slow, creeping paces from him. Then he shouted. Muggs wavered on past him into the hallway grumbling to himself but the Fuller man went on shouting. I think mother had to throw a pan of cold water on him before he stopped.

That was the way she used to stop us boys when we got into fights.

Muggs died quite suddenly one night. Mother wanted to bury him in the family lot under a marble stone with some such inscription as "Flights of angels sing thee to they rest" but we persuaded her it was against the law. In the end we just put up a smooth board above his grave along a lonely road. On the board I wrote with an indelible pencil "Cave Canem." Mother was quite pleased with the simple classic dignity of the old Latin epitaph.

There's No Place Like Home *by Sir Edwin Landseer*

Stickeen

by JOHN MUIR

I
N the summer of 1880 I set out from Fort Wrangell in a canoe to continue the exploration of the icy region of southeastern Alaska, begun in the fall of 1879. After the necessary provisions, blankets, etc., had been collected and stowed away, and my Indian crew were in their places ready to start, while a crowd of their relatives and friends on the wharf were bidding them good-bye and good luck, my companion, the Reverend S. H. Young, for whom we were waiting, at last came aboard, followed by a little black dog that immediately made himself at home by curling up in a hollow among the baggage. I like dogs, but this one seemed so small and worthless that I objected to his going, and asked the missionary why he was taking him.

"Such a little helpless creature will only be in the way," I said; "you had better pass him up to the Indian boys on the wharf, to be taken home to play with the children. This trip is not likely to be good for toy-dogs. The poor silly thing will be in rain and snow for weeks or months, and will require care like a baby."

But his master assured me that he would be no trouble at all; that he was a perfect wonder of a dog, could endure cold and hunger like a bear, swim like a seal, and was wondrous wise and cunning, etc., making out a list of virtues to show he might be the most interesting member of the party.

Nobody could hope to unravel the lines of his ancestry. In all the wonderfully mixed and varied dog-tribe I never saw any creature very much like him, though in some of his sly, soft, gliding motions and gestures he brought the fox to mind. He was short-legged and bunchy-bodied, and his hair, though smooth, was long and silky and slightly waved, so that when the wind was at his back it ruffled, making him look shaggy. At first sight his only noticeable feature was his fine tail, which was about as airy and shady as a squirrel's, and was carried curling forward almost to his nose. On closer inspection you might notice his thin sensitive ears, and sharp eyes with cunning tan spots above them. Mr. Young told me that when the little fellow was a pup about the size of a woodrat he was presented to his wife by an Irish prospector at Sitka, and that on his arrival at Fort Wrangell he was adopted with enthusiasm by the Stickeen Indians as a sort of new good-luck totem, was named "Stickeen" for the tribe, and became a universal favorite; petted, protected and admired wherever he went, and regarded as a mysterious fountain of wisdom.

On our trip he soon proved himself a queer character—odd, concealed, independent, keeping invincibly quiet and doing many little puzzling things that piqued my curiosity. As we sailed week after week through the long intricate channels and inlets among the innumerable islands and mountains of the coast, he spent most of the dull days in sluggish ease, motionless and apparently as unobserving as if in deep sleep. But I discovered that somehow he always knew what was going on. When the Indians were about to shoot at ducks or seals, or when anything along the shore was exciting our attention, he would rest his chin on the edge of the canoe and calmly look out like a dreamy-eyed tourist. And when he heard us talking about making a landing, he immediately roused himself to see what sort of a place we were coming to, and made ready to jump overboard and swim ashore as soon as the canoe neared the beach. Then, with a vigorous shake to get rid of the brine in his hair, he ran into the woods to hunt small game. But though always the first out of the canoe, he was always the last to get into it. When we were ready to start he could never be found, and refused to come to our call. We soon found out, however, that though we could not see him at such times, he saw us, and from the cover of the briers and huckleberry bushes in the fringe of the woods was watching the canoe with wary eye. For as soon as we were fairly off he came trotting down the beach, plunged into the surf and swam after us, knowing well that we would cease rowing and take him in. When the contrary little vagabond came alongside, he was lifted by the neck, held at arm's length a moment to drip and dropped aboard. We tried to cure him of this trick by compelling him to swim a long way, as if we had a mind to abandon him; but this did no good: the longer the swim the better he seemed to like it.

Though capable of great idleness, he never failed to be ready for all sorts of adventures and excursions. One pitch-dark rainy night we landed about ten o'clock at the mouth of a salmon stream when the water was phosphorescent. The salmon were running, and the myriad fins of the onrushing multitude were churning all the stream into a silvery glow, wonderfully beautiful and impressive in the ebon darkness. To get a good view of the show I set out with one of the Indians and sailed up through the midst of it to the foot of a rapid about half a mile from camp, where the swift current dashing over rocks made the luminous glow most glorious. Happening to look back down the stream, while the Indian was catching a few of the struggling fish, I saw a long spreading fan of light like the tail of a comet, which we thought must be made by some big strange animal that was pursuing us. On it came with its magnificent train, until we imagined we could see the monster's head and eyes; but it was only Stickeen, who, finding I had left the camp, came swimming after me to see what was up.

When we camped early, the best hunter of the crew usually went to the woods for a deer, and Stickeen was sure to be at his heels, provided I had not gone out. For, strange to say, though I never carried a gun, he always followed me, forsaking the hunter and even his master to share my wanderings. The days that were too stormy for sailing I spent in the woods, or on the adjacent mountains, wherever my studies called me; and Stickeen always insisted on going with me, however wild the weather, gliding like a fox through dripping huckleberry bushes and thorny tangles of panax and rubus, scarce stirring their rain-laden leaves; wading and wallowing through snow, swimming icy streams, skipping over logs and rocks and the crevasses of glaciers with the patience and endurance of a determined mountaineer, never tiring or getting discouraged. Once he followed me over a glacier the surface of which was so crusty and rough that it cut his feet until every step was marked with blood; but he trotted on with Indian fortitude until I noticed his red track, and, taking pity on him, made him a set of moccasins out of a handkerchief. However great his troubles he never asked help or made any complaint, as if, like a philosopher, he had learned that without hard work and suffering there could be no pleasure worth having.

Yet none of us was able to make out what Stickeen was really good for. He seemed to meet danger and hardships without anything like reason, insisted on having his own way, never obeyed an order, and the hunter could never set him on anything or make him fetch the birds he shot. His equanimity was so steady it seemed due to want of feeling; ordinary storms were pleasures to him, and as for mere rain, he flourished in it like a vegetable. No matter what advances you might make, scarce a glance or a tail-wag would you get for your pains. But though he was apparently as cold as a glacier and about as impervious to fun, I tried hard to make his acquaintance, guessing there must be something worthwhile hidden beneath so much courage, endurance, and love of wild-weathery adventure. No superannuated mastiff or bulldog grown old in office surpassed this fluffy midget in stoic dignity. He sometimes reminded me of a small, squat, unshakable desert cactus. For he never displayed a single trace of the merry, tricksy, elfish fun of the terriers and collies that we all know, nor of their touching affection and devotion. Like children, most small dogs beg to be loved and allowed to love; but Stickeen seemed a very Diogenes, asking only to be let alone: a true child of the wilderness, holding the even tenor of his hidden life with the silence and serenity of nature. His strength of character lay in his eyes. They looked as old as the hills, and as young, and as wild. I never tired of looking into them: it was like looking into a landscape; but they were small and rather deep-set, and had no explaining lines around them to give out particulars. I was accustomed to look into the faces of plants and animals, and I watched the little sphinx more and more keenly as an interesting study. But there is no estimating the wit and wisdom concealed and latent in our lower fellow mortals until made manifest by profound experiences; for it is through suffering that dogs as well as saints are developed and made perfect.

After exploring the Sum Dum and Tahkoo fiords and their glaciers, we sailed through Stephen's Passage into Lynn Canal and thence through Icy Strait into Cross Sound, searching for unexplored inlets leading toward the great fountain ice-fields of the Fairweather Range. Here, while the tide was in our favor, we were accompanied by a fleet of icebergs drifting out to the ocean from Glacier Bay. Slowly we paddled around Vancouver's Point, Wimbledon, our frail canoe tossed like a feather on the massive heaving swells coming in past Cape Spenser. For miles the sound is bounded by precipitous mural cliffs, which, lashed with wave-spray and their heads hidden in clouds, looked terribly threatening and stern. Had our canoe been crushed or upset we could have made no landing here, for the cliffs, as high as those of Yosemite, sink sheer into deep water. Eagerly we scanned the wall on the north side for the first sign of an opening fiord or harbor, all of us anxious except Stickeen, who dozed in peace or gazed dreamily at the tremendous precipices when he heard us talking about them. At length we made the joyful discovery of the mouth of the inlet now called "Taylor Bay," and about five o'clock reached the head of it and encamped in a spruce grove near the front of a large glacier.

While camp was being made, Joe the hunter climbed the mountain wall on the east side of the fiord in pursuit of wild goats, while Mr. Young and I went to the glacier. We found that it is separated from the waters of the inlet by a tide-washed moraine, and extends, an abrupt barrier, all the way across from wall to wall of the inlet, a distance of about three miles. But our most interesting discovery was that it had recently advanced, though again slightly receding. A portion of the terminal moraine had been plowed up and shoved forward, uprooting and overwhelming the woods on the east side. Many of the trees were down and buried, or nearly so, others were leaning away from the ice-cliffs, ready to fall, and some stood erect, with the bottom of the ice plow still beneath their roots and its lofty crystal spires towering high above their tops. The spectacle presented by these century-old trees standing close beside a spiry wall of ice, with their branches almost touching it, was most novel and striking. And when I climbed around the front, and a little way up the west side of the glacier, I found that it had swelled and increased in height and width in accordance with its advance, and carried away the outer ranks of trees on its bank.

On our way back to camp after these first observations I planned a far-and-wide excursion for the morrow. I awoke early, called not only by the glacier, which had been on my mind all night, but by a grand floodstorm. The wind was blowing a gale from the north and the rain was flying with the clouds in a wide passionate horizontal flood, as if it were all passing over the country instead of falling on it. The main perennial streams were booming high above their banks, and hundreds of new ones, roaring like the sea, almost covered the lofty gray walls of the inlet with white cascades and falls. I had intended making a cup of coffee and getting something like a breakfast before starting, but when I heard the storm and looked out I made haste to join it; for many of Nature's finest lessons are to be found in her storms, and if careful to keep in right relations with them, we may go safely abroad with them, rejoicing in the grandeur and beauty of their works and ways, and chanting with the old Norsemen, "The blast of the tempest aids our oars, the hurricane is our servant and drives us whither we wish to go." So, omitting breakfast, I put a piece of bread in my pocket and hurried away.

Mr. Young and the Indians were asleep, and so, I hoped, was Stickeen; but I had not gone a dozen rods before he left his bed in the tent and came boring through the blast after me. That a man should welcome storms for their exhilarating music and motion, and go forth to see God making landscapes, is reasonable enough; but what fascination could there be in such tremendous weather for a dog? Surely nothing akin to human enthusiasm for scenery or geology. Anyhow, on he came, breakfastless, through the choking blast. I stopped and did my best to turn him back. "Now don't," I said, shouting to make myself heard in the storm, "now don't, Stickeen. What has got into your queer noddle now? You must be daft. This wild day has nothing for you. There is no game abroad, nothing but weather. Go back to camp and keep warm, get a good breakfast with your master and be sensible for once. I can't carry you all day or feed you, and this storm will kill you."

But Nature, it seems, was at the bottom of the affair, and she gains her ends with dogs as well as with men, making us do as she likes, shoving and pulling us along her ways, however rough, all but killing us at times in getting her lessons driven hard home. After I had stopped again and again, shouting good warning advice, I saw that he was not to be shaken off; as well might the earth try to shake off the moon. I had once led his master into trouble, when he fell on

one of the topmost jags of a mountain and dislocated his arm; now the turn of his humble companion was coming. The pitiful wanderer just stood there in the wind, drenched and blinking, saying doggedly, "Where thou goest I will go." So at last I told him to come on if he must, and gave him a piece of the bread I had in my pocket; then we struggled on together, and thus began the most memorable of all my wild days.

The level flood, driving hard in our faces, thrashed and washed us wildly until we got into the shelter of a grove on the east side of the glacier near the front, where we stopped awhile for breath and to listen and look out. The exploration of the glacier was my main object, but the wind was too high to allow excursions over its open surface, where one might be dangerously shoved while balancing for a jump on the brink of a crevasse. In the mean time the storm was a fine study. Here the end of the glacier, descending an abrupt swell of resisting rock about five hundred feet high, leans forward and falls in ice-cascades. And as the storm came down the glacier from the north, Stickeen and I were beneath the main current of the blast, while favorably located to see and hear it. What a psalm the storm was singing, and how fresh the smell of the washed earth and leaves, and how sweet the still small voices of the storm! Detached wafts and swirls were coming through the woods, with music from the leaves and branches and furrowed boles, and even from the splintered rocks and ice-crags overhead, many of the tones soft and low and flutelike, as if each leaf and tree, crag and spire were a tuned reed. A broad torrent, draining the side of the glacier, now swollen by scores of new streams from the mountains, was rolling boulders along its rocky channel, with thudding, bumping, muffled sounds, rushing toward the bay with tremendous energy, as if in haste to get out of the mountains; the waters above and beneath calling to each other, and all to the ocean, their home.

Looking southward from our shelter, we had this great torrent and the forested mountain wall above it on our left, the spiry ice-crags on our right, and smooth gray gloom ahead. I tried to draw the marvelous scene in my notebook, but the rain blurred the page in spite of all my pains to shelter it, and the sketch was almost worthless. When the wind began to abate, I traced the east side of the glacier. All the trees standing on the edge of the woods were barked and bruised, showing high-ice mark in a very telling way, while tens of thousands of those that had stood for centuries on the bank of the glacier farther out lay crushed and being crushed. In many places I could see down fifty feet or so beneath the margin of the glacier-mill, where trunks from one to two feet in diameter were being ground to pulp against outstanding rock-ribs and bosses of the bank.

About three miles above the front of the glacier I climbed to the surface of it by means of ax-steps made easy for Stickeen. As far as the eye could reach, the level, or nearly level, glacier stretched away indefinitely beneath the gray sky, a seemingly boundless prairie of ice. The rain continued, and grew colder, which I did not mind, but a dim snowy look in the drooping clouds made me hesitate about venturing far from land. No trace of the west shore was visible, and in case the clouds should settle and give snow, or the wind again become violent, I feared getting caught in a tangle of crevasses. Snow-crystals, the flowers of the mountain clouds, are frail, beautiful things, but terrible when flying on storm-winds in darkening, benumbing swarms or when welded together into glaciers full of deadly crevasses. Watching the weather, I sauntered about on the crystal sea. For a mile or two out I found the ice remarkably safe. The marginal crevasses were mostly narrow, while the few wider ones were easily avoided by passing around them, and the clouds began to open here and there.

Thus encouraged, I at last pushed out for the other side; for Nature can make us do anything she likes. At first we made rapid progress, and the sky was not very threatening, while I took bearings occasionally with a pocket compass to enable me to find my way back more surely in case the storm should become blinding; but the structure lines of the glacier were my main guide. Toward the west side we came to a closely crevassed section in which we had to make long, narrow tacks and doublings, tracing the edges of tremendous transverse and longitudinal crevasses, many of which were from twenty to thirty feet wide, and perhaps a thousand feet deep—beautiful and awful. In working a way through them I was severely cautious, but Stickeen came on as unhesitating as the flying clouds. The widest crevasse that I could jump he would leap without so much as halting to take a look at it. The weather was now making quick changes, scattering bits of dazzling brightness through the wintry gloom; at rare intervals, when the sun broke forth wholly free, the glacier was seen from shore to shore with a bright array of encompassing mountains partly revealed, wearing the clouds as garments, while the prairie bloomed and sparkled with irised light from myriads of washed crystals. Then suddenly all the glorious show would be darkened and blotted out.

Stickeen seemed to care for none of these things, bright or dark, nor for the crevasses, wells, moulins or swift flashing streams into which he might fall. The little adventurer was only about two years old, yet nothing seemed novel to him, nothing daunted him. He showed neither caution nor curiosity, wonder nor fear, but bravely trotted on as if glaciers were playgrounds. His stout, muffled body seemed all one skipping muscle, and it was truly wonderful to see how swiftly and to all appearance heedlessly he flashed across nerve-trying chasms six or eight feet wide. His courage was so unwavering that it seemed to be due to dullness of perception, as if he were only blindly bold; and I kept warning him to be careful. For we had been close companions on so many wilderness trips that I had formed the habit of talking to him as if he were a boy and understood every word.

We gained the west shore in about three hours; the width of the glacier here being about seven miles. Then I pushed northward in order to see as far back as possible into the fountains of the Fairweather Mountains, in case the clouds should rise. The walking was easy along the margin of the forest, which, of course, like that on the other side, had been invaded and crushed by the swollen, overflowing glacier. In an hour or so, after passing a massive headland, we came suddenly on a branch of the glacier, which, in the form of a magnificent ice-cascade two miles wide, was pouring over the rim of the main basin in a westerly direction, its surface broken into wave-shaped blades and shattered blocks, suggesting the wildest updashing, heaving, plunging motion of a great river cataract. Tracing it down three or four miles, I found that it discharged into a lake, filling it with icebergs.

I would gladly have followed the lake outlet to tidewater, but the day was already far spent, and the threatening sky called for haste on the return trip to get off the ice before dark. I decided therefore to go no farther and, after taking a general view of the wonderful region, turned back, hoping to see it again under more favorable auspices. We made good speed up the canyon of the great ice-torrent, and out on the main glacier until we had left the west shore about two miles behind us. Here we got into a difficult network of crevasses, the gathering clouds began to drop misty fringes, and soon the dreaded snow came flying thick and fast. I now began to feel anxious about finding a way in the blurring storm. Stickeen showed no trace of fear. He was still the same silent, able little hero. I noticed, however, that after the storm-darkness came on he kept close up behind me. The snow urged us to make still greater haste, but at the same time hid our way. I pushed on as best I could, jumping innumerable crevasses, and for every hundred rods or so of direct advance traveling a mile in doubling up and down in the turmoil of chasms and dislocated ice-blocks. After an hour or two of this work we came to a series of longitudinal crevasses of appalling width, and almost straight and regular in trend, like immense furrows. These I traced with firm nerve, excited and strengthened by the danger, making wide jumps, poising cautiously on their dizzy edges after cutting hollows for my feet before making the spring, to avoid possible slipping or any uncertainty on the farther sides, where only one trial is granted—exercise at once frightful and inspiring. Stickeen followed seemingly without effort.

Many a mile we thus traveled, mostly up and down, making but little real headway in crossing, running instead of walking most of the time as the danger of being compelled to spend the night on the glacier became threatening. Stickeen seemed able for anything. Doubtless we could have weathered the storm for one night, dancing on a flat spot to keep from freezing, and I faced the threat without feeling anything like despair; but we were hungry and wet, and the wind from the mountains was still thick with snow and bitterly cold, so of course that night would have seemed a very long one. I could not see far enough through the blurring snow to judge in which general direction the least dangerous route lay, while the few dim, momentary glimpses I caught of mountains through rifts in the flying clouds were far from encouraging either as weather signs or as guides. I had simply to grope my way from crevasse to crevasse, holding a general direction by the ice-structure, which was not to be seen everywhere, and partly by the wind. Again and again I was put to my mettle, but Stickeen followed easily, his nerve apparently growing more unflinching as the danger increased. So it always is with mountaineers when hard beset. Running hard and jumping, holding every minute of the remaining daylight, poor as it was, precious, we doggedly persevered and tried to hope that every difficult crevasse we overcame would prove to be the last of its kind. But on the contrary, as we advanced they became more deadly trying.

At length our way was barred by a very wide and straight crevasse, which I traced rapidly northward a mile or so without finding a crossing or hope of one; then down the glacier about as far, to where it united with another uncrossable crevasse. In all this distance of perhaps two miles there was only one place where I could possibly jump it, but the width of this jump was the utmost I dared attempt, while the danger of slipping on the farther side was so great that I was loath to try it. Furthermore, the side I was on was about a foot higher than the other, and even with this advantage the crevasse seemed dangerously wide. One is liable to underestimate the width of crevasses where the magnitudes in general are great. I therefore stared at this one mighty keenly, estimating its width and the shape of the edge on the farther side, until I thought that I could jump it if necessary, but that in case I should be compelled to jump back from the lower side I might fail. Now, a cautious mountaineer seldom takes a step on unknown ground which seems at all dangerous that he cannot retrace in case he should be stopped by unseen obstacles ahead. This is the rule of mountaineers who live long, and, though in haste, I compelled myself to sit down and calmly deliberate before I broke it.

Retracing my devious path in imagination as if it were drawn on a chart, I saw that I was recrossing the glacier a mile or two farther up stream than the course pursued in the morning, and that I was now entangled in a section I had not before seen. Should I risk this dangerous jump, or try to regain the woods on the west shore, make a fire and have only hunger to endure while waiting for a new day? I had already crossed so broad a stretch of dangerous ice that I saw it would be difficult to get back to the woods through the storm before dark, and the attempt would most likely result in a dismal night-dance on the glacier; while just beyond the present barrier the surface seemed more promising, and the east shore was now perhaps about as near as the west. I was therefore eager to go on. But this wide jump was a dreadful obstacle.

At length, because of the dangers already behind me, I determined to venture against those that might be ahead, jumped and landed well, but with so little to spare that I more than ever dreaded being compelled to take that jump back from the lower side. Stickeen followed, making nothing of it, and we ran eagerly forward, hoping we were leaving all our troubles behind. But within the distance of a few hundred yards we were stopped by the widest crevasse yet encountered. Of course I made haste to explore it, hoping all might yet be remedied by finding a bridge or a way around either end. About three-fourths of a mile upstream I found that it united with the one we had just crossed, as I feared it would. Then, tracing it down, I found it joined the same crevasse at the lower end also, maintaining throughout its whole course a width of forty to fifty feet. Thus to my dismay I discovered that we were on a narrow island about two miles long, with two barely possible ways to escape: one back by the way we came, the other ahead by an almost inaccessible sliver-bridge that crossed the great crevasse from near the middle of it!

After this nerve-trying discovery I ran back to the sliver-bridge and cautiously examined it. Crevasses, caused by strains from variations in the rate of motion of different parts of the glacier and convexities in the channel, are mere cracks when they first open, so narrow as hardly to admit the blade of a pocket-knife, and gradually widen according to the extent of the strain and the depth of the glacier. Now some of these cracks are interrupted, like the cracks in wood, and in opening, the strip of ice between overlapping ends is dragged out, and may maintain a continuous connection between the side, just as the two sides of a slivered crack in wood that is being split are connected. Some crevasses remain open for months or even years, and by the melting of their sides continue to increase in width long after the opening strain has ceased; while the sliver-bridges, level on top at first and perfectly safe, are at length melted to thin, vertical, knife-edged blades, the upper portion being most exposed to the weather; and since the exposure is greatest in the middle, they at length curve downward like the cables of suspension bridges. This one was evidently very old, for it had been weathered and wasted until it was the most dangerous and inaccessible that ever lay in my way. The width of the crevasse was here about fifty feet, and the sliver crossing diagonally was about seventy feet long; its thin knife-edge near the middle was depressed twenty-five or thirty feet below the level of the glacier, and the up-curving ends were attached to the sides eight or ten feet below the brink. Getting down the nearly vertical wall to the end of the sliver and up the other side were the main difficulties, and they seemed all but insurmountable. Of the many perils encountered in my years of wandering on mountains and glaciers none seemed so plain and stern and merciless as this. And it was presented when we were wet to the skin and hungry, the sky dark with quick driving snow, and the night near. But we were forced to face it. It was a tremendous necessity.

Beginning, not immediately above the sunken end of the bridge, but a little to one side, I cut a deep hollow on the brink for my knees to rest in. Then, leaning over, with my short-handled ax I cut a step sixteen or eighteen inches below, which on account of the sheerness of the wall was necessarily shallow. That step, however, was well made; its floor sloped slightly inward and formed a good hold for my heels. Then, slipping cautiously upon it, and crouching as low as possible, with my left side toward the wall, I steadied myself against the wind with my left hand in a slight notch, while with the right I cut other similar steps and notches in succession, guarding against losing balance by glinting of the ax, or by wind-gusts, for life and death were in every stroke and in the niceness of finish of every foothold.

After the end of the bridge was reached I chipped it down until I had made a level platform six or eight inches wide, and it was a trying thing to poise on this little slippery platform while bending over to get safely astride of the sliver. Crossing was then comparatively easy by chipping off the sharp edge with short, careful strokes, and hitching forward an inch or two at a time, keeping my balance with my knees pressed against the sides. The tremendous abyss on either hand I studiously ignored. To me the edge of that blue sliver was then all the world. But the most trying part of the adventure, after working my way across inch by inch and chipping another small platform, was to rise from the safe position astride and to cut a stepladder in the nearly vertical face of the wall—chipping, climbing, holding on with feet and fingers in mere notches. At such times one's whole body is eye, and common skill and fortitude are replaced by power beyond our call or knowledge. Never before had I been so long under deadly strain. How I got up that cliff I never could tell. The thing seemed to have been done by somebody else. I never have held death in contempt, though in the course of my explorations I have oftentimes felt that to meet one's fate on a noble mountain, or in the heart of a glacier, would be blessed as compared with death from disease, or from some shabby lowland accident. But the best death, quick and crystal-pure, set so glaringly open be-fore us, is hard enough to face, even though we feel gratefully sure that we have already had happiness enough for a dozen lives.

But poor Stickeen, the wee, hairy, sleekit beastie, think of him! When I had decided to dare the bridge, and while I was on my knees chipping a hollow on the rounded brow above it, he came behind me, pushed his head past my shoulder, looked down and across, scanned the sliver and its approaches with his mysterious eyes, then looked me in the face with a startled air of surprise and concern and began to mutter and whine; saying as plainly as if speaking with words, "Surely you are not going into that awful place." This was the first time I had seen him gaze deliberately into a crevasse, or into my face with an eager, speaking, troubled look. That he should have recognized and appreciated the danger at the first glance showed wonderful sagacity. Never before had the daring midget seemed to know that ice was slippery or that there was any such thing as danger anywhere. His looks and tones of voice when he began to complain and speak his fears were so human that I unconsciously talked to him in sympathy as I would to a frightened boy, and in trying to calm his fears perhaps in some measure moderated my own. "Hush your fears, my boy," I said, "we will get across safe, though it is not going to be easy. No right way is easy in this rough world. We must risk our lives to save them. At the worst we can only slip, and then how grand a grave we will have, and by and by our nice bones will do good in the terminal moraine."

But my sermon was far from reassuring him: he began to cry, and after taking another piercing look at the tremendous gulf, ran away in desperate excitement, seeking some other crossing. By the time he got back, baffled of course, I had made a step or two. I dared not look back, but he made himself heard; and when he saw that I was certainly bent on crossing he cried aloud in despair. The danger was enough to daunt anybody, but it seems wonderful that he should have been able to weigh and appreciate it so justly. No mountaineer could have seen it more quickly or judged it more wisely, discriminating between real and apparent peril.

When I gained the other side, he screamed

louder than ever, and after running back and forth in vain search for a way of escape, he would return to the brink of the crevasse above the bridge, moaning and wailing as if in the bitterness of death. Could this be the silent, philosophic Stickeen? I shouted encouragement, telling him the bridge was not so bad as it looked, that I had left it flat and safe for his feet, and he could walk it easily. But he was afraid to try. Strange so small an animal should be capable of such big, wise fears. I called again and again in a reassuring tone to come on and fear nothing; that he could come if he would only try. He would hush for a moment, look down again at the bridge, and shout his unshakable conviction that he could never, never come that way; then lie back in despair, as if howling, "O-o-oh! what a place! No-o-o, I can never go-o-o down there!" His natural composure and courage had vanished utterly in a tumultuous storm of fear. Had the danger been less, his distress would have seemed ridiculous. But in this dismal, merciless abyss lay the shadow of death, and his heart-rending cries might well have called Heaven to his help. Perhaps they did. So hidden before, he was now transparent, and one could see the workings of his heart and mind like the movements of a clock out of its case. His voice and gestures, hopes and fears, were so perfectly human that none could mistake them; while he seemed to understand every word of mine. I was troubled at the thought of having to leave him out all night, and of the danger of not finding him in the morning. It seemed impossible to get him to venture. To compel him to try through fear of being abandoned, I started off as if leaving him to his fate, and disappeared back of a hummock; but this did no good; he only lay down and moaned in utter hopeless misery. So, after hiding a few minutes, I went back to the brink of the crevasse and in a severe tone of voice shouted across to him that now I must certainly leave him, I could wait no longer, and that, if he would not come, all I could promise was that I would return to seek him next day. I warned him that if he went back to the woods the wolves would kill him, and finished by urging him once more by words and gestures to come on, come on.

He knew very well what I meant, and at last, with the courage of despair, hushed and breathless, he crouched down on the brink in the hollow I had made for my knees, pressed his body against the ice as if trying to get the advantage of the friction of every hair, gazed into the first step, put his little feet together and slid them slowly, slowly over the edge and down into it, bunching all four in it and almost standing on his head. Then, without lifting his feet, as well as I could see through the snow, he slowly worked them over the edge of the step and down into the next and the next in succession in the same way, and gained the end of the bridge. Then, lifting his feet with the regularity and slowness of the vibrations of a seconds pendulum, as if counting and measuring *one-two-three,* holding himself steady against the gusty wind, and giving separate attention to each little step, he gained the foot of the cliff, while I was on my knees leaning over to give him a lift should he succeed in getting within reach of my arm. Here he halted in dead silence, and it was here I feared he might fail, for dogs are poor climbers. I had no cord. If I had had one, I would have dropped a noose over his head and hauled him up. But while I was thinking whether an available cord might be made out of clothing, he was looking keenly into the series of notched steps and finger-holds I had made, as if counting them, and fixing the position of each one of them in his mind. Then suddenly up he came in a springy rush, hooking his paws into the steps and notches so quickly that I could not see how it was done, and whizzed past my head, safe at last!

And now came a scene! "Well done, well done, little boy! Brave boy!" I cried, trying to catch and caress him; but he would not be caught. Never before or since have I seen anything like so passionate a revulsion from the depths of despair to exultant, triumphant, uncontrollable joy. He flashed and darted hither and thither as if fairly demented, screaming and shouting, swirling round and round in giddy loops and circles like a leaf in a whirlwind, lying down and rolling over and over, sidewise and heels over head and pouring forth a tumultuous flood of hysterical cries and sobs and gasping mutterings. When I ran up to him to shake him,

In Charge *by J. Bateman*

fearing he might die of joy, he flashed off two or three hundred yards, his feet in a mist of motion; then, turning suddenly, came back in a wild rush and launched himself at my face, almost knocking me down, all the time screeching and screaming and shouting as if saying, "Saved! saved! saved!" Then away again, dropping suddenly at times with his feet in the air, trembling and fairly sobbing. Such passionate emotion was enough to kill him. Moses' stately song of triumph after escaping the Egyptians and the Red Sea was nothing to it. Who could have guessed the capacity of the dull, enduring little fellow for all that most stirs this mortal frame? Nobody could have helped crying with him!

But there is nothing like work for toning down excessive fear or joy. So I ran ahead, calling him in as gruff a voice as I could command to come on and stop his nonsense, for we had far to go and it would soon be dark. Neither of us feared another trial like this. Heaven would surely count one enough for a lifetime. The ice ahead was gashed by thousands of crevasses, but they were common ones. The joy of deliverance

burned in us like fire, and we ran without fatigue, every muscle with immense rebound glorying in its strength. Stickeen flew across everything in his way, and not till dark did he settle into his normal foxlike trot. At last the cloudy mountains came in sight, and we soon felt the solid rock beneath our feet, and were safe. Then came weakness. Danger had vanished, and so had our strength. We tottered down the lateral moraine in the dark, over boulders and tree trunks, through the bushes and devil-club thickets of the grove where we had sheltered ourselves in the morning, and across the level mudslope of the terminal moraine. We reached camp about ten o'clock, and found a big fire and a big supper. A party of Hoona Indians had visited Mr. Young, bringing a gift of porpoise meat and wild strawberries, and Hunter Joe had brought in a wild goat. But we lay down, too tired to eat much, and soon fell into a troubled sleep. The man who said, "The harder the toil, the sweeter the rest," never was profoundly tired. Stickeen kept springing up and muttering in his sleep, no doubt dreaming that he was still on the brink of the crevasse; and so did I, that night and many others long afterward, when I was overtired.

Thereafter Stickeen was a changed dog. During the rest of the trip, instead of holding aloof, he always lay by my side, tried to keep me constantly in sight, and would hardly accept a morsel of food, however tempting, from any hand but mine. At night, when all was quiet about the campfire, he would come to me and rest his head on my knee with a look of devotion as if I were his god. And often as he caught my eye he seemed to be trying to say, "Wasn't that an awful time we had together on the glacier?"

Nothing in after years has dimmed that Alaska storm-day. As I write it all comes rushing and roaring to mind as if I were again in the heart of it. Again I see the gray flying clouds with their rain-floods and snow, the ice-cliffs towering above the shrinking forest, the majestic ice-cascade, the vast glacier outspread before its white mountain-fountains, and in the heart of it the tremendous crevasse—emblem of the valley of the shadow of death—low clouds trailing over it, the snow falling into it; and on its brink I see little Stickeen, and I hear his cries for help and his shouts of joy. I have known many dogs, and many a story I could tell of their wisdom and devotion; but to none do I owe so much as to Stickeen. At first the least promising and least known of my dog-friends, he suddenly became the best known of them all. Our storm-battle for life brought him to light, and through him as through a window I have ever since been looking with deeper sympathy into all my fellow mortals.

None of Stickeen's friends knows what finally became of him. After my work for the season was done I departed for California, and I never saw the dear little fellow again. In reply to anxious inquiries his master wrote me that in the summer of 1883 he was stolen by a tourist at Fort Wrangell and taken away on a steamer. His fate is wrapped in mystery. Doubtless he has left this world—crossed the last crevasse—and gone to another. But he will not be forgotten. To me Stickeen is immortal.

Elegy for a Dead Labrador

by LARS GUSTAFSSON

Here there may be, in the midst of summer,
a few days when suddenly it's fall.
Thrushes sing on a sharper note.
The rocks stand determined out in the water.
They know something. They've always known it.
We know it, too, and we don't like it.
On the way home, in the boat, on just such even-
    ings,
you would stand stock-still in the bow, collected,
scouting the scents coming across the water.
You read the evening, the faint streak of smoke
from a garden, a pancake frying
half a mile away, a badger
standing somewhere in the same twilight
sniffing the same way. Our friendship
was of course a compromise; we lived
together in two different worlds: mine,
mostly letters, a text passing through life;
yours, mostly smells. You had knowledge
I would have given much to have possessed:
the ability to let a feeling—eagerness, hate, or
    love—
run like a wave through your body
from nose to tip of tail, the inability
ever to accept the moon as fact.
At the full moon you always complained loudly
    against it.
You were a better Gnostic than I am. And conse-
    quently

you lived continually in paradise.
You had a habit of catching butterflies on the
    leap
and munching them, which some people thought
    disgusting.
I always liked it. Why
couldn't I learn from you? And doors.
In front of closed doors you lay down and slept,
sure that sooner or later the one would come
who'd open up the door. You were right.
I was wrong. I ask myself, now this
long mute friendship is forever finished,
if possibly there was anything I could do
which impressed you. Your firm conviction
that I called up the thunderstorms
doesn't count. That was a mistake. I think
my certain faith that the ball existed,
even when hidden behind the couch,
somehow gave you an inkling of my world.
In my world most things were hidden
behind something else. I called you "dog."
I really wonder whether you conceived of me
as a larger, noisier "dog,"
or as something else, forever unknown,
something that is what it is, existing in that attri-
    bute
it exists in, a whistle
in the nocturnal park one has got used to
returning to without actually knowing

39

what it is one is returning to. About you,
and who you were, I knew no more.
One might say, from this more objective
standpoint, we were two organisms. Two
of those places where the universe makes a knot
in itself, short-lived, complex structures
of proteins that have to complicate themselves

more and more in order to survive, until everything
breaks and turns simple once again, the knot
dissolved, the riddle gone. You were a question
asked of another question, nothing more,
and neither had the answer to the other.

The Friend in Suspense *by Sir Edwin Landseer*

(Translated, from the Swedish, by Yvonne L. Sandstroem.)

Kooa's Song

by FARLEY MOWAT

THE new location of the summer den was ideal from the wolves' point of view, but not from mine, for the clutter of boulders made it difficult to see what was happening. In addition, caribou were now trickling back into the country from the north, and the pleasures of the hunt were siren calls to all three adult wolves. They still spent most of each day at or near the summer den, but they were usually so tired from their nightly excursions that they did little but sleep.

I was beginning to find time hanging heavy on my hands when Uncle Albert* rescued me from boredom by falling in love.

When Mike departed from the cabin shortly after my first arrival there he had taken all his dogs with him—not, as I suspected, because he did not trust them in the vicinity of my array of scalpels, but because the absence of caribou made it impossible to feed them. Throughout June his team had remained with the Eskimos, whose camps were in the caribous' summer territory; but now that the deer were returning south the Eskimo who had been keeping the dogs brought them back.

Mike's dogs were of aboriginal stock, and

*Uncle Albert, George and Angeline are nicknames Mowat gave to three members of a small wolf pack he has been studying.—*Ed.*

were magnificent beasts. Contrary to yet another myth, Eskimo dogs are not semidomesticated wolves—though both species may well have sprung from the same ancestry. Smaller in stature than wolves, true huskies are of a much heavier build, with broad chests, shorter necks and bushy tails which curl over their rumps like plumes. They differ from wolves in other ways too. Unlike their wild relations, husky bitches come into heat at any time of the year with a gay disregard for seasons.

When Mike's team returned to the cabin one of the bitches was just coming into heat. Being hot-blooded by nature, and amorous by inclination, this particular bitch soon had the rest of the team in an uproar and was causing Mike no end of trouble. He was complaining about the problem one evening when inspiration came to me.

Because of their continent habits, my study of the wolves had so far revealed nothing about their sexual life and, unless I was prepared to follow them about during the brief mating season in March, when they would be wandering with the caribou herds, I stood no chance of filling in this vital gap in my knowledge.

Now I knew, from what Mike and Ootek had already told me, that wolves are not against miscegenation. In fact they will mate with dogs, or vice versa, whenever the opportunity arises. It does not arise often, because the dogs are almost invariably tied up except when working, but it *does* happen.

I put my proposition to Mike and to my delight he agreed. In fact he seemed quite pleased, for it appeared that he had long wished to discover for himself what kind of sled dogs a wolf-husky cross would make.

The next problem was how to arrange the experiment so that my researches would benefit to the maximum degree. I decided to do the thing in stages. The first stage was to consist of taking the bitch, whose name was Kooa, for a walk around the vicinity of my new observation site, in order to make her existence and condition known to the wolves.

Kooa was more than willing. In fact, when we crossed one of the wolf trails she became so enthusiastic it was all I could do to restrain her impetuosity by means of a heavy chain leash. Dragging me behind her she plunged down the trail, sniffing every marker with uninhibited anticipation.

It was with great difficulty that I dragged her back to the cabin where, once she was firmly tethered, she reacted by howling her frustration the whole night through.

Or perhaps it was not frustration that made her sing; for when I got up next morning Ootek informed me we had had a visitor. Sure enough, the tracks of a big wolf were plainly visible in the wet sand of the riverbank not a hundred yards from the dog-lines. Probably it was only the presence of the jealous male huskies which had prevented the romance from being consummated that very night.

I had been unprepared for such quick results, although I should have foreseen that either George or Albert would have been sure to find some of Kooa's seductively scented billets-doux that same evening.

I now had to rush the second phase of my plan into execution. Ootek and I repaired to the observation tent and, a hundred yards beyond it in the direction of the summer den, we strung a length of heavy wire between two rocks about fifty feet from one another.

The next morning we led Kooa (or more properly, were led *by* Kooa) to the site. Despite her determined attempts to go off wolf seeking on her own, we managed to shackle her chain to the wire. She retained considerable freedom of movement with this arrangement, and we could command her position from the tent with rifle fire in case anything went wrong.

Rather to my surprise she settled down at once and spent most of the afternoon sleeping. No adult wolves were in evidence near the summer den, but we caught glimpses of the pups occasionally as they lumbered about the little grassy patch, leaping and pouncing after mice.

About 8:30 P.M. the wolves suddenly broke into their prehunting song, although they themselves remained invisible behind a rock ridge to the south of the den.

The first sounds had barely reached me when Kooa leaped to her feet and joined the chorus. And *how* she howled! Although there is not, as far as I am aware, any canine or lupine blood in my veins, the seductive quality of Kooa's siren song was enough to set me thinking longingly of other days and other joys.

That the wolves understood the burden of her plaint was not long in doubt. Their song stopped in mid-swing, and seconds later all three of them came surging over the crest of the ridge into our view. Although she was a quarter of a mile away, Kooa was clearly visible to them. After only a moment's hesitation, both George and Uncle Albert started toward her at a gallop.

George did not get very far. Before he had gone fifty yards Angeline had overtaken him and, while I am not prepared to swear to this, I had the distinct impression that she somehow tripped him. At any rate he went sprawling in the muskeg, and when he picked himself up his interest in Kooa seemed to have evaporated. To do him justice, I do not believe he was interested in her in a sexual way—probably he was simply taking the lead in investigating a strange intruder into his domain. In any event, he and Angeline withdrew to the summer den, where they lay down together on the lip of the ravine and watched proceedings, leaving it up to Uncle Albert to handle the situation as he saw fit.

I do not know how long Albert had been celibate, but it had clearly been too long. When he reached the area where Kooa was tethered he was moving so fast he overshot. For one tense moment I thought he had decided we were competing suitors and was going to continue straight on into the tent to deal with us; but he got turned somehow, and his wild rush slowed. Then when he was within ten feet of Kooa, who was awaiting his arrival in a state of ecstatic anticipation, Albert's manner suddenly changed. He stopped dead in his tracks, lowered his great head and turned into a buffoon.

It was an embarrassing spectacle. Laying his ears back until they were flush with his broad skull, he began to wiggle like a pup while at the same time wrinkling his lips in a frightful grimace which may have been intended to register infatuation, but which looked to me more like a symptom of senile decay. He also began to whine in a wheedling falsetto which would have sounded disgusting coming from a Pekinese.

Kooa seemed nonplussed by his remarkable behavior. Obviously she had never before been wooed in this surprising manner, and she seemed uncertain what to do about it. With a half-snarl she backed away from Albert as far as her chain would permit.

This sent Albert into a frenzy of abasement. Belly to earth, he began to grovel toward her while his grimace widened into an expression of sheer idiocy.

I now began to share Kooa's concern, and thinking the wolf had taken complete leave of his senses I was about to seize the rifle and go to Kooa's rescue, when Ootek restrained me. He was grinning; a frankly salacious grin, and he was able to make it clear that I was not to worry; that things were progressing perfectly normally from a wolfish point of view.

At this point Albert shifted gears with bewildering rapidity. Scrambling to his feet he suddenly became the lordly male. His ruff expanded until it made a huge silvery aura framing his face. His body stiffened until he seemed to be made of white steel. His tail rose until it was as high, and almost as tightly curled, as a true husky's. Then, pace by delicate pace, he closed the gap.

Kooa was no longer in doubt. *This* was something she could understand. Rather coyly she turned her back toward him and as he stretched out his great nose to offer his first caress she spun about and nipped him coyly on the shoulder. . . .

My notes on the rest of this incident are fully detailed but I fear they are too technical and full of scientific terminology to deserve a place in this book. I shall therefore content myself by summing up what followed with the observation that Albert certainly knew how to make love.

My scientific curiosity had been assuaged, but Uncle Albert's passion hadn't, and a most difficult situation now developed. Although we waited with as much patience as we could muster for two full hours, Albert showed not the slightest indication of ever intending to depart from his new-found love. Ootek and I wished to return to the cabin with Kooa, and we could not wait forever. In some desperation we finally made a sally toward the enamored pair.

Albert stood his ground, or rather he ignored us totally. Even Ootek seemed somewhat uncertain how to proceed after we reached a point not fifteen feet from the lovers without Albert's having given any sign that he might be inclined to leave. It was a stalemate which was only broken when I, with much reluctance, fired a shot into the ground a little way from where Albert stood.

The shot woke him from his trance. He leaped high into the air and bounded off a dozen yards, but having quickly recovered his equanimity he started to edge back toward us. Meanwhile we had untied the chain, and while Ootek dragged the sullenly reluctant Kooa off toward home, I covered the rear with the rifle.

Albert stayed right with us. He kept fifteen to twenty yards away, sometimes behind, sometimes on the flanks, sometimes in front; but leave us he would not.

Back at the cabin we again tried to cool his

ardor by firing a volley in the air, but this had no effect except to make him withdraw a few yards farther off. There was obviously nothing for it but to take Kooa into the cabin for the night; for to have chained her on the dog-line with her teammates would have resulted in a battle royal between them and Albert.

It was a frightful night. The moment the door closed, Albert broke into a lament. He wailed and whooped and yammered without pause for hours. The dogs responded with a cacophony of shrill insults and counterwails. Kooa joined in by screaming messages of undying love. It was an intolerable situation. By morning Mike was threatening to do some more shooting, and in real earnest.

It was Ootek who saved the day, and possibly Albert's life as well. He convinced Mike that if he released Kooa, all would be well. She would not run away, he explained, but would stay in the vicinity of the camp with the wolf. When her period of heat was over she would return home and the wolf would go back to his own kind.

He was perfectly right, as usual. During the next week we sometimes caught glimpses of the lovers walking shoulder to shoulder across some distant ridge. They never went near the den esker, nor did they come close to the cabin. They lived in a world all their own, oblivious to everything except each other.

They were not aware of us, but I was uncomfortably aware of them, and I was glad when, one morning, we found Kooa lying at her old place in the dog-line looking exhausted but satiated.

The next evening Uncle Albert once more joined in the evening ritual chorus at the wolf esker. However, there was now a mellow, self-satisfied quality to his voice that I had never heard before, and it set my teeth on edge. Braggadocio is an emotion which I have never been able to tolerate—not even in wolves.

Poor Tweed

by IAN NIALL

THE life of a working dog is short, especially a dog that is out in all weathers, earning his keep by shepherding. The dog's coat gets wet and only his continual exertions dry the long hair on most occasions. This is not to say that shepherds are callous towards their dogs. It is impossible to mollycoddle a dog that travels twenty miles on a wet or damp and misty day. The dog steams out by the fire. The onset of rheumatism is inevitable. His master almost certainly suffers from it himself. They are both used to sheltering and shivering on the lea sides of drystone walls or close under a dripping peat bank that shields them from the wind. A procession of dogs accompanied me through my childhood and adolescence. I would come back on holiday and find the faces changed and a new dog there being trained. I suppose most of these faithful animals had a working life of six or seven years and were pensioned off but where they all came from I was never able to find out. I suppose my grandfather met a hill shepherd at the market and arranged to buy a useful or partly-trained dog and there were more where this one came from. Tweed may have been one of these. Grandfather was reckoned to be a very good judge of horseflesh. He bred some good Clydesdales and I suppose in a lifetime he must have acquired an eye for a dog, but dogs weren't his business by any stretch of imagination. He once

in a while bought the wrong horse (and quickly got rid of it again) and he should have done this with poor Tweed, but there it was. Tweed came at the wrong time, when my brothers were there to accompany me into the wilderness and we were all as wild as the hare itself. Tweed was about the same mental age, a young dog, not sure what life was meant to be about. He was there to be trained and he no more wanted training than I wanted the schoolroom. He wanted to be free. I suppose the only people he understood were children. The old working dog looked upon him with disapproval and often nipped him for some misdemeanor or out of downright meanness. He wanted to escape and hated to be made to stand by in case he might be needed. When we were off for the morning he would slip out after us, slinking up the hedgeside and only attaching himself to us when he thought he wouldn't be sent home. We didn't send him home unless we encountered one of the family, an adult who commanded us to send him home. As soon as he discovered that we were the next best thing to a pack of hunting dogs, Tweed was our inseparable companion. He would follow us anywhere. He taught himself to hunt with us, to cooperate in the jungle way of beating through a great gorse clump to drive out a hare that had foolishly taken shelter there instead of racing off across the open ground. There was never anything that made my hackles rise as much as this tension. Tweed's hair ruffed too. He would pause and look at us and words were no longer necessary. A moment later the hare would bolt and we would throw our sticks to bring him down if we could. Sometimes it wasn't a hare that came out but an old cock pheasant, running as fast as any hare, and arrowing for the shelter of a bank or a thicket to which we would all charge like savages to renew the hunt. Often these prolonged chases ended with our quarry crossing a deep drain or taking to the air with a great clatter as cock pheasants will. Tweed and his accomplices would slow down for a hundred yards or so until a rabbit was startled out of the round rushes and bolted for a bush a few yards farther on. We knew every warren and almost every burrow in every warren. We had Tweed to dig for us, a thing he would do almost lying on his side and using his forefeet furiously as he built a mound of black earth behind him and sometimes threw the stuff in our eyes. We had ways of smoking rabbits out by lighting little fires of gorse on the windward side of a bank and making sure the suffocating smoke was fanned into the burrow. We were barbarians and when I think of it all now I am sorry for Tweed. He came to be a sheep dog and he might have been one if he hadn't been led astray. He might never have met his executioner, I think, but for the fact that his dog youth was misspent.

"The boys are ruining that dog," someone would say. We didn't think so. We loved him and he loved to be with us. He was wild and we were wild. No one said we were ruining ourselves. Did we corrupt him or did he corrupt us? I don't think anyone was to blame. When we ran with Tweed or he ran with us, barking and dancing round us as we sprang down from the drystone wall, we were doing what man and dog had done almost since the beginning of time. If there was any perversion of natural instinct it was in making the dog nursemaid to stupid sheep. How many days we hunted the bracken, the great sea of round rushes in the low bog, the mossy hags and heather banks, the gorse hills and long grass of the hay fields with him! Our elders were too busy to concern themselves with what was hap-

pening. Everyone had work to do, harrowing newly sown oats, cleaning out the stable, feeding hens, carting peats, mowing rushes for rickyard thatch.

We went back to London and returned again for another holiday. In London I would think of Tweed while I struggled with my homework and even when I sat in the classroom. The schoolmaster knew the idlers and the daydreamers only too well. He would prod me with the blackboard pointer when I was five hundred miles away on a stubble hill watching a covey of partridges whirring in a hollow and looking at Tweed when he turned and looked at me. What did the dreary theorems of Euclid matter? Even in the chalk dust I could breathe the scent of the moss and follow Tweed's swaying tail as he bustled through scrub bushes and old, blackened gorse the shepherd had fired in spring. "Come back to earth!" the schoolmaster would urge, and I came back to triangles and arcs and radii. They never meant a thing to me but I did know where you could put up a hare and Tweed knew where to cut it off. Even if he didn't we could run on and find another or put a rabbit out and knock him down with a stick. The schoolmaster never knew the kind of savage he was trying to teach. He knew the boys who lingered late at night in the gaslight pools of almost deserted streets. He knew those whose dreams were of finding a sixpence and going to the pictures, but he didn't know me and if he had he would have shuddered. In a year or two I would spend all of every holiday wandering with a gun, fishing for trout or looking for plovers' nests, but this was to come. I would be put on the train back north fearful only that in the meantime Tweed would have been turned into a sober old working dog who couldn't be persuaded to join in and hunt the woods, even the keeper's preserves when we knew he was engaged elsewhere. Tweed didn't change. The damage was done. He was a renegade. He had reverted to ancestors back beyond his herding forebears, his servile father and grandfather. His failure as a working dog was already well-known and accepted. When people came to visit they would remark upon him for he was black and brown, a sort of brindly color, not unlike dyed Harris tweed I suppose. The adults of the family would look at him and shrug. He was a waster, something to be ashamed of, hidden away like an alcoholic relative. "The boys spoilt him," they would say. They didn't mean that he had been spoiled as a child is indulged, but ruined. Poor Tweed knew it. He would creep in under the table, aware of the shame. We were sorry for him. The world was cruel. All he wanted to do was to enjoy his young life. His development had been arrested, I suppose a psychiatrist might say. He had been turned into a permanent adolescent.

When we couldn't hunt the fields because it was too wet or too cold even for the hardiest of us, there was always a cat hunt. The farm had more than its share of cats. They were never the sleek, well-fed cats of the old ladies but lean and hungry, Cassius cats that lived by their wits. They had tattered ears and patches of baldness on their heads or backs. They growled more than they purred. They snarled and sprang at one another like angry tigers. A misguided compassion made my aunts put out churn lids of milk for these wild strays. They said it was by way of reward for all the mice and rats they must kill, but come threshing day there were always just as many mice and rats in the rick bottoms. We hunted these hungry cats in a wild stampede from stable to barn and high granary, from the open-sided shed to the piggery and up the byre walks. If anyone heard us yelling in pursuit they would come out and give us a lecture that would leave us all with hanging heads. Only Tweed escaped, for he would be off on the top of the hay or the at back of the straw house, cornering one of those spitting, long-clawed wild cats in the hope that we might eventually come up with him. It was all very reprehensible. It had to stop. Father lectured us and threatened us with all kinds of punishment. Grandfather raged as only he could. Tweed was forbidden to hunt. We were forbidden ever to take him to the fields again, or hiss him on to chase the most scabby of the cat intruders. It wasn't just cruel. It was the ruin of a dog. His end would come, tied to a stake and looking up at the barrels of a twelve-bore.

Poor Tweed slunk about with his tail between his legs. When we went away he began to take himself hunting. People reported him far and wide, loping along a wall like a wolf, standing all by himself on some big field of feathery ryegrass and looking guilty as a sheep-worrier, which was the only crime he hadn't yet committed. It wasn't just that he roamed and neighbors saw their flocks crowding in a corner as he passed, but that he was recognized as our dog. This was like one of the family making a fool of himself in public, at market or on a cattle show day. His name was the family's name. He had to be chained and kept in the stable. There was nothing else for it. I have felt guilty about it ever since but what is one dog more or less, some people will say. Man is a superior animal and dogs are expendable.

It happened that Tweed had been kept on the chain so long that although he had a fine bed of dry straw and could sleep the clock round and find his food dish full, he became morose. He began to snarl at those who came near him. The chain held him in the manger. He saw nothing. He heard very little except the horses grinding their oats and the cock crowing. It was wrong and someone should have done something about it. A young cousin came into the stable for something one day and walked past poor sleeping Tweed who came awake in a frenzy of rage, leapt up and tore at him. The boy staggered back with a frightful wound on his upper lip. The doctor had to stitch it. There was even some anxiety in case such a wild, roaming dog could have contracted rabies. They did what had become inevitable. Tweed was taken on the end of the chain and led to the place of execution where a hole had been dug and a pile of quicklime tipped from a cauldron. The chain was fastened to a stake. Tweed crouched on all fours and looked at the farmhand with the gun. He surely knew in that moment where his life had finally led him, or perhaps he didn't. Perhaps he wondered why the gun came to bear on his head and was steadied for a moment. The shot echoed back from the walls of the steading and Tweed slumped, blood coloring his black-and-tan head. His body was tipped into the pit and the lime shoveled in on top with a long-handled lime shovel. When I came on holiday again I saw the place where he was buried. The stake was still in the ground. I choked a little and wiped a tear from my cheek because he had been part of my boyhood and my brothers' boyhood too. He had been as close a companion as any of us had known and we had brought him to this.

Grandfather was philosophical about it. A dog bites a man and he must be put down, he said. Mind you, the man was often as much to blame as the dog, whether he was aware of it or not. This is the truth of it. A dog bites because he is frightened, because he is driven out of his mind, because he has been brutally used. We can find in it all the reasons we find for human misdeeds. We make our dogs what they are. It is a long time since Tweed was shot. No other dog the family had was "put down," as country folk call it. I can't forget him. I hunt with him still, not because I long for the wildness, but because I would love to know again the exhilaration, the tense excitement of the days we ran wild together, young and free as the wind blowing across the moss. It saddens me when I look at myself past middle age and at my brothers and know how impossible it is for us to ever know such excitement again.

Shepherd's Dog *by P. Reinagle*

De Re Rustica

by MARCUS TERENTIUS VARRO

ABOUT dogs then: there are two kinds, one for hunting connected with the wild beasts of the woods, the other trained for purposes of defense, and used by shepherds.

In the first place you must obtain dogs of the proper age; puppies and old dogs are no good to themselves or to the sheep either and sometimes become the prey of wild beasts. They should possess a handsome shape, and be of great size, their eyes black or yellowish, with nostrils to match; the lips should be blackish or red, the upper lips neither turned up too much nor hanging down too low. The lower jaw should be short and the two teeth that spring from it on the right and on the left side should project a little, while the upper teeth should be rather straight. The incisors should be covered by the lip; the head and ears large, and the latter broad and hanging; the neck and throat thick, the parts between the joints long, the legs straight and turned out rather than in; the feet big and broad, spreading out as they walk; the toes being well separated, and the claws hard and curved. The soles be neither horny nor overhard, but rather sponge-like and soft; the body tucked in near the top of the thighs, the spine neither prominent nor curved, and the tail thick. The bark should be deep, the stretch of the jaw extensive, the color preferably white, because they are then more easily recognized in the dark, and their appearance should be lionlike. Breeders also prefer that the bitches should have breasts with teats of equal size. One must also see that they come of a good breed. . . .

Be careful not to buy dogs from hunters or from butchers, for the dogs of butchers are too idle to follow the flock, while hunting dogs, if they see a hare or a stag, will chase after it instead of after the sheep. Thus the best is one that has been bought from shepherds and has been trained to follow sheep or has had no training at all. For a dog acquires a habit more quickly than other animals, and the attachment to the shepherds which results from familiar intercourse with them is stronger than that which he feels for the sheep. . . .

It is of importance that your dogs should be of the same blood, for when they are akin they are also the greatest protection to one another. . . .

A dog's food is more like a man's than a sheep's, for it feeds on scraps of meat and bones; not on grass or on leaves. You must be very careful to give them food, for if you do not, hunger will drive them to hunt for it and to desert the flock. . . . And you must give them barley-bread, and the bread should be well soaked in milk, for when once accustomed to such diet they are slow to desert the flock. They must not be allowed to

49

Water Spaniel *by P. Reinagle*

eat the flesh of a dead sheep for fear that the good flavor might weaken their restraint. They are also given bone soup or the bones themselves after they have been broken up, for this makes their teeth stronger, and the mouth wider because of the vigor with which their jaws are extended as they eagerly enjoy the marrow. Dogs are usually fed in the daytime when they go out to the pasture, and in the evening when they come back to the stalls.

As to breeding, this is usually arranged to commence with the beginning of spring; for it is then that they are in heat, that is, show their desire for mating. Bitches that are covered about this time of the year litter about the summer solstice, for gestation usually lasts three months. During pregnancy barley rather than wheaten bread should be given, for this will nourish them

better, and they will give a greater supply of milk.

And now we come to the rearing of the puppies: if there are many of them you should choose immediately after birth those you mean to keep and get rid of the rest. The fewer you leave the better they thrive, because they obtain an abundance of milk. Put chaff or something of a like nature for them to lie on, for the more comfortable their bed, the more easily are they reared. Puppies begin to see at twenty days old. For the first two months after birth they are not separated from their mother, but they learn gradually to do without her. . . . They are trained at first to be tied up with light leather thongs, and they are beaten if they try to gnaw them away, until they drop the habit. . . . Some people castrate them, thinking them less likely to leave the flock. Others do not because they believe that it kills their courage. . . . To prevent them from being wounded by wild beasts, collars are put on them; the collar, called "melium," is a band made of stout leather going round the neck and furnished with nails that have heads on them. Under these heads a piece of soft leather is sewn, so that the hardness of the iron may not hurt the neck of the dog. If a wolf or any other animal has been wounded by this collar, it makes all other dogs safe from him, even those who do not wear a collar.

The number of dogs is usually fixed in proportion to the size of the flock, and in most cases it is considered proper for one dog to follow each shepherd. As to the number, however, people differ in their estimates. If the district is one in which there is an abundance of wild beasts, more dogs will be necessary, and this is the case with those who have to travel with their flocks to summer and winter quarters by long tracks through the forest. But for a flock staying at the farmhouse two are considered sufficient, one male and one female. For so they hold better to their work. For the same dog when he has a companion grows keener than before, and if one or the other fall ill, the flock need not be without a dog.

A Robust Matter of Some Delicacy

by JAMES HERRIOT

I like women better than men.

Mind you, I have nothing against men —after all, I am one myself—but in the RAF there were too many of them. Literally thousands, jostling, shouting, swearing; you couldn't get away from them. Some of them became my friends and have remained so until the present day, but the sheer earthy mass of them made me realise how my few months of married life had changed me.

Women are gentler, softer, cleaner, altogether nicer things and I, who always considered myself one of the boys, had come to the surprising conclusion that the companion I wanted most was a woman.

My impression that I had been hurled into a coarser world was heightened at the beginning of each day, particularly one morning when I was on fire picket duty and had the sadistic pleasure of rattling the dustbin lids and shouting "Wakey-wakey!" along the corridors. It wasn't the cursing and the obscene remarks which struck deepest, it was the extraordinary abdominal noises issuing from the dark rooms. They reminded me of my patient, Cedric, and in an instant I was back in Darrowby answering the telephone.

The voice at the other end was oddly hesitant.

"Mr. Herriot . . . I should be grateful if you would come and see my dog." It was a woman, obviously upper class.

"Certainly. What's the trouble?"

"Well . . . he . . . er . . . he seems to suffer from . . . a certain amount of flatus."

"I beg your pardon?"

There was a long pause. "He has . . . excessive flatus."

"In what way, exactly?"

"Well . . . I suppose you'd describe it as . . . windiness." The voice had begun to tremble.

I thought I could see a gleam of light. "You mean his stomach . . .?"

"No, not his stomach. He passes . . . er . . . a considerable quantity of . . . wind from his . . . his . . ." A note of desperation had crept in.

"Ah, yes!" All became suddenly clear. "I quite understand. But that doesn't sound very serious. Is he ill?"

"No, he's very fit in other ways."

"Well then, do you think it's necessary for me to see him?"

"Oh yes, indeed, Mr. Herriot. I wish you would come as soon as possible. It has become quite . . . quite a problem."

"All right," I said. "I'll look in this morning. Can I have your name and address, please?"

"It's Mrs. Rumney, The Laurels."

The Laurels was a very nice house on the edge of the town standing back from the road in a large garden. Mrs. Rumney herself let me in and

I felt a shock of surprise at my first sight of her. It wasn't just that she was strikingly beautiful; there was an unworldly air about her. She would be around forty but had the appearance of a heroine in a Victorian novel—tall, willowy, ethereal. And I could understand immediately her hesitation on the phone. Everything about her suggested fastidiousness and delicacy.

"Cedric is in the kitchen," she said. "I'll take you through."

I had another surprise when I saw Cedric. An enormous Boxer hurled himself on me in delight, clawing at my chest with the biggest, horniest feet I had seen for a long time. I tried to fight him off but he kept at me, panting ecstatically into my face and wagging his entire rear end.

"Sit down, boy!" the lady said sharply, then, as Cedric took absolutely no notice, she turned to me nervously. "He's so friendly."

"Yes," I said breathlessly, "I can see that." I finally managed to push the huge animal away and backed into a corner for safety. "How often does this . . . excessive flatus occur?"

As if in reply an almost palpable sulphurous wave arose from the dog and eddied around me. It appeared that the excitement of seeing me had activated Cedric's weakness. I was up against the wall and unable to obey my first instinct to run for cover, so I held my hand over my face for a few moments before speaking.

"Is that what you meant?"

Mrs. Rumney waved a lace handkerchief under her nose and the faintest flush crept into the pallor of her cheeks.

"Yes," she replied almost inaudibly. "Yes . . . that is it."

"Oh well," I said briskly. "There's nothing to worry about. Let's go into the other room and we'll have a word about his diet and a few other things."

It turned out that Cedric was getting rather a lot of meat and I drew up a little chart cutting down the protein and adding extra carbohydrates. I prescribed a kaolin antacid mixture to be given night and morning and left the house in a confident frame of mind.

It was one of those trivial things and I had entirely forgotten it when Mrs. Rumney phoned again.

"I'm afraid Cedric is no better, Mr. Herriot."

"Oh I'm sorry to hear that. He's still . . . er . . . still . . . yes . . . yes . . ." I spent a few moments in thought. "I tell you what—I don't think I can do any more by seeing him at the moment, but I think you should cut out his meat completely for a week or two. Keep him on biscuits and brown bread rusked in the oven. Try him with that and vegetables and I'll give you some powder to mix in his food. Perhaps you'd call round for it."

The powder was a pretty strong absorbent mixture and I felt sure it would do the trick, but a week later Mrs. Rumney was on the phone again.

"There's absolutely no improvement, Mr. Herriot." The tremble was back in her voice. "I . . . I do wish you'd come and see him again."

I couldn't see much point in viewing this perfectly healthy animal again but I promised to call. I had a busy day and it was after six o'clock before I got round to The Laurels. There were several cars in the drive and when I went into the house I saw that Mrs. Rumney had a few people in for drinks; people like herself—upper-class and of obvious refinement. In fact I felt rather a lout in my working clothes among the elegant gathering.

Mrs. Rumney was about to lead me through to the kitchen when the door burst open and Cedric bounded delightedly into the midst of the company. Within seconds an aesthetic-looking gentleman was frantically beating off the attack as the great feet ripped down his waistcoat. He got away at the cost of a couple of buttons and the Boxer turned his attention to one of the ladies. She was in imminent danger of losing her dress when I pulled the dog off her.

Pandemonium broke out in the graceful room. The hostess's plaintive appeals rang out above the cries of alarm as the big dog charged around, but very soon I realized that a more insidious element had crept into the situation. The atmosphere in the room became rapidly charged with an unmistakable effluvium and it was clear that Cedric's unfortunate malady had reasserted itself.

I did my best to shepherd the animal out of the room but he didn't seem to know the meaning of obedience and I chased him in vain. And as the embarrassing minutes ticked away I began to realize for the first time the enormity of the problem which confronted Mrs. Rumney. Most dogs break wind occasionally but Cedric was different; he did it all the time. And while his silent emanations were perhaps more treacherous there was no doubt that the audible ones were painfully distressing in a company like this.

Cedric made it worse, because at each rasping expulsion he would look round inquiringly at his back end then gambol about the room as though the fugitive zephyr were clearly visible to him and he was determined to corner it.

It seemed a year before I got him out of there. Mrs. Rumney held the door wide as I finally managed to steer him towards it but the big dog wasn't finished yet. On his way out he cocked a leg swiftly and directed a powerful jet against an immaculate trouser leg.

After that night I threw myself into the struggle on Mrs. Rumney's behalf. I felt she desperately needed my help, and I made frequent visits and tried innumerable remedies. I consulted my colleague Siegfried on the problem and he suggested a diet of charcoal biscuits. Cedric ate them in vast quantities and with evident enjoyment but they, like everything else, made not the slightest difference to his condition.

And all the time I pondered upon the enigma of Mrs. Rumney. She had lived in Darrowby for several years but the townsfolk knew little about her. It was a matter of debate whether she was a widow or separated from her husband. But I was not interested in such things; the biggest mystery to me was how she ever got involved with a dog like Cedric.

It was difficult to think of any animal less suited to her personality. Apart from his regrettable affliction he was in every way the opposite to herself; a great thickheaded rumbustious extrovert totally out of place in her gracious menage. I never did find out how they came together but on my visits I found that Cedric had one admirer at least.

He was Con Fenton, a retired farm worker who did a bit of jobbing gardening and spent an average of three days a week at The Laurels. The Boxer romped down the drive after me as I was leaving and the old man looked at him with undisguised admiration.

"By gaw," he said. "He's a fine dog, is that!"

"Yes, he is, Con. He's a good chap, really." And I meant it. You couldn't help liking Cedric when you got to know him. He was utterly amiable and without vice and he gave off a constant aura not merely of noxious vapors but of bonhomie. When he tore off people's buttons or sprinkled their trousers he did it in a spirit of the purest amity.

"Just look at them limbs!" breathed Con, staring rapturously at the dog's muscular thighs. "By heck, 'e can jump ower that gate as if it weren't there. He's what ah call a dog!"

As he spoke it struck me that Cedric would be likely to appeal to him because he was very like the Boxer himself; not overburdened with brains, built like an ox with powerful shoulders and a big constantly-grinning face—they were two of a kind.

"Aye, ah allus likes it when t'missus lets him out in t'garden," Con went on. He always spoke in a peculiar snuffling manner. "He's grand company."

I looked at him narrowly. No, he wouldn't be likely to notice Cedric's complaint since he always saw him out of doors.

On my way back to the surgery I brooded on the fact that I was achieving absolutely nothing with my treatment. And though it seemed ridiculous to worry about a case like this, there was no doubt the thing had begun to prey on my mind. In fact I began to transmit my anxieties to Siegfried. As I got out of the car he was coming down the steps of Skeldale House and he put a hand on my arm.

"You've been to The Laurels, James? Tell me," he queried solicitously, "how is your farting Boxer today?"

"Still at it, I'm afraid," I replied, and my colleague shook his head in commiseration.

We were both defeated. Maybe if chlorophyll tablets had been available in those days they might have helped but as it was I had tried everything. It seemed certain that nothing would alter the situation. And it wouldn't have been so bad if the owner had been anybody else but Mrs. Rumney; I found that even discussing the thing with her had become almost unbearable.

Siegfried's student brother Tristan didn't help, either. When seeing practice he was very selective in the cases he wished to observe, but he was immediately attracted to Cedric's symptoms and insisted on coming with me on one occasion. I never took him again because as we went in the big dog bounded from his mistress's side and produced a particularly sonorous blast as if in greeting.

Tristan immediately threw out a hand in a dramatic gesture and declaimed: "Speak on, sweet lips that never told a lie!" That was his only visit. I had enough trouble without that.

I didn't know it at the time but a greater blow awaited me. A few days later Mrs. Rumney was on the phone again.

"Mr. Herriot, a friend of mine has such a sweet little Boxer bitch. She wants to bring her along to be mated with Cedric."

"Eh?"

"She wants to mate her bitch with my dog."

"With Cedric . . .?" I clutched at the edge of the desk. It couldn't be true! "And . . . and are you agreeable?"

"Yes, of course."

I shook my head to dispel the feeling of unreality. I found it incomprehensible that anyone should want to reproduce Cedric, and as I gaped into the receiver a frightening vision floated before me of eight little Cedrics all with his complaint. But of course such a thing wasn't hereditary. I took a grip of myself and cleared my throat.

"Very well, then, Mrs. Rumney, you'd better go ahead."

There was a pause. "But Mr. Herriot, I want you to supervise the mating."

"Oh really, I don't think that's necessary." I dug my nails into my palms. "I think you'll be all right without me."

"Oh but I would be much happier if you

were there. Please come," she said appealingly.

Instead of emitting a long-drawn groan I took a deep breath.

"Right," I said. "I'll be along in the morning."

All that evening I was obsessed by a feeling of dread. Another acutely embarrassing session was in store with this exquisite woman. Why was it I always had to share things like this with her? And I really feared the worst. Even the daftest dog, when confronted with a bitch in heat, knows instinctively how to proceed, but with a really ivory-skulled animal like Cedric I wondered. . . .

And next morning all my fears were realized. The bitch, Trudy, was a trim little creature and showed every sign of willingness to cooperate. Cedric, on the other hand, though obviously delighted to meet her, gave no hint of doing his part. After sniffing her over, he danced around her a few times, goofy-faced, tongue lolling. Then he had a roll on the lawn before charging at her and coming to a full stop, big feet outsplayed, head down, ready to play. I sighed. It was as I thought. The big chump didn't know what to do.

This pantomime went on for some time and, inevitably, the emotional strain brought on a resurgence of his symptoms. Frequently he paused to inspect his tail as though he had never heard noises like that before.

He varied his dancing routine with occasional headlong gallops round the lawn and it was after he had done about ten successive laps that he seemed to decide he ought to do something about the bitch. I held my breath as he approached her but unfortunately he chose the wrong end to commence operations. Trudy had put up with his nonsense with great patience but when she found him busily working away in the region of her left ear it was too much. With a shrill yelp she nipped him in the hind leg and he shot away in alarm.

After that whenever he came near she warned him off with bared teeth. Clearly she was disenchanted with her bridegroom and I couldn't blame her.

"I think she's had enough, Mrs. Rumney," I said.

I certainly had had enough and so had the poor lady, judging by her slight breathlessness, flushed cheeks and waving handkerchief.

"Yes . . . yes . . . I suppose you're right," she replied.

So Trudy was taken home and that was the end of Cedric's career as a stud dog.

This last episode decided me. I had to have a talk with Mrs. Rumney and a few days later I called in at The Laurels.

"Maybe you'll think it's none of my business," I said. "But I honestly don't think Cedric is the dog for you. In fact he's so wrong for you that he is upsetting your life."

Mrs. Rumney's eyes widened. "Well . . . he is a problem in some ways . . . but what do you suggest?"

"I think you should get another dog in his place. Maybe a poodle or a corgi—something smaller, something you could control."

"But Mr. Herriot, I couldn't possibly have Cedric put down." Her eyes filled quickly with tears. "I really am fond of him despite his . . . despite everything."

"No, no, of course not!" I said. "I like him too. He has no malice in him. But I think I have a good idea. Why not let Con Fenton have him?"

"Con . . .?"

"Yes, he admires Cedric tremendously and the big fellow would have a good life with the old man. He has a couple of fields behind his cottage and keeps a few beasts. Cedric could run to his heart's content out there and Con would be able to bring him along when he does the garden. You'd still see him three times a week."

Mrs. Rumney looked at me in silence for a few moments and I saw in her face the dawning of relief and hope.

"You know, Mr. Herriot, I think that could work very well. But are you sure Con would take him?"

"I'd like to bet on it. An old bachelor like him must be lonely. There's only one thing worries me. Normally they only meet outside and I wonder how it would be when they were indoors and Cedric started to . . . when the old trouble . . ."

"Oh, I think that would be all right," Mrs.

Rumney broke in quickly. "When I go on holiday Con always takes him for a week or two and he has never mentioned any . . . anything unusual . . . in that way."

I got up to go. "Well, that's fine. I should put it to the old man right away."

Mrs. Rumney rang within a few days. Con had jumped at the chance of taking on Cedric and the pair had apparently settled in happily together. She had also taken my advice and acquired a poodle puppy.

I didn't see the new dog till it was nearly six months old and its mistress asked me to call to treat it for a slight attack of eczema. As I sat in the graceful room looking at Mrs. Rumney, cool, poised, tranquil, with the little white creature resting on her knee I couldn't help feeling how right and fitting the whole scene was. The lush carpet, the trailing velvet curtains, the fragile tables with their load of expensive china and framed miniatures. It was no place for Cedric.

Con Fenton's cottage was less than half a mile away and on my way back to the surgery, on an impulse I pulled up at the door. The old man answered my knock and his big face split into a delighted grin when he saw me.

"Come in, young man!" he cried in his strange snuffly voice. "I'm right glad to see tha!"

I had hardly stepped into the tiny living room when a hairy form hurled itself upon me. Cedric hadn't changed a bit and I had to battle my way to the broken armchair by the fireside. Con settled down opposite and when the Boxer leaped to lick his face he clumped him companionably on the head with his fist.

"Siddown, ye great daft bugger," he murmured with affection. Cedric sank happily on to the tattered hearthrug at his feet and gazed up adoringly at his new master.

"Well, Mr. Herriot," Con went on as he cut up some villainous-looking plug tobacco and began to stuff it into his pipe. "I'm right grateful to ye for gettin' me this grand dog. By gaw, he's a topper and ah wouldn't sell 'im for any money. No man could ask for a better friend."

"Well, that's great, Con," I said. "And I can see that the big chap is really happy here."

The Dog and the Shadow *by Sir Edwin Landseer*

The old man ignited his pipe and a cloud of acrid smoke rose to the low, blackened beams. "Aye, he's 'ardly ever inside. A gurt strong dog like 'im wants to work 'is energy off, like."

But just at that moment Cedric was obviously working something else off because the familiar pungency rose from him even above the billowings from the pipe. Con seemed oblivious of it but in the enclosed space I found it overpowering.

"Ah well," I gasped. "I just looked in for a moment to see how you were getting on together. I must be on my way." I rose hurriedly and stumbled towards the door but the redolence followed me in a wave. As I passed the table with the remains of the old man's meal I saw what seemed to be the only form of ornament in the cottage, a cracked vase holding a magnificent bouquet of carnations. It was a way of escape and I buried my nose in their fragrance.

Con watched me approvingly. "Aye, they're lovely flowers, aren't they? T'missus at Laurels lets me bring 'ome what I want and I reckon them carnations is me favorite."

"Yes, they're a credit to you." I still kept my nose among the blooms.

"There's only one thing," the old man said

pensively. "Ah don't get t'full benefit of 'em."

"How's that, Con?"

He pulled at his pipe a couple of times. "Well, you can hear ah speak a bit funny, like?"

"No . . . no . . . not really."

"Oh aye, ye know ah do. I've been like it since I were a lad. I 'ad a operation for adenoids and summat went wrong."

"Oh, I'm sorry to hear that," I said.

"Well, it's nowt serious, but it's left me lackin' in one way."

"You mean . . .?" A light was beginning to dawn in my mind, an elucidation of how man and dog had found each other, of why their relationship was so perfect, of the certainty of their happy future together. It seemed like fate.

"Aye," the old man went on sadly. "I 'ave no sense of smell."

A Gentleman's Dogs

by an ANONYMOUS NINETEENTH-CENTURY SPORTSMAN

SMOAKER was a deer greyhound of the largest size, but of his pedigree I know nothing. In speed he was equal to any hare greyhound; at the same time, in spirit he was indomitable. He was the only dog I ever knew who was a match for a red stag, singlehanded. From living constantly in the drawing room and never being separated from me, he became acquainted with almost the meaning of every word —certainly of every sign. His retrieving of game was equal to any of the retrieving I ever saw in any other dogs. He would leap over any of the most dangerous spikes at a sign, walk up and come down any ladder, and catch, without hurting it, any particular fowl out of a number that was pointed out to him. If he missed me from the drawing room and had doubts about my being in the house, he would go into the hall and look for my hat: if he found it, he would return contented; but if he did not find it, he would proceed upstairs to a window at the very top of the house, and look from the window each way, to ascertain if I were in sight. One day in shooting at Cranford, with his late Royal Highness the Duke of York, a pheasant fell on the other side of the stream. The river was frozen over; but in crossing to fetch the pheasant the ice broke and let Smoaker in, to some inconvenience. He picked up the pheasant, and instead of trying the ice again, he took it many hundred yards round to

the bridge. Smoaker died at the great age of eighteen years. His son Shark was also a beautiful dog. He was by Smoaker out of a common greyhound bitch, called Vagrant, who had won a cup at Swaffham. Shark was not so powerful as Smoaker; but he was, nevertheless, a large-sized dog, and was a first-rate deer greyhound and retriever. He took his father's place on the rug, and was inseparable from me. He was educated and entered at deer under Smoaker. When Shark was first admitted to the house, it chanced that one day he and Smoaker were left alone in a room with a table on which luncheon was laid. Smoaker might have been left for hours with meat on the table, and he would have died rather than have touched it; but at that time Shark was not proof against temptation. I left the room to hand some lady to her carriage, and as I returned by the window, I looked in. Shark was on his legs, smelling curiously round the table; whilst Smoaker had risen to a sitting posture, his ears pricked, his brow frowning, and his eyes intently fixed on his son's actions. After tasting several viands, Shark's long nose came in contact with about half a cold tongue; the morsel was too tempting to be withstood. For all the look of curious anger with which his father was intently watching, the son stole the tongue and conveyed it to the floor. No sooner had he done so than the offended sire rushed upon him, rolled him over,

61

beat him and took away the tongue. Instead, though, of replacing it on the table, the father contented himself with the punishment he had administered, and retired with great gravity to the fire.

I was once waiting by moonlight for wild ducks on the Ouze in Bedfordshire, and I killed a couple on the water at a shot. The current was strong; but Shark, having fetched one of the birds, was well aware there was another. Instead, therefore, of returning by water to look for the second, he ran along the banks as if aware that the strong stream would have carried the bird further down; looking in the water till he saw it at least a hundred yards from the spot where he had left it in bringing the first; when he also brought that to me. Nothing could induce either of these dogs to fetch a glove or a stick: I have often seen game fall close to me, and they would not attempt to touch it. It seemed as if they simply desired to be of service when service was to be done; and that when there were no obstacles to be conquered, they had no wish to interfere. Shark died at a good old age, and was succeeded by his son Wolfe. Wolfe's mother was a Newfoundland bitch. He was also a large and powerful dog, but of course not so speedy as his ancestors. While residing at my country house, being my constant companion, Wolfe accompanied me two or three times a day in the breeding season to feed the young pheasants and partridges reared under hens. On going near the coops, I put down my gun, made Wolfe a sign to sit down by it and fed the birds with some caution, that they might not be in any way scared. I mention this, because I am sure that dogs learn more from the manner and method of those they love, than they do from direct teaching. In front of the windows on the lawn there was a large bed of shrubs and flowers into which the rabbits used to cross, and where I had often sent Wolfe in to drive them for me to shoot. One afternoon, thinking that there might be a rabbit, I made Wolfe the usual sign to go and drive the shrubs, which he obeyed; but ere he had gone some yards beneath the bushes, I heard him make a peculiar noise with his jaws, which he always made when he saw anything he did not like, and he came softly back to me with a sheepish look.

I repeated the sign, and encouraged him to go; but he never got beyond the spot he had been to in the first instance, and invariably returned to me with a very odd expression of countenance. Curiosity tempted me to creep into the bushes to discover the cause of the dog's unwonted behavior; when there, I found, congregated under one of the shrubs, eight or nine of my young pheasants, who had for the first time roosted at a distance from their coop. Wolfe had seen and known the young pheasants, and would not scare them.

Wolfe was the cause of my detecting and discharging one of my gamekeepers. I had forbidden my rabbits to be killed until my return; and the keeper was ordered simply to walk Wolfe to exercise on the farm. There was a large stone quarry in the vicinity, where there were a good many rabbits, some parts of which were so steep, that though you might look over the cliff, and shoot a rabbit below, neither man nor dog could pick him up without going a considerable way round. On approaching the edge of the quarry to look over for a rabbit, I was surprised at missing Wolfe, who invariably stole off in another direction, but always the same way. At last, on shooting a rabbit, I discovered that he invariably went to the only spot by which he could descend to pick up whatever fell to the gun; and by this I found that somebody had shot rabbits in his presence at times when I was from home.

Wolfe accompanied me to my residence in Hampshire, and there I naturalized, in a wild state, some white rabbits. For the first year the white ones were never permitted to be killed, and Wolfe saw that such was the case. One summer's afternoon I shot a white rabbit for the first time, and Wolfe jumped the garden fence to pick the rabbit up; but his astonishment and odd sheepish look, when he found it was a white one, were curious in the extreme. He dropped his stern, made his usual snap with his jaws, and came back looking up in my face, as much as to say, "You've made a mistake and shot a white rabbit, but I've not picked him up." I was obliged to assure him that I intended to shoot it, and to encourage him before he would return and bring the rabbit to me. Wolfe died when he was about nine years old, and was succeeded by my present favorite, Brenda, a hare greyhound of the highest caste. Brenda won the Oak Stakes of her year, and is a very fast and stout greyhound. I have taught her to retrieve game to the gun, to drive home the game from dangerous sands, and, in short, to do everything but speak; and this she attempts, by making a beautiful sort of bark when she wants her dinner.

I have the lop-eared rabbit naturalized, and in a half-wild and wild state, and Brenda is often to be seen with some of the tamest of them asleep in the sun on the lawn together. When the rabbits have been going out into a dangerous vicinity, late in the evening, I have often sent Brenda to drive them home, and to course and kill the wild ones if she could. I have seen one of the wild-bred lop-ears get up before her, and I have seen her make a start to course it; but when she saw that it was not a native of the soil she would stop and continue her search for others. The next moment I have seen her course and kill a wild rabbit. She is perfectly steady from hare if I tell her not to run, and is, without any exception, one of the prettiest and most useful and engaging creatures ever seen. She is an excellent rat-killer also, and has an amazing antipathy to a cat. When I have been absent from home for some time, Mrs. B. has observed that she is alive to every sound of a wheel, and if the doorbell rings she is the first to fly to it. When walking on the sea-beach during my absence, she is greatly interested in every boat she sees, and watches them with the most intense anxiety, as in the yachting season she has known me return by sea. Brenda would take my part in a row, and she is a capital house dog. If ever the heart of a creature was given to man, this beautiful, graceful and clever animal has given me hers, for her whole existence is either passed in watching for my return or in seeking opportunities to please me when I am at home. It is a great mistake to suppose that severity of treatment is necessary to the education of a dog, or that it is serviceable in making him steady. Manner—*marked and impressive manner*—is that which teaches obedience, and example rather than command forms the desired character.

I had two foxhounds when I hunted stag,— my pack were all foxhounds,—they were named Bachelor and Blunder. We used to play with them together, and they got to know each other by name. In returning from hunting, my brother and myself used to amuse ourselves by saying in a peculiar tone of voice—the one we used to use in playing with them—"Bachelor, where's Blunder?" On hearing this, Bachelor's stern and bristles rose, and he trotted about among the pack, looking for Blunder, and when he found him he would push his nose against his ear and growl at him. Thus Bachelor evidently knew Blunder by name, and this arose from the way in which we used to play with them. At this moment, when far away from home, and after an absence of many weeks, if I sing a particular song, which I always sing to a dog named Jessie, Brenda, though staying in houses where she had never seen Jessie, will get up much excited, and look to the door and out of the window in expectation of her friend. I have a great pleasure in the society of all animals, and I love to make my house a place where all may meet in rest and good fellowship. This is far easier to achieve than people would think for when dogs are kindly used, but impressed with ideas of obedience.

The gazelle which came home from Acre in the Thunderer, was one evening feeding from Mrs. B.'s plate at dessert, when Odion, the great deerhound, who was beaten in my match against the five deer by an unlucky stab in the first course, came in by special invitation for his biscuit. The last deer he had seen previous to the gazelle he had coursed and pulled down. The strange expression of his dark face was beautiful when he first saw her; and halting in his run up to me, he advanced more slowly directly to her; she met him also in apparent wonder at his great size, and they smelled each others' faces. Odion then kissed her, and came to me for his biscuit, and never after noticed her. She will at times butt him if he takes up too much of the fire; but this she will not do to Brenda, except in play; and if she is eating from Mrs. Berkeley's hand, Brenda by a peculiar look can send her away and take her place. Odion, the gazelle, Brenda, and the rabbits will all quietly lay on the lawn together, and the gazelle and Bruiser, an immense house dog between the bloodhound and mastiff, will run and play together.

Terriers *by P. Reinagle*

I had forgotten to mention a bull-and-mas-tiff dog that I had, called Grumbo. He was previous to Smoaker, and was indeed the first four-footed companion established in my confidence. I was then very young, and of course inclined to anything like a row. Grumbo, therefore, was well entered in all kinds of strife—bulls, oxen, pigs, men, dogs, all came in turn as combatants; and Grumbo had the oddest ways of making men and animals the *aggressors* I ever knew. He seemed to make it a point of honor never to begin, but on receiving a hint from me; some one of his enemies was sure to commence the battle, and then he or both of us would turn to as an oppressed party. I have seen him walk leisurely out into the middle of a field where oxen were grazing, and then throw himself down. Either a bull or the oxen were sure to be attracted by the novel sight,

and come dancing and blowing round him. All this he used to bear with the most stoical forti-tude, till some one more forward than the rest touched him with the horn. "War to the knife, and no favor," was then the cry; and Grumbo had one of them by the nose directly. He being engaged at odds, I of course made in to help him, and such a scene of confusion used to follow as was scarce ever seen. Grumbo tossed in the air, and then some beast pinned by the nose would lie down and bellow. I should all this time be swinging round on to some of their tails, and so it would go on till Grumbo and myself were tired and our enemies happy to beat a retreat. If he wished to pick a quarrel with a man, he would walk listlessly before him till the man trod on him, and then the row began. Grumbo was the best assistant in the world, night or day, for catching delinquents. As a proof of his thoughtful sagacity, I give the following fact. He was my sole companion when I watched two men steal a quantity of pheasants' eggs: we gave chase; but before I could come near them, with two hundred yards start of me, they fled. There was no hope of my overtaking them before they reached the village of Harlington, so I gave Grumbo the office. Off he went, but in the chase the men ran up a headland on which a cow was tethered. They passed the cow; and when the dog came up to the cow he stopped, and, to my horror, contemplated a grab at the tempting nose. He was, however, uncertain as to whether or not this would be right, and he looked back to me for further assurance. I made the sign to go ahead, and he understood it, for he took up the running again and disappeared down a narrow pathway leading through the orchards to the houses. When I turned that corner, to my infinite delight I found him placed in the narrow path directly in front of one of the poachers, with such an evident determination of purpose that the man was standing stock still, afraid to stir either hand or foot. I came up and secured the offender, and bade the dog be quiet.

Nuptials

by J. R. ACKERLEY

Soon after Tulip* came into my possession I set about finding a husband for her. She had had a lonely and frustrated life hitherto; now she should have a full one. A full life naturally included the pleasures of sex and maternity. . . .

It is necessary to add that she is beautiful. People are always wanting to touch her, a thing she cannot bear. Her ears are tall and pointed, like the ears of Anubis. How she manages to hold them constantly erect, as though starched, I do not know, for with their fine covering of mouse-gray fur they are soft and flimsy; when she stands with her back to the sun it shines through the delicate tissue, so that they glow shell-pink as though incandescent. Her face also is long and pointed, basically stone-gray but the snout and lower jaw are jet black. Jet, too, are the rims of her amber eyes, as though heavily mascaraed, and the tiny mobile eyebrow tufts that are set like accents above them. And in the midst of her forehead is a kind of Indian caste-mark, a black diamond suspended there, like the jewel on the brow of Pegasus in Mantegna's *Parnassus,* by a fine dark thread, no more than a penciled line, which is drawn from it right over her poll midway between the tall ears. A shadow extends across her forehead from either side of this caste-mark,

*A German shepherd. In Britain the breed is known as "Alsatian."—*Ed.*

so that, in certain lights, the diamond looks like the body of a bird with its wings spread, a bird in flight.

These dark markings symmetrically divide up her face into zones of pale pastel colors, like a mosaic, or a stained-glass window; her skull, bisected by the thread, is two primrose pools, the center of her face light gray, the bridge of her nose above the long, black lips fawn, her cheeks white, and upon each a *patte de mouche* has been tastefully set. A delicate white ruff, frilling out from the lobes of her ears, frames this strange, clownish face, with its heavily leaded features, and covers the whole of her throat and chest with a snowy shirt front.

For the rest, her official description is sable gray: she is a gray dog wearing a sable tunic. Her gray is the gray of birch bark; her sable tunic is of the texture of satin and clasps her long body like a saddle-cloth. No tailor could have shaped it more elegantly; it is cut round the joints of her shoulders and thighs and in a straight line along the points of her ribs, lying open at the chest and stomach. Over her rump it fits like a cap, and then extends on in a thin strip over the top of her long tail down to the tip. Viewed from above, therefore, she is a black dog; but when she rolls over on her back she is a gray one. Two dark ribbons of fur, descending from her tunic over her shoulders, fasten it at her sternum, which

67

seems to clip the ribbons together as with an ivory brooch.

Tulip's next heat—the third of her life, but the first since she entered mine—was close at hand. I could not rely upon a chance encounter. Might not a vet help? Any vet would probably include an Alsatian or two among his patients; it would be easy for him to sound the owners and put me in touch. All this a local vet obligingly did. He provided me with the address of a Mr. Blandish who lived in Sheen and owned a good Alsatian named Max whom he was willing to lend. . . . He added that I should find out whether Max had had any previous sexual history. Why? I asked. With a weary smile the vet replied that mating dogs was not always so simple a matter as I seemed to suppose, and that since Tulip was inexperienced it would be helpful to have a sire who knew the ropes. He then turned his back on me.

The house was large, solid and detached, and that it was probably the right one was indicated, as I pressed the bell, by a short rumble of gruff barks within. Max was then revealed as a heavy, handsome dog with the grave deportment of the old family retainer. His stolid figure silently barred my entry, until a quiet word from his master authorized him to admit me. When I was invited into the sitting room he followed after and, assuming a dignified posture on the hearthrug, kept me under close surveillance: the house and its management clearly belonged to him. To have offered him any kind of familiarity, it was plain, would have been as shocking a breach of etiquette as if one had attempted to stroke the butler.

Mr. Blandish, who was hearty, prosperous, middle-aged and bald, seated himself beside me on the sofa and gave me a cigarette.

"Matches! Matches!" he then exclaimed, in a petulant voice. "Are there no matches in the house!"

Considerably startled by this outburst, I said soothingly: "Oh, never mind. I think I've got some."

But before I could begin to fumble, Max had lumbered to his feet and, with a swaying motion

of the hips, crossed the room. Picking up an outsize box that was lying on a stool he brought it to his master. Mr. Blandish accepted it without comment and lighted our cigarettes, while Max stood obsequiously at his elbow.

"Thank you, Max," he then said, in a negligent manner, and handed the box back to the dog, who replaced it on the stool and gravely resumed his watchful position on the rug.

This unnerving incident was not permitted to interrupt the Blandishes' flow of polite conversation. They plied me with questions about Tulip and expressed their delight at the projected alliance. They had had Max for six years and had always wished for an opportunity of this kind; his happiness was their only concern in the transaction. These remarks gave me the opening I needed to put the question the vet had advised me to put, but the alarming exhibition of canine sagacity I had just witnessed had so shaken me that I hardly knew how to frame the inquiry in Max's presence. Avoiding his eye, I stammered:

"Then will this be his first experience of—with the opposite sex? The vet seemed to think there might be difficulties unless—"

But Mr. Blandish displayed no sense of delicacy.

"Oh, you needn't worry about that!" said he, with a guffaw. "Max knows his oats all right!"

I coughed.

"He's been married before, then?"

"He's never been churched, it's true," said Mr. Blandish, "but when we were down in the country a couple of years ago, he happened upon a stray bitch in heat—not at all a classy one, either—and had his wicked way with her on the spot. He'll be delighted to repeat the performance with Tulip, I can assure you!" he added gleefully.

"Oh, then that's all right. It was only that, Tulip being a virgin, the vet thought—"

"Leave it all to me," said Mr. Blandish gaily. "I've got a very reliable little book—not that Max will need to look anything up in it!"

I was then invited to bring Tulip along for a formal introduction to her betrothed. When I got up to go, Max preceded me into the hall and, interposing his bulk between myself and my hat, required another permissive word from his master before I was able to pick it up, in case, Mr. Blandish explained, I took the wrong one.

The formal introduction was effected a few days later, and if Tulip failed to make a bad impression on the Blandishes, it was not, I thought, for any want of trying. Of the kind of impression she made on Max there seemed to me no doubt at all. The sound of his throaty rumble as we advanced up the drive announced that he was on duty, and the opening door disclosed him, planted squarely on the threshold as before, his master's hand upon his collar. The affianced pair gingerly sniffed each other's noses, and Max's tail rose higher in the air and began to wave majestically from side to side: he was clearly preparing to do the canine honors. Much gratified by this exhibition of tender feeling, Mr. Blandish bade us enter, and both animals were released in the hall. But no sooner had Max approached Tulip, in the most affable manner, to extend his acquaintance with her, than she rounded vigorously upon him and drove him down the passage into what appeared to be the pantry with his tail between his legs. From then on, it seemed to me, she behaved abominably. She investigated all round the Blandishes' sitting room in a thorough, dubious and insulting way, as though she could scarcely believe her nose, and then refused to sit or lie down, but constantly interrupted our conversation by nattering at me to take her away, staring at me imperiously with her exclamatory face. When I pretended not to notice her, she tried to pull me out of my chair by her own lead, which I always carried clipped round my neck. To the Blandishes and their overtures of friendship she paid not the slightest heed; they might, indeed, not have been present; and whenever Max was emboldened to emerge from the pantry to join us, she instantly chased him back into it again.

I apologized for her behavior, but I need not have done so. The Blandishes had taken no offense. On the contrary, they were positively enchanted by her beauty and the femininity, as they termed it, of her conduct; and every time she drove poor Max out of his own sitting room, Mr. Blandish was, indeed, so excessively amused,

remarking with a chuckle that she was a sweet and proper little bitch and that he could see they would get along famously together when her time came, that I could not help wondering from what source of knowledge such optimism derived and found my gaze dwelling speculatively upon Mrs. Blandish, who was a pretty little woman considerably younger than her husband.

Tulip's time would come, said he, between her seventh and ninth day. The nuptials, he added jovially, would take place in his back garden. I ventured to remark that my own information was that a later day in the second week might be better, but he replied firmly that I was mistaken, his reliable little book recommended the seventh to the ninth days and I could safely leave matters to his judgment. His assertiveness overbore me, but I was dissatisfied nevertheless. Ignorant though I was, it seemed to me a pity that the two animals should have no opportunity to get better acquainted before the moment arrived, and I therefore suggested diffidently, that, since we were neighbors, they might be exercised together occasionally between now and the event.

"What a good idea!" cried Mrs. Blandish. But her husband was instantly and flatly opposed. It was Mrs. Blandish, he observed drily, who took Max for his walks while he himself was at work, and he could not permit her to have any part in this business, at any rate in his absence. When we left, Max was again withdrawn from hiding to say good-bye to Tulip, but he could not be induced to approach her closely. This restored Mr. Blandish to his previous good humor.

"His other wife bit him in the shoulder," he chortled, rubbing his hands; "but he won't at all mind a few more bites when his time with Tulip comes!" He said this with such gusto that I glanced again involuntarily at Mrs. Blandish, who was smiling roguishly at him with her small, even teeth . . .

It was scarcely to be expected that Mr. Blandish would relish being reminded of his engagement, for the country had lain under snow for many days. He complained that, and sounded as if, he had a heavy cold, but he kept his word and appointed an afternoon in the following week, Tulip's eighth or ninth day: since I was too inexperienced to know precisely when one started to count, whether at the first faint smear of blood or when the discharge became more copious, I was uncertain which. The day dawned colder, if possible, than any that had preceded it, and it was in no very cheerful frame of mind that I deserted my fireside and set out with her across Putney Common. Tulip, however, was in an ecstasy of joy; this was the first snow she had ever seen and, warmly clad in her fine sable-gray coat, she flew about in it with childish glee. She was still bleeding a little, and my most recent piece of lore on the subject was that dogs would not copulate with bitches until the flow of blood had ceased. Be that as it may, we were accompanied as usual by a small escort of ardent admirers. They did not trouble me much, however, partly because they all looked too small to be a serious menace, partly because she herself was so obedient. And eventually she lost many of them for me by delaying tactics worthy of Hippomenes—if that was her intention and she was not, on the contrary, a bungling Ariadne with a too brittle thread. I had already noticed that her urine, in her present condition, appeared to provide her wooers with a most gratifying cordial, for they avidly lapped it up whenever she condescended to void it, which she frequently did. So heady was its effect that their jaws would at once start to drip and chatter together, not merely visibly but audibly. Now, squatting here and there upon other dogs' droppings or whatever odor attracted her, like some famous chef adding to a prepared dish the final exquisite flavor, the crowning touch, she left behind her in the snow as she flew a series of sorbets, and her crazed attendants were so often and so long delayed in licking them up that they eventually fell far behind.

Though his heavy cold persisted, Mr. Blandish received us amiably. I told him that Tulip was still bleeding, but he said that did not matter, he had his reliable little book and we would now see a marked change in Max's demeanor. This was perfectly true. The moment Tulip's scent reached him, he quickly discarded his servile role and was seen to be capable of manly emotions.

Unhappily there was no corresponding change on Tulip's side. Never mind, said Mr. Blandish cheerfully, picking up the umbrella stand which had been overturned by Max in his headlong flight, everything would be quite all right when the two animals were left alone together in the garden, they would soon "get down to business" then. But to be left alone together in the garden, it could not have been more evident, was the last thing that either of the two animals wished; Tulip's single purpose was not to be separated from me, while Max needed peremptory orders to withdraw him from the servants' quarters. Eventually, however, both of them were pushed out of the back door, at which Tulip barked and rattled until I commanded her to stop. Silence then fell, while Mr. Blandish and I gazed hopefully out of the kitchen window into the bleak and snow-patched garden. It was all the view we had, for the two dogs were nowhere to be seen—until Tulip's face with its pricked ears rose suddenly up to confront me accusingly through the glass.

I then told Mr. Blandish that if she was to pay any attention at all to Max I felt convinced she would have none to spare while so much of it was focused anxiously upon myself, and that I had better set her mind at rest by joining her outside. I added politely that, in view of his seedy condition, it would be unwise of him to take the risk of coming too.

"No, dear, you really shouldn't!" chimed in Mrs. Blandish, who had just come in. "Let *me* go out with Mr. Ackerley."

No speech could have been more considerate or more unwise.

"Nonsense!" said Mr. Blandish. "I cannot allow you to venture out. I shall be quite all right," and struggling into a thick overcoat and a pair of galoshes he accompanied me into the garden, where Tulip cast herself into my arms with an ardor I could have wished to see directed elsewhere. Max at first could not be found; he was eventually located skulking under the laurels at the front of the house.

The end of this fiasco will already be apparent. I do not remember how long we stood stamping our feet in that icy garden exhorting the two dogs, when they were momentarily together, to sexual intercourse, nor how many times Max was propelled from and stampeded back into the house. Tulip, whose fixed determination clearly was that he should approach neither me nor her, enjoyed herself hugely. Considering that Max was almost twice her size and weight, his conduct seemed to me craven.

At length Mr. Blandish, who had omitted to bring his hat, began to feel a chill on his bald head and said he must have a covering. I offered to fetch it for him, but he said no, Max would bring it, it was one of his household duties. He spoke with pride; it was obviously another of Max's "turns." He therefore shouted up to Mrs. Blandish to send out his cap, and with it, Max, like a well-trained servant, albeit warily, soon emerged from the french windows.

"Thank you, Max," said Mr. Blandish, extending a casual hand. But Tulip was having no nonsense of that sort. First by one barely distinct garden path, then by another, did Max (who had been taught not to walk on the beds) endeavor to carry out his master's wishes, which soon turned into vexed commands; but he was headed off and driven back over and over again, until, totally demoralized, he dropped the cap in the snow and slunk off for good, his proud mission unfulfilled.

This marked the end of Mr. Blandish's indulgence and our visit. I diffidently suggested that it might be worth while seeing whether the animals got on any better together when Tulip's heat was further advanced, but he replied, rather stuffily, that he feared he had no time to arrange it. On that we took our leave. "You bad girl!" I said to Tulip as we trudged away through the snow; but she was now, when she had me back to herself, in her most disarming mood, and as soon as we were home she attempted to bestow upon my leg and my overcoat all the love that the pusillanimous Max had been denied.

My vet could help no further. Tulip's receptive period, he agreed, would continue for some days, but he had no more Alsatians on his books. He observed, tiresomely, that he had told me that mating dogs was not always a simple matter,

and added, even more tiresomely, the belated information that when they were inexperienced it was often necessary to hold the bitch's head and guide the dog into position: the application of a little Vaseline to the bitch sometimes helped to excite and define the interest besides acting as a lubricant. But I am not easily deterred. I had seen a number of Alsatians on Putney Heath at various times, and I went in search of one now. I drew a blank. But the following day fortune favored me. A solitary gentleman with his dog was visible in the distance. I hastened after him and caught him up. It is even easier to talk to people about their dogs than about their children, and in this case the animal himself provided the introduction by coming up to be petted.

"Nice dog," I said, thinking what a poor specimen he looked. "What's his name?"

"Chum," said his owner gloomily.

"He's friendly for an Alsatian."

"That's just it! He goes up to anyone, and often goes off with them too. Other dogs as well. Sometimes I have quite a job to get him back, he's grown so disobedient. I don't know what's come over him. He was more of a pal once . . ."

"Has he a pedigree?" I asked politely, examining Chum with increasing dismay. Was he really good enough for Tulip? His ears managed to stand up, but he had scarcely any ruff and a pale, lean body like a greyhound.

"Oh yes, I paid quite a bit for him. I specially wanted an Alsatian, they're said to be so devoted . . ."

"How long have you had him?"

"Getting on for three years. And he's well looked after. I take a lot of trouble to please him. Oh yes, he has the best of everything, and I always feed him myself. Yet he's jumped the garden wall twice lately and run away. The police brought him back on both occasions. I don't know what to do . . ."

"He *seems* fond of you," I said. Chum, who had a blunt, foolish face, was gazing up at him sentimentally.

"Yes, he is, you know," said the gentleman, brightening a little. "That's the funny part of it. He's as pleased as Punch to see me when I come home—sometimes he won't eat his dinner till I've left him, no matter how hungry he is; yet the next minute he buzzes off. I've made a run for him in the garage now; well, I can't trust him alone in the garden any more, and the wife's got enough to do already without having to keep an eye on him. She's not that keen on dogs, anyway . . . Fact is, I'm afraid he may be a bit lonely, for I can't spend as much time with him now as I did before I married, and I've been wondering whether he mightn't settle down better if I found *him* a wife, too."

Was ever wish so miraculously granted! I at once described my own problem with Tulip, and Mr. Plum, as we will call him, for such he seemed to be, positively begged me to bring her along to his place on the following Saturday afternoon: his engagements unfortunately precluded him from inviting us earlier. Mr. Plum's place was off Putney Hill.

"Now do try to be serious!" I said to Tulip as, with a tin of Vaseline in my pocket, I rang Mr. Plum's bell. He at once emerged and led us to the garage, which was built onto the side of the house. Here Chum was discovered at home, lying on a heap of clean straw, surrounded by quantities of dog biscuits, in a huge wire-netting cage which had been constructed in that part of the garage which did not contain Mr. Plum's car. Uttering no bark, he welcomed us all, and particularly Tulip, into his lair. But, although the signs were momentarily encouraging, I apprehended almost at once that we were probably in for much the same sort of afternoon that we had spent at the Blandishes. Tulip was friendlier to Chum than she had been to Max. She played and flirted with him a little, while, he on his side, though half Max's age and quite without experience, put up an infinitely better show than his predecessor. The warmth of his feelings was, indeed, plainly and frequently visible. But though he tried constantly to take her, awares and unawares, she slid out of his grasp every time and repulsed him. As before, her attention was fixed upon myself.

Mr. Plum was wonderfully kind and patient. He gave her presents and did what he could to placate her and to understand the cause of her

nervous excitement. Might it not be a good idea, he asked, to leave them together for a bit? Perhaps Tulip would concentrate better if my distracting presence were removed, and (he looked at his watch) Mrs. Plum had a cup of tea for us in the flat. I did not think it at all a good idea, but, except for the matter of Vaseline, which I now mentioned and which he said we must certainly try out later, had none better to offer, and a nice cup of tea, after the chill of the garage, would be most welcome. We accordingly edged our way out of the cage and shut the wire door. Thwarted in her attempt to push out with me, poor Tulip rose up frantically against it, while Chum tried in vain to take her in the midst of her woe.

The striking thing about Mr. Plum's flat was its cleanliness. The kitchen, into which I was led, was almost dazzling; it was more like a model kitchen in an Ideal Home Exhibition than a room actually lived in and used. Everything was spotlessly clean and tidy, everything shone, the blue and white enamel paint on the walls, the polished linoleum, the white wood table and pale blue chairs, the gleaming pots and pans; everything looked brand new, everything was neatly arranged in its proper place, not a speck of dust was to be seen. Except, reprehensibly one felt, in the shaft of wintry sunlight that fell from a high window and illumined, like a spotlight, the erect figure of the mistress of the house. A pretty, neat, unsmiling young woman, Mrs. Plum stood in the midst of her immaculate kitchen, holding in her arms the most doll-like baby I ever saw. Two cups of tea were already poured out. They stood, precisely placed, with a sugar bowl, on the table, and Mrs. Plum, inclining her head a little as I bowed to her, invited me to accept one. I thanked her and took it up. It was not tepid, it was cold. It must have been poured out for a quarter of an hour at least. From this I inferred that one had to enter into Mrs. Plum's scheme of things, that punctuality played an important part therein, and that we were late. Presumably Mr. Plum's tea was as cold as my own but he did not flinch. I then congratulated Mrs. Plum on the beauty of her kitchen, and added that it was a marvel to keep a place so clean when it contained a dog.

"He's not allowed into the house," said

she, in a grave voice. "Dogs make things dirty."

Throughout this short interlude Tulip's faint but heart-rending cries had been audible from the garage. Unable to bear them any longer, I suggested to Mr. Plum that we should return and see how the courtship was progressing—though I was under no illusion that her cries were due to physical pain. He agreed, and when I had thanked Mrs. Plum for her delightful hospitality we made good our escape.

Tulip was exactly where we had left her, by the wire door, though now sitting down, presumably for safety's sake, while Chum hovered wearily in the background. For the next half hour we did our best to effect a conjunction between them. I smeared Tulip lavishly with Vaseline and tried to hold her still while Mr. Plum strove to guide Chum, whom fatigue had made erratic, to a more accurate aim. But it was all of no use. Tulip either squirmed her posterior aside or sat down upon it, and at length began to appeal to me with such obvious distress, uttering quavering, beseeching cries and rising up to lick my face, that I realized that our efforts to please had turned into cruelty and said we must stop. Mr. Plum, sweet fellow, at once agreed. But we were both of us disappointed and perplexed. What was Tulip trying to tell us? Had I lost her ready time? Had I brought her to Max too early and to Chum too late? Was neither dog personally acceptable to her? Or did she simply not know what to do? Or was her devotion to myself all the love she needed? Or could it be, as Mr. Plum suggested, that the *mise en scène* was unpropitious and that she might relax more if the action were transferred to my own flat? This was a characteristically sensitive thought, and when he then offered to bring Chum to call upon Tulip next day I accepted with gratitude.

The most conspicuous result of Mr. Plum's visit was that my flat was rapidly transformed into a condition which, had it been her place, would have caused Mrs. Plum instantly to swoon away. A thaw had set in, and although I foresaw the consequences of this and did what I could to protect my carpets from the forthcoming invasion by laying sheets of newspaper over them, I need not have troubled myself. Tulip greeted Chum with infantile pleasure and at once in-stituted nursery games, romping with him on my large, now messy, terrace, and then chasing him, or being chased by him, in and out of the flat, scattering the newspapers like leaves in the wind. He still found her attractive, but of sexual interest on her side there was no sign.

Later on we took them out for a walk together on Putney Common. It was a fine day and an agreeable expedition, though more agreeable to me than to Mr. Plum, for the contrast in behavior of our two animals was now too plainly seen. Chum soon got bored with Tulip's scoldings and flew constantly off in pursuit of other dogs, paying no attention at all to Mr. Plum's commands, while Tulip kept a vigilant eye upon me and deferred to my opinion about everything she did. Poor Mr. Plum observed her with envy.

"I thought Chum was going to be like that," said he, "but—well, I don't like to blame him, I've a feeling I let him down. I'm fond of walking, and we've had some jolly good hikes together, but of course when you're married you've got other people to consider. This Sunday walk's his weekly treat now, not that I wouldn't take him out more often, especially of a summer's evening, but you can't always please yourself when you're married, and it's natural, after all, that the wife should want one's company too. Chummy! Chummy!" But Chummy had vanished. "There you are, you see . . ."

When we had retrieved him, I said:

"It's a pity you can't have him with you in the flat. After all, dogs do like company and to busy themselves about their masters."

Mr. Plum sighed:

"Yes, I'm afraid he mopes. And of course I'd love to have him in with me like I did in my bachelor days, but, well you know what women are, house-proud and so on, and I can quite see the place would get a bit mucky, not that I should mind that . . ."

But I had left off listening to Mr. Plum's sorrowful reflections. Cutting across our path was a curious figure who instantly caught my attention. This was a rough, thick-set man with the cauliflower ears and battered face of a pugilist. He was wearing a roll-necked sweater and a tiny cap. What riveted my interest upon him, however, was the fact that he was being hauled along by two powerful young Alsatian dogs on a chain. A boy walked at his side. To let such a man pass at such a moment would have been to fly in the face of providence, and I accosted him. He was readily conversable. Yes, he knew all about Alsatians, he bred them as a sideline to his work, and these two splendid young dogs who were trying to get at Tulip had been reared by him. Craving his indulgence, I described my perplexities and requested his valuable advice. He studied Tulip with a beady eye.

"I wouldn't be surprised," he then remarked darkly, "if she's a barren bitch."

"Barren!" I cried. "How can you tell?"

"Ah, I'm not laying it down, but that'd be my guess. Too nervous and 'ighly strung for my liking. But if you showed me 'er pedigree I could tell from that."

"I haven't got it on me," I said dejectedly.

"Well, you could fetch it along some other time. Any road, I reckon 'e wouldn't stand much chance with 'er," he continued, casting at Chum a disparaging glance. "Too young and flimsy, if you take my meaning. Now if it 'adn't been a Sunday and so many people about and me 'aving the young lad with me an' all, I wouldn't 'ave minded unleashing one of me own dogs on 'er, 'ere and now. They'd soon find out if she was a barren bitch or not!"

"But isn't it too late in her season? It must be her fourteenth or fifteenth day."

"Seeing as 'ow she's carrying on with that there mongrel," he replied, "I'd say she could still be done. And if I was you, I'd watch out!"

"Tulip!" I said reproachfully.

We had been followed for some time by a small dog, one of those smooth, tight-skinned, busy and bouncing little creatures who, if dogs wore hats, would certainly have worn a bowler. He had attached himself to Tulip in very nearly the closest sense of the word, and was receiving from her all those marks of favor which she had declined to bestow upon Max or Chum. Indeed, she was clearly vastly amused by this artful little dodger, who was making repeated attempts to jump her, an ambition which I had already been pondering whether he was too small to achieve, and although she skipped her bottom from side to side when I admonished her, she was accepting from him, with an appearance of absent-mindedness, a shameful amount of familiarity. Our oracle observed all this with interest.

"Aye," said he, "I believe she'd stand for that little bloke where she wouldn't stand for Chum; and if she'd stand for 'im, she wouldn't get away from *my* dogs once they'd got a grip on 'er."

All this was extremely tantalizing.

"There aren't really many people about," I said. "Can't we go over into those bushes? No one would see us there."

"I'm right sorry to disoblige you. I'd 'ave been pleased to try; but I couldn't do that, not in front of the young lad." . . . That was the end of my first attempt to marry Tulip.

Mr. Plum saw us home and I invited him up for a glass of sherry; but although he was clearly tempted, he thought, after studying his watch, that he had better not, it might make him late for his Sunday dinner, and, well, you know, when one was married that didn't do. I had already learnt that it didn't do to be late for tea, so I did not press him and he hurried off, this good, kind, once adventurous, now lost young man to his doom, while I ascended in the elevator with mine.

. . . I wanted as many rods in the next fire as I could muster; but at the same time there seemed to me—I had felt it all along—something unnatural about bringing two dogs, total strangers, together for an hour or so for the purpose of copulation, not to mention having to stimulate them into taking an interest in each other. I perceived that I might be influenced in this feeling by the fact that my royal bitch was, of course, so infinitely superior to anything else in her domesticated species that she seemed scarcely to belong to it at all. I perceived, too, or thought I perceived, the danger of translating human emotions into beastly breasts. But whether or not my recent fiasco with Tulip could be attributed to such personal causes, that neither of her two suitors had been attractive to her, there was no doubt that in normal times she displayed decided preferences in her canine relationships. There were two or three mongrels in my district for whom she had a special fancy; to one in particular she was so devoted that it was quite a romance. It was even quite a menace. Ordinarily far less interested in dogs than in many other things, and possessed of an exemplary road sense, she was nevertheless liable to cross the street, without permission or precaution, if she perceived this favorite of hers upon the other side. He was a very small and rather wooden terrier, with a mean little face streaked black-and-white like a badger, and I had only to pronounce his name, which was Watney, for her to prick up her ears and lead me excitedly to the public house in which he lived. Hastening across the Saloon Bar to the counter, she would stand up on her hind legs and peer over it to see if he was there. The publican, who was privy to the romance, would let the little dog out, and Tulip would greet him with all her prettiest demonstrations of pleasure, curtsying down to him on her elbows in her play attitude, with her rump and its waving tail up in the air. Every now and then, as he rotated round her, she would place a paw on his back as though to hold him still for contemplation.

What she saw, or smelt, in this dreary little dog I never could understand. Disillusioned women often upbraid their husbands with: "You only like me for one thing!" and this might well have been the case between Tulip and Watney. During her heats he practically lived on our doorstep and, when she appeared, clung like a limpet to one of her hind legs—he could reach no higher—while she patiently stood and allowed him to do with her as he would and could. But when, in the long intervals between, she visited him in his pub in all her fond and radiant beauty, he never found for her more than a moment to spare. Having trotted round her once and ascertained, with a sniff, that there was nothing doing, he would retire stiffly on his apparently hingeless legs to his duties behind the bar (he guarded the till and rang the bell at closing time)—duties which he totally neglected when she was in season—leaving her sitting, frustrated and forlorn, in the saloon.

"Never mind, Tulip dear," I would say, as she turned her mournful gaze upon me. "It's the way of the world, I fear." . . .

It was during this time that Miss Canvey* entered my life, and I carried my problem to her. She was immediately helpful. She had two or three Alsatian-owners on her books whom she was willing to approach; but she added what seemed to me a far more satisfactory proposition: her own kennel-maid possessed an Alsatian, named Timothy, of whom I could have the use, a possible advantage of this choice being, said Miss Canvey, that she herself would supervise the operation. On the other hand, it had to be admitted, Timothy, though "quite good," was not a highly bred dog, and perhaps I ought to see him before making up my mind. But my mind was already made up. What could be better than to hand the whole thing over to dear Miss Canvey? I inspected Timothy nevertheless. He was the smallest Alsatian I had ever seen, no larger in height and build than Tulip herself; but he was nicely shaped in his small-scale way and had an extremely intelligent face. He was reputed to be as devoted to his mistress as Tulip was to me, which may have explained why, when the two animals were given a preliminary opportunity to meet, they took of each other no notice whatever. But never mind, the matter was now in Miss Canvey's capable hands. She told me to phone her as soon as Tulip's heat began, and with everything so ideally arranged I gave up hunting for other dogs.

On August 22, spots of blood appeared again on Tulip's shins and I phoned the news to Miss Canvey. When should I bring her along? Miss Canvey at once supplied the clue I had missed in the autumn:

"Bring her as soon as she starts to hold her tail sideways when you stroke her."

Wonderful Miss Canvey! No other vet, nor any dog book I had ever read, had thought fit to provide this inestimably important piece of information, a truth, like many another great truth,

*A veterinarian—*Ed.*

so obvious in its simplicity when it is pointed out that I wondered how I could have failed to notice it before and draw from it its manifest conclusions. Tulip herself supplies the answer to the question of her readiness. At the peak of her heat, from her ninth or tenth day, her long tail, as soon as she is touched anywhere near it, or even if a feint of touching her is made, coils away round one flank or the other, leaving the vaginal passage free and accessible. This pretty demonstration of her physical need goes on for several days; during all of these she is receptive.

I took her down to Miss Canvey on September 1. The arrangement was that I should leave her there on my way to work and call for her on my return. There was a stable yard attached to Miss Canvey's old-fashioned establishment, and there the two animals were to spend the intermediate hours together, under observation from the surgery windows. Tulip evidenced no particular pleasure at meeting Timothy again; her desolate cries followed me as I left. When I rejoined her in the evening I was told that he had penetrated her but had not tied.* This, I gathered, had not been achieved without help. Miss Canvey was displeased and asked me to fetch her back in a couple of days for another go. On this second occasion, again with help, the animals tied for ten minutes, and Miss Canvey declared herself satisfied. After a lapse of three weeks I was to produce Tulip for examination. I did so. She was not pregnant. She was not to be a mother after all.

This was the end of my second attempt to mate her, and since it had seemed successful, it was a greater disappointment than the first.

In the months that followed this second failure to mate Tulip my mind was ceaselessly engaged in planning for the future, and soon I had three more suitors lined up for her, all belonging to people with leisure to afford them a proper courtship. I had not worked out the mechanics, but my intention was to let her make her own

*Or locked. The dog's penis only reaches full erectal size after entering the bitch. It cannot then be withdrawn until detumescence occurs. Foxes and wolves have the same coital pattern.

choice among these three. An unforeseen fate ruled otherwise.

The human emotions that brought about her change of residence from London to Sussex do not belong to this history, which concerns itself with the canine heart; but a few words of explanation are necessary. A cousin of mine, who had no fixed abode, had rented a bungalow in Ferring for the winter months. Aware that I had been looking in vain for holiday accommodation that would accept an Alsatian dog, she invited us down to stay. We went. Newly painted white with a broad blue band round it, like a ribbon round a chocolate box, "Mon Repos" was a trim little place. It had a garden fore and aft which my cousin, whose knowledge of gardening was slender to the point of invisibility, had undertaken to "keep up." The front one contained a rockery with flowering shrubs, among which were tastefully disposed figurines of the Seven Dwarfs. It was quite the prettiest bungalow in Witchball Lane. That we had not, however, been invited entirely disinterestedly soon appeared: my cousin confessed to being nervous of staying in Mon Repos alone. Arguments were therefore advanced, when the end of my holiday approached, for prolonging a situation that suited her: Tulip was enjoying herself, it was nice for her to have a garden to play in, and the walks round about were superior to anything that Putney had to offer; she was looking better already for the change; why not leave her there to profit from the wonderful sea air and come down myself at weekends to join her? The value of sea air to canine health was an idea that had not occurred to me, but I saw that there was some small substance in the rest of the argument. On the other hand I did not want to be separated from Tulip throughout the week and believed that all her present amusements combined were as nothing to her anxiety not to be separated from me; nor had I the slightest inclination to make a railway journey to Mon Repos every weekend. But when women have set their hearts on something, the wishes and convenience of others are apt to wear a flimsy look; my own point of view, when I ventured it, was quickly dismissed as selfishness. I was sorry for my cousin and consented. I only stipulated that Tulip must be removed to

London before her next heat, which was due in March. This was agreed to.

To recall the weeks that followed is no pleasure, but since this is the story of Tulip's love life they should not be passed over in silence. An alarm clock woke me at 6:45 every Monday morning; I then had half an hour in which to get up and catch the bus at the top of Witchball Lane for the station a couple of miles away. Tulip, who slept always in my room, would get up too and follow me about as I tiptoed between bedroom, bathroom and kitchen. I knew, without looking at her, that her gaze was fixed unswervingly upon me, that her tall ears were sharp with expectation. I knew that, the moment she caught my attention, they would fall back as though I had caressed her, then spring up again while she continued to search my face with that unmeetably poignant inquiry in which faith and doubt so tragically mingled: "Of course I'm coming with you—aren't I?" Avoiding her eyes for as long as I could, I would go about my preparations; but the disappointing had to be done at last. As I picked up my bag in the bedroom, she would make her little quick participating movement with me through the door, and I would say casually, as though I were leaving her for only a moment, "No, old girl, not this time." No more was needed. She would not advance another step but, as if the words had turned her to stone, halt where she was outside the bedroom door. Now to go without saying good-bye to her I could not, though I knew what I should see, that stricken look, compounded of such grief, such humility, such despair, that it haunted me all the journey up. "Good-bye, sweet Tulip," I would say and, returning to her, raise the pretty disconsolate head that drooped so heavily in my hands, and kiss her on the forehead. Then I would slip out into the darkness of Witchball Lane. But the moment the door had closed behind me she would glide back into the bedroom, which was on the front of the bungalow, and rearing up on her hind legs at the window, push aside the curtains with her nose and watch me pass. This was the last I would see of her for five days, her gray face, like a ghost's face, at the window, watching me pass.

The year turned, the date of our departure drew near, and my cousin's mind got busy, as I guessed it would, with the problem of obstructing it. She really could not see the necessity for taking Tulip away. Why should she not have her heat in Ferring?

"Because I've fixed up her love affairs in Putney."

"None of your dogs could possibly be as good as Mountjoy, and Mrs. Tudor-Smith is frightfully keen on the marriage."

This was a high card. Mountjoy belonged to some people a little further down Witchball Lane. He was an Alsatian of such ancient and aristocratic ancestry that Mrs. Tudor-Smith had been heard to declare that his genealogy went back even further than her own. She had paid as much as a hundred guineas for the privilege of possessing him. He gave, indeed, in his appearance and manners, so instant a conviction of the bluest of blood that it would have been both superfluous and impertinent to ask to see his pedigree. More like a lion than a dog, with his magnificent tawny coat and heavy ruff, he was often to be viewed in the grounds of the bungalow in which he resided, or just outside its gates, standing always in the classic attitude as though he had invented it. Perpetually posing, it seemed, for cameras that were his customary due and were doubtless somewhere about, he gave the impression not so much of looking up or down Witchball Lane as of gazing out over distant horizons. He had neither any objection nor any wish to be stroked; he accepted caresses from strangers in the aloof manner in which a king might receive tribute from his subjects; when he felt he had done his duty by the human race, he would stalk majestically back into the house; and if he had ever emitted any sound louder than a yawn I had not heard it, certainly nothing so coarse as a bark. But it was not on account of his nobility that he was more advantageous than my Putney dogs; I was not greatly interested in the canine Debrett; it was simply that his situation with regard to Tulip made everything far easier. To get one animal to the other was a matter of only a minute's walk; they were already on friendly terms and often in each other's company.

I hesitated. Cashing in on this, my cousin added:

"If you want a second string, Colonel Finch says you can have Gunner whenever you like."

During my weekends in Ferring I had met many of its dogs and their owners, and although Gunner was a far less impressive card than Mountjoy, he too was an Alsatian and therefore eligible for Tulip's hand. Gunner was an unlovable dog, as ill-favored as the hyena he somewhat resembled and of bad local character. His master, who doted on him, always averred that he was a positive lamb and would not hurt a fly, but his habit was to lie all day on the colonel's porch on Ferring front and charge out like the Light Brigade at every dog that passed. Constant was the hot water into which Gunner got his master. It was the commonest thing, as one walked down the path by their bungalow, to hear the colonel's dominating voice on the further side of the hedge assuring some other dog-lover, whose animal had just been stampeded into the sea, that it was only Gunner's little bit of fun. And, indeed, there may well have been some truth in this, for the colonel's own sense of humor was of a similar cast, and since we are said to get like our pets, perhaps vice versa, master and dog may have grown to understand one another in an imitative kind of way. The very first time I met Colonel Finch, he gave Tulip an appraising look and rapped out at me:

"Hm! Pampered bitch, I can see! I bet she sleeps on your bed!"

Much taken aback by this unprovoked attack, I confessed apologetically:

"I'm afraid she does. It's wrong, I suppose. Where does Gunner sleep?"

"On the bed, of course!" roared the colonel, delighted to have teased me so successfully. "The best bed in the house!"

But Tulip failed to take of Gunner's "little bit of fun" the tolerant view I took of his master's. Having received from him, as *their* first introduction, one of his famous broadsides before he perceived her sex and attempted to recover his mistake by a belated display of awkward gallantry, she never accorded him the condescension she showed to Mountjoy, and I did not

therefore pin much hope on Colonel Finch's lamb. Nevertheless, with my resolutions now weakened—they needed little to undermine them, for, in truth, I was not looking forward to Tulip's next heat—I said:

"In any case, you've no idea of the difficulties. You couldn't cope."

"You're exaggerating," said my cousin. "If you can cope, so can I."

Tulip entered her heat on the first of March, and even I never envisaged the consequences that rapidly developed. Within a few days Mon Repos was in a state of siege. My cousin began by thinking this rather amusing, and sent me cheerful accounts of the "sweet" little Scotties and Sealyhams who had come to call. She found it less amusing when they accumulated and would not go away; when the larger dogs took to scrambling over the whitewashed wall in front, which, by repeated leapings against the winter jasmine that had been carefully trained to ornament it, they could just manage to do; when their smaller associates, not to be outdone and left behind, contrived to smash the flimsy latch of the gate by constant rattling at it, and all camped out all night, quarrelling and whining, among the Seven Dwarfs. Nor did she find it amusing when the other ladies of Ferring, deprived of and anxious about their pets who returned not home even for their dinners, called round to retrieve them, not once but every day and a number of times a day, in a progressively nastier frame of mind. The soft answer that turneth away wrath is no part of the diplomatic equipment women claim to possess; my cousin was not one to be spoken to sharply without giving as good as she got. Very soon to the sound of Tulip's excited voice within and the replies of her devotees without was added a recurrent chorus of equally incontinent human voices raised in revilement and recrimination. And my cousin found it less amusing still when she tried to take Tulip for walks and fell into the error I had made of attempting to beat off her escort, which resulted not only in a more formidable incursion of enraged owners complaining that she had been seen ill-treating their pets, but, more affectingly, in her clothes and flesh getting torn. Before the first week was over, Tulip was not taken out at all; but now there was no lovely elevator to waft her out of sight, sound and scent of her admirers; good though she always was, no desirable and desiring bitch could be expected to behave with restraint in a small bungalow all the windows of which presented her with the spectacle of a dozen or so of her male friends awaiting her outside; she barked at them incessantly, hastening from window to window; they barked back; then, like the siren, she would break into song; the expensive net curtains were soon all in tatters, and these, in the end, I had to replace.

I could not replace Mon Repos itself. By the close of the affair it is no exaggeration to say that it was practically wrecked. The walls still stood, of course; but what walls! A tepid rain had been falling for some time to add to the general melancholy of the scene, and their fresh white paint was liberally stippled with filthy paw marks where the excited creatures had tried to clamber in at the windows; the pale blue paint of the doors, at which they had constantly knocked, was scratched and scored; the Seven Dwarfs were prostrate in a morass that had once been a neat grassy border. Siege became invasion. The back of the bungalow held out a little longer than the front; its garden was protected by a fence; but as Tulip's ready time approached and the frustrated besiegers realized that this was where she now took the sea air, they set about discovering its weak spots. This did not take long. By the time I was able to come down for my second visit during this period, to stay now and supervise the marriage, they had already forced their way in at several points, and my cousin was hysterically engaged in ejecting dogs of all shapes and sizes from dining room, sun parlor and even in the night from her bedroom.

Into the midst of this scene of chaos Mountjoy, at the appropriate moment, was introduced. Tulip had not seen much of him during her wooing week; the Tudor-Smiths had thought it undesirable that he should mix in such low company; she was pleased to see him now. As soon as he made his wishes clear she allowed him to mount her and stood quietly with her legs apart and her tail coiled away while he clasped her round the waist. But, for some reason, he failed to achieve his purpose. His stabs, it looked to me standing beside them, did not quite reach her. After a little she disengaged herself, and, assuming her play attitude, began to flirt in front of him. But he had graver ends in view. Again she stood, with lowered head and flattened ears, her gaze slanted back, apprehensively, I thought, to what he was doing behind. This time he appeared to have moved further forward, and now it did look as though he would succeed; but suddenly she gave a nervous cry and escaped from him once more. They tried again and again, but the same thing always happened; whenever he seemed about to enter her she protested, as though she were still a virgin, and pulled herself free. And now it was quite upsetting to watch, his continual failure to consummate his desire and the consequent frustration of these two beautiful animals who wished to copulate and could not manage to do so. Nor could I see any way to help them, except to lubricate Tulip, which I did, for they seemed to be doing themselves all that could be done, except unite. It was, indeed, very moving, it was sorrow, to watch them trying to know each other and always failing, and it was touching to see Tulip give him chance after chance. But of course she was getting tired, she was panting; compared with him she was a small, slender creature, and it could not have been anything but burdensome for her to have the weight of his massive body upon her back and the clutch of his leonine arms about her waist. Yet, at the same time, he was as gentle with her as he could be; he took hold of her in a careful kind of way, or so it looked, maneuvering his arms tentatively upon her as though to get a purchase that did not grip her too hard; and sometimes, when she made a nervous movement or uttered an anxious cry, he would dismount and, going round to her head, put his nose to hers as if to say: "Are you all right?" But at last, in his own weariness, his jabs got wilder and wilder, quite wide of the mark; finally she would have no more to do with him and, whenever he approached her, drove him away.

Now what to do I did not know. Who would

have supposed that mating a bitch could be so baffling a problem? Perhaps, in spite of her coiling tail, she was not ready. I set them together the following day, and the day after, only to watch them go through the same agonizing performance. And now it was her twelfth day. Was there truly something wrong with her, or was I muddling away her third heat like the others? I sent for the local vet. Next morning he came and stood with me while the animals repeated their futile and exhausting antics.

"It's the dog's fault," he said. "He can't draw."

This term had to be explained to me. It meant that his foreskin was too tight to enable him to unsheathe, a disability that could have been corrected when he was a puppy. Besides this, the vet announced after examining him, which Mountjoy permitted with extraordinary dignity, he was a "rig" dog, that is to say, he had an undescended testicle, a not uncommon thing, said the vet, and a serious disqualification in mating, since it was heritable. It is scarcely necessary to add that neither of these terms, nor any of this information, is mentioned in the dog books, at least in none that I have ever come across. Mountjoy's owners themselves, who had never offered him a wife before, were totally ignorant of these facts, if facts they were, and therefore of the corollary that their noble and expensive beast was relatively worthless.

There was nothing now to be done but to phone Colonel Finch. In the late afternoon Tulip was hustled into a taxi and conveyed to Gunner. Of the outcome of this I never was in doubt and was not therefore disappointed. She would have nothing to do with him at all. He was willing, she was not; it was the bully's turn to be bullied, and when the colonel decided that his positive lamb had had enough, Tulip reentered her taxi and was driven back to Mon Repos.

Dusk was now falling. I restored her to the ravaged garden, and it was while I stood with her there, gazing in despair at this exquisite creature in the midst of her desire, that the dog-next-door emerged through what remained of the fence. He had often intruded before, as often been ejected. Now he hung there in the failing light,

half in, half out of the garden, his attention fixed warily upon me, a disreputable, dirty mongrel, Dusty by name, in whom Scottish sheepdog predominated. I returned the stare of the disconcertingly dissimilar eyes, one brown, one pale blue, of this ragamuffin with whom it had always amused Tulip to play, and knew that my intervention was at an end. I smiled at him.

"Well, there you are, old girl," I said. "Take it or leave it. It's up to you."

She at once went to greet him. Dusty was emboldened to come right in. There was a coquettish scamper. She stood for him. He was too small to manage. She obligingly squatted, and suddenly, without a sound, they collapsed on the grass in a heap. It was charming. They lay there together, their paws all mixed up, resting upon each other's bodies. They were panting. But they looked wonderfully pretty and comfortable—until Tulip thought she would like to get up, and found she could not. She tried to rise. The weight of Dusty's body, united with her own, dragged her back. She looked round in consternation. Then she began to struggle. I called to her soothingly to lie still, but she wanted to come over to me and could not, and her dismay turned to panic. With a convulsive movement she regained her feet and began to pull Dusty, who was upside down, along the lawn, trying from time to time to rid herself of her incubus by giving it a nip. The unfortunate Dusty, now on his back, now on his side, his little legs scrabbling wildly about in their efforts to find a foothold, at length managed, by a kind of somersault, to obtain it. This advantage, however, was not won without loss, for his exertion turned him completely round, so that, still attached to Tulip, he was now bottom to bottom with her and was hauled along in this even more uncomfortable and abject posture, his hindquarters off the ground, his head down and his tongue hanging out. Tulip gazed at me in horror and appeal. Heavens! I thought, this is love! These are the pleasures of sex! As distressed as they, I hastened over to them, persuaded Tulip to lie down again for poor Dusty's sake, and sat beside them to caress and calm them. It was a full half-hour before detumescence occurred and Nature released Dusty, who instantly fled home through the gap in the fence and was seen no more. As for Tulip, her relief, her joy, her gratitude (she seemed to think it was I who had saved her) were spectacular. It was more as though she had been freed from some dire situation of peril than from the embraces of love.

The following day I removed her to London and the haven of my flat. The house agent of Mon Repos had been apprised of our activities and was belatedly on the warpath. Even my cousin had had enough. A car was summoned to take us to the station. When all was ready for immediate departure—the engine running, the car door open—I emerged from the ruined bungalow with Tulip on the lead and ran the gauntlet of dogs down the garden path. We rushed into the car, slammed the door, and were off. But the frenzied animals were not so easily balked. They pursued us in a pack so far down the country lanes that, though their number gradually diminished, I was suddenly terrified that the more pertinacious would gain the station and invade the train. If there had been any comedy in the situation ever, it was no longer present; the scene had the quality of nightmare. But the car outstripped them all at last and we got safely away.

Tulip was not a barren bitch. Three weeks after the events described I walked her over to Miss Canvey, who pronounced her pregnant.

Bachelor and Blunder *by A. Cooper*

The Origin of the Dog

by EDWIN H. COLBERT

To the casual observer the numerous breeds of domestic dogs would seem to have reached the farthest possible limits of diversity among animals that may still be called by one name. And so they have, in one sense of the word. Compare, for a moment, the Great Dane with the Scotch terrier, the Old English sheepdog with the Chihuahua, or the greyhound with the bulldog. Certainly there appears to be but little in common between these dogs, at least in their outer form, even though they are all dogs. One wonders what some future zoologist or paleontologist might do with the breeds of modern dogs, were he to find their bones among the ruins of what we are pleased to call our present-day civilization.

Yet we know that the collie and the Yorkshire terrier and the Pomeranian are all dogs, because we have seen them originate and develop—so to speak—under the controlling influence of man's hand. Moreover, we know that they are all dogs because of their habits, for in spite of the dissimilarities in their appearances, they act much alike—they are all dogs by instinct and by reason of their peculiar psychology and the workings of their canine brains.

And when we get down to such a fundamental comparison as this we bump into the fact that the domestic dog, no matter what his looks may make him, is under the skin nothing more nor less than a tractable wolf—or, to look at it from another angle, the wolf is nothing more nor less than a wild dog.

The origin of the dog is lost in the mists of antiquity, for of all the animals domesticated by man, the dog was the first. Since the time when the question of the dog's origin was first seriously investigated, numerous attempts have been made to ferret out what his ancestors might have been, but despite diligent studies toward this end no definite conclusions have been reached. Indeed, zoologists differ among themselves, and at best they can for the most part only indulge in scientific speculations regarding the ultimate ancestry of the dog.

Generally speaking, most authorities agree that the dog is largely descended from the Eurasiatic wolf. Perhaps the story of the origin of the dog is a complex one, in that wild dogs have been severally and independently domesticated by man at different times in different parts of the world, while on top of this the dog after his domestication has perhaps often been crossed back with various wild dogs at different periods during the rise of human cultures. Certainly we know that the Eskimos, for instance, not infrequently cross their sledge dogs with wolves, to maintain the strength and endurance of the breed.

Which is to get back to a point made before,

83

that the dog is nothing more than a tractable wolf —or tame wild dog, if you will. And to understand this question of the domestication of the dog, it may be well, perhaps, to review the story of the origin and evolution of the dog and his cousins—to get a glimpse at the background of the dog tribe, the better to appreciate those characters that make dogs what they are.

The dogs, the wolves and their relatives belong to a family of carnivorous mammals known as the *Canidae*. This family includes, in addition to the dogs and wolves, the jackals, coyotes, dingos, the various dogs and foxes of South America, the Japanese "raccoon-dog," the numerous northern foxes and the fennec, and finally the African hunting dog, the East Indian wild dog, or dhole, and the South American bush dog. Even to the nonzoologist, these creatures are clearly recognizable as being related to each other, because of their general doglike or wolflike appearance. And in addition to these modern dogs there is a host of extinct canids, for the most part known only to the trained paleontologist—many of them of course very much like our modern dogs, but many more quite different from anything in the canid line surviving to the present day.

The canid or dog family (and here we use the word "dog" in an inclusive sense, to designate the numerous canids listed above) had its beginning some forty million years ago, during the transition from the Eocene to the Oligocene period of geologic history. Those were the days when horses were no larger than small sheep, and had three toes on each foot, when rhinoceroses were still small horselike running animals, quite hornless and probably completely lacking in the ferocity that so distinguishes their modern descendants; when camels were dainty, gazellelike creatures; and when the first ancestors of the great apes and man were small, tree-dwelling monkeys.

In those far-off days there lived a small carnivorous mammal known as *Miacis*, the offspring of some very primitive Eocene carnivores that had passed through the heyday of their evolutionary supremacy and were on their way to extinction.

Miacis was a small carnivore with a long body and relatively short legs—not so different in appearance from some of the modern East Indian or African civets, which are but the slightly changed descendants of this primitive ancestor. Perhaps *Miacis* spent a considerable part of his time in the trees, for it would seem probable that the earliest true carnivores dwelt in the primitive forests that sheltered so many ancestral mammalian types. This early carnivore, structurally and mentally in a low stage of development, seems to us to have taken but a slight step in the direction leading to its progressive heirs, yet in spite of its primitive form it had the potentialities that were destined to lead into a large and varied group of highly advanced mammals.

During the Oligocene period the first canids evolved in North America as the direct lineal descendants of *Miacis*. Of these there were two types, one a large, heavy, long-tailed dog known as *Daphaenus*, the other a much smaller, more slender animal, going by the name of *Cynodictis*.

Daphaenus was the first of the "bear-dogs," an animal as large as a coyote but longer-bodied, with relatively shorter legs, with a massive skull and an unbelievably long, heavy tail. These animals became progressively larger as time went on, until during late Miocene days (some ten million years or so ago) they grew to truly gigantic proportions. Then some of them followed a line of evolution that involved a marked increase in weight, a secondary change from the typical running habits of the canids to a lumbering type of walk—due to the shortening of the feet—and profound modifications of the skull and teeth. Thus the bears arose, as descendants of the bear-dogs, in early Pliocene times.

As this first of the "bear-dogs" began to develop in the direction of the bears, the grandfather of all the dog family appeared. This animal, *Cynodictis*, retained the long body and short legs of the primitive carnivores. Indeed, like its ancestor, *Miacis*, it must have resembled to a considerable extent the modern Old World civets. And it was still so close to its earlier tree-climbing ancestors that it retained partially retractile claws, something like those of a cat.

This ancestor of the true canids gave rise to two distinct types of "grandchildren" in lower Miocene days.

One of these canids, *Temnocyon*, was ancestral to an evolutionary line that culminated in the modern hunting dogs of Africa and India. The African hunting dog, *Lycaon*, is a large, mongrel-looking canid with erect, rounded ears, and marked by irregular brown and yellow spots. The East Indian hunting dog, or dhole, is very doglike in its general appearance, with a long, pointed face, a bushy tail and a reddish coat. These canids, so like ordinary dogs to the casual observer, are in reality of quite an independent ancestry, and it would seem that the peculiar South American bush-dog, *Icticyon*, with an abbreviated face and a short tail, is, strangely enough, related to the Old World hunting dogs.

The other of these two lower Miocene canids, *Cynodesmus*, was the ancestor of a large and varied group of dogs, including our modern Eurasiatic and American dogs, wolves and foxes, which went through a major portion of their evolutionary development in North America.

Among the offspring of this ancestor of our common dogs (*Cynodesmus*), one branch, completely North American in its distribution and destined to become extinct, developed along a peculiar line whereby its members became very large, and strangely enough, hyenalike. This does not mean, of course, that they are to be related to the hyenas, but rather that they developed by *parallelism* in a way similar to the hyenas, because they lived the same kind of a life that the hyenas live today. These dogs were the "hyenas" of their time, occupying a role in North America that the hyenas, which were just beginning to evolve along their strange line of evolutionary development, were learning to play in the Old World. These "hyena-dogs," the most characteristic of which were *Hyaenognathus* and *Borophagus*, had heavy, bulldoglike skulls, with extraordinarily strong blunt teeth, adapted to crushing bones, rather than to slashing or tearing, for like the hyena, these dogs were carrion feeders.

Finally, we may consider the true dogs as we know them, which evolved between upper Miocene and recent times as an offshoot from the *Cynodesmus* stem and had their immediate origin in a genus known as *Tomarctus*.

Tomarctus must have been very doglike in its general appearance, and with but little change, except for the important one of the growth of intelligence, it grew into the wolves and wild dogs that spread throughout the northern world and surrounded primitive man in the East. From this ancestral form there evolved also, along a somewhat different line, the foxes, and the fenecs, small desert foxes of Africa.

Reducing these facts to their simplest terms, it may be said then that the canids, or "dogs" have followed four general lines or trends of evolutionary development. These were first, the gigantic bear-dogs, the direct ancestors of the bears, dogs in which size was at a premium and giantism was the final result of evolutionary progress. Secondly there were the hyenalike or "hyaenognathid" dogs, which, though true canids through and through, imitated to some extent the hyenas in their adaptations to life. Finally there were the two branches of dogs as we know them; on the one hand the hunting dogs of Africa and India, very much like the more familiar wolves and dogs but having a quite separate family history, and on the other hand the group of wolves, wild dogs and foxes, which may be considered as the central stem in this tree of canid history.

These were the particular specializations in the canid world. But throughout this melange of varying adaptations to different means of existence, there ran the central, unifying ties in the family history of the *Canidae*, like a strong warp weaving in and out among the varied threads of a patterned rug. These were: first, the universal adaptations among all of the canids toward a running mechanism of the body, capable of great speed; secondly, the attainment of a remarkably high degree of intelligence, commonly coupled with an extraordinarily well-developed sense of sociability; and lastly, the retention of a surprising amount of adaptability.

To continue our survey of the physical evolution among the dogs, the running habits so common to these animals must be stressed. The earliest dogs, such as *Cynodictis,* already showed some progress in this direction, although in these primitive forms the legs were relatively short as compared to the length of the body. But from the beginnings of canid history down to the point where man took a hand and produced specialized breeds, the story of evolution among these animals has been for the most part a tale of ever increasing limb length—a series of progressive adaptations for the running down and seizing of prey. In this respect the dogs differ from almost all of the other carnivorous mammals. The bears, their closest relatives, are huge lumbering creatures living for the most part on a diet of absurdly trifling items, and depending, when they do kill, on their great strength and size, while the raccoons, also close relatives, are primarily climbers. Of the other carnivores (except for the cheetah—an aberrant and quite uncatlike cat) only the hyenas may be classified as primarily running animals. And the hyenas do not rank at all with the canids when it comes to fast running—for they are not hunters but carrion feeders.

Thus we must think of the dogs—even the aberrant types that long since have become extinct—as the chasers of game, trailing their quarry mile after mile, hour after hour, until by the very diligence of their efforts and the cleverness of their methods they are able to overtake their prey. Of course, these remarks do not apply in their entirety to all of the canids, but they outline the general rule for the adaptations in this family of carnivores.

The running adaptations in the canids have led to a method of life that has been very important in deciding the "social" life of these animals. For, early in the history of their development, these hunters must have discovered that it is much easier for a family to act together in running down a fleet victim than is such a feat for a single individual. Thus was born the habit of family hunting. And from this it was but a short step to the banding together of several families at advantageous times, to hunt as groups or packs.

Now this communal life, so characteristic of most of the dogs, led to the growth of sociability

and a spirit of cooperation among the individual members of the group. Therefore, the dogs, instead of being individualists, such as the cats, became responsible members of a cooperative group, all working together toward a common end. Needless to say, animals living a life such as this are bound to exercise their intelligence to the utmost—they stimulate each other, and by working together they learn faster and build up the capabilities of their brains faster than would probably be the case if they were solitary.

Of course, generalizations such as these do not always hold. For among the canids, the foxes are strict individualists, and yet they are among the most gifted of the dog family, when it comes to a question of brains. Perhaps the answer is that the Miocene ancestors of the later canids were already extraordinarily intelligent animals, so that their descendants were bound to grow in wisdom, no matter what direction that growth followed. So it is that the foxes early in their history followed the solitary mode of life; but, living by their wits in much the same way that their wolf and wild-dog cousins lived, they naturally developed a sharp intellect. They became intelligent, as did all of the canids, because—among other things—of their heritage from precocious ancestors.

It is interesting to notice a few of the means whereby this sociability is expressed. The tales of hunting by relays are so often told as to be almost trite. A number of wolves or wild dogs will map out a "course" over which the quarry is to be pursued. Then, several dogs will distribute themselves along this course—usually circular—and take their turns in chasing the antelope or deer, until the animal is fatigued to a point of exhaustion. In this manner it is relatively easy for several animals working together to accomplish their purpose with a minimum amount of effort on the part of the individual.

Indeed the spirit of cooperation is so highly developed within some of the canids that there are well authenticated records of wolves supplying food for an infirm and aged member of the pack.

One of the social habits of the wild dogs that is retained by their domestic relatives, is the rather annoying one (to us) of marking trees and posts with urine. I suppose that the average person gives but little thought to the origin of this habit, or its significance. Yet it is really quite a remarkable and characteristic adaptation among the *Canidae,* for it is a method whereby individuals are able to communicate with each other. The wolf has a series of bulletin boards scattered through his domain; these may be trees, rocks, bushes or other like objects. To these signposts he pays periodic visits, marking them to show other members of his group that he has been this way, and this is a part of his kingdom. And by sniffing at these posts he is able to determine what other wolves have been past in the last day or two, and whether or not they have had a right to be in his region. He learns whether the other visitors were male or female, young or old, well or ill, unworried or hunted. And through the use of these markers wolves seem to be able to spread the news of danger, so that when one animal is threatened, the entire community soon becomes aware of the threat. Thus an analysis of this habit shows that it is a highly developed trait among the canids, one in keeping with their sociability and their gregariousness, and one that is of the utmost importance in the scheme of their lives.

Examples might be multiplied ad infinitum, but perhaps these are enough to demonstrate the rare combination of mental acuteness and cooperation typical of the wild dogs.

It is very difficult, and more than a little bit risky, to dogmatize as to the ranking in intelligence among the mammals, but certainly it is safe to say that the canids are among the most intelligent of the warm-blooded animals. In a large part this intelligence is innate, just as it is among all of the carnivorous mammals. But it is quite definitely augmented by the sociability of the dogs and their relatives, thereby making a combination of qualities that particularly suit these animals to live commensally with another intelligent species—Man.

Then, there is the remarkable adaptability of the canids, a trait that has been of immeasurable worth in enabling them to become suited to their surroundings. Structurally the canids are not highly specialized. Except for their long legs and compact feet as adaptations to running, and their highly developed brains, they are on the whole rather generalized carnivores. Hence they are unusually plastic, both physically and psychically, and are able to adapt themselves readily to changing conditions.

Contrast, if you will, the numerous types of wild canids with the cats. Cats, whether they be small or large, are generally speaking of one pattern, for these animals became highly specialized early in their phylogenetic history, and have been rigidly fixed ever since. Consequently a tiger and a puma and a house cat are much the same, except as to color and size, whereas the canids in their wild state show a rather wide range of adaptive radiation. This plasticity among the canids is illustrated artificially but none the less effectively by the extraordinarily numerous breeds of the domestic dogs, showing a range in size between the Chihuahua and the Great Dane and a range in form between the bulldog and the greyhound. What a contrast these artificial adaptations among the domestic dogs afford, as compared with fixity of the domestic cats.

But this plasticity in the canids is not confined to physical makeup alone, for these animals—at least the gregarious canids—are remarkably adaptable in their mentality. It is this fact that has made the dogs so amenable to domestication; the dog has been domesticated because he has been willing to conform to the ways of man, not only in his habits but even in his manner of thinking.

To thoroughly appreciate and really understand the domestic dog, it is necessary to become acquainted with his heritage from numerous ancestors, running back in an unbroken line for many millions of years, and to keep in mind the many ties that bind him to his wild relatives of the present day. When we take this comprehensive view of the dogs as we know them, we get an inkling of the various factors of heredity, environment and behavior that have worked together to bring about that combination of characters and traits which we recognize as being typical of the *Canidae.* Thus we see that the dogs are members of a varied and a highly interesting family of carnivorous mammals—a family of swift runners, characterized by the attainment of a high degree of intelligence, by a general feeling of sociability, and by a trait of adaptability that has enabled them to adjust themselves to a rapidly changing environment. Is it any wonder, then, that they should be the first animals to fall under the all-prevailing influence of Man?

Italian Greyhounds *by P. Reinagle*

An Honest Dog

by DONALD McCAIG

IF you were a range ewe, you'd be afraid of sharp noises, flickers of movement in tall grass, strange countryside and loneliness.

Unless they were on horseback, or inside a pickup truck, you'd fear men. A distant bark carried on the wind—you'd crane your neck and cock your ears and peer your head around and stamp your forefoot, wary as any deer.

Paradise is a broad hilltop with short graze, water, salt, some shade—maybe a breeze to keep off the worst flies—and forty or fifty pals for company.

It's best in the center of the flock because the outside ewes get pulled down first (everybody knows that), and it's a wise ewe who protects herself with the bodies of her friends.

Hell is a tight spot—a trap-place you can't get out of—a pen on strange ground with no more company than strangers can offer; two sheep not from your own flock and thus aliens, barbarians.

You'd be afraid of dogs.

The member clubs of the American Kennel Club (AKC) publish breed standards for their respective breeds. For practical purposes, these standards are definitions of the breed. Great Dane males "should be not less than thirty inches at the shoulders," Doberman pinscher ears are "normally cropped and carried erect," the Lhaso apso's "length from wither to point of buttocks is longer than height at withers." Black hair is a fault in the Irish setter but required in the schipperke.

At bench shows, judges evaluate dogs according to these standards and since AKC champions have many more breeding opportunities than nonchampions, a breed gradually becomes its standard.

These standards can provoke great controversy among fanciers. And, in practical judging, some features (for example, the bulldog's facial wrinkle) are deemed more important than other features (the bulldog's gait). Infrequently, revised standards are published with the hope of emphasizing those features modern fanciers find particularly attractive. The AKC publishes a compendium of purebred dogs with each breed's history, standard and a photograph or two. The AKC *Dogbook* contains very many photographs of beautiful dogs.

For rare or miscellaneous breeds, there are real advantages to gaining full AKC recognition. Only AKC dogs can compete for AKC bench championships. Pups with an AKC number fetch a premium. (Twelve-week-old pups from AKC Champions can bring $2000.)

For many years, owners and managers of professional baseball teams insisted that Major League baseball players must be white.

Across the country there are many putting greens less kempt than the ordinary bluegrass pasture at Walnut Hall Farm. Walnut Hall is one of the great Kentucky horse farms (standardbreds; pacers and trotters). It's partly farm, partly breeding factory, overall a great estate. Farm roads are smoothly asphalted. The tremendous black walnuts could provide enough veneer to panel every townhouse from Lexington, Kentucky to Pacolet Mills, South Carolina. Young trees are fenced from nibbling horses and the herd of buttermilk-white Charolais cows.

With its breeding barns, horse cemetery and miles of white board fence, Walnut Hall would have made a grand location for a forties movie, perhaps a remake of *National Velvet*.

Twenty-three years ago, the farm staff formed the Kentucky Stock Dog Association and their Bluegrass National Open Sheep Dog Trials have become the most important in North America. Other trials offer better prize money but every year, America's top sheepdog handlers return to Lexington for the oldest and toughest trial of all.

Pope Robertson is here with his young dog, Bill, and his imported dog, Sweep. Pope's won this trial three times with dogs he trained himself.

Ralph Pulfer brought Imported Bess and Imported Spot. It's said Ralph can get more out of a dog than anybody on this side of the ocean.

In 1978, Ada Karrasch's Nan finished the third leg of her CDX Obedience title, whelped a litter of puppies and six weeks later was reserve champion here.

John Bauserman brought Rory and his own Imported Bess (probably the best little bitch in Virginia). Lewis Pence has two young dogs: Diamond and Star. Lewis won here in '66, '70 and '73. His protege, young Bruce Fogt, has come to run his first Bluegrass.

Jack Knox has won three of the last ten Bluegrass Trials. A native Scot, he's lived in this country long enough to rub some of the burr off. He keeps a flock of 350 sheep and, at any one time, between twenty and forty border collies. He breeds them, buys, imports, trains, sells and handles them. Jack Knox is an even-tempered man.

The day before Bluegrass qualifications, Jack's in Ohio, teaching a sheep-dog clinic. Occasionally you find other breeds at these training clinics. Usually the dogs are border collies and this clinic's no exception. Sixteen dogs—some have worked sheep before; others are exposed to sheep for the first time in this training ring.

Jack and the owner command the dog trotting around the worried sheep. "That's a six-year-old dog who never saw sheep. You see its interest? That's the instinct. It's up to you to bring out what's inside your dog."

The next dog is younger, an obedience-trained dog. "I do not want the dog to be watching you. I want him watching his sheep."

"I don't care if the dog has its flanking commands [its left and right] if it has no balance. Keep your dog back off the sheep."

And the sun burns down and the dogs circle sheep in the small ring and the spectator dogs lie along the fence like so many silent torpedoes watching every move.

"You cannot correct a dog when it's half a mile from you. You must correct him in the small ring where you can go to him."

"Think what the dog is thinking," he says. "Some dogs you can tell what to do; others, you must ask."

Round the dogs go. Go left. Go right. Get back. Lie down. They get to the head of their sheep to take control.

"Always watch your dog's tail. The tail's like a rudder to them. When the dog's out of balance, the tail will start to rise."

"There are no dumb dogs. They remember."

Jack has three dogs entered for the Bluegrass: Jan, Mick and Jed. When he filed his papers he had high hopes for Jed, but now he doesn't know whether he'll run her or not. He hasn't worked her for several weeks.

"I soured her. You tune a dog for the big

trials, just bring her up to the peak. We'd not been on the trial circuit for a long time and when I started with Jed, I was looking for miracles. One day I worked her too hard, too rough, and the next day I couldn't do a thing with her. When a dog gets sour, you just have to put it back into the kennel until it's ready to work for you again."

Later in the afternoon Jack gives a penning demonstration. The pen is a six-by-eight-foot rectangle, open at one end. To the sheep it is perfectly obvious: once inside the pen, they're trapped. They are quite reluctant to stroll inside. Jack takes his big male, Craig, and coaxes five sheep into the pen. When he slams the gate shut on their rumps, the students applaud.

"I guess I'll show off now," he says and frees the sheep. He lays Craig down inside the pen and whistles for Jed. If the sheep were unwilling before, they're doubly so with a large dog lying inside the pen where they're supposed to go. They turn to bolt, but Jed's at their heads, turning them back, anticipating their escapes, pushing them steadily. Hating every step, they back inside and Jack Knox closes the gate on five sheep and two dogs.

Jed is a short, long-bodied bitch. Her coat is black, her breast merle (mottled blue-gray) and the tip of her tail is dull. She's extremely keen, fixed on Jack and her sheep. In 1979, she won the Bluegrass.

In motion, Jed's stylish and extremely fast. At rest she's very homely. The last time I saw a dog that looked like her, it was raiding garbage cans.

The great Scottish breeder, David McTeir, has said, "The first thing I look for in a young dog is honesty. It is something in the way they look at you. If it is there, it can be seen immediately. An honest dog will never let you down when you are in difficulties."

Border collies work by a process of specific intimidation, crouched low to the ground, creeping toward the sheep they bend to their will. They are low-slung as a filmstar's sportscar and just as fluid. Anyone who hunts bird dogs will remark the similarity between Jed's approach and a hunting dog's point. Anyone who's ever seen a red fox slipping up behind an unsuspecting young woodchuck has seen Jed's delicacy.

Sometimes, at play, a border collie pup will eye a human like it eyes its sheep. It's odd and unpleasant.

They do not bark at sheep and must not bite. On slow, heavy farm sheep, they work at a walk. With wild range sheep, the herding takes place at a dead run, a trick not unlike playing chess while running windsprints through an obstacle course.

They are commanded by voice or whistle and can master more than two hundred separate commands. They think well for themselves and a strong dog will need a strong handler.

The United States Border Collie Club is the only major breed organization which resists full AKC recognition. The club was organized, in part, to defend the border collie against those who would put it on the bench. Listed as a miscellaneous breed, border collies can be worked in obedience trials (where they do quite well) but there is no effective breed standard for them and if the dog's friends have their way, there never will be.

The AKC is filled with beautiful hunters that no longer hunt, shepherds that cannot herd sheep and working dogs that do not work. As one border collie man put it, "I breed worker to worker. I don't breed pretty to pretty."

One consequence of this stand is terrible puppy prices. From one to three hundred dollars will buy the best border collie pups in the land. In a curious reversal of usual purebreed practice, border collies are often worth more as they get older, and three-year-old trained dogs can bring three or four thousand dollars. Jack Knox has turned down five thousand for Jed.

Most of the very best trial dogs were trained in Scotland and imported, ready to run. Most Bluegrass winners have been imported dogs and of this year's sixty-five entrants, only fifteen are homegrown.

The entrants have prick ears, flop ears or

bent ears. They have blunt noses and snip noses. They are sixty-five pounds or thirty pounds. Some have the familiar collie ruff. Jed is black, Lewis Pence's Diamond is almost completely white, Bernie Ryan's dog, Jim, is a red dog and Bruce Fogt's Hope is black and merle.

It is not what they look like that makes them alike. They are alike in what they can do.

Just like baseball players.

The first handler is ready to qualify his dog. Nice morning. Acres and acres of green horse-pasture rising away from the handler's circle. There's a dip at the head of the pasture where dog and sheep can be lost to sight and you want to keep your dog out of it if you can. The dog trembles. The pasture is fenced into a long diamond—handler's circle at one tip and, at the other tip, 300 yards away, the sheep are released. The spectators and judges are behind the handler's circle and the pen.

Three sets of white board panels are on the slope. Each is two sections of fence with a narrow opening between. If this were a baseball diamond, the fetch panel would be second base and the two drive panels would be shortstops.

Without leaving the circle, you direct your dog's outrun, his first contact with the sheep (the lift) and his bringing the sheep through the fetch panel to your feet. Next, the dog drives them through the left drive panel, across the diamond in front of you through the second drive panel, and back to the pen where you shut them up. Ten minutes.

The sheep bolt like rabbits; the dog is in hot pursuit, and getting the sheep through those panels is like threading an embroidery needle at seventy mph. These sheep have never been a flock before so they break apart: a whiteface to the right; both blackfaces drifting downhill toward the drive panel.

A real chill falls over the watching handlers.

"Last time those sheep saw a dog, it was a coyote eating their mama."

"Out west they got a way of handling sheep that like to break off like that. A rifle."

"I don't mind that those sheep don't know each other. But those sheep aren't even speaking to each other."

Three terrified range ewes, careening every which way. They are healthy yearlings, in the peak of their strength, and by God, they can outrun a dog for a couple hundred yards.

At the pen, one ewe crashes right over the dog. The dog doesn't bite.

"Last year, thirty-six points won this trial." (There are sixty points possible. The dog loses points each time it fails to accomplish some portion of the trial.)

The morning wears on, short-tempered and fleet. Working fifty yards off the sheep, the dogs can scarcely control them and twenty-one dogs run before anyone (Edgar Gould with Roy) pens his sheep.

After a run, it takes three or four men, dogs and sometimes a station wagon to clear the sheep off the course.

You can hear the dogs panting sixty feet away. It's possible to work a sheep dog to death. Dogs only sweat through their tongues and the pads of their feet and if they're kept at it too long, they go into shock, overwhelmed by their own wastes. After each dog finishes its run, it flops into a cattle tank, immersed to cool off.

As the sun climbs, the sheep slow a bit and there are a few more good runs. Ralph Pulfer pushes too hard at the pen and his sheep blow up. John Bauserman shakes his head, "That's one of the very few mistakes you'll ever see Ralph make."

Jack Knox's Jan whirls her sheep into the pen, tight as a spinning top.

Bruce Fogt qualifies with a tight, controlled run. The handlers remember the first time they ever qualified in a major trial and give young Bruce a nice hand.

Jed's sheep are drifting at the start and her outrun is a shallow hook. Jack Knox gives no commands. Three hundred yards out, Jed is on her own. Two whiteface sheep, one blackface. They separate: two and one. The blackface wants to make tracks.

Jed drops down, well behind them and

centered. The group re-collects and bolts away from the dog, lickety-split. No chance to make the fetch panel. Jed is full-tilt and the sheep are full-tilt too. They stop, reluctant to enter the mowed handler's circle. Jack Knox steps back, gives them room, and three nervous sheep prance onto the short grass. (Wild sheep will sometimes balk at a chalk line.)

Jack is using his voice to advantage now, easing Jed onto the sheep, moving them steadily toward the first drive panel. Left they go, right, left again. Each time Jed turns them. For some sheep reason, they don't want to go through the panels though freedom is clear as air on the other side. When they bolt through the opening, the spectators applaud, though no one's supposed to make a sound until the run's finished.

Jed makes a fine crossdrive and just misses the far drive panel.

Jack Knox glances at his watch. Not much time for the pen. (When Jed was younger, she lacked power. Every time a ewe would stamp her foot, Jed would back up five or ten feet and finally a tough ewe ran Jed right off the trial field. Jack took Jed home and used her in the lambing yards. Ewes with newborn lambs are rough, slamming and battering a dog whenever they feel their lambs threatened. Jack told Jed to bite and Jed made the wool fly. Jed returned to the trial field with plenty of power and she does not bite as she presses these wild sheep toward Jack Knox and the pen.)

It's hot. Down near the ground where Jed is, it's hotter. She's created a flock from what had been three individuals and she slips carefully forward as the sheep twist this way and that, seeking an opening to break past her. Steadily, Jed comes on, her nose barely off the ground, tongue out, drooling. Two inside. The blackface breaks. Before the sheep's half around the pen, Jed heads it and brings it back to the others.

Jack Knox speaks to his dog, whispers to his dog, croons to her. The sheep stamp their feet and lower their heads and Jed pauses at each threat and waits for the ewe's second (more rational) thoughts. A half-step at a time, the sheep back. With seconds left, Jack slams the gate closed and grins and the crowd hollers for him and his honest dog.

Two judges score every run, mapping it like cartographers, rewarding the direct line. Since a trial depicts the work a farm dog does at home (gathering, driving sheep through gates and penning them) the scores are weighted to the dog who accomplishes his tasks.

Twenty dogs qualify. For the championship next day, the dogs will work five sheep, one ribboned. After penning, the dog must take its sheep to the handler's circle where it is to shed off the ribboned sheep and hold her, all alone. The shed extends the time limit to twelve minutes. No matter how soon a dog gets to the shedding ring, it has only three minutes to make the shed.

The championship attracts a good crowd of a thousand or so. There's an Egyptian-Arabian horseshow and a saluki show next door at the Kentucky Horse Park and the horse and dog people have come over to watch the sheep dogs run.

The sheep-dog handlers wear fancy Western garb: straw cowboy hats, pointy boots, pearl-buttoned shirts and wide ties. The handlers who've won silver and gold belt buckles at other trials wear them today. Everyone has a shepherd's crook over his arm.

The announcer notes that this handler is a retired grain farmer, this one's an unemployed machinist. One handler's a vet, another has 600 sheep and 1000 acres of cropland.

Fresh sheep. None of them has ever been worked by a dog.

Trial dogs are quite sensitive and when they sense excitement in their handler's voice (or whistle) they amplify the excitement into big trouble. Jack Knox gets nervy, overcommands, and Jan fails to pen her sheep.

Bruce Fogt makes a lovely slow run, penning his sheep in 11:59.

John Bauserman's Bess runs brilliantly. John loses points for helping her at the pen.

Jed's sheep take off like a shot and never

stop running. They zoom past the fetch panel and both drive panels and a slower dog would lose them completely. Her tail twitches in annoyance. When she gets her sheep to the pen, she slams them in about as sentimental as a jailer in the Tombs. She pens in a remarkable 7:50. Jed has a full three minutes in the shedding ring and she needs this shed to have a chance at first.

"Jed! Come by! Back! Way to me! Get back! On your feet! Lie Down! Walk on! Jed, Jed, Jed! Way Jed!"

The commands come nonstop. The ribboned sheep (a blackface) is absolutely unwilling to find herself outside the flock. She hides in the middle and her mates roil around her like an eddy.

Jack Knox slips to one side, to the other, seeking the line Jed can dart through to shed that ribboned sheep. Once she's got the sheep shed, Jed can hold her; no doubt about that.

Jed moves left, moves right, presses, withdraws pressure but the sheep are tight as a knot. For three gut-wrenching minutes they work, man and dog, seeking the line, pouring it on.

"Time! Sorry, Jack!"

"Jed, that'll do. That'll do now, Jed." And gives his dog a pat for thanks and walks off the course with a hard-earned sixth place.

The Twenty-Third Bluegrass National Open Sheep Dog Trials were won by Bruce Fogt with a dog he trained himself. A dog named Hope.

Catching a Poacher

Dogs, and the Tug of Life

by EDWARD HOAGLAND

IT used to be that you could tell just about how poor a family was by how many dogs they had. If they had one, they were probably doing all right. It was only American to keep a dog to represent the family's interests in the intrigues of the back alley; not to have a dog at all would be like not acknowledging one's poor relations. Two dogs meant that the couple were dog lovers, with growing children, but still might be members of the middle class. But if a citizen kept three, you could begin to suspect he didn't own much else. Four or five irrefutably marked the household as poor folk, whose yard was also full of broken cars cannibalized for parts. The father worked not much, fancied himself a hunter; the mother's teeth were black. And an old bachelor living in a shack might possibly have even more, but you knew that if one of them, chasing a moth, didn't upset his oil lamp some night and burn him up, he'd fetch up in the poorhouse soon, with the dogs shot. Nobody got poor feeding a bunch of dogs, needless to say, because the more dogs a man had, the less he fed them. Foraging as a pack, they led an existence of their own, but served as evidence that life was awfully lonesome for him and getting out of hand. If a dog really becomes a man's best friend his situation is desperate.

That dogs, low-comedy confederates of small children and ragged bachelors, should have turned into an emblem of having made it to the middle class—like the hibachi, like golf clubs and a second car—seems at the very least incongruous. Puppies which in the country you would have to carry in a box to the church fair to give away are bringing seventy-five dollars apiece in some of the pet stores, although in fact dogs are in such oversupply that one hundred and fifty thousand are running wild in New York City alone.

There is another line of tradition about dogs, however. Show dogs, toy dogs, foxhounds for formal hunts, Doberman guard dogs, bulldogs as ugly as a queen's dwarf. An aristocratic Spanish lady once informed me that when she visits her Andalusian estate each fall the mastiffs rush out and fawn about her but would tear to pieces any of the servants who have accompanied her from Madrid. In Mississippi it was illegal for a slave owner to permit his slaves to have a dog, just as it was to teach them how to read. A "Negro dog" was a hound trained by a bounty hunter to ignore the possums, raccoons, hogs and deer in the woods that other dogs were supposed to chase, and trail and tree a runaway. The planters themselves, for whom hunting was a principal recreation, whooped it up when a man unexpectedly became their quarry. They caught each other's slaves and would often sit back and let the dogs do the punishing. Bennet H. Barrow of West Feliciana Parish in Louisiana, a rather moderate and representative plantation owner, recounted in his diary of the 1840s, among several similar incidents, this for November 11, 1845: "[In] 5 minutes had him up & a going, And never in my life did I ever see as excited beings as R & myself, ran 1/2 miles & caught him dogs soon tore him naked, took him Home Before the other negro(es) at dark & made the dogs give him another over hauling." Only recently in Louisiana I heard what happened to two Negroes who happened to be fishing in a bayou off the Blind River, where four white men with a shotgun felt like fishing alone. One was forced to pretend to be a scampering coon and shinny up a telephone pole and hang there till he fell, while the other impersonated a baying, bounding hound.

Such memories are not easy to shed, particularly since childhood, the time when people can best acquire a comradeship with animals, is also when they are likely to pick up their parents' fears. A friend of mine hunts quail by jeep in Texas with a millionaire who brings along forty bird dogs, which he deploys in eight platoons that spell each other off. Another friend though, will grow apprehensive at a dinner party if the host lets a dog loose in the room. The toothy, mysterious creature lies dreaming on the carpet, its paws pulsing, its eyelids open, the nictitating membranes twitching; how can he be certain it won't suddenly jump up and attack his legs under the table? Among Eastern European Jews, possession of a dog was associated with the hard-drinking *goyishe* peasantry, traditional antagonists, or else with the gentry, and many carried this dislike to the New World. An immigrant fleeing a potato famine or the hunger of Calabria might be no more equipped with the familiar British-German partiality to dogs—a failing which a few rugged decades in a great city's slums would not necessarily mend. The city had urbanized plenty of native farmers' sons as well, and so it came about that what to rural America had been the humblest, most natural amenity—friendship with a dog—has been transmogrified into a piece of the jigsaw of moving to the suburbs: there to cook outdoors, another bit of

absurdity to the old countryman, whose toilet was outdoors but who was pleased to be able to cook and eat his meals inside the house.

There are an estimated forty million dogs in the United States (nearly two for every cat). Thirty-seven thousand of them are being destroyed in humane institutions every day, a figure which indicates that many more are in trouble. Dogs are hierarchal beasts, with several million years of submission to the structure of a wolf pack in their breeding. This explains why the Spanish lady's mastiffs can distinguish immediately between the mistress and her retainers, and why it is about as likely that one of the other guests at the dinner party will attack my friend's legs under the table as that the host's dog will, once it has accepted his presence in the room as proper. Dogs need leadership, however; they seek it, and when it's not forthcoming quickly fall into difficulties in a world where they can no longer provide their own.

"Dog" is "God" spelled backwards—one might say, way backwards. There's "a dog's life," "dog days," "dog-sick," "dog-tired," "dog-cheap," "dog-eared," "doghouse," and "dogs" meaning villains or feet. Whereas a wolf's stamina was measured in part by how long he could go without water, a dog's is becoming a matter of how long he can *hold* his water. He retrieves a rubber ball instead of coursing deer, chases a broom instead of hunting marmots. His is the lowest form of citizenship: that tug of life at the end of the leash is like the tug at the end of a fishing pole, and then one doesn't have to kill it. On stubby, amputated-looking feet he leads his life, which if we glance at it attentively is a kind of cutout of our own, all the more so for being riskier and shorter. Bam! A member of the family is dead on the highway, as we expected he would be, and we just cart him to the dump and look for a new pup.

Simply the notion that he lives on four legs instead of two has come to seem astonishing—like a goat or cow wearing horns on its head. And of course to keep a dog is a way of attempting to bring nature back. The primitive hunter's intimacy, telepathy, with the animals he sought, surprising them at their meals and in their beds, then stripping them of their warm coats to expose a frame so like our own, is all but lost. Sport hunters, especially the older ones, retain a little of it still; and naturalists who have made up their minds not to kill wild animals nevertheless appear to empathize primarily with the predators at first, as a look at the tigers, bears, wolves, mountain lions on the project list of an organization such as the World Wildlife Fund will show. This is as it should be, these creatures having suffered from our brotherly envy before. But in order to really enjoy a dog, one doesn't merely try to train him to be semihuman. The point of it is to open oneself to the possibility of becoming partly a dog (after all, there are plenty of sub- or semihuman beings around whom we don't wish to adopt). One wants to rediscover the commonality of animal and man—to see an animal eat and sleep that hasn't forgotten how to enjoy doing such things—and the directness of its loyalty.

The trouble with the current emphasis on preserving "endangered species" is that, however beneficial to wildlife the campaign works out to be, it makes all animals seem like museum pieces, worth saving for sentimental considerations and as figures of speech (to "shoot a sitting duck"), but as a practical matter already dead and gone. On the contrary, some animals are flourishing. In 1910 half a million deer lived in the United States, in 1960 seven million, in 1970 sixteen million. What has happened is that now that we don't eat them we have lost that close interest.

Wolf behavior prepared dogs remarkably for life with human beings. So complete and complicated was the potential that it was only a logical next step for them to quit their packs in favor of the heady, hopeless task of trying to keep pace with our own community development. The contortions of fawning and obeisance which render group adjustment possible among such otherwise forceful fighters—sometimes humping the inferior members into the shape of hyenas—are what squeezes them past our tantrums, too. Though battling within the pack is mostly accomplished with body checks that do no damage,

a subordinate wolf bitch is likely to remain so in awe of the leader that she will cringe and sit on her tail in response to his amorous advances, until his female coequal has had a chance to notice and dash over and redirect his attention. Altogether, he is kept so busy asserting his dominance that this top-ranked female may not be bred by him, finally, but by the male which occupies the second rung. Being breadwinners, dominant wolves feed first and best, just as we do, so that to eat our scraps and leavings strikes a dog as normal procedure. Nevertheless, a wolf puppy up to eight months old is favored at a kill, and when smaller can extract a meal from any pack member—uncles and aunts as well as parents—by nosing the lips of the adult until it regurgitates a share of what it's had. The care of the litter is so much a communal endeavor that the benign sort of role we expect dogs to play within our own families toward children not biologically theirs comes naturally to them.

For dogs and wolves the tail serves as a semaphore of mood and social code, but dogs carry their tails higher than wolves do, as a rule, which is appropriate, since the excess spirits that used to go into lengthy hunts now have no other outlet than backyard negotiating. In addition to an epistolary anal gland, whose message-carrying function has not yet been defined, the anus itself, or stool when sniffed, conveys how well the animal has been eating—in effect, its income bracket—although most dog foods are sorrily monotonous compared to the hundreds of tastes a wolf encounters, perhaps dozens within the carcass of a single moose. We can speculate on a dog's powers of taste because its olfactory area is proportionately fourteen times larger than a man's, its sense of smell at least a hundred times as keen.

The way in which a dog presents his anus and genitals for inspection indicates the hierarchal position that he aspires to, and other dogs who sniff his genitals are apprised of his sexual condition. From his urine they can undoubtedly distinguish age, build, state of sexual activity and general health, even hours after he's passed by. Male dogs dislike running out of urine, as though an element of potency were involved, and try to save a little; they prefer not to use a scent post again until another dog has urinated there, the first delight and duty of the ritual being to stake out a territory, so that when they are walked hurriedly in the city it is a disappointment to them. The search is also sexual, because bitches in heat post notices about. In the woods a dog will mark his drinking places, and watermark a rabbit's trail after chasing it, as if to notify the next predator that happens by exactly who it was that put such a whiff of fear into the rabbit's scent. Similarly, he squirts the tracks of bobcats and of skunks with an aloof air unlike his brisk and cheery manner of branding another dog's or fox's trail, and if he is in a position to do so, will defecate excitedly on a bear run, leaving behind his best effort, which no doubt he hopes will strike the bear as a bombshell.

The chief complaint people lodge against dogs is their extraordinary stress upon lifting the leg and moving the bowels. Scatology did take up some of the slack for them when they left behind the entertainments of the forest. The forms of territoriality replaced the substance. But apart from that, a special zest for life is characteristic of dogs and wolves—in hunting, eating, relieving themselves, in punctiliously maintaining a home territory, a pecking order and a love life, and educating the resulting pups. They grin and grimace and scrawl graffiti with their piss. A lot of inherent strategy goes into these activities: the way wolves spell each other off, both when hunting and in their governess duties around the den, and often "consult" as a pack with noses together and tails wagging before flying in to make a kill. (Tigers, leopards, house cats base their social relations instead upon what ethologists call "mutual avoidance.") The nose is a dog's main instrument of discovery, corresponding to our eyes, and so it is that he is seldom offended by organic smells, such as putrefaction, and sniffs intently for the details of illness, gum bleeding and diet in his master and his fellows, and for the story told by scats, not closing off the avenue for any reason—just as we rarely shut our eyes against new information, even the tragic or unpleasant kind.

Though dogs don't see as sharply as they smell, trainers usually rely on hand signals to instruct them, and most firsthand communication in a wolf pack also seems to be visual—by the expressions of the face, by body English and the cant of the tail. A dominant wolf squares his mouth, stares at and "rides up" on an inferior, standing with his front legs on its back, or will pretend to stalk it, creeping along, taking its muzzle in his mouth, and performing nearly all of the other discriminatory pranks and practices familiar to anybody who has a dog. In fact, what's funny is to watch a homely mutt as tiny as a shoebox spin through the rigmarole which a whole series of observers in the wilderness have gone to great pains to document for wolves.

Dogs proffer their rear ends to each other in an intimidating fashion, but when they examine the region of the head it is a friendlier gesture, a snuffling between pals. One of them may come across a telltale bone fragment caught in the other's fur, together with a bit of mud to give away the location of bigger bones. On the same impulse, wolves and free-running dogs will sniff a wanderer's toes to find out where he has been roaming. They fondle and propitiate with their mouths also, and lovers groom each other's fur with tongues and teeth adept as hands. A bitch wolf's period in heat includes a week of preliminary behavior and maybe two weeks of receptivity—among animals, exceptionally long. Each actual copulative tie lasts twenty minutes or a half an hour, which again may help to instill affection. Wolves sometimes begin choosing a mate as early as the age of one, almost a year before they are ready to breed. Dogs mature sexually a good deal earlier, and arrive in heat twice a year instead of once—at any season instead of only in midwinter, like a wolf, whose pups' arrival must be scheduled unfailingly for spring. Dogs have not retained much responsibility for raising their young, and the summertime is just as perilous as winter for them because, apart from the whimsy of their owners, who put so many of them to sleep, their nemesis is the automobile. Like scatology, sex helps fill the gulf of what is gone.

The scientist David Mech has pointed out how like the posture of a wolf with a nosehold on a moose (as other wolves attack its hams) are the antics of a puppy playing tug-of-war at the end of a towel. Anybody watching a dog's exuberance as it samples bites of long grass beside a brook, or pounds into a meadow bristling with the odors of woodchucks, snowshoe rabbits, grouse, a doe and buck, field mice up on the seedheads of the weeds, kangaroo mice jumping, chipmunks whistling, weasels and shrews on the hunt, a plunging fox, a porcupine couched in a tree, perhaps can begin to imagine the variety of excitements under the sky that his ancestors relinquished in order to move indoors with us. He'll lie down with a lamb to please us, but as he sniffs its haunches, surely he must remember atavistically that this is where he'd start to munch.

There is poignancy in the predicament of a great many animals: as in the simple observation which students of the California condor have made that this huge, most endangered bird prefers the carrion meat of its old standby, the deer, to all the dead cows, sheep, horses and other substitutes it sees from above, sprawled about. Animals are stylized characters in a kind of old saga—stylized because even the most acute of them have little leeway as they play out their parts. (*Rabbits,* for example, I find terribly affecting, imprisoned in their hop.) And as we drift away from any cognizance of them, we sacrifice some of the intricacy and grandeur of life. Having already lost so much, we are hardly aware of what remains, but to a primitive snatched forward from an earlier existence it might seem as if we had surrendered a richness comparable to all the tapestries of childhood. Since this is a matter of the imagination as well as of animal demographics, no Noah projects, no bionomic discoveries on the few sanctuaries that have been established are going to reverse the swing. The very specialists in the forefront of finding out how animals behave, when one meets them, appear to be no more intrigued than any ordinary Indian was.

But we continue to need—as aborigines did, as children do—a parade of morality tales which are more concise than those that politics, for instance, later provides. So we've had Aesop's and medieval and modern fables about the grasshop-per and the ant, the tiger and Little Black Sambo, the wolf and the three pigs, Br'er Rabbit and Br'er Bear, Goldilocks and her three bears, Pooh Bear, Babar and the rhinos, Walt Disney's animals, and assorted humbler scary bats, fat hippos, funny frogs and eager beavers. Children have a passion for clean, universal definitions, and so it is that animals have gone with children's literature as Latin has with religion. Through them they first encountered death, birth, their own maternal feelings, the gap between beauty and cleverness, or speed and good intentions. The animal kingdom boasted the powerful lion, the mothering goose, the watchful owl, the tardy tortoise, Chicken Little, real-life dogs that treasure bones, and mink that grow posh pelts from eating crawfish and mussels.

In the cartoons of two or three decades ago, Mouse doesn't get along with Cat because Cat must catch Mouse or miss his supper. Dog, on the other hand, detests Cat for no such rational reason, only the capricious fact that dogs don't dote on cats. Animal stories are bounded, yet enhanced, by each creature's familiar lineaments, just as a parable about a prince and peasant, a duchess and a milkmaid, a blacksmith and a fisherman, would be. Typecasting, like the roll of a metered ode, adds resonance and dignity, summoning up all of the walruses and hedgehogs that went before: the shrewd image of Br'er Rabbit to assist his suburban relative Bugs Bunny behind the scenes. But now, in order to present a tale about the contest between two thieving crows and a scarecrow, the storyteller would need to start by explaining that once upon a time crows used to eat a farmer's corn if he didn't defend it with a mock man pinned together from old clothes. Crows are having a hard go of it and may soon receive game-bird protection.

One way childhood is changing, therefore, is that the nonhuman figures—"Wild Things" or puppet monsters—constructed by the best of the new artificers, like Maurice Sendak or the *Sesame Street* writers, are distinctly humanoid, ballooned out of faces, torsos met on the subway. The televised character Big Bird does not resemble a bird the way Bugs Bunny remained a rabbit—though

Comical Dogs *by Sir Edwin Landseer*

already he was less so than Br'er or Peter Rabbit. Big Bird's personality, her confusion, haven't the faintest connection to an ostrich's. Lest she be confused with an ostrich, her voice has been slotted unmistakably toward the prosaic. Dr. Seuss did transitional composites of worldwide fauna, but these new shapes—a beanbag like the *Sesame Street* Grouch or Cookie Monster or Herry Monster, and the floral creations in books—have been conceived practically from scratch by the artist ("in the night kitchen," to use a Sendak phrase), and not transferred from the existing caricatures of nature. In their conversational conflicts they offer him a fresh start, which may be a valuable commodity, whereas if he were dealing with an alligator, it would, while giving him an old-fashioned boost in the traditional manner, at the same time box him in. A chap called Alligator, with that fat snout and tail, cannot squirm free of the solidity of actual alligators. Either it must stay a heavyweight or else play on the sternness of reality by swinging over to impersonate a cream puff and a Ferdinand.

Though animal programs on television are popular, what with the wave of nostalgia and "ecology" in the country, we can generally say about the animal kingdom, "The king is dead, long live the king." Certainly the talent has moved elsewhere. Those bulbous Wild Things and slant-mouthed beanbag puppets derived from the denizens of Broadway—an argumentative night news vendor, a lady on a traffic island —have grasped their own destinies, as characters on the make are likely to. It was inevitable they would. There may be a shakedown to remove the elements that would be too bookish for children's literature in other hands, and another shakedown because these first innovators have been more city-oriented than suburban. New authors will shift the character sources away from Broadway and the subway and the ghetto, but the basic switch has already been accomplished —from the ancient juxtaposition of people, animals, and dreams blending the two, to people and monsters that grow solely out of people by way of dreams.

Which leaves us in the suburbs, with dogs as a last link. Cats are too independent to care, but dogs are in an unenviable position, they hang so much upon our good opinion. We are coming to *have* no opinion; we don't pay enough attention to form an opinion. Though they admire us, are thrilled by us, heroize us, we regard them as a hobby or a status symbol, like a tennis racquet, and substitute leash laws for leadership—expect them not simply to learn English but to grow hands, because their beastly paws seem stranger to us every year. If they try to fondle us with their handyjack mouths, we read it as a bite; and like used cars, they are disposed of when the family relocates, changes its "bag," or in the scurry of divorce. The first reason people kept a dog was to acquire an ally on the hunt, a friend at night. Then it was to maintain an avenue to animality, as our own nearness began to recede. But as we lose our awareness of all animals, dogs are becoming a bridge to nowhere. We can only pity their fate.

A Boston Terrier

by E. B. WHITE

I would like to hand down a dissenting opinion in the case of the Camel ad which shows a Boston terrier relaxing. I can string along with cigarette manufacturers to a certain degree, but when it comes to the temperament and habits of terriers, I shall stand my ground.

The ad says: "A dog's nervous system resembles our own." I don't think a dog's nervous system resembles my own in the least. A dog's nervous system is in a class by itself. If it resembles anything at all, it resembles the New York Edison Company's power plant. This is particularly true of Boston terriers, and if the Camel people don't know that, they have never been around dogs.

The ad says: "But when a dog's nerves tire, he obeys his instincts—he relaxes." This, I admit, is true. But I should like to call attention to the fact that it sometimes takes days, even weeks, before a dog's nerves tire. In the case of terriers it can run into months.

I knew a Boston terrier once (he is now dead and, so far as I know, relaxed) whose nerves stayed keyed up from the twenty-fifth of one June to the sixth of the following July, without one minute's peace for anybody in the family. He was an old dog and he was blind in one eye, but his infirmities caused no diminution in his nervous power. During the period of which I speak, the famous period of his greatest excitement, he not only raised a type of general hell which startled even his closest friends and observers, but he gave a mighty clever excuse. He said it was love.

"I'm in love," he would scream. (He could scream just like a hurt child.) "I'm in love and I'm going *crazy.*"

Day and night it was all the same. I tried everything to soothe him. I tried darkness, cold water dashed in the face, the lash, long quiet talks, warm milk administered internally, threats, promises, and close confinement in remote locations. At last, after about a week of it, I went down the road and had a chat with the lady who owned the object of our terrier's affection. It was she who finally cleared up the situation.

"Oh," she said, wearily, "if it's that bad, let him out."

I hadn't thought of anything as simple as that myself, but I am a creature of infinite reserve. As a matter of record, it turned out to be not so simple—the terrier got run over by a motor car one night while returning from his amorous adventures, suffering a complete paralysis of the hip but no assuagement of the nervous system; and the little Scotty bitch returned to Washington, D.C., and a caesarian.

I am not through with the Camel people yet. Love is not the only thing that can keep a dog's nerves in a state of perpetual jangle. A dog, more than any other creature, it seems to me, gets

Comparisons Are Odious

interested in one subject, theme, or object, in life, and pursues it with a fixity of purpose which would be inspiring to Man if it weren't so troublesome. One dog gets absorbed in one thing, another dog in another. When I was a boy there was a smooth-haired fox terrier (in those days nobody ever heard of a fox terrier that *wasn't* smooth-haired) who became interested, rather late in life, in a certain stone. The stone was about the size of an egg. As far as I could see, it was like a million other stones—but to him it was the Stone Supreme.

He kept it with him day and night, slept with it, ate with it, played with it, analyzed it, took it on little trips (you would often see him three blocks from home, trotting along on some shady errand, his stone safe in his jaws). He used to lie by the hour on the porch of his house, chewing the stone with an expression half tender, half

petulant. When he slept he merely enjoyed a muscular suspension: his nerves were still up and around, adjusting the bed clothes, tossing and turning.

He permitted people to throw the stone for him and people would. But if the stone lodged somewhere he couldn't get to he raised such an uproar that it was absolutely necessary that the stone be returned, for the public peace. His absorption was so great it brought wrinkles to his face, and he grew old before his time. I think he used to worry that somebody was going to pitch the stone into a lake or a bog, where it would be irretrievable. He wore off every tooth in his jaw, wore them right down to the gums, and they became mere brown vestigial bumps. His breath was awful (he panted night and day) and his eyes were alight with an unearthly zeal. He died in a fight with another dog. I have always suspected it was because he tried to hold the stone in his mouth all through the battle. The Camel people will just have to take my word for it: that dog was a living denial of the whole theory of relaxation. He was a paragon of nervous tension, from the moment he first laid eyes on his slimy little stone till the hour of his death.

The advertisement speaks of the way humans "prod" themselves to endeavor—so that they keep on and on working long after they should quit. The inference is that a dog never does that. But I have a dog right now that can prod himself harder and drive himself longer than any human I ever saw. This animal is a dachshund, and I shall spare you the long dull inanities of his innumerable obsessions. His particular study (or mania) at the moment is a black-and-white kitten that my wife gave me for Christmas, thinking that what my life needed was something else that could move quickly from one place in the room to another. The dachshund began his research on Christmas Eve when the kitten arrived "secretly" in the cellar, and now, five months later, is taking his Ph.D. still working late at night on it, every night. If he could write a book about that cat, it would make *Middletown* look like the work of a backward child.

I'll be glad to have the Camel people study this animal in one of his relaxed moods, but they will have to bring their own seismograph. Even curled up cozily in a chair, dreaming of his cat, he quivers like an aspen.

Guard and War Dogs in History

by JERROLD MUNDIS

MILLENNIA past, Nature experienced a moment of whimsey and decreed that two grossly differing species would be given an opportunity to become friends. Incredibly, they did: *Homo sapiens* and *Canis familiaris*, buddies. There is no comparable relationship in the natural world. More than 27 million dogs are registered in the United States alone, roughly one per every eight humans. Yet most dog owners, even those who have lived with several different animals over a period of years, have little or no real knowledge of the history and nature of the creatures with whom they share their lives.

It's beyond the scope of this book to render a detailed account of the dog's evolution and of his relationship to man, but some basic understanding is essential in order to deal successfully with the dog as a protector of men.

Three major schools of thought seek to explain the origin of the domestic dog. Each argues persuasively, but each lacks definitive fossil evidence. Direct descent is claimed from the Eurasiatic wolf *(Canis lupus)*, from the Golden or Oriental jackal *(Canis aureus)*, and from an extinct animal known as *Tomarctus*, which evolved some fifteen to twenty million years ago during the Upper Miocene epoch. Of the first two theories, the bulk of the evidence favors the wolf (despite the championing of the jackal by scientists as

redoubtable as Konrad Lorenz), but assigning the honors to the wolf raises nearly as many questions as it puts to rest. *Tomarctus* is generally agreed to have been the father of wolves, jackals, foxes and all similar canines, and it would seem logical that he also sired the earliest forms of *Canis familiaris* (all this, of course, throughout several millions of years). Such a view would have the common dog cousin to the wolf and jackal rather than descendant, neatly resolving many present difficulties that plague the first two schools. Perhaps too neatly. We will have to wait for the discovery of empiric and conclusive proofs before we can end the controversy with any confidence.

Whatever his origin, the dog is indisputably a carnivore. This is obvious—but its implications are generally overlooked by dog owners, often in deference to fragile sensibilities. A current television dog food advertisement features a delicate and affectionate Shetland sheepdog (a miniature collie) and a man who croons to it, "It's hard to believe such a pretty little thing like you is a carnivore. Why, the very word makes you think of big jungle tigers." Well, no tiger, just good old shoe-chewing Spot, but he *is* a carnivore—which means that he is a hunter by nature, a predatory killer. He is also a pack-animal, one whose social relationships with other members of the pack are diverse and sophisticated. With few exceptions, any pet dog sundered from its family and denied other human contact will revert to a wild state in short order. Not only will he survive but he will usually flourish. Countless times dogs "gone natural" in the forests of this country have formed into small packs and have thrived quite well on available game. In the northern reaches they have brought down prey as large as deer and moose, and it is not unusual for a wolf bitch to join the pack and, in little time, increase its numbers with wolf-dog pups.

The two significant aspects of the domestic dog's heritage, then, are his impulse to hunt and his pack membership. Man, in his relentless pragmatism, has capitalized on both throughout the history of his relationship with *Canis familiaris* (indeed, there would have been no relationship had the dog not been able to work for man), and depends heavily on them today in the training and employment of guard dogs.

It's been postulated that the first nonaggressive contact between dog and man—that is, contact in which one party was not attempting to eat the other—took place some fifty thousand years ago, and that the dog became domesticated, actually moved into man's cave, tent, lean-to or stickhouse roughly thirty thousand years later. The former is a reasonable speculation, or educated guess, but the latter is probably no more than wishful thinking.

Fifty millennia ago, man wasn't much more than a predatory pack-animal himself, a nomadic hunter who followed the movements of his prey into new territory. The dog, or something that was the forerunner of the present dog, was fair —albeit difficult—game for hungry man. And an irksome competitor as well. But somewhere a particularly bright human was chasing an elusive thought through the chaos of his newly emergent mind, and after days, even months, he grunted his equivalent of "Aha!" Several weeks probably passed before he was able to make his fellow pack members understand. But eventually they did, or at least a few of them did. Since dogs and men hunt the same meat animals, why not follow dog spoor to the prey, or run to the sound of baying while the dogs course some animal to its death, and then either beat them to the kill, or

drive them off the carcass, or even—what luck!— locate the nearby herd from which the quarry has been cut? This was fine for the men, but not especially advantageous for the dogs. Tough. But move the clock ahead several thousand years and observe men making their kill, completing the butchery, and leaving behind the offal: guts, head, tough, muscley shanks and bones with ragged hunks of meat. And perhaps the men even kill more meat than they can use and abandon it, or they wound a beast but lose it in the chase. The dogs move in when the men have left, and finish up. Or they find that the beast the men have wounded is slow and greatly weakened and can be killed with minimum effort. The dog begins to see some profit here. He decides that the biped, particularly since the biped refrains from trying to make a meal of him unless times are hard, offers some interesting possibilities. Providing man keeps a reasonable distance, say half a mile or so, the dog no longer flees from him, and possibly even refrains from making a meal of a stray, young or sickly man. Unless, of course, times are hard.

So, somewhere around 15,000 B.C., we find a pack of predatory bipeds settling down for the night around fires and, in proximity of maybe a quarter of a mile, a pack of dogs turning, sniffing, then dropping down to the grass themselves. A few thousand years more and the greatest leap is made, the one of massive consequence. He is either a young, terribly curious and foolish dog, or a large, bold and aggressive one. He moves slowly, quivering with nervousness, to the very edge of the human camp, and he remains rigid several agonizing moments until, finally, he can bear no more and he goes streaking back to the safety of his pack. It is a monumental event. Man's Best Friend has been born.

Regardless of romantic claims, man did not begin to look upon the dog as a pet, loosely defined for our purposes as a rewarding social companion (with no thought to utilitarian function), until the late Middle Ages. The Chinese, the Japanese and—to a smaller extent—the Babylonians, Egyptians and Romans are the only exceptions of any import. No, man's relationship with the dog was loose and unstructured, based solely on practical concerns, and sustained through mutual respect of rights. By the seventh or eighth millennium B.C., dogs were probably traveling with man from hunting ground to hunting ground and wandering through his small villages and camps in relative ease. On occasion, one might even endure some human's impulse to touch or stroke him. Certainly, no man would have presumed to place any kind of collar or restraint upon a dog.

Dog buffs are quick to point to Pyrenees cave paintings (dated by some authorities at twelve thousand to seventeen thousand years ago), which depict men, meat animals and—it is claimed—dogs. These are offered as proof that the dog was domesticated at this time. Most definitely, doglike creatures are featured in the paintings, but whether they are dogs or wolves— or something else—is moot, and one must strain imagination to discern any conscious working relationship between the hunters and the dog creatures. Attempting to establish an ancient bond between man and dog is predestined to failure. The final word on this belongs to Brian Vesey-FitzGerald, a British dog authority, who writes: "It is noticeable that most English historians of the dog are at pains to stress not only their subject's ancient lineage as a domestic animal, but also man's ancient lineage as a dog-lover. The Stone Age dog, we are assured, was 'temperamentally trustful and friendly, and liked to be petted.' The implication, of course, is that Stone Age man—English Stone Age man, at any rate— was a friendly soul who liked to pet his dog. It really is astonishing how much information can be obtained from a fossil skull."

Archaeological evidence suggests that the dog shifted from the status of a semiwild creature to that of a domestic animal somewhere around the fifth or sixth millennium B.C. While man probably held a certain degree of affection for his dog, quite clearly it was not what contemporary man feels for his dog; rather, it was the same prideful fondness he experienced when looking upon a fleet mount or a fine weapon.

In becoming domesticated the dog retained his wild heritage, surrendering only his wariness of man. This served man's purposes admirably.

He prized the dog solely for his functional value and used him in the two most important activities of the day, hunting and defense. We can divide this early dog more or less into two types: There were fat dogs and there were skinny dogs. The skinny dogs, structured for speed, were used to run swift game—such as deer, antelope and wild horses—to bay or to their deaths. Aristotle wrote, "Those dogs which are fondest of hunting are all narrow in the waist," and Oppian, more than six hundred years later, "The hunting dog has a long hardy body . . . outstretched mouth, short ears, long neck and strong chest . . . the rows of ribs crosswise, loins fleshy but not obese, a stout and long stretched out tail." The others, he remarks, used for defense, were "somewhat flat of face, and they show a terrible frown in the skin which overhangs the eyebrows, and they display bright eyes that gleam with fire, and all their skin is covered with shaggy hair, and they are of a powerful build, with broad backs, and great internal strength though it be without speed; and their strength is incredible and unalloyed, and their courage imperturbable." Naturally, there was some overlapping of function. These latter dogs were used to hunt large and dangerous quarry—wild boar and bulls, bear and lion— which demanded the heavier and more ferocious dogs. Theodore Gaza, a fifteenth-century Greek scholar, rhapsodized on the pleasures of hunting such perilous game and noted the necessity of dogs: "For, led out to the chase, they spot the animals and hunt them, or catching the trail they conduct us by means of this after the animals running themselves, while we run after as fast as we can; and they fight along with and in defence of us." Though varying in demeanor over the centuries, these fat dogs and skinny dogs were more or less the prototypes of present-day greyhounds or salukis, and mastiffs.

Champions of various breeds labor to prove the antiquity of their dogs, but of the 116 breeds currently recognized by the American Kennel Club, less than 20 can be traced with surety back more than 200 years. Studying the art and literature of history, the best one can say is: This is a Great Dane kind of dog, that refers to a German shepherd-type, and so on.

Defense was focused upon the guarding of herds—which called for a dog strong enough to defeat a wolf, lion or armed thief—and the protection of the village and home. Speed was of minimal importance here; strength and savagery were the cardinal virtues.

Consider a moment the psychological effect of a dog on the attack. Many men have little or no fear of other men. They will readily fight a larger and more powerful man, face an adversary with a knife, assault a policeman or even disregard the threat of a leveled gun. But very few will stand up to a raging dog. The rationale is found in the dog's animalhood, and in its physiognomy. Its animalhood negates the civilizing forces by which a man might reasonably expect a human opponent to be influenced—essentially the weight of a cultural and ethical past that makes him somewhat reluctant to wreak any potentially serious damage upon a fellow man. The dog is unencumbered by such strictures and may well spark primordial fears of the predator, the voracious beast whose single goal is to kill.

Physically, a man is severely disadvantaged in combat with a dog. The dog is quicker, his powerful jaws are studded with teeth an inch to an inch and three-quarters long, he is less vulnerable than a human, and the usual tactics employed against men are ineffectual: you can't gouge his eyes or kick him in the groin with any success, it is exceedingly difficult to strangle him and arms thrown up against his onslaught block no blows and result only in ripped flesh. A large dog on the attack can demoralize nearly any man.

Never a sluggard in warfare, and unencumbered by sentimental notions of pethood, man was quick to introduce the dog to the battlefield. Egyptian hieroglyphics of five thousand years ago depict large dogs attacking enemy troops under the direction of handlers. Assyrian bas-reliefs feature war dogs straining at the leash. Cambyses of Persia maintained a squadron of five hundred war dogs and used them in the vanguard of battle. Early Babylonian art contains numerous representations of war dogs. Greek dogs fought with their masters against Darius the Great on the plain of Marathon, one with such valiance that the citizens of Athens voted to include him in a painting honoring the day's heroes. War dogs wore wide, heavy leather collars studded with metal, and Xenophon, a Greek general, also advised the use of body straps, suggesting that "spikes should be sewn in, so as to protect the breed." The Celts bred particularly large and savage dogs and fashioned leather cuirasses for them that were equipped with sharp metal blades. The teeth and blades of these dogs played havoc with Belgian and Gallic infantry and successfully routed and stampeded cavalry. Pliny wrote: "There was a king of the Garamants exiled, and recovered his royal state again by means of two hundred dogs that fought for him against all those that made resistance, and brought him home in spite of his enemies. The Colophonians and Catabaleans maintained certain squadrons of massive dogs for their war service: and those were put in the forward to make the head and front of the battle and were never known to draw back and refuse combat. These were their trustiest auxiliaries and aid-soldiers and never so needy as to call for pay." He also noted several other tribes who employed similar dog squadrons.

Antiquity's most famous breed was the *molossus*, the Molossian hound. This was a huge brute developed by the Molossi, a people living in Epirus, a district in northern Greece. He was without peer in the known Mediterranean world, and was either a forerunner or cousin to the mastiff. A single Molossian hound was considered the match of any bull, bear or lion, and was reputedly capable of tearing down both horses and riders in battle. Writers of the period inevitably compared all dogs with the Molossian hound and, just as inevitably, the other dogs ended second best.

Dogs were used as guards in various Greek and Roman temples and were reported to have been gentle with true worshipers and to have attacked the impious. Obviously, a dog gives not a damn for piety; what is probable, though, is that priests or functionaries used the animals to keep "undesirables" from the temple grounds.

The Romans staked dogs around the perimeters of their night camps to serve as sentries. These were called ban dogs, and the term is still in use in some areas of Europe. Roman house guards were in such common use that they were awarded their own name, *Canis ostiarius* (literally, Dog of the Portal), and small paintings frequently appeared over exterior doors to warn would-be intruders. War dogs, known as *Canis bellator,* were held in such regard that handler and dog were often buried together if killed in battle. The column erected in the Forum, honoring Marcus Aurelius, included spike-collared war dogs. The Romans were definitely fonder of their dogs than any other Western people, but, though some were kept as pets by the rich, the Romans were not truly dog-loving. As always, the dog's major value was utilitarian. Rome used them by the hundreds of thousands in the gladiatorial arenas, and crucified many cowardly and nonbarking dogs once each year, in memory of a night on which the Gauls had nearly taken the Capitol because of the failure of sentry dogs to give warning. A third-century Roman spoke for the majority when, in a treatise on dogs, he mentioned "those worthless, greedy pet dogs that attend at table." The most accomplished appropriators in history (religion, art, political theory, *anything*), the Romans had nothing but admiration for the fearsome dogs the wild and painted tribes of Briton sent against the legionnaires. They were mastiff-types, Molossian hounds several degrees improved, larger, and more powerful. The Romans promptly christened the breed *Pugnaces molossi* and proceeded to ship them back by the thousands to Rome, where they fought in the arenas, were mustered into service as war dogs and were purchased by private citizens to guard homes. One commentator wrote, "When a great work is to be done and courage to be displayed and the hazard of approaching war gives the final summons, then you would not admire even the well-known Molossian hounds so much as these."

After the end of the Roman Empire, the dog continued to hunt for man, defend him, and go to war with him. The Swiss, for example, used dogs against Charles the Bold at the Battle of Murten. A fifteenth-century treatise on dogs instructs: "The war dog ought to be trained up to fight from his earliest years. Accordingly some man or other is fitted out with a coat of thick skin, which the dog will not be able to bite through, as a sort of dummy; the dog is then spurred on against this man, upon which the man in the skin runs away and then allows himself to be caught and, falling down on the ground in front of the dog, to be bitten. The day following he ought to be pitted against another man protected in the same manner, and at the finish he can be trained to follow any person upon whose tracks he has been placed . . . from time to time it is a good thing to go for this dog with drawn swords: in this way . . . the dog will develop his spirit and courage to the utmost; and then of course you can lead him against real enemies." The log of an early traveler journeying through Turkey mentions "dogs the size of asses who are used in war to tear men from their horses." In the sixteenth century, King Henry VIII, well known for his use of mastiffs in battle, sent four hundred of the animals "garnished with good yron collars" to King Charles I of Spain for use against the invading French. The Conquistadors fought the Indians of South America with dogs, and Nikolaus Federman, a bootlegging German who followed Quesada to Colombia, equipped his force with a large brigade of battle dogs that slaughtered and terrorized the Cibchas.

The invention of gunpowder and its application to warfare eliminated the dog from the battlefield proper. Although he continued to serve as a courier and, with superior olfactory and auditory senses, as sentry, he no longer participated in actual combat. But he did remain popular as a guardian of home and property. Dr. Caius, one of the earliest and most renowned English dog authorities, wrote of the watchdog in the sixteenth century: "For when the master goes to bed and a hundred brazen bolts close everything . . . then if the master tells the dog to go out, he goes all through the estate more carefully than any bailiff, and if he finds any stranger, be it man or animal, he drives them off, but leaves domestic animals and servants alone. . . . One should be careful of these because they mean to inflict injury at some time, but do not attack them, for they are provoked by anger to bite." One of the earlier references to Great Danes (1732) advises that it is an excellent animal with which to travel, for it will "carry a Lantern before you on a dark night . . . [and] if you

Chevy Chase *by Sir Edwin Landseer*

should sleep in any strange place, while he is near you, nobody dare touch you or any thing belonging to you." Great Danes became common companions on the road, loping alongside the master's coach during the day and protecting him at night.

A good dog was indispensable for both working flocks and herds and protecting them from predators. An English sportsman on holiday reported the kind of fanatical devotion that owners sometimes developed for these dogs: "Though every flock that one meets with has one or more of these redoubtable guardians attached to it, I have never seen them used as sheep-dogs,

according to our acceptance of the term . . . [they] are simply used to guard the flocks against depredators—biped as well as quadruped. . . . So much importance do the Albanian shepherds attach to the fierceness of their 'skillies' that however savagely the innocent wanderer in search of woodcocks may be attacked, the owner of the dog will never call him off, for fear of spoiling him." Strangers were warned that they must not under any circumstances shoot such a dog if they did not wish to be shot in turn. However, it was considered proper to defend oneself with a knife if attacked.

Dogs continued to hunt for man, their importance in this function attested by the frequency with which they appear in works of art down through the ages. Certainly, no nobleman would mount a hunt without including several good dogs, and for the peasant, who might well go hungry if his afternoon's hunting was unsuccessful, a dog was an absolute necessity.

The Eastern world had long looked upon the dog as a pet as well as a practical functionary; the Chinese, Babylonians and Japanese wrote of him as such, centuries before the birth of Christ. But it was not until the end of the Middle Ages that Western man began to make a pet of his dog. The change was slow. In the beginning, only the nobility possessed the time and the money necessary to the enjoyment of such a frivolity as a pet. Not unexpectedly, they often indulged in ludicrous and pathetic excess. Witness King Henry III of France, carrying his miniature dog in a basket slung from his neck so that he need never be parted from it, not even in church or at the highest functions of state. But the sentiment gradually seeped down through the various strata of society, and here and there you might find a tradesman saving a pup from his watchdog's unwanted litter so that his daughter might play with it. Or a shepherd maintaining, in addition to his two fine sheep dogs, some smaller cur who, while useless with the flocks, was funny and affectionate, good company and not that expensive to feed, after all. The Industrial Revolution completed the adjustment by creating a large bourgeoisie, a comfortable middle class for whom pet-keeping was not only possible, but emotionally gratifying. With the Industrial Revolution came a consequent expansion of towns and cities into the first megalopolises. And for the great numbers of people uprooted from rural heritages the dog made an ideal pet: he adapted well to city life and he provided a kind of link back to more open and freer spaces, greener, less dirty, and more pleasant days.

By the mid-eighteenth century, it can be said without argument that Western man had granted his dog the status of pet as well as property, and by the early nineteenth century this attitude was shared by all class levels.

The dog at first glance seems to have been amenable to the change. However, I think it is more likely that he is as yet unaware of his new state and that he still considers himself party of the first or second part to a two-way working agreement, the only modification being that the relationship is friendlier than ever it was before.

Were he capable of abstraction, it is probable that he would consider pethood an affront to his dignity and would be properly outraged.

He has lived with man for perhaps ten thousand years now, but, while he is usually willing to deport himself in a civilized and social manner, he has certainly not undergone any major alteration of his basic nature. He remains a predatory pack-animal—just as his Best Friend, while usually willing to deport *himself* in a civilized and social manner, has also failed to undergo any substantial change of nature, and remains in large part what he originally was, a belligerent ape.

Our Friend, the Dog

by MAURICE MAETERLINCK

I

I have lost, within these last few days, a little bulldog. He had just completed the sixth month of his brief existence. He had no history. His intelligent eyes opened to look out upon the world, to love mankind, then closed again on the cruel secrets of death.

The friend who presented me with him had given him, perhaps by antiphrasis, the startling name of Pelléas. Why rechristen him? For how can a poor dog, loving, devoted, faithful, disgrace the name of a man or an imaginary hero?

Pelléas had a great bulging, powerful forehead, like that of Socrates or Verlaine; and, under a little black nose, blunt as a churlish assent, a pair of large hanging and symmetrical chops, which made his head a sort of massive, obstinate, pensive and three-cornered menace. He was beautiful after the manner of a beautiful, natural monster that has complied strictly with the laws of its species. And what a smile of attentive obligingness, of incorruptible innocence, of affectionate submission, of boundless gratitude and total self-abandonment lit up, at the least caress, that adorable mask of ugliness! Whence exactly did that smile emanate? From the ingenuous and melting eyes? From the ears pricked up to catch the words of man? From the forehead that unwrinkled to appreciate and love, or from the stump of a tail that wriggled at the other end to testify to the intimate and impassioned joy that filled his small being, happy once more to encounter the hand or the glance of the god to whom he surrendered himself?

Pelléas was born in Paris, and I had taken him to the country. His bonny fat paws, shapeless and not yet stiffened, carried slackly through the unexplored pathways of his new existence his huge and serious head, flat-nosed and, as it were, rendered heavy with thought.

For this thankless and rather sad head, like that of an overworked child, was beginning the overwhelming work that oppresses every brain at the start of life. He had, in less than five or six weeks, to get into his mind, taking shape within it, an image and a satisfactory conception of the universe. Man, aided by all the knowledge of his own elders and his brothers, takes thirty or forty years to outline that conception, but the humble dog has to unravel it for himself in a few days: and yet, in the eyes of a god, who should know all things, would it not have the same weight and the same value as our own?

It was a question, then, of studying the ground, which can be scratched and dug up and which sometimes reveals surprising things; of casting at the sky, which is uninteresting, for there is nothing there to eat, one glance that does away with it for good and all; of discovering the grass, the admirable and green grass, the springy and cool grass, a field for races and sports, a friendly and boundless bed, in which lies hidden the good and wholesome couch-grass. It was a question, also, of taking promiscuously a thousand urgent and curious observations. It was necessary, for instance, with no other guide than pain, to learn to calculate the height of objects from the top of which you can jump into space; to convince yourself that it is vain to pursue birds who fly away and that you are unable to clamber up trees after the cats who defy you there; to distinguish between the sunny spots where it is delicious to sleep and the patches of shade in which you shiver; to remark with stupefaction that the rain does not fall inside the houses, that water is cold, uninhabitable and dangerous, while fire is beneficent at a distance, but terrible when you come too near; to observe that the meadows, the farmyards and sometimes the roads are haunted by giant creatures with threatening horns, creatures good-natured, perhaps, and, at any rate, silent, creatures who allow you to sniff at them a little curiously without taking offense, but who keep their real thoughts to themselves. It was necessary to learn, as the result of painful and humiliating experiment, that you are not at liberty to obey all nature's laws without distinction in the dwelling of the gods; to recognize that the kitchen is the privileged and most agreeable spot in that divine dwelling, although you are hardly allowed to abide in it because of the cook, who is a considerable, but jealous power; to learn that doors are important and capricious volitions, which sometimes lead to felicity, but which most often, hermetically closed, mute and stern, haughty and heartless, remain deaf to all entreaties; to admit, once and for all, that the essential good things of life, the indisputable blessings, generally imprisoned in pots and stewpans, are almost always inaccessible; to know how to look at them with laboriously-acquired indifference and to practice to take no notice of them, saying to yourself that here are objects which are probably sacred, since merely to skim them with the tip of a respectful tongue is enough to let loose the unanimous anger of all the gods of the house.

And then, what is one to think of the table on which so many things happen that cannot be guessed; of the derisive chairs on which one is forbidden to sleep; of the plates and dishes that are empty by the time that one can get at them; of the lamp that drives away the dark? . . . How many orders, dangers, prohibitions, problems, enigmas has one not to classify in one's overburdened memory! . . . And how to reconcile all this with other laws, other enigmas, wider and more imperious, which one bears within one's self, within one's instinct, which spring up and develop from one hour to the other, which come from the depths of time and the race, invade the blood, the muscles and the nerves and suddenly assert themselves more irresistibly and more powerfully than pain, the word of the master himself, or the fear of death?

Thus, for instance, to quote only one example, when the hour of sleep has struck for men, you have retired to your hole, surrounded by the darkness, the silence and the formidable solitude of the night. All is sleep in the master's house. You feel yourself very small and weak in the presence of the mystery. You know that the gloom is peopled with foes who hover and lie in wait. You suspect the trees, the passing wind and the moonbeams. You would like to hide, to suppress yourself by holding your breath. But still the watch must be kept; you must, at the least sound, issue from your retreat, face the invisible and bluntly disturb the imposing silence of the earth, at the risk of bringing down the whispering evil or crime upon yourself alone. Whoever the enemy be, even if he be man, that is to say, the very brother of the god whom it is your business to defend, you must attack him blindly, fly at his throat, fasten your perhaps sacrilegious teeth into human flesh, disregard the spell of a hand and voice similar to those of your master, never be silent, never attempt to escape, never allow yourself to be tempted or bribed and, lost in the night without help, prolong the heroic alarm to your last breath.

There is the great ancestral duty, the essential duty, stronger than death, which not even man's will and anger are able to check. All our humble history, linked with that of the dog in our first struggles against every breathing thing, tends to prevent his forgetting it. And when, in our safer dwelling places of today, we happen to punish him for his untimely zeal, he throws us a glance of astonished reproach, as though to point out to us that we are in the wrong and that, if we lose sight of the main clause in the treaty of alliance which he made with us at the time when we lived in caves, forests and fens, he continues faithful to it in spite of us and remains nearer to the eternal truth of life, which is full of snares and hostile forces.

But how much care and study are needed to succeed in fulfilling this duty! And how complicated it has become since the days of the silent caverns and the great deserted lakes! It was all so simple, then, so easy and so clear. The lonely hollow opened upon the side of the hill, and all that approached, all that moved on the horizon of the plains or woods, was the unmistakable enemy. . . . But today you can no longer tell. . . . You have to acquaint yourself with a civilization of which you disapprove, to appear to understand a thousand incomprehensible things. . . . Thus, it seems evident that henceforth the whole world no longer belongs to the master, that his property conforms to unintelligible limits. . . . It becomes necessary, therefore, first of all to know exactly where the sacred domain begins and ends. Whom are you to suffer, whom to stop? . . . There is the road by which everyone, even the poor, has the right to pass. Why? You do not know; it is a fact which you deplore, but which you are bound to accept. Fortunately, on the other hand, here is the fair path which none may tread. This path is faithful to the sound traditions; it is not to be lost sight of; for by it enter into your daily existence the difficult problems of life.

Would you have an example? You are sleeping peacefully in a ray of the sun that covers the threshold of the kitchen with pearls. The earthenware pots are amusing themselves by elbowing and nudging one another on the edge of the shelves trimmed with paper lacework. The copper stew-pans play at scattering spots of light over the smooth white walls. The motherly stove hums a soft tune and dandles three saucepans

blissfully dancing; and, from the little hole that lights up its inside, defies the good dog who cannot approach, by constantly putting out at him its fiery tongue. The clock, bored in its oak case, before striking the august hour of meal time, swings its great gilt navel to and fro; and the cunning flies tease your ears. On the glittering table lie a chicken, a hare, three partridges, besides other things which are called fruits— peaches, melons, grapes—and which are all good for nothing. The cook guts a big silver fish and throws the entrails (instead of giving them to you!) into the dustbin. Ah, the dustbin! Inexhaustible treasury, receptacle of windfalls, the jewel of the house! You shall have your share of it, an exquisite and surreptitious share; but it does not do to seem to know where it is. You are strictly forbidden to rummage in it. Man in this way prohibits many pleasant things, and life would be dull indeed, and your days empty if you had to obey all the orders of the pantry, the cellar and the dining room. Luckily, he is absentminded and does not long remember the instructions which he lavishes. He is easily deceived. You achieve your ends and do as you please, provided you have the patience to await the hour. You are subject to man, and he is the one god; but you none the less have your own personal, exact and imperturbable morality, which proclaims aloud that illicit acts become most lawful through the very fact that they are performed without the master's knowledge. Therefore, let us close the watchful eye that has seen. Let us pretend to sleep and to dream of the moon. . . .

Hark! A gentle tapping at the blue window that looks out on the garden! What is it? Nothing; a bough of hawthorn that has come to see what we are doing in the cool kitchen. Trees are inquisitive and often excited; but they do not count, one has nothing to say to them, they are irresponsible, they obey the wind, which has no principles. . . . But what is that? I hear steps! . . . Up, ears open; nose on the alert! . . . It is the baker coming up to the rails, while the postman is opening a little gate in the hedge of lime-trees. They are friends; it is well; they bring something; you can greet them and wag your tail discreetly twice or thrice, with a patronizing smile. . . .

Another alarm! What is it now? A carriage pulls up in front of the steps. The problem is a complex one. Before all, it is of consequence to heap copious insults on the horses, great, proud beasts, who make no reply. Meantime, you examine out of the corner of your eye the persons alighting. They are well-clad and seem full of confidence. They are probably going to sit at the table of the gods. The proper thing is to bark without acrimony, with a shade of respect, so as to show that you are doing your duty, but that you are doing it with intelligence. Nevertheless, you cherish a lurking suspicion and, behind the guests' backs, stealthily, you sniff the air persistently and in a knowing way, in order to discern any hidden intentions.

But halting footsteps resound outside the kitchen. This time it is the poor man dragging his crutch, the unmistakable enemy, the hereditary enemy, the direct descendant of him who roamed outside the bone-cramped cave which you suddenly see again in your racial memory. Drunk with indignation, your bark broken, your teeth multiplied with hatred and rage, you are about to seize their reconcilable adversary by the breeches, when the cook, armed with her broom, the ancillary and forsworn scepter, comes to protect the traitor, and you are obliged to go back to your hole, where, with eyes filled with impotent and slanting flames, you growl out frightful but futile curses, thinking within yourself that this is the end of all things, and that the human species has lost its notion of justice and injustice. . . .

Is that all? Not yet; for the smallest life is made up of innumerous duties, and it is a long work to organize a happy existence upon the borderland of two such different worlds as the world of beasts and the world of men. How should we fare if we had to serve, while remaining within our own sphere, a divinity, not an imaginary one, like to ourselves, because the offspring of our own brain, but a god actually visible, ever present, ever active and as foreign, as superior to our being as we are to the dog?

We now, to return to Pelléas, know pretty well what to do and how to behave on the mas-ter's premises. But the world does not end at the house door, and, beyond the walls and beyond the hedge, there is a universe of which one has not the custody, where one is no longer at home, where relations are changed. How are we to stand in the street, in the fields, in the marketplace, in the shops? In consequence of difficult and delicate observations, we understand that we must take no notice of passersby; obey no calls but the master's; be polite, with indifference, to strangers who pet us. Next, we must conscientiously fulfill certain obligations of mysterious courtesy toward our brothers the other dogs; respect chickens and ducks; not appear to remark the cakes at the pastry-cook's, which spread themselves insolently within reach of the tongue; show to the cats, who, on the steps of the houses, provoke us by hideous grimaces, a silent contempt, but one that will not forget; and remember that it is lawful and even commendable to chase and strangle mice, rats, wild rabbits and, generally speaking, all animals (we learn to know them by secret marks) that have not yet made their peace with mankind.

All this and so much more! . . . Was it surprising that Pelléas often appeared pensive in the face of those numberless problems, and that his humble and gentle look was often so profound and grave, laden with cares and full of unreadable questions?

Alas, he did not have time to finish the long and heavy task which nature lays upon the instinct that rises in order to approach a brighter region. . . . An ill of a mysterious character, which seems specially to punish the only animal that succeeds in leaving the circle in which it is born; an indefinite ill that carries off hundreds of intelligent little dogs, came to put an end to the destiny and the happy education of Pelléas. And now all those efforts to achieve a little more light; all that ardor in loving, that courage in understanding; all that affectionate gaiety and innocent fawning; all those kind and devoted looks, which turned to man to ask for his assistance against unjust death; all those flickering gleams which came from the profound abyss of a world that is no longer ours; all those nearly human little habits lie sadly in the cold ground, under a flowering elder tree, in a corner of the garden.

II

Man loves the dog, but how much more ought he to love it if he considered, in the inflexible harmony of the laws of nature, the sole exception, which is that love of a being that succeeds in piercing, in order to draw closer to us, the partitions, ever elsewhere impermeable, that separate the species! We are alone, absolutely alone on this chance planet; and amid all the forms of life that surround us, not one, excepting the dog, has made an alliance with us. A few creatures fear us, most are unaware of us, and not one loves us. In the world of plants, we have dumb and motionless slaves; but they serve us in spite of themselves. They simply endure our laws and our yoke. They are impotent prisoners, victims incapable of escaping, but silently rebellious; and, so soon as we lose sight of them, they hasten to betray us and return to their former wild and mischievous liberty. The rose and the corn, had they wings, would fly at our approach like the birds.

Among the animals, we number a few servants who have submitted only through indifference, cowardice or stupidity: the uncertain and craven horse, who responds only to pain and is attached to nothing; the passive and dejected ass, who stays with us only because he knows not what to do nor where to go, but who nevertheless, under the cudgel and the pack-saddle, retains the idea that lurks behind his ears; the cow and the ox, happy so long as they are eating, and docile because, for centuries, they have not had a thought of their own; the affrighted sheep, who knows no other master than terror; the hen, who is faithful to the poultry-yard because she finds more maize and wheat there than in the neighboring forest. I do not speak of the cat, to whom we are nothing more than a too large and uneatable prey: the ferocious cat, whose sidelong contempt tolerates us only as encumbering parasites in our own homes. She, at least, curses us in her mysterious heart; but all the others live beside us

as they might live beside a rock or a tree. They do not love us, do not know us, scarcely notice us. They are unaware of our life, our death, our departure, our return, our sadness, our joy, our smile. They do not even hear the sound of our voice, so soon as it no longer threatens them; and, when they look at us, it is with the distrustful bewilderment of the horse, in whose eye still hovers the infatuation of the elk or gazelle that sees us for the first time, or with the dull stupor of the ruminants, who look upon us as a momentary and useless accident of the pasture.

For thousands of years, they have been living at our side, as foreign to our thoughts, our affections, our habits as though the least fraternal of the stars had dropped them but yesterday on our globe. In the boundless interval that separates man from all the other creatures, we have succeeded only, by dint of patience, in making them take two or three illusory steps. And, if, tomorrow, leaving their feelings toward us untouched, nature were to give them the intelligence and the weapons wherewith to conquer us, I confess that I should distrust the hasty vengeance of the horse, the obstinate reprisals of the ass and the maddened meekness of the sheep. I should shun the cat as I should shun the tiger; and even the good cow, solemn and somnolent, would inspire me with but a wary confidence. As for the hen, with her round, quick eye, as when discovering a slug or a worm, I am sure that she would devour me without a thought.

III

Now, in this indifference and this total want of comprehension in which everything that surrounds us lives; in this incommunicable world, where everything has its object hermetically contained within itself, where every destiny is self-circumscribed, where there exist among creatures no other relations than those of executioners and victims, eaters and eaten, where nothing is able to leave its steel-bound sphere, where death alone establishes cruel relations of cause and effect between neighboring lives, where not the smallest sympathy has ever made a conscious leap from one species to another, one animal alone, among all that breathes upon the earth, has succeeded in breaking through the prophetic circle, in escaping from itself to come bounding toward us, definitely to cross the enormous zone of darkness, ice and silence that isolates each category of existence in nature's unintelligible plan. This animal, our good familiar dog, simple and unsurprising as may today appear to us what he has done, in thus perceptibly drawing nearer to a world in which he was not born and for which he was not destined, has nevertheless performed one of the most unusual and improbable acts that we can find in the general history of life. When was this recognition of man by beast, this extraordinary passage from darkness to light, effected? Did we seek out the poodle, the collie or the mastiff from among the wolves and the jackals, or did he come spontaneously to us? We cannot tell. So far as our human annals stretch, he is at our side, as at present; but what are human annals in comparison with the times of which we have no witness? The fact remains that he is there in our houses, as ancient, as rightly placed, as perfectly adapted to our habits as though he had appeared on this earth, such as he now is, at the same time as ourselves. We have not to gain his confidence or his friendship: he is born our friend; while his eyes are still closed, already he believes in us: even before his birth, he has given himself to man. But the word "friend" does not exactly depict his affectionate worship. He loves us and reveres us as though we had drawn him out of nothing. He is, before all, our creature full of gratitude and more devoted than the apple of our eye. He is our intimate and impassioned slave, whom nothing discourages, whom nothing repels, whose ardent trust and love nothing can impair. He has solved, in an admirable and touching manner, the terrifying problem which human wisdom would have to solve if a divine race came to occupy our globe. He has loyally, religiously, irrevocably recognized man's superiority and has surrendered himself to him body and soul, without afterthought, without any intention to go back, reserving of his independence, his instinct and his character only the small part indispensable to the

continuation of the life prescribed by nature. With an unquestioning certainty, an unconstraint and a simplicity that surprise us a little, deeming us better and more powerful than all that exists, he betrays, for our benefit, the whole of the animal kingdom to which he belongs and, without scruple, denies his race, his kin, his mother and his young.

But he loves us not only in his consciousness and his intelligence: the very instinct of his race, the entire unconsciousness of his specie, it appears, think only of us, dream only of being useful to us. To serve us better, to adapt himself better to our different needs, he has adopted every shape and been able infinitely to vary the faculties, the aptitudes which he places at our disposal. Is he to aid us in the pursuit of game in the plains? His legs lengthen inordinately, his muzzle tapers, his lungs widen, he becomes swifter than the deer. Does our prey hide under wood? The docile genius of the species, forestalling our desires, presents us with the basset, a sort of almost footless serpent, which steals into the closest thickets. Do we ask that he should drive our flocks? The same compliant genius grants him the requisite size, intelligence, energy and vigilance. Do we intend him to watch and defend our house? His head becomes round and monstrous, in order that his jaws may be more powerful, more formidable and more tenacious. Are we taking him to the south? His hair grows shorter and lighter, so that he may faithfully accompany us under the rays of a hotter sun. Are we going up to the north? His feet grow larger, the better to tread the snow; his fur thickens, in order that the cold may not compel him to abandon us. Is he intended only for us to play with, to amuse the leisure of our eyes, to adorn or enliven the home? He clothes himself in a sovereign grace and elegance, he makes himself smaller than a doll to sleep on our knees by the fireside, or even consents, should our fancy demand it, to appear a little ridiculous to please us.

You shall not find, in nature's immense crucible, a single living being that has shown a like suppleness, a similar abundance of forms, the same prodigious faculty of accommodation to our wishes. This is because, in the world which

A Litter *by A. Cooper*

we know, among the different and primitive geniuses that preside over the evolution of the several species, there exists not one, excepting that of the dog, that ever gave a thought to the presence of man.

It will, perhaps, be said that we have been able to transform almost as profoundly some of our domestic animals: our hens, our pigeons, our ducks, our cats, our horses, our rabbits, for instance. Yes, perhaps; although such transformations are not comparable with those undergone by the dog and although the kind of service which these animals render us remains, so to speak, invariable. In any case, whether this impression be purely imaginary or correspond with a reality, it does not appear that we feel in these transformations the same unfailing and preventing good will, the same sagacious and exclusive love. For the rest, it is quite possible that the dog, or rather the inaccessible genius of his race, troubles scarcely at all about us and that we have merely known how to make use of various aptitudes offered by the abundant chances of life. It matters not: as we know nothing of the substance of things, we must needs cling to appearances; and it is sweet to establish that, at least in appearance, there is on the planet where, like unacknowledged kings, we live in solitary state, a being that loves us.

However the case may stand with these appearances, it is none the less certain that, in the aggregate of intelligent creatures that have rights, duties, a mission and a destiny, the dog is a really privileged animal. He occupies in this world a preeminent position enviable among all. He is the only living being that has found and recognizes an indubitable, tangible, unexceptionable and definite god. He knows to what to devote the best part of himself. He knows to whom above him to give himself. He has not to seek for a perfect, superior and infinite power in the darkness, amid successive lies, hypotheses and dreams. That power is there, before him, and he moves in its light. He knows the supreme duties which we all do not know. He has a morality which surpasses all that he is able to discover in himself and which he can practice without scruple and without fear. He possesses truth in its fulness. He has a certain and infinite ideal.

IV

And it was thus that, the other day, before his illness, I saw my little Pelléas sitting at the foot of my writing table, his tail carefully folded under his paws, his head a little on one side, the better to question me, at once attentive and tranquil, as a saint should be in the presence of God. He was happy with the happiness which we, perhaps, shall never know, since it sprang from the smile and the approval of a life incomparably higher than his own. He was there, studying, drinking in all my looks; and he replied to them gravely, as from equal to equal, to inform me, no doubt, that at least through the eyes, the most immaterial organ that transformed into affectionate intelligence the light which we enjoyed, he knew that he was saying to me all that love should say. And, when I saw him thus, young, ardent and believing, bringing me, in some wise, from the depths of unwearied nature, quite fresh news of life and trusting and wonder-struck, as though he had been the first of his race that came to inaugurate the earth and as though we were still in the first days of the world's existence, I envied the gladness of his certainty, compared it with the destiny of man, still plunging on every side into darkness, and said to myself that the dog who meets with a good master is the happier of the two.

Lurchers

by LESLIE NORRIS

WHEN my great-grandfather came out of the hills above Llandovery in 1864, his furniture on a flat cart, his pans in clanking bundles, his pots in wicker baskets, his two small boys kicking their legs over the backboard, you can be sure he brought his dogs with him. He was not migrating very far— not more than fifty miles—but he was leaving behind the green, Welsh-speaking county in which he had been born. He never went back. He walked with his wife at the mare's head through the hamlets of Halfway and Llywel, and his cousins the Gardners ran out to wish them luck and to give them parting gifts—small luster jugs, packets of tea. Reaching Sennybridge, they turned south to climb the gaunt and sneering heights of the Brecon Beacons. Here the little boys climbed down to lighten the load as, dwarfed by height, silenced by darkness, the family crawled for hours under black Fan Frynach before they reached the top of the pass, at the Storey Arms inn. Then they could see below them the spoiled valleys of Glamorgan, their sides already pocked with the heaped detritus of the Industrial Revolution, their skies lit by leaping flames from the furnaces or hidden by rolling smoke.

Yes, my great-grandfather brought the dogs. He needed them. He was not going to the foundries or the coal mines but to a farm on the clear hills above the newly smoking town. He would have a white house, thick-walled, four-square to the winds; he would have an enclosure of over forty acres and grazing rights on twelve long miles of open mountain. On those high, unhindered moors he would raise his sheep— not your demure symbols of meekness, all soft fleece and gentle bleating, but stubborn, short-tempered animals, malevolent and cunning, able to grow stout on the shortest grass, yellow-eyed as goats, fluent as goats on the rock faces. They could outrun the mountain fox, they could lie snug for days under a fall of snow in the hollow, fetid caves of their own warm breathing.

To contain such animals without dogs would have been impossible. They would have been among my great-grandfather's most valued possessions—more prized than the corner cupboard given to him by his mother, more valuable than the dresser and the six oak dining chairs made for him by Jonah Jenkins of Trecastle. He needed his dogs more than he needed the tough brown mare that pulled the cart. Without them he could not have commanded the long slab of the mountain, acres of sloping turf and bracken on which his sheep were to feed, he could not have stood alone and calm while the dogs worked above him, extensions of his will. Each obedient to its own set of signals, his sheepdogs ran, crouched, sidled and slunk close, and faultlessly gathered in his butting and recalcitrant animals. Panting, they brought in the sheep for lambing and dipping and marking, they held and penned them for shearing, they cut out the sick and injured so that my great-grandfather could treat them with his homemade drenches and salves. And after his death, in my grandfather's day, the descendants of those dogs still ran the hills, hard, strong, heavy-coated, their names repeated generation after generation: Bob, Gyp, Mot, Fan, Meg, Dick, Carl—monosyllables easy to shout against the wind.

They were the strong aristocrats of the farm, moving stiff-legged and contemptuous through the yard, scattering the silly Buff Orpington and Light Sussex fowl my grandfather so admired, or sleeping thin-eyed in a patch of sun by the barn. They lived only for my grandfather, they had no existence without him. When he appeared around the dim back door and walked down the path, they swung in behind him, heads low, waiting only for the twitch of his hand to send them racing for the flocks. Wherever he went, two or three dogs padded silently behind him, as natural as his shadow. They were as close to him as his hands.

On warm afternoons we would sit together, old man and boy, talking. We spoke with wonder of the world outside the farm, for we shared an ignorance of that community which did not live directly, as we did, by what it produced. We believed completely that the rest of society was in some sense an immoral growth, a parasite like mistletoe, hanging without purpose from the great oak of our work. At such times we would look with pride at our dogs, seeing them as symbols of those puritan qualities we admired; they were staunch, loyal, infinitely hardworking, shy —like us—and sometimes sullen with strangers. And yet, although I loved my grandfather's sheepdogs and could work Bob myself, I did not want one of my own. I yearned for another kind of dog altogether—a long, silent hunter, a dog outside the law. I wanted a lurcher.

Sometimes a group of men—small men, dark, wary-eyed—would move through our big field on the way to the mountain. Beyond a nod in our direction, or a muttered good morning, they rarely greeted us. They were gypsies. They would have with them four or five lurchers, a kind of dog unchanged since the time of the pharaohs, with the lines of greyhounds but quieter, more secretive. Most of them would have long hair. They were bred from working greyhounds, with an occasional cross of sheepdog or, sometimes, deerhound blood. They were beautiful. It was their sheepdog ancestry that enabled them to hunt silently, that made them hardy and resourceful, and instantly obedient, despite the raging instinct of the chase which came from the greyhound.

My grandfather would stand unspeaking, rigid with distaste, when such a little group crossed our ground. The gypsies would climb the stile and cross the railway line, the gray dogs would wind themselves sinuously through the wire or, effortlessly, without fuss, leap the fence. When the men had vanished, quietly with their quiet dogs, my grandfather would turn away, two sharp, unaccustomed spots of color on his cheekbones, his mouth stern beneath his white mustache. He was a short, generally smiling man, extravagantly generous. He could whistle like a thrush. He knew where the early flowers grew, the windflower and the primrose, and where the mistle thrush, first of birds to nest, kept her spotted eggs. He never seemed to hurry. His speech was slow and quiet. But his rare anger was terrible. He hated lurchers—I could see that. I dared not ask him for one—though I wanted one of those lean outlaws far more than respectability— because I had no wish to set my grandfather's violence alight.

Still, once the old man had turned away, I would follow the gypsies at a timid distance. Standing in the shadow of a clump of stubby hawthorn, or almost hidden in bracken waist-high to a man, I would watch the hills for the lurchers—long, slim as stems, powerful, coursing and turning the blue hares of the mountain. I stood one morning in the red ferns, powder of winter frost unthawed on every brittle frond, when a tall lurcher stopped in front of me. I saw its eyes. They were large and gentle, curiously distant and impersonal. It opened its mouth in a kind of laugh, and I had a glimpse of the terrifying white teeth before it was whistled away and I ran downhill, frightened and elated, in the thin tracks made by the sheep. A lurcher can pull down a grown deer. According to record, in Cowdray Park, in Sussex, in the summer of 1591, Queen Elizabeth saw "sixteen bucks, all having fair play, pulled down after dinner" by dogs very much like these lurchers.

Too soon, we had to leave the farm. We went to live at the edge of town, in a row of houses almost where the fields began, and every day my grandfather walked out into the country, smiling as best he could, and wrecked by age. Of our dogs we took only Bob with us. The big orange-and-white sheepdog, dignified and brilliantly handsome, was too old to work with a new master. He settled down well, sat mildly on our front lawn, was gentle with passing children. He lived a long time, dying when I was seventeen, a year or two older than he was. It was June, and we buried him in the garden and planted a cherry tree over him.

That summer I found a holiday job in a fruit-and-vegetable warehouse. I used to rise early and walk through the streets as the summer dawn gradually brought the town awake. I used to hump boxes of fruit onto the trucks for delivery to shops all down the valley. I liked it very much. On Saturdays I used to work right through to late afternoon, loading up, checking invoices and delivery notes, taking new deliveries from the growers, and then I'd get paid. I had never known such wealth. The whole world grew docile and manageable under the power of the three pound notes I carried away each Saturday. Whole perfumed empires opened up for my inspection—cafés, theaters, gentlemen's outfits with real silk ties. It was a heady time. On my last Saturday Mr. Frimpton put three pound notes into my hand, and then, with a light smile, two more. "You've been a good lad," he said. "Buy yourself something special."

That evening I went alone to swim in the river. September was already chilling the water,

but it seemed warmer when the sun had gone down. It was my last freedom before school began again, and it was fine to be there, washing summer off my summer skin, lazing softly downstream. I got out in the dusk, as the bats were beginning to fly, and walked down the lane for home. A ghost of the moon was out in a sky still full of daylight. Long grass in the hedgerows was ripe and heavy, there was a faint odor of hay as the dew settled.

Three people were standing in the lane, and one of them was singing. The singer was Talbot Hamer, famous in our town as an outrageous firebrand, a drinker and a fighter. He sang with his head slightly raised and his arms at shoulder height in front of him, palms upward as if he held on his hands the airy weight of his lovely voice. He was singing "The Last Rose of Summer," and he was not drunk. His two companions, men of his own age—thirty, perhaps—were listening seriously, and Talbot filled the lane with his perfect singing, as a river fills its bed.

"All her lovely companions," sang Talbot Hamer, "are faded and gone." It was unbearably beautiful. We waited until the final note, sweet and poignant beyond our understanding, had died in the darkening lane. Talbot stood there, smiling down at us, amused at our stillness.

"I didn't know you'd gone in for singing, Talbot," said one of the men.

"I have," said Talbot, nodding dreamily, still aware of the song inside his head. "I've been taking lessons for two years now."

The music still held us, a sense quieter and more intense than silence. We stood there respectfully, not knowing what to do.

"Do you want to buy a dog?" said the other man at last, looking at me.

It was as if I were being asked to take part in a ceremony of gratitude. I looked at the long, pale dog standing at the man's knees.

"He's a good one," said Talbot Hamer. The spell of his song was with him; he looked at the evening with an exalted eye.

"Yes," I said. "I'll buy him."

"Two pounds," the man said.

I took the two carefree pounds Mr. Frimpton had given me and handed them over. The man put them in his pocket without a glance. "He'll catch anything that moves," the man said. "Retrieve to hand. Gentle, obedient. I'd not sell him to anyone but you."

"I believe you," I said.

He handed over the dog's leash. The whole affair was so tenuous that I was startled by the weight and touch of the leash; it was heavy, smooth and heavy—real saddler's leather, and hand-stitched. It was pliable and slightly oily with use, about eighteen inches long, and fastened by a spring clip to the dog's wide collar.

"I'll take him, then," I said.

The men stood aside and I walked past them, the dog going with me, unprotesting. He didn't look back.

"The name's Ben," the man called. "He's a good one, mind. You look after him and he'll look after you."

I trotted away as Talbot Hamer sang again. *"Una furtiva lagrima,"* he sang. *"Negli occhi suoi spunto, quelle festose giovani . . ."*

I turned the corner and could hear him no more.

I took Ben into the house and had a look at him. He was bigger than I'd thought—all of twenty-nine inches at the shoulder—and rough-coated. He was mostly white, but there were patches of orange on his body—on the ribs and the right shoulder—and his ears were deep orange, almost red. He might have been two years old. I fed him in the kitchen—a bowl of crusts softened in milk. He ate thoroughly, carefully cleaning every particle of food from the dish, and then looked thoughtfully about him. His expression was both cynical and mournful, and he never looked any different all the years I had him. That's how I came to own my first lurcher.

Talbot Hamer was quite right; the dog was a good one. When he was with us, he was vastly obedient, without ever letting us believe that he was at all humble or subservient; he followed at our heels, alert for any order. But he was also independent, roaming the town at will. I often saw him swinging down the High Street with his long, economical stride—deep-ribbed, solitary, detached from the scene, as if he were some thoughtful philosopher engrossed in a pro-

foundly satisfying problem. On such occasions he did not seem to recognize me; he looked away tactfully, as if to let me know that he was his own man with his own concerns. He roamed very far afield. Men from outlying villages, seeing him with me, would often come up and tell me of his exploits in their parishes, for he was a famous lover, visiting for miles around.

He was also very fond of beer. He was at his best in small inns on winter evenings, when the talk was good. His method was a simple one, I was told. He would sidle in quietly, offering a token wag of the tail if anyone looked at him, sigh gently and lie down out of the way in some corner. His eyes would grow soft as he looked beyond the walls at some distant and innocent memory. In a little while everybody would forget all about him. The old drinkers sat on their benches, laughed, pulled at their beer, wiped the foam from their mouths and put their mugs on the floor, the better to illustrate a point in some hot debate. Casually, Ben would saunter over and join the group, stretching almost invisibly in the shadow of a bench or a chair. And then, dreamily and in complete silence, he would lap up the beer. Men who knew him would chase him out the moment his long head appeared around the inn door, and he often had to move very smartly. On the other hand, he also managed to drink a lot of beer.

He was wonderful in the country, an incomparable craftsman. He and I worked together. A little shift of his head would lead me unerringly to some animal—a hedgehog, maybe, curled up in his leaves and just about to stir, or a bird. I had never seen a snipe until Ben turned one out for me one heavy winter morning when the ground was hard and the only place for such shy creatures was on the softness at the edge of a stream. Ben held back, looking to make sure I was attending, and then moved noiselessly into the willows. At once, a snipe came rocketing out, breaking into erratic flight, uttering two stiff cries. Ben looked at me sardonically and then stretched his long body in a gallop over the frozen meadow. He was a hunter all his life, he could not be kept from hare or game bird. Well, that was long ago.

Talbot Hamer is dead, the summer of his voice a memory.

The most beautiful lurcher I ever saw was Georgie Todd's Dagger—a spectacular, golden dog Georgie owned when I first knew him, about fifteen years back. Oh, he was lovely, a great beauty, over seventy pounds in weight, and he moved like thistledown. His yellow coat was harsh to the touch, his eyes were dark and kind. He and Georgie were very like each other— large, quiet, diffident and very gentle.

Georgie has a fruit farm the other side of the Downs, toward Pulborough. He grows apples mainly—Bramley's, Cox's, russets—but he has a few pear trees and a couple of acres of strawberries. The house is an old Georgian farmhouse, simply and beautifully preserved. The furniture is good, too, each piece shrewdly chosen. Georgie and his wife have taken great pains over it, bought carefully over the years, and have never been impulsive or haphazard. I always thought it strange that so neat and methodical a pair as Georgie and Phyllis Todd should have a dog at all, even one as striking as Dagger.

Their greatest enthusiasm is for the history of this part of Sussex—the Weald and the South Downs—and they are very serious about it, very knowledgeable. Between them, they've done some first-class research; Georgie does the field work, and Phyllis, a meticulous woman, looks after records and documents. Dagger was very much Georgie's dog. Without being in any way unkind, Phyllis seemed hardly aware that the animal was about. One day, in the Welldigger's Arms at lunchtime, looking at Dagger as he lay at our feet, I asked Georgie to sell me the dog.

"I shan't sell him," Georgie said. "We get along very nicely; he's a sweet old dog."

"Where did you buy him, Georgie?" I said.

"I didn't buy him," Georgie said.

He told me how, three years before, he had been walking down Bury Hill. It was a day of quite exceptional heat, after a succession of very hot days. Georgie had got up in the cool of the morning and tramped off to visit a church in one of the villages; he was tracing the ramifications of an old local family and had gone to look at the gravestones in the churchyard. Now, in the late morning, the heat was growing intense. Traffic wasn't as heavy in those days, and you could walk the roads with pleasure, but that day the dust was everywhere—chalk dust off the Downs, very thick, like powder. It rose in little puffs as Georgie plodded down the hill, getting into his nose and throat, making him think of the long, cool drink he'd have when he reached home. He sat on a stone at the side of the road to watch a gypsy caravan, pulled by a bay mare, climbing the hill toward him. It was a barrel caravan, its canvas stretched neatly over its hooped ribs, and it was in good shape, but the mare was finding the going hard; she was distressed and blowing as she dug into the steep of the hill. A thin young man walked with her, a surly young man, lean and dark in the face. They came slowly by, the caravan heavily laden, well down on its two creaking springs.

"You've got a load on," said Georgie, smiling.

The man didn't lift his head. Georgie stood up. At the tail of the caravan, tied to a spar by a rope heavy enough to hold a lion, was a lurcher puppy. He tottered and swayed, yelping each time he was dragged by the neck as the mare pulled gamely on. He was so dirty that Georgie could not guess at his color. He was far gone. Georgie, surprised by his own anger, ran to the front of the van.

"Do something about the dog!" he shouted. "You're killing him!"

Very quietly and deliberately the young gypsy led his mare to the roadside grass and dropped the reins over her head. She stood there, exhausted. The man said nothing at all. He took from his pocket a black-handled clasp knife and opened it with his thumbnail. The blade was long and glittering, thin with use and viciously sharp. Georgie knew that his last moments had come and prepared to meet his death as well as he could. All he could think of, he told me, smiling, was to stand erect and die bravely. But the gypsy walked slowly past him, down the side of the van, disappeared around the tail. The puppy began to scream, and Georgie's quick relief turned to indignation.

"My God," he thought, starting to run after the man, "he's going to kill the dog." But then the young man came back toward him, in one hand the open knife and in the other the heavy rope, its fibers freshly cut. The dog, unhurt, howled at the other end. The young man bent down and lifted the animal, holding it to Georgie. "Take it," he said. "Take it away." His voice was thick and trembling, as if he held his violence in check only by the severest effort.

"That was the first time I saw his face clearly," said Georgie. "The man was desperate, and I became even more frightened. I still believe that if I hadn't taken the dog—well, the fellow would have knifed me. I grabbed the pup and ran downhill as fast as I could go."

Georgie carried the dog home and, in time and with patience, turned him into Dagger. He was a lovely dog, noble and unassuming. After his death Georgie never had another.

There's a parti-colored dog that lives on the coast road with an old gypsy couple. I saw this dog when it was a sapling, running loose on Clymping beach, and I followed it home. The old man was sitting on the step of his caravan, a wooden van, traditionally painted. The old people travel the road from Littlehampton to Portsmouth and back again. I often see them parked on some small plot of grass, their skewbald gelding hobbled close by.

"That's a nice dog," I said to the old man.

"He'll come," said the old man. "In time, he'll come."

"What's his name?" I said.

"Toro," said the old man. "It's a good name. You should always give a dog a name he can grow up to. I've had three dogs named Toro in my life, and they've all been good. Belle is a good name, too."

The old man would not live well without Toro. There will not be many nights when the dog will not be silently quartering some rich man's fields, bringing almost apologetically to the pot the fresh spoils of the countryside—hare, rabbit, a pheasant so gently killed that the bronze feathers are not displaced.

The lurcher I have now, Jess, came to me from the dogs' home when she was twelve weeks old—a pathetic little waif, very ugly and awkward. But you could tell she'd be elegant; the length was already apparent in leg and back. At that time she couldn't manage herself at all well. Even her slight weight was sometimes too much for her, and she'd slowly collapse, spread-eagled, unable to rise and yelling with pain. At first we couldn't give her enough food—she ate all day long—and as she grew stronger she began to forage for herself. A poor sparrow once flew into the garden wall. It had hardly fallen to the ground when she'd swallowed it at a gulp. She began to catch wood pigeons. Slow to get up the birds would be, in their first clatter of flying, and she would grab one of them and, running on, take it to a corner of the field. Later I'd find two small pink feet—all that would be left of Jess's meal. But she's big now, a sturdy animal, full of grace and power.

I know quite a lot about her—where she was bred, her parentage, her precise age. When she was about twelve months and beginning to look as she should, I had her out on the lawn, chasing a ball. A young man came over and leaned on the gate, watching us. "She's growing nicely," he said. He was a pleasant young man—heavy-shouldered, thick, tousled fair hair above a round face. "We've been keeping an eye on her," he went on. "We knew you'd got her."

"Oh?" I said.

"I bred her," the young man said. "I had to leave her. And the rest of them—eight pups altogether. I put them in a box in the middle of the field and rang the dogs' home. Told them where to find the pups."

"Why did you abandon them?" I said sternly.

"Had to. I was running," he said, as if it were the most obvious explanation in the world.

I was mystified. "Running?" I said.

"Yes," he said. "From the police. I had to leave everything—the van, wife, kids, everything. It's all blown over now."

"What had you done?" I asked.

"Nothing," he said, so virtuously I knew he was lying. "I hadn't done a thing."

We looked at Jess galloping about the garden, pouncing on invisible game behind the lilac trees.

"She's big," the young man said. "And fast. I'll buy her back. I'll give you a good profit, mister."

"No, thanks," I said. "I quite like her." I started to walk toward the house when I remembered something. "Tell me," I asked. "How was she bred?"

He took a small notebook out of his pocket and turned the pages. "Here it is," he said. "I keep all the details in this book. Her father was a first-cross greyhound-deerhound. She favors him a lot—same gray color, same little whiskers. And her mother was a little brindle greyhound, very fast. I gave her to my brother after these pups were born, but she got killed up on the Downs. Ran into a fence and broke her neck. Yes, it's all down here. Born April 12, your dog was, one of eight pups."

Gypsies call here pretty regularly, to offer me a profit. Jess would be a good dog for a traveling man. She's very fast, but it's not just her speed—she's a thinking runner. I've seen her catch seagulls on the beach, racing on the very last inch of sand next to the water so that the birds on land are unable to fly directly out to sea. They have to take off and turn back over Jess's head, and any gull that isn't above her astonishing leap is in real danger.

When I first had her, I kept her about the house for a week or two before taking her out. I put her in the back of the car one day, thinking to let her have a run near the river. When I reached the top of the village, I saw Alec Dougan come out of the post office. Alec owns a lot of land around here—a couple of thousand acres of arable land, enough pasture for a large and famous herd of Ayrshires, and a stretch of woodland it takes days to cover. I stopped to talk to him.

"How are you, old son?" said Alec, eyes alight, smiling. I could see he was going to tell me the latest racy tale of local high life. And then he turned the smile off. I watched the harsh resurrection of my grandfather's dislike of lurchers

come into his face—the same downturn of the lips, the same stiffening of the neck.

"What's that you've got?" he said.

"Nice, isn't she?" I said.

"You've got trouble there," he said.

"Come away, Alec," I said. "She's only a baby."

"She'll hunt," he said. "You won't be able to stop her." I could see him thinking of his pheasants. "We're old friends," he said. "I won't ask you to keep her off my land, but watch her. And don't say I didn't warn you." He went off shaking his head.

She hasn't been too hard to train, though, and she no longer hunts indiscriminately. But I have had moments of panic. Last spring, we walked on a holiday Sunday in the public woods. The paths were full of strolling groups come to see the renewed foliage of the beeches. Children ran through the grass. I had Jess on her lead, and she walked demurely at my side. Without breaking step, she dipped her long neck to a tussock and, raising her head, gave me—put gently into my hand—a live cock pheasant. His gape wide with fright, he sat heavily in my hand. It had all been done so gracefully, so entirely without fuss, that nobody noticed at all. Completely unhurt, the bird sat there, and then, indignant, blundered off, his long tail feathers streaming.

Although I can safely whistle Jess off any chase at all now, she can still startle me. This morning the fields are covered with a light snow. It lies in the furrows and is blown in midget drifts in the lee of trees. The ground is so hard that it rings when you stamp on it. We went out early into the field behind Dr. Medlicott's house, and I slipped Jess at once. Normally she bounds immediately into a frolic, running in circles, tossing twigs in the air, but this morning her moving was quite unlike play, and I should have recognized at once that she was on to something. There is a frightening directness and velocity about her serious running, a concentration of effort that involves the whole dog, bending everything to a single purpose, that of catching and killing. Before I could purse my cold lips to a single recall, she had picked up a rabbit in the shadow of a hedge. It was a run of at least two hundred yards

Sleeping Bloodhound *by Sir Edwin Landseer*

and the poor creature hadn't time to turn away, hadn't time to squeal before its back was snapped and Jess was bringing it back, hanging loose from her killing jaws. It's easy to understand why landowners are wary of men who walk the fields with lurchers.

It wasn't always so. Such dogs were once owned only by princes. In ancient Wales, the gift of a rough-coated greyhound was a mark of the highest royal favor, and great poets, skilled in the strict measures, wrote complex odes to their lords begging such gifts. The young hero Culhwch, journeying to Arthur's court in search of initiation and adventure, went on horseback, dressed as a prince, miraculously accoutred. His horse was a light gray, four winters old, well

ribbed and shell-hoofed. His saddle was of gold, his tubular bridle bit was of gold, his battle-axe was keen enough to draw blood from the wind, his sword was hilted with gold, and his buckler was of gold and ivory. But his ultimate treasures were the two greyhounds, white-breasted, brindled, that danced and cavorted in front of him as he rode. Sufficient evidence of his nobility in themselves, they each wore a wide collar of red gold, fitting from shoulder to ear. They would have been the old, rough-coated greyhounds, exactly like the lurchers I've studied for so long, since the brindle color did not exist in smooth-haired greyhounds until Lord Orford, in the eighteenth century, introduced a bulldog cross in order to improve the courage of his strain. What I am calling a lurcher is a dog that has come down unchanged through the ages; except that he was known until the seventeenth century as a greyhound, everything about him is the same. A strong, hardy dog, his lines the dominant graceful outline of the greyhound we know today, his coat longer and weather-resisting, from the occasional judicious crosses of sheepdog and deerhound, he is valued for his intelligence and ability in the field. His likeness can be seen in a thousand paintings and tapestries, because he was as necessary to the life of the court as he is now to the traveling man. Culhwch's dogs would have been true hunting dogs, bred for efficiency in all weathers, long-coated, tough. King Canute, a notably sensible man, laid down in his laws that none but a gentleman could own a greyhound, and I'm delighted by this evidence of the legitimacy of lurchers.

It wouldn't surprise me to find the lurcher becoming a fashionable dog in a year or two. It has many virtues: it is tactful, not quarrelsome; will curl up in the smallest space; is not noisy. Lurchers are big enough to be very efficient guards. I saw one walking along the Charles River in Boston two years ago, and it was evident to me that the girl who owned him was safe. It would be a desperate mugger who'd willingly face a lurcher; he'd very likely lose an arm. And they're gratifyingly good to look at; they'd cause a sensation in Greenwich Village. I saw, in a fashionable journal recently, a slim and disdainful lady, posed to display the perfection of her expensive clothes. She held on two leads two splendid lurchers. They're coming back. If I wear my country tweeds and carry an ashplant, my lurcher takes me into the most rarefied social circles; she becomes a sporting dog rather than the companion of gypsies, thieves and tramps. Retired colonels write books about them, they are to be seen with rich racehorse owners and young men-about-town.

They are likely to be very useful very soon. As an experiment, a group of people in Wiltshire have been living for a year exactly as the ancient Celts did, raising scrubby animals, growing meager wheat, sleeping in a thatched, circular hut. They have with them two dogs—lurchers—and are loud in their praise of these animals, which have proved essential to the success of their project. Come the destruction, when the last warhead has exploded and the world is an untechnical ruin and small groups of people live desperately on what they can catch, we lurcher owners will no doubt be the new aristocrats. Because of Jess I expect I'll have a gray horse of four winters, gold all over him. I shall be a prince.

Rufus

by H. ALLEN SMITH

MY most intimate friend died two days ago.

While the vet was putting him away, I went into the deep woods back of the house and wandered around for an hour, trying to fight off a sickish feeling and not succeeding at all. It was one of the worst hours I've ever had.

His name was Rufus and he had been my constant companion for all of thirteen years of his life. He was a black cocker spaniel and during those years, from early morning to late at night, he was forever at my feet. As has been stated, my office is across a breezeway from the house and each morning, when I had finished breakfast, I'd address him as "Miss Blue"—recalling the secretary in the old Amos 'n' Andy radio show ("Miss Blue, buzz me!").

"All right, Miss Blue," I'd say, and head for the office, and he'd be right at my heels, ready for the day's work, ready to supervise everything I did. Sometimes there in the privacy of the office I'd talk to him. He was the first to hear the plots of two novels I wrote. He never said anything, one way or another, even after the books came out. I didn't expect him to. I didn't want him to. I wasn't looking for critical comment—I simply wanted to talk about those stories. He thought I was tetched. Whenever I talked to him at some length, he would twist his head to one side and keep it there, staring at me, telling me quite clearly that I was off my rocker. It never bothered me, because a lot of people look at me the same way.

On those occasions when I did leave the property for an hour or a day or a week, he would plant himself in the middle of the driveway and sit there staring patiently toward the road, until he heard my car horn beyond the curve. He could distinguish my horn from a hundred others and sometimes, on hearing it, he'd start racing around in a circle—he was that happy over my return.

Rufus had faults and failings that were almost human. He was, in fact, more of a "person" than many of my neighbors; he could be depended upon to react in certain definite ways to certain definite stimuli. He was a real oddball in many of his traits. For example, he was afraid of rabbits. Several times in his later years I saw him skulk in the presence of a rabbit. There was a reason for it. When he was younger he chased rabbits like any other dog. One day we were going down the hill to the mailbox when a cottontail took off across the field. Rufus gave it the old college try, running as hard as he could, and then something happened to his back legs. Both of them were somehow thrown out of joint and I had to carry him to the house and then to the vet. He couldn't walk for a couple of weeks and then the legs got better and pretty soon he was sound again. But he had learned something about rabbits, and he had no use for them after that. He had a feeling, I think, that a rabbit was possessed of a secret weapon—a sort of crippling ray. He had been a good fifty feet from that rabbit when the ray hit his back legs.

He was a real milquetoast. He rarely left our property except for an occasional daring expedition up or down the road, traveling no more than a quarter of a mile and then he'd get frightened at the immensity of the world and come hurrying home. He could do a job of ferocious barking, usually at the wrong people; his most hysterical outbursts were always directed against the delivery truck which brought his meat. Because of his superficial ferocity everyone considered him to be a fine watchdog and said so. Yet he was the world's worst. He'd charge at any and all invaders, barking furiously, so long as I was on the scene to back him up. But we found out later that whenever we were away from the house he had a tendency to crawl off somewhere and hide. A friend arrived one day while we were in New York City, and she went searching for Rufus. Eventually she found him upstairs, under a bed, almost trembling with fright.

He used to go at the laundryman as if he meant to chew the guy to pieces; at the same time he would whine and tremble and cling to my side at a distant rumble of thunder. He didn't seem to know that more dogs have been knocked head over heels by laundrymen than by all the thunderclaps since time began.

My affection for Rufus was a little strange considering the fact that during the years in which I lived in New York City I was a dog-hater. It wasn't a mere distaste for dogs, but a wild and untrammeled bitterness, born of ten thousand meetings with them on the pavements and sidewalks of the city. In later years I realized that my animus wasn't actually directed against dogs, but rather against the people who owned them, and kept them in the prison of apartments, and put little raincoats and rubber booties on them when they walked them in the rain.

Then I moved to the country and almost immediately, by command of my children, I acquired Rufus. It came about through my reading of a classified ad in the local paper, an ad that was somewhat confusing in its terminology. After studying it for quite a while I concluded that a man named Paul Ganz was giving away cocker spaniels. He lived over in Yorktown, on Baptist Church Road, and when I telephoned him and asked him if it was true, he said it certainly was not true. What the ad meant was that he had some girl dogs that he wanted to stash around at different homes, and they wouldn't really belong to the people who kept them, and occasionally Mr. Ganz would come around with boy dogs, and then something would happen that I never did quite understand, and that's all there was to it, except that there was some mention of puppies. This didn't sound good to me—I said I just wanted to buy a dog, not operate a house of ill fame. So Mr. Ganz drove over one evening, walked into the living room, reached into his coat pocket and pulled out a little black ball and set it on the floor and it promptly peed on the carpet.

A few days later Mr. Ganz sent me a certificate of pedigree—a thing I didn't even have for myself. I didn't like the looks of that pedigree. The dogs involved in the production of Rufus all seemed to be close relatives—first cousins and uncles and aunts and brothers and sisters—and the more I studied the thing the more I thought that I might have an idiot dog on my hands. Rufus was a My Own Brucie cocker. Of his eight great-grandparents, two were My Own Brucie—the same fellow both times—and one was My Own Miss Brucie, and one was Blackstone Brucie (a dog lawyer?) and one was My Own Old Lace, and one was My Own Clear Doubt. Kinfolks. Close-knit. Clannish. Carrying on under the same roof. Then one of the grandfathers named Pooh-Bah of Angelfear romanced My Own Clear Doubt and to this union was born Rustum of Angelfear and Rustum of Angelfear fell in love with Rebel Beauty of Angelfear (could they have been brother and sister?) and they begat Rufus and Rufus peed on the carpet. His real name was Black Rebel of Mount Kisco but I don't think he ever knew it. He was named Rufus after my friend Rufus Blair of Hollywood. Rufus Blair's daughter, Sandra, when she was about twelve, developed a deep resentment over my having named a dog for her father. She got back at me. One day she came home with an ancient tomcat, and announced to the family that its name was H. Alley Cat.

Any dog that has My Own Brucie for a great-grandfather, twice over, has something to be genuinely proud about, but I'm sure Rufus never gave the matter any thought. He was as common as dirt. He didn't act superior, was opposed to bathing and ate sticks. It took a long time to get him housebroken. Bluebloods are harder to train in that respect than ordinary dogs; whether this also applies to people is a thing I wouldn't know. After we did get him housebroken it turned out that he was broken to only one house. Whenever he got into a house other than his own, the first thing he looked for was the piano. He seemed to have some prejudice against pianos, or perhaps against music generally. If he couldn't find a piano, he'd use people. One evening when he was still a puppy we had company in, and among the guests was a lady of considerable dignity and poise. She was standing by the fireplace with a cocktail in her hand, gassing about Henry James, when her left foot began to feel warmish. She took a sip of her drink and then glanced down at her foot and Rufus was there, just finishing up a great job of work. He had filled her shoe, but there was a saving circumstance. She had on open-toed slippers, and it all ran down and out through the vent in the front. This is the only time I ever saw an application of the practical value of open-toed shoes.

(I wrote a few things about Rufus once in a book, including the incident of the open-toed shoe. Maureen McKernan told me later that there was an eighty-year-old priest down-country who, about once every two or three months, would call his assistant and say, "Get the book and read me the part about Rufus and the shoe again." He expressed the wish to meet Rufus before he died, but unhappily I didn't know about it so it never came to pass.)

I must mention that at the same time we got Rufus we acquired two cats and he grew up with them and for a long time I'm sure he believed himself to be a cat. He acquired certain cat hab-its, the most noteworthy of which was the expert use of his paws. He boxed and slapped with his paws, the way a cat does, and showed a certain dexterity in handling objects with his paws. And he did more licking of his pelt, cat fashion, than any other dog of my acquaintance.

He knew no tricks. He jumped through no hoops. We never tried to get him to heel by saying "heel" to him. That would only have bewildered him because we used the word in another connection at our house. He had an extensive vocabulary, insofar as understanding words was concerned, and we sometimes had to spell out things that we didn't want him to hear. Like most dogs he was daffy about riding in automobiles, and knew the word "car" and when he heard it, he'd get so excited he'd almost swoon. Consequently it was necessary for us sometimes to refer to the C-A-R in his presence. It will not be generally believed, but I take oath that eventually he learned to understand the word when it was spelled out.

I did things for him that I shouldn't have done. I often fed him things that were forbidden. I blush to confess that on several occasions I sprinkled Accent on his horsemeat to make it taste better. My attitude toward him was much the same as that of an old man I knew when I was a boy—Old Man Carter. He lived alone with a venerable hound named Jeff and the two of them were inseparable. On Saturday nights Old Man Carter would get loaded on home brew and then he'd take to grieving over the plight of his dog in *merely being a dog*. He'd get to weeping, beerily, and talking to Jeff, and he'd wail, "You're nothin' but a dog—jist a dog—you won't never be nothin' else but a dog—I'd do somethin' about it if I could, but I cain't—Oh God I woosht I could do somethin' about it!"

As I have mentioned, I regarded myself as a dog-hater before Rufus came into my life. And then one evening I realized to the full just how drastically I had changed. We were playing cards in the living room and Rufus was lying at my feet. At the conclusion of the game I stood up and lifted the chair away from the table. It came down on Rufus's paw and being a heavy chair, hurt him. He let out a yell, jumped about three feet across the carpet, and then began crying, looking at me as if I were the most unprincipled villain on earth.

I confess that I went a little out of my head, and got panicky. I was *so* distraught, *so* upset about it, *so* sorry. I hadn't done it on purpose. And the feeling that took possession of me was a desperate desire to let him know, somehow, that it was an accident, that I loved him, that I would never be capable of hurting him deliberately. I just *had* to get it across to him . . .

So I whipped the chair.

Another dog? Certainly not. What would I want with a dog? Rufus was not a dog. He was Rufus.

Waiting for the Countess *by Sir Edwin Landseer*

Dog-Fighting and Baiting Sports

by PHIL DRABBLE

FOR centuries the men who frequented bull rings and bear pits had enjoyed watching two dogs fight, but it was only with the abolition of bull baiting that dogs were bred and trained specifically for the sport.

It had been found that bulldogs were the only dogs which possessed the requisite courage for the dog-pit but that they lacked the necessary agility. Various bulldog crosses were tried, mainly with terriers, until eventually a specific breed of bull terriers was produced which was fast, strong and utterly game.

From that time dog-fighting increased in popularity. It was spectacular and as searching a test of gameness and capacity to give and take punishment as ever a bull bait was. There was little initial interference from the law, since it was possible to fight two dogs in any hollow or shed without attracting much attention, for fighting dogs fight silently. They were easy to get away afterwards, as they could aways be carried in a sack if their condition was likely to draw suspicion. And dog-fighting had the advantage over bull- or bear-baiting in that at least both animals wanted to fight instead of the victim having to be fastened with a rope or chain with no chance of escape.

Early fighting dogs were of all sorts of shapes, sizes and colors since their breeding was very promiscuous. By about 1860 they more or less fell into one of two groups, from one of which the English bull terrier was developed and from the other the Staffordshire bull terrier. Both breeds were initially very game, since nobody would keep a bull terrier which was not, but men soon bred the English variety for show, and looks were "improved" at the expense of courage. The Staffordshire bull terrier continued to be bred for the pit and, though not very standardized even yet (despite being shown for more than ten years) there is no living breed so game.

There is nothing very complicated in the rules of dog-fighting. The important thing is not so much to kill the other dog as to be game enough to try.

In days when the sport was still legal and at the height of its popularity, between 1820 and 1830, dog-fights were a regular part of the sport at such famous centers of attraction to "the fancy" as the Westminster Pit. The arena here was used indiscriminately for dog-fights, rat-killing contests, cock fights and various freak contests between dog and racoon or even monkey.

The pit itself was roughly twelve to eighteen feet across, with a boarded surround about three feet high, over which the spectators could watch. Each dog was handled by his second and, after the preliminary formalities concerning the stakes had been completed, each dog was weighed in the pit. It is common for owners of bull terriers

137

which develop a taste for fighting to boast that their dogs will "kill anything" and that this dog or that "killed an Alsatian" (or something equally big) "in ten minutes." They would alter their tune if they met a *real* fighting terrier. So much does sheer weight count that matches were rarely made at more than a maximum excess of one pound over the stipulated weight. If a match were made to be fought at "thirty-eight pounds give or take a pound," a dog coming to the pit so much as a few ounces over thirty-nine pounds would be disqualified and forfeit the stakes. And two good dogs would sometimes take as much as two hours to decide which was the better and rarely less than twenty-five or thirty minutes. However good a dog was known to be, nobody but a fool would match him against anything but a cur outside his weight class. And the men who kept fighting terriers considered all breeds to be curs which were not game in the pit.

There was often a good deal of trickery, of the lowest sort, employed to ensure a particular dog winning. He would be rubbed over with acid or pickle or pepper or anything to discourage his opponent from biting him. To avoid this a common butt of water was provided from which both dogs had to be washed, or sometimes milk was used to "kill" the acid. As an additional precaution, each setter was allowed to "taste" (or lick) his opponent's dog both before and after fighting to satisfy himself that nothing pernicious had been used.

When the preliminaries had been completed a coin was tossed to decide which dog should "scratch" first.* They were taken to opposite corners of the pit where each second held his dog between his knees so that the other dog got a fair unobstructed view of his opponent's head. On a word from the referee, the dog which had to "scratch" first was liberated and had to go across the pit to attack his opponent. A line was drawn cross the center of the pit, which was known as the scratch, and the opposing dog

*Alternatively it was customary in some parts to commence by loosing both dogs simultaneously. The setters could not leave the pit until they commenced fighting, and the first to "fault" had to scratch next time when the battle continued as described above.

could not be loosed until the attacker had crossed this line. When he had crossed the scratch the other setter could loose his dog whenever he liked and it was judgment here that won or lost many battles.

If a setter thought his opponent was not "fast" (or aggressive) he might risk holding his dog quite still and, if the other dog did not begin to fight him, he automatically lost the battle. But if his judgement had been wrong and the other dog did fight at once, the dog which had been held still, until his opponent caught hold of him where he wanted to, was at an obvious disadvantage. If, on the other hand, the setter thought his opponent was pretty fast, his obvious tactics were to loose his dog the moment the other dog crossed the scratch so that they could meet on equal terms. Sometimes a setter opposed to a fast dog would hold his till the last moment and slip him to one side, so that the other dog rushed harmlessly by. He then loosed him, in the hope that he could get a hold before his adversary had recovered his balance. This was an obvious case of "not showing his dog's head fair to scratch" and should have been penalized by the referee.

When both dogs commenced to fight, and not before, the setters could leave the pit and though they could encourage their own dogs they were forbidden to speak to their opponent's dog. Neither dog could be touched again until both stopped fighting, which would eventually happen when they were short of wind or otherwise exhausted. When this happened either setter would pick up his dog. If the opposing dog showed fight he was obliged to put it down again and allow them to continue. If he could get him away unmolested he could take him to his corner and the round had expired. One minute was allowed for sponging down and making ready for the next round, and the referee gave warning after fifty seconds so that both should be ready when the minute was up.

This time the dog who scratched first was held while his opponent came to the scratch and the battle went on again for no set time but until both dogs "faulted" again. Sometimes these rounds lasted for twenty minutes or more. Towards the end of a battle, when both dogs were becoming weak or short of breath, there might only be a few minutes between scratches. A battle of an hour or more might have twenty scratches, or one dog might be killed in the first scratch. It was very like the old prize ring rules where men did not fight for a stipulated time but until one fell to the ground.

The battle was lost by the first dog to fail to come to scratch in his turn. It was not necessarily the dog which killed the other who won but the dog which proved most game. If a dog was killed in the pit the other had to stay at him for ten minutes at least and he could still not be handled by his setter till he faulted. Then he was taken to his corner. If it was the dead dog's turn to scratch the battle was automatically lost. If it was the live dog's turn and he did not scratch, he lost the battle although he had killed his opponent. Dog-fighting has become illegal since the days of the Westminster Pit and by the middle of last century it had to be carried on surreptitiously. It was very popular in London until the beginning of this century and a little has been carried on in the Midlands at intervals since then. Police interference has increased until all organized dog-fighting in this country has now been stamped out, but game terriers are still bred and exported to America where the sport is still perfectly legal in some states.

It is natural that a sport demanding such gameness should produce some remarkable dogs. I saw a dog only last year which refused to mate a bitch which was dead-hot in season. Every time he was loosed he went straight for her throat and we had to choke him off eight times before he eventually mated her and he even tried to worry her when he was knotted. No damage was done as it happened, since she was wearing her broad leather collar. Puppies will fight to kill at three months and bitches are as keen as dogs. Yet some strains are remarkably friendly to other dogs and will put up with unusual insults before being goaded into fighting. When once they get a taste for it, they would rather fight than do anything in the world.

If sheer love of fighting is the prime necessity of the successful fighting dog, correct physique and complete physical fitness are almost equally important. A dog fights with his mouth, and the only places he can sweat are through his tongue and the pores of his feet. And no dog can do much damage with his tongue lolling out.

The first considerations in getting a dog fighting fit are therefore his wind and the removal of all surplus fat. He must be given constant hard exercise to get him muscled up and in dead-hard condition, this can be best achieved by giving small quantities of highly nutritious food with an absence of starchy food during training. The jelly from cows' feet and an adequate supply of fresh green food forms a good basis. Plenty of hard walking on a lead with a wide collar so that he can lay himself down and pull helps to strengthen his back and loin muscles. An old motor tire or other piece of rubber hung up so that he can jump up, catch hold and shake himself about on it is simply vital. The damage a fighting dog does is not so much by the sheer force of his bite as by shaking when he has got hold. And his neck and back muscles are essential for this. Plenty of running and jumping for a ball that bounces well strengthens all the muscles he uses in turning and twisting, and produces the required agility.

When he is thoroughly fit, the fighting dog is the very personification of energy. His coat glistens until it seems to exude good health. His eye is bright and there is a rippling mass of muscle from his cheeks, and down his neck and shoulders to his loins. He dances like a boxer in the ring and once he has tried fighting he will attack anything that moves, from a mouse to a mule. Although there is no definite type of fighting dog, the breed which was developed for this specific purpose was the Staffordshire bull terrier. Many successful dogs were shipped to America, where they became known as "pit bull terriers" and American periodicals devoted to dog-fighting and cockfighting regularly give round-by-round commentaries of the battles their dogs have, at what they call "pit bull terrier conventions."

Despite the illegality of the sport in this country it has always been carried on spasmodically to a small extent. Periodically the press write of "orgies" of dog-fighting which are alleged to have been carried on for fabulous stakes, usually behind locked doors in the presence of beautiful women gambling away their fortunes or their honor on the gory result of some battle. In point of fact the reports are usually an elaboration woven round scraps of conversation overheard through the fumes of some bar-parlor.

The battle which may or may not have been described will have taken place in some cellar or pigsty or barn in the presence of from three to five men, all of whom are intimately known to each other. They never fight in the same place twice. They rarely even keep the dogs they fight, usually collecting them for the occasion from the men who trained them and who will be busily engaged in securing a watertight alibi elsewhere. And the whole proceedings will be notable more for their sordidness than glamor. Nobody but the people concerned know when or where the next "job" is coming off and the sum total of battles fought is very small, so that chances of detection are negligible.

The dogs themselves take to fighting like a spaniel to the gun and their absolute craziness to get at each other has to be seen to be believed. The men who watch them are of an equally unusual type. That they have little imagination goes without saying. But I find it surprising what a low percentage appear to have taken any purely sadistic delight. They almost worship the quality of aggressive gameness and they are usually as willing to fight each other as to watch their dogs.

> Experienced men, inured to city ways,
> Need not the calendar to count their days.
> When through the town, with slow and solemn
>   air,
> Led by the nostrils, walks the muzzled bear,
> Behind him moves, majestically dull,
> The pride of Hockley Hole, the surly bull.
> Learn hence the periods of the week to name—
> Mondays and Thursdays are the days of game.
> Gray, Trivia

No sport which has ever been carried out in England can have been more cruel than bull-baiting. No sport can have been more popular with the masses. No dogs gamer than the bulldogs which were developed for no other purpose and which became synonymous with English courage and determination because of the feats they performed.

The remarkable thing is that bull-baiting did not begin as a sport at all. It was once illegal to slaughter a bull unless it had first been baited with dogs. The reason for this was twofold. Firstly it was considered that flesh which had died after prolonged exertion was more tender than if the end had been sudden—and a similar belief still exists which maintains, for instance, that a coursed hare is more tender than one which has been shot. I shouldn't wonder if there wasn't something in it. Secondly, if the whole community had had the chance to attend a publicly announced bull-bait, the local butchers would have difficulty in foisting the carcass off at prime beef prices.

There is no shadow of doubt that the populace soon developed a hearty appetite for this baiting of bulls, if their appreciation of the resulting meat was less keen. At first the dogs which were used were the fierce animals the butchers used to drive their cattle and hold them if necessary. The English "bandogges" were also favorites for the sport because of their phenomenal strength and fierceness. They were direct descendants of the great dogs of war for which the Romans developed such respect when they invaded our islands that they took them back to fight various wild animals in the arena in Rome. These bandogs were still being used for baiting bulls in the time of Queen Elizabeth, whose tastes in sport were anything but spinsterish by our standards. It is recorded that she and her unfortunate sister Mary were "well pleased" with extremely gory spectacles including bull-baiting, and there is an excellent account of a most catholic baiting of all sorts of animals which was staged for Elizabeth's benefit at Kenilworth.

It was not very long, however, before tastes began to alter. In 1620 James I refused to license houses for bull-baiting, which was also forbidden on Sundays. This was not so much because bull-baiting was considered cruel, but as a sop to the prevailing zeal to make the sabbath as austere and unpleasant for the masses as possible. Work would presumably seem less unpleasant on Monday by comparison. Along with other baiting sports, bull-baiting underwent various vicissitudes from this time on. Cromwell forbade them altogether because, like most dictators, he was rightly afraid of anything which gave men the excuse to gather together in groups. But the Restoration saw a great revival and the diarist Evelyn says that on June 16, 1670 he went to the Bear Garden "where was cockfighting with dog-fighting, Bear-and-Bull-baiting, it being a famous day for butcherly sports." The sports which these men of all classes enjoyed are simply unbelievable. In 1710 the Bear Gardens at Hockley-in-the-Hole did not only provide customers with the spectacles of bull- and bear-baiting but a mad ass was baited, a bull was loosed with fireworks all over him and a dog was drawn up with fireworks. That such amusements were attractive to normal members of the public only a couple of hundred years ago seems hardly possible.

Nevertheless, bull- and bear-baiting were, in fact, so widely popular that a very specialized type of dog was bred for the purpose. The object in bull-baiting was to grip the bull in a tender enough part of the face to hold him still or throw him. Tremendous power of jaw was necessary for this and nostrils set far enough back to allow normal breathing without letting go.

Do not imagine that the monstrosities wheezing at modern dog shows in the classes for bulldogs are like the animals which were used for baiting bulls. Instead of being disproportionately squat and broad, like some great toad, the bulldogs which were used in the ring were finely proportioned dogs, little heavier in build than a modern Staffordshire bull terrier, and taller for their size. Weight ranged from about thirty-three pounds to fifty pounds and they might be any color though brindle, red and pied dogs were commonest.

By the beginning of the nineteenth century bull-baiting had been developed into a highly intoxicating sport which was the indispensable stimulant of the masses on every holiday or wake. Men earned their livings by taking a "game bull"

from one jollification to the next. In every town was a "bull ring" or "bull stake" and the "bullots," or men who owned the bulls, would march their animal round the town, suitably attended by trumpeters and criers to advertise the sport. The bull was gaily bedecked with ribbons and favors, and some of the bullots were born showmen. Jack Willets, for instance, of Walsall, went to Spain to learn all he could of foreign customs and when he returned he paraded in costume, complete with a sword which he used impartially to finish off the bull, to discourage enthusiasts from approaching too close or to sever the piece of living bull a dog had pinned, to save himself the trouble of choking him off.

When all was ready the bull was tethered to the stake by a rope about fifteen yards long attached to the base of his horns. The owner of each dog had to pay a fee of sixpence to five shillings a run at the bull and the first dog was slipped. He would not rush madly at the quarry but creep on his belly, stealthily, as close as possible. If the bull was a "green" bull, which had never been baited before, he would bellow and lower his head towards the dog but do little else, for he didn't know what he'd got coming to him. If, on the other hand, he was a "game" bull, which had been baited before and proved his mettle in the ring, he would not get at the extremity of his rope but would leave himself enough slack to charge when necessary. He would lower his head and keep his forelegs close to prevent the dog slipping between them and getting hold. The aim of the dog would be to creep along and wait for an opening, when he would dart in and "pin" the bull by laying hold of his tongue, eyepiece, lip or nose. The bull would not try to impale him but slip his horn under his belly and toss him high enough into the air to suffer damage when he fell. The dog's owner was well aware of this and he would be ready to try and break his fall by catching him in his apron or deftly slide a light pole under him, in mid-air, down which he could slide in comparative immunity. If the bull was successful and the dog not much hurt he was let go again since he was expected to be game enough to go back so long as he had still the strength to crawl. That all the dogs were not game to go back is apparent from a contemporary account of a bait at Clerkenwell which says,

Some stretched out in field lie dead; and some,
Dragging their entrails, run howling home.

But if the dog was successful and pinned the bull, he would hang grimly on whilst the bull lashed him about, in a paroxysm of pain, trying to shake him off. Sometimes the flesh the dog was gripping was torn away so that the bulldog was slung away still clenching a fragment of his quarry. Sometimes the agony of the bull forced him to surrender and lie still while his tormentors prized the dog's jaws apart with staves, for in no other way could he be induced to loose. Sometimes, the frantic struggle of the tortured bull snapped his rope and he charged the crowd. A roar would go up for "A lane, a lane" and men would trample each other in their frenzy to avoid the danger into which they had so glibly urged their dogs. Sometimes all went well, as when a bull, which had a horn shattered with a club, broke loose and charged the crowd at Bilston Wake in 1743. Jack Willets, the Walsall bullot who had been to Spain, was the Master of Ceremonies, and the incident is described in the doggerel of the time:

"A lane, a lane" was all the cry
As fast they ran away,
Leaving Jack Willets there to die
Or live as best he may.

On this occasion there was no loss of human life because Jack put into practice the lessons he had learned in Spain and struck the bull dead with his sword. But the spectators did not always escape so lightly, and another poem, supposed to be a description of what was seen by the weathercock on Willenhall church, retails how the bull broke loose and tossed one of his torturers high in the air, continuing:

As he falls to the ground, with sullen sound,
Shrieks, groans and cries are heard around.

Then gathered they round, with moisten'd eye,
Silently watching their comrade die.

The depraved reverence for gameness occasionally went even further than setting bulldogs onto bulls, and a man at Toll End, near Tipton, once, very rashly, matched himself to pin a bull. Possessing none of the requisite qualities of the bulldog but gameness, he was instantly gored through the neck and killed on the spot.

By the late 1820s public opinion was beginning to harden against such bestiality and, oddly enough, the great epidemic of cholera in 1832 which swept the Bilston district was indirectly responsible for finally inflaming the indignation which gave it its death blow. Despite the terrible misery caused by this epidemic, which wiped out whole families, unruly mobs persisted in roaming through areas prostrated by grief, even jostling the dead on their way to burial. This was too much. The outcry became overwhelming, and the last bull-bait took place about 1838.

Bulls were by no means the only animals to be tormented in an endeavor to prove the gameness of dogs which were bred for sport. Perhaps the second favorite quarry were bears, which were led from town to town by "bearwards," who corresponded to the bullots of the bull ring. But the bears did not provide such good sport as the bulls. For one thing too much manipulation was necessary to prevent the dog from being killed. Claws had to be blunted and the bear had to be attached by a collar to a rope passed through a ring placed in the wall about six feet from the ground. When the dog came to grips, the bear lay on him and would quickly "hug" him to death if he were not hauled on to his hind legs by the rope through the ring on the wall. Although this method was practiced at such establishments as the famous Westminster Pit, the old bearpits used to have scaffolding on which the spectators could climb to watch the fun in safety from on high. Like the bulls taken round by bullots, these poor bears were usually a mass of festering fly-blown sores which had resulted from the lacerations of earlier "baits." They were led by a chain and ring in the nose and their muzzles were scarred or raw from the chafing of their chains. The sport they gave was neither so spectacular for the spectators nor so searching for the dogs as was bull-baiting and by about 1750 the popularity had waned practically to extinction.

Men thought so highly of the gameness of their dogs that they stopped at no barbarity to prove it. It was by no means unknown to wager that a bulldog would allow his legs to be amputated without loosing his hold and even that he would run at the bull on his stumps. Perhaps the most fantastic wager of all was when six dogs were matched against a lion at Warwick in 1825. The lion was owned by Mr. Wombwell, who had a collection of wild beasts. According to the articles of the match, three dogs could be slipped at once and any turning tail was to be deemed beaten and not allowed a second run. None of the second trio was to be allowed in until twenty minutes after the first bout concluded.

A stage was set in a factory yard at Warwick to which admission was charged varying from half a sovereign to three sovereigns. This high price, combined with the fact that the whole affair was generally regarded as a hoax, kept the number of spectators down to six or seven hundred.

At seven o'clock on Tuesday evening, July 26, the contest began. Two of the first three dogs were cross bulldog and mastiff, weighing fifty to sixty pounds, while the third, Turk, was a pure bulldog of thirty-six pounds. One of the mongrels lasted but a very short time, and the second did not take an undue hiding before deeming discretion the better part of valor. Turk, the little bulldog, stayed at it eleven minutes, making Nero, the lion, turn tail before his owner drew him out of the cage. The second trio of dogs were all dead game and they pinned him by the nose and held him still on the floor until Mr. Wombwell admitted defeat.

Nero, although a large five-year-old lion, had been caged and handled all his life and showed no gameness and surprisingly little desire even to defend himself.

A second match was made against a lion called Wallace which proved a very different proposition and very quickly disposed of three pairs of extremely game dogs, "watched," it is said, "by several well-dressed females" from the upper apartments of the factory.

There are countless other instances recorded of the supreme, and often useless, gallantry of these English bulldogs. Generations of careful selection had produced such courage that literally nothing which moved could daunt them. Some of the feats which they were asked to perform were barbaric in their callousness. If the example of their courage did something towards creating the doggedness for which our nation is famed, they did not die, perhaps, in vain.

I have always been extremely fond of badgers. They are noctural by nature and so unobtrusive that they have created about themselves a false impression of rarity. The fact is that they are far commoner than is believed, even by most countrymen, and they are to be found by the observant in most country which offers suitable harborage.

In localities where it is discovered that they abound, you will usually also find, sooner or later, a Badger Club. And these Badger Clubs are very remarkable institutions. They are begun in a spate of enthusiasm, they flourish for a time and increase with incredible vigor—and die as suddenly as they began. Almost before they have been decently interred a fresh one is started in the same area.

The trouble with badger digging is not the exertion necessary to tunnel down to old "Brock" but the exertion necessary to fill up the holes again. The most casual of followers and the laziest of members is always willing to help with the business of "bagging" poor Brock. But, the moment the fun is over, it is miraculous how silently folk fade away, how many must get home by lighting-up time, how many must call for their wives from some friends. Only the hard core of enthusiasts are left to refill the holes, to level off the ground and to perform all the chores which have none of the glamor of the chase. This palls even with the keenest of badger men who, being as incurably optimistic as all enthusiasts, are perpetually starting a new club in which all the members shall be as keen as themselves.

The physical exertions necessary to bring a badger successfully to bag should not be underestimated. Badgers live in a sett, or extensive warren, often enlarged from the workings of foxes or rabbits. And they frequently choose a locality where they can tunnel directly into the side of a hill. They are fascinating animals about which less is known than most of our fauna. It is known that they are fastidious in their habits to the extent of bringing their bedding to the mouth of their holes for a daily airing; that they use clearly defined latrines at a distance from the sett; that they will often change their quarters rather than endure the odorous discomfort of sharing with foxes. It is beginning to be more widely appreciated that they are unjustly blamed for many of the crimes of foxes, too. In a word, badgers are comparatively harmless creatures of very unusual interest and it seems unnecessary to kill them.

No well-run Badger Club does kill them nowadays. In areas where they are considered to be too thick on the ground or harmful to game preservation, they are "bagged" when caught, and turned down in other localities where landowners and naturalists will welcome their presence.

The chief requisites for badger-digging are willing and capable diggers and game terriers. These need to be hardbitten little dogs, low enough to stand up in a nine-inch diameter hole, and they should not weigh more than fifteen to eighteen pounds, and even lighter are often all right. Their purpose is to seek out the badger and bark at him incessantly from the minimum safe distance. If they go in and "mix it" they won't last long, and if they are too big they will be too cramped to move about in the hole rapidly enough to avoid punishment if the badger charges them.

Several terriers are necessary, but all but one should be securely chained out of sight of operations. If they are fastened by anything but a chain they will chew through it; and if they can see what is going on they will yap their heads off to join the fray. The terrier which is to be used

first has his collar removed to prevent his getting hung up on a root, and is turned in to one of the holes. He will wander about below ground until he comes on a badger when he will immediately "speak" and his approximate locality can be determined by listening to the sound. If the badger does not happen to be in a blind hole he will retreat to one where he will turn at bay and face the terrier. This is realized when the sounds coming from below come steadily from the same place for some time, and digging can begin.

The simplest thing to do is to dig straight in from the nearest hole to the sound until a fork is reached, when it can be decided along which branch to dig by listening to the direction from which the terrier is "speaking." Sometimes it is possible to avoid a lot of laborious following of holes by taking bearings on the position of the terrier from several directions and sinking a hole from above. A steel rod thrust into the ground will transmit sound from below surprisingly clearly, and another aid to location is the rabbiter's simple dodge of lying with ear to ground in various spots until the noise seems nearest. When the hole goes straight into the side of a hill there just aren't any short cuts. It is best to tunnel straight in, the tunnel being large enough to allow earth to be removed in baskets and the roof shored up if necessary. When roots and rocks are encountered it will test the enthusiasm of the keenest, but when once the terrier is in, nothing on earth must stop operations to reach him.

Besides these natural hazards, everything may not go well with the terriers. The original dog may get exhausted or too hot and come up for a breather, in which case it is advisable to catch him and turn a fresh one in. And during the interval the badger may have moved to another part of the sett, or the fresh dog may find a new badger, so that all the digging to the first dog will have been in vain and it will be necessary to start all over again. Sometimes a terrier will be mute, so that it is not possible even to guess where he or the badger is, and such a dog is useless and should be discarded. Occasionally a terrier is fainthearted and if the badger discovers this he will turn round and proceed to dig himself farther in much faster than the mere men with spades can come at him from above. A good dog will sail right in and bite him just where it hurts the most, so that he is forced to face the right way and is prevented from boring deeper. Should the badger charge, the terrier must retreat only until the charge is spent, when the quarry will return to the end of the hole followed by the terrier screaming his song of hate. Perhaps worst of all, two dogs will get into the sett at the same time, and then the fun is apt to start. At best they will get in each other's way so that, if the badger charges, the nearest can't avoid trouble. But they are quite likely to be jealous and resent each other's presence to the extent of a pitched battle between themselves.

If all goes well the terrier will be sighted after anything up to eight hours' digging. During this time a basket is kept over the mouth of the hole so that the air can never be completely cut off by subsidence for more than a minute or so. A little more digging and the terrier's job is done and he can be hauled out and there, blinking into the light at the blind end of his hole, is Brock himself. Sometimes this blind end is just the same diameter as the rest of the burrow and sometimes it is a compartment about the size of a large oven, with a shelf over the entrance. Brock lies on this shelf and bites down into anything foolish enough to thrust itself in (I have known rats adopt exactly similar tactics with ferrets.)

The normal way of removing the quarry is with a large pair of steel tongs similar to those used by blacksmiths. This has always seemed an unromantic end to a strenuous day's sport and something of an anticlimax. Some people who own bull terriers which they consider can kill anything on four legs, are occasionally persuaded to "draw" the badger with their dog. Provided the badger is still in his own chosen hole this is quite legal and no prosecution for baiting can be successful. But, if the badger is transferred to another hole or put on top of the ground to see if the bull terrier will have a go, then that is technically baiting and therefore illegal. In any case the idea is to see if the dog will sail right in, grip the badger and drag him forth.

A good dog will do this and a wise owner will break him off as soon as possible.

I have heard lots of owners offer bets that their dog will kill a badger in a stipulated time. I have even heard men with ordinary terriers, as opposed to bull terriers, claim that their dogs would kill a badger. But I have never met anyone who has seen it done. A badger can bite at least as hard as any dog and about twice as fast. As his skin is exceedingly tough he can stand much more from a dog than a dog could stand. So, if it is full grown, you are safe in backing the badger. Although the bull terrier won't kill old Brock, it is quite on the cards that he will draw him, and if he does he is a good dog.

But the right and proper end to a badger dig, in my humble opinion, is for the badger to be "tailed." Now this tailing is performed by a member of the hunt, and anyone who can tail a badger has as much of my respect as a dog who can draw one. The idea is to thrust in an arm, grab the badger by the tail, draw him out and hold him up so that his snapping jaws snap nothing but air. It is a case of the quickness of the hand deceiving the badger, and if it is successfully accomplished it makes badger digging a very humane sport, for nobody is hurt. The terriers have sat just out of range yodeling directions to the diggers above; and when the badger has been reached he has been painlessly extracted. To make the day quite perfect he should be released either in his own country or in an area where more badgers are wanted. At worst he should be painlessly killed, although I see no reason for this, since he is such an attractive animal and comparatively harmless.

An amusing alternative, though far less common, method of catching badgers is to hunt them. Since they are by nature nocturnal and do not often lie up above ground far from their setts by day, this hunting has to take place by night. Which adds all sorts of possibilities. Almost any sort of dogs will do to hunt him if they have good noses. A few old foxhounds will do, or even terriers entered to badger. Someone is deputed to sit very quietly outside the sett on a moonlit night until he sees Brock sally forth on his foraging expedition. When it is considered that he has had time to get out of earshot the watcher creeps to the sett and does a little quick "earth stopping" to prevent his returning. A well-pegged sack or so over chosen holes will act as sort of "purse-nets" in reverse. The next thing to do is to inform the members of the hunt, who are probably whiling away the time at the nearest pub, and as soon as they can be dragged away they will bring their "hounds" and lay them on the line by which Brock has left his sett. The idea is that the hounds hunt the line and try to catch up with their quarry before he can get back home, which he will begin to do as soon as he hears the disturbance. If the "hounds" catch up with him in the open they will not be able to kill him as they would a fox because he is a very much tougher customer. He will amble on, keeping them at a respectful distance, unless they include something really tough which can bring him to a standstill until the "field" arrives. But the chances are, if he is caught up before he gets home, that he will be hustled into one of the sacks.

Despite this possibility, the odds are heavily in favor of the badger. Hounds may strike the line of fox or hare and decide that is more attractive. They may even "riot" after rabbit. And they are not easy to control by moonlight. Neither are the followers by any means certain to complete the course. Ditches are deceptively seductive; barbed wire is amorously clinging; the alcoholic fumes, imbibed while waiting for Brock to come out, are not very effective aids to locomotion; even the sounds of the hunt floating on the still night air do not always come from the expected direction. The quarry, in fact, has an unusually sporting chance.

In days gone by, nobody worried very much about the quarry having any chance at all. And the badger used for badger-baiting could not be described as quarry at all. He was merely a victim. The baiting usually took place in one of the establishments kept for all sorts of baiting sports, and the idea was to test the gameness of the various dogs brought for the purpose. By far the most successful breed was bull terriers. The badger was allowed to take refuge in an artificial earth rather like a deep, narrow barrel laid on its side. The dog was let go and he dived into the barrel; if he was game he caught hold of the badger and tried to draw him out into the open. Sometimes he was helped by his handler who "tailed" him, or caught hold of him by the root of his tail and steadily drew him out when he had got a grip, so that he, in turn, brought the badger with him. Sometimes this was not allowed and the dog was expected to perform the whole job himself. I have before me a handbill advertising that a very famous rat-killing bitch, The Kentish Bitch, would "draw the badger without tailing at the Westminster Pit on Tuesday August 23rd, 1825." If the badger was fit and well this must have been a very grueling contest for both animals. As the badger became mauled after frequent baitings, and despondent from pining for the privacy and wildness of his native land, he frequently became easier to draw. Whether this was from progressive weakness or because he found his agonies ended upon emergence is impossible to say. I like to think that his intelligence was greater than some of the patrons who bet against the dogs.

Of all the baiting sports which have now been made illegal, I only regret the passing of rat-pits. For one thing, I hate rats and anyhow their end was extremely sudden. For another I love to see a good dog kill rats and I have caught them for a hobby since I was a lad.

My dogs have always worked with ferrets and would have been of very little use in the rat-pit, which required a rather specialized technique. And some of the results were astounding. The main thing was to have a dog which could kill rats more quickly than his rivals. As proof of the pudding, a specified number of rats would be loosed in the rat-pit. This was the same pit which was used for dog-fighting, cockfighting, matches between dogs and monkeys and similar forms of entertainment. It could be either round or square and was boarded to a height of two or three feet. If it was a square pit, bits of metal had to be nailed at the top of the corners because the rats were quite capable of climbing up these if not prevented.

A match would be made between two or more dogs to decide which was the more efficient at vermin destruction. Sometimes the match would be to decide which dog could kill the most rats in a specified time and sometimes which could kill a specified number in the shortest time. This way was the most popular. When all was ready, the stakes paid up and the bets made, the rats were turned into the pit and the first dog brought along. He was held where he could see the quarry, his handler waited a favorable opportunity when the rats were placed as he wanted them, and dropped his dog into the pit. The match had now begun and the timekeeper started taking the time. If the pit was square the rats would bunch in a corner but if it was round they would form into smaller groups, one way suiting some dogs and the other way suiting the rest. The moment the dog touched the pit he started killing rats. He did not bother to pick them up and shake them but just gave each one a hard bite and left him for the next. The dog which liked the square pit would slip quietly up to the bunch in the corner and begin to pick off the nearest rats to him. Any which tried to break from the bunch were nipped as they passed and he would not have much running about to do, if he was clever, until all but a few were killed. He would work rather like a sheepdog keeping a flock bunched to be brought out singly for dipping. If the pit was round, the dog would get the rats on the move and remain more or less where he was, just picking them off as they passed. This continued until the last rat was caught, when the dog was picked up, which was noted by the timekeeper as the end of the performance for that dog.

This was where the wrangles used to start. The side which owned the dog claimed all the rats were dead and the side which had backed against the dog said some of them were still alive. The point was that a good terrier did not waste time by shaking rats. He simply snapped them and one good grab stopped the rat all right, though sometimes it only broke his back, which left a bit of kick in him though he could not crawl away. The method of deciding if he was technically "alive" was a bit rough and ready. He was

picked up and put in a chalk circle about as big as a dinner plate. Someone, who had backed against the dog and was therefore interested in proving the rat alive was given a bit of wood rather like a grocer's butter-pat. The rat's tail was then smacked sharply with the edge of this piece of wood, which must have been distinctly painful to any rats which were physically alive, whether they were technically dead or not. If they were able to wriggle out of the chalk circle, when thus "encouraged," the verdict was that the dog had not killed them. If, on the other hand, they were too far gone to be persuaded to bestir themselves they were technically dead whatever they felt about it.

What happened if they were alive depended upon the articles under which the match had been made. Sometimes it was stated that in the event of any rats remaining alive after the dog had been picked up, that dog was disqualified. At others he merely had to be put back in the pit, where he was re-timed until he had disposed of all his quarry. Occasionally it would be stipulated that the dog could only have one bite at any rat and that if he touched him after once putting him down he lost the match. I have often wondered how these rat-pit terriers would work with ferrets. I imagine that there would be complications at first, because they would not know where to stand so as to give the rats room to bolt clear of the holes, and the ferrets would be in imminent danger. Conversely, a dog used to ferrets would race into a bunch like a bull in a china shop, scatter them all over the pit so that it would take longer to catch up with them than it would take a trained dog to kill them.

That was how the rats were actually killed when a dog was put in the pit with them, and obviously a great many rats would be needed for a match since these specialist dogs could kill at a simply phenomenal rate. For instance, I have an advertisement for a match at the Westminster Pit on May 15, 1825. Billy, a very famous dog of his time, was matched to kill 100 rats against The Kentish Bitch, which was almost equally famous. On this particular occasion the official rat-catchers for the pit had failed to provide the requisite 200 adult rats so that the match had to be

The Bull and Mastiff *by Howitt*

declared "No-Go." The result with the rats available was that Billy disposed of ninety in seven and one-half minutes and The Kentish Bitch killed sixty-five in eight minutes, forty-five seconds. Which was a pretty good performance.

Another time this same Billy was matched to kill 100 rats at the Cockpit in Tufton Street in twelve minutes for twenty pounds and bets. The floor of the pit was whitened, to give him every chance, and he had stopped the last one kicking within seven minutes, thirty seconds. And so it goes on. I will not be dogmatic as to what dog got the world's record, for the contemporary accounts I have been able to trace have not been complete, but this dog Billy once killed 100 in five minutes and thirty seconds, which must have taken some beating. Certainly no dog of his day could hold a candle to him and when he was five or six years old, in June 1826, he killed his hun-

dred in eight and one-half minutes against a young dog which took twelve minutes and was still considered very good. I have been told that the greatest feat in the world was when a Liverpool dog killed 1000 rats in under three minutes over an hour, but I have no documentary proof of this and I would not like to vouch for it. In any case, I should be extremely proud to own a dog which could kill his hundred rats in any reasonably short time, for it would certainly demand plenty of stamina and guts. But rats are not easy to get in such quantities.

In addition to straight matches for which dog could kill a certain quantity of rats quickest, irrespective of the weight of the dog, it was common to have handicaps based on weight. The champion Billy, which was white but for a patched head, weighed twenty-seven pounds and had fought in the dog-pit and baited bear besides his wonderful performance in the rat-pit. As time went on, however, rats became difficult to obtain in such numbers and it became fashionable to run handicaps. These were arranged so that the heavier the dog was the more rats he had to kill. Various handicaps were set ranging from one rat being added to a dog's quota for every three pounds additional weight over his rival to a rat for every pound. This was perhaps the favorite, and it was frequent to arrange a handicap where each dog had to kill as many rats as there were pounds in his weight, the dog disposing of his quota the quickest being the winner. For instance, a ten-pound dog would only have to kill ten rats while Billy killed twenty-seven. This put rather a premium on small dogs and breeds were developed specially for this sport. The little smooth black-and-tan teriers of Manchester and the rough Yorkshire terriers were particularly good for this sport and a friend of mine owns a picture of three famous terriers ranging in weight from five and one-quarter pounds to seven pounds. That dogs so small were game enough to kill large rats at all always surprises me. That they could kill twenty in less than three minutes seems nothing short of miraculous.

Occasionally freak wagers were made. Dogs would be matched to kill a given number of cats in a covered pit. Once there was a famous monkey called Jacko Maccacco which was matched against famous fighting dogs. I have a contemporary print of him performing at the Westminster Pit and he is gripping the dog round the neck with his arms and tearing at his entrails with his feet. The most fantastic challenge of all was made by old Sam Wedgebury, a famous setter of the time who handled one of the dogs which fought the lion at Warwick. He backed his son, Young Wedgebury, a lad of under twelve, to kill rats quicker than any twenty-four pound dog. I once saw Hairy Kelly, our local rat-catcher, kill a tethered rat on a pub table by biting it, but speed was by no means the essence of his show.

Taken all in all, I regret the passing of rat-pits very much. They did not go as early as other baiting sports, party because they were less conspicuous and partly because there was no general sympathy towards rats. There is, fortunately, a passable alternative which is encouraged by the powers that be. When ricks are threshed after Christmas there are often a lot of rats in them. Persuade the farmer to allow you to surround the rick with one-inch wire-netting and take your dogs when the rick is getting low. If you catch between fifty and one hundred in an afternoon you will have had some good sport. Then go home and dream of the dogs which could kill as many in five or ten minutes.

On a Spaniel Called Beau Killing a Young Bird

by **WILLIAM COWPER**

Spaniel and Game *by A. Cooper*

A Spaniel, Beau, that fares like you,
Well-fed, and at his ease,
Should wiser be, than to pursue
Each trifle that he sees.

But you have kill'd a tiny bird,
Which flew not till to-day,
Against my orders, whom you heard
Forbidding you the prey.

Nor did you kill, that you might eat,
And ease a doggish pain,
For him, though chas'd with furious heat,
You left where he was slain.

Nor was he of the thievish sort,
Or one whom blood allures,
But innocent was all his sport,
Whom you have torn for yours.

151

My dog! what remedy remains,
Since, teach you all I can,
I see you, after all my pains,
So much resemble man!

BEAU'S REPLY

Sir! when I flew to seize the bird,
In spite of your command,
A louder voice than yours I heard
And harder to withstand:

You cried—Forbear!—but in my breast
A mightier cried—Proceed!
'Twas nature, Sir, whose strong behest
Impell'd me to the deed.

Yet much as nature I respect,
I ventur'd once to break
(As you perhaps may recollect)
Her precept, for your sake;

And when your linnet, on a day,
Passing his prison-door,
Had flutter'd all his strength away,
And panting press'd the floor,

Well knowing him a sacred thing,
Not destin'd to my tooth,
I only kiss'd his ruffled wing,
And lick'd the feathers smooth.

Let my obedience then excuse
My disobedience now,
Nor some reproof yourself refuse
From your aggriev'd Bow-wow!

If killing birds be such a crime,
(Which I can hardly see)
What think you, Sir, of killing Time
With verse address'd to me?

Laudatio Canis: A Scholar of Revival and Learning Addresses Mohammed II

by THEODORE GAZA

I am conscious at the start, Your Grace, that I am doing what is strange and out of the common, and perhaps even ludicrous, in this sense, that whereas other men cheapen and minimize the value of the gifts they send to their friends, I, on the contrary, am taking the opposite cause by exaggerating and puffing the value of my gift. Still, I am not without a precedent for this, and a plausible excuse. As to a precedent, I would refer to a man, not certainly to be met anywhere or one of a crowd, or of small estimation, but a man who has acquired all the culture of his time; I mean the emperor who conducted the war against the Christians and inflicted no small loss upon them, and whose pursuits, too, were very much like mine. And my excuse will be my belief that you will find this by-work as pleasing as my work, or may perhaps judge it to be my serious work, and regard my digression as more valuable than the work itself. For as every man fond of literature should, you enjoy beautiful things, and the intellectual pleasures more than any; and it was my consciousness of this that induced me to undertake this effort.

The gift which I am sending you is called the dog, and is in fact the most precious and valuable possession of mankind. For while other animals are each of them of use to us in virtue of one particular quality, and possess a special and distinguishing excellence, this one animal is re-sponsible for many and all kinds of benefits to us, and is adorned with the greatest and highest points of excellence. A lion excels in courage, an ox in reliability and adaptability to agriculture, the horse in intelligence and speed, the ass and the mule, as is stated by the poets, in patience and hard work; and other animals have other good points: this one animal combines the excellence of all the others without any exception. He is naturally adapted to a life in cities or in the country, suitable for war work and the pursuits of peace, and equally fitted to be of use and to be a pleasant companion. It would not be easy, as you will believe, to enumerate all the excellences and all the services to ourselves of this animal. It will be sufficient if I essay to outline a few, and then my demonstration will be reasonably adequate, and the instruction that you will derive also.

And in the first place, the hunting of quadrupeds, which is generally agreed to be a pursuit of value and one which increases the amenities of life, retains the name which it originally derived from the dog, and is literally "dog-leading." And the gods followed this pursuit, and the men of the Heroic Age; and Greeks no less than barbarians both now, and in ancient times, and in all countries. And the patroness of the sport was Artemis, the sister of Apollo, the most honorable of the goddesses in heaven. Of heroes one might add Cheiron and Cephalus, and Asclepius, and Melanus, and Nestor, and indeed so many that it would be tedious to enumerate them. And does not Homer introduce the wisest of the Greeks hunting with Autolycus, and wounded in the thigh by a boar? His words are: "And him a boar wounded with his tusk when he had gone a-hunting to Parnassus with the sons of Autolycus."

Sparta, the most warlike city of antiquity, honored this pursuit above all others; and they actually passed a law according to which a man who appeared at a banquet following the festival of Artemis without having hunted with the hounds was deemed to be guilty of an illegality and was punished. In the case of a young man the punishment was a pitcher of water poured over the head, and in the case of older men poured over the fingers of his hand: which so far as the pain endured goes, would seem to the reader slight enough; but was severe so far as the social disgrace it involved is concerned.

The attitude of the Macedonians towards the chase was similar, for the man who had wounded a boar without the use of nets was allowed as a concession to recline at dinner instead of being seated, which was considered a great honor amongst the people. The same thing holds good of the Persians, amongst whom the king was as much devoted to the chase as he was to military pursuits, leading out the young men on hunting expeditions, and taking care that they actually performed their share of the task. And it was not without reason that they acted in this way, for hunting is the very best preparatory school for soldiers; this is so because it gets a man into the habit of rising early and going to bed late, and working during the night, and of enduring heat and cold and hunger and thirst. Yes, and more important still it teaches him to run over smooth and level ground not more readily than through wild precipitous places, and to shoot and to wound, and not retreat if hit, and to put up with every kind of pain and danger and inconvenience; and the benefit one derives from such a life towards soldiering is incredible. And if you want to test by actual observation what good hunting is in war, just compare a hunting man and one who has had no experience of hunt-

ing and has never had anything to do with it, and you will at once see what an immense advantage the former has in the military field.

Or one might cite the authority of Plato. In his *Laws* he advises young men to go in for this pursuit, if they wish to become properly acquainted with their own country; but perhaps it would be more advisable to quote a passage from the text itself. He says: "I should imagine that one of the worthiest aims of public education would be to impart to every man an accurate knowledge of his own country. No doubt hunting either with dogs or in other ways is pleasant to any man and profitable to him also; but the scientific knowledge which he obtains is the real reason why a young man should pay attention to it." So much for the teaching of Plato. But by what voluntary assistance do we engage in hunting? Is it not clear that we do this by means of dogs? For, led out to the chase, they spot the animals and hunt them, or catching the trail they conduct us by means of this after the animals running themselves, while we run after as fast as we can; and they fight along with and in defense of us; and it often happens that before the huntsmen have followed up the track the hounds have torn the prey in pieces.

Enough for the help afforded us by dogs in hunting.

And without any great trouble it would be possible to prove point by point that if hunting had not been practiced, the world had been full of wild animals dealing destruction to mankind and besieging them in the cloistered safety of cities; from all such horrors, then, it is the help of dogs and hunting with dogs that has delivered us.

And what animal, again, is a better keeper than a dog, a more faithful custodian of that which one gives to be kept? And so we naturally entrust the control of flocks to them; and they lead them out to pasture, and conduct them, and look after the safety of those that are conducted, and bring back all the objects of their care safe home again: to sheep they are gentle, towards wolves suspicious, to shepherds obedient: wherefore while they are alive wolves do not attack the herds, but when they are dead they tear them to pieces. And so the wolves we are familiar with in Aesop offer treaties of peace and alliance to the flocks on the terms of having the dogs, those rough and harsh and hateful beasts handed over, being well aware that having once conquered them, it is an easy matter to subdue the other animals.

And why should I mention the well-known Capparus to you? Or rather why should I not tell the story of the guardian of the temple of Asclepius?

The story is that a burglar slipped into the sacred precincts, and was stealing the most valuable objects when the dog uttered the loudest bark it could; but as the attendants did not wake up but gave the thief an opportunity to escape, the dog gave chase to the thief, and would not leave off following him; then when daylight came the dog made up to everybody he met and kept on barking at the thief, following him up by night as well, until at last those who had been in pursuit learnt the story of the dog's exploits along the way, and so caught the thief and brought him back to Athens. And the dog followed exultingly, as though he were bringing back a trophy from war, a splendid and most gratifying object to the spectators. In return for all this the Athenians passed a resolution that the dog should be sustained at the public charge, and they gave orders to the temple servants to look after him properly.

It was with such considerations as these in his mind that Plato, the great master we have already mentioned, when he was wondering who would be the most suitable guardian for his beautiful and wonderful Republic, was not able to find a better simile than one derived from the world of dogs. For he says in the third book of the *Republic*, where he is describing the guardian: "Do you think there is much difference between a noble dog and a young nobleman so far as guarding a city is concerned? If there is, what? For just consider how quick each of them should be in perception, and quick to follow up the perceived object, yes, and strong enough to fight, if need be, after taking it, for the possession of it."

And a little later on: "You know, of course, the disposition of a well-bred dog towards those with whom he lives and is familiar he is as gentle as gentle can be, but just the opposite to strangers?"

"Oh yes, I know that much."

"Well, then," I said, "it would seem that our task is not an impossible one, and that the guardian we are trying to find could not be called 'unnatural'!"

"It seems so."

"But don't you think too, that in addition to courage, our guardian ought to have another qualification, I mean the possession of the philosophic nature?"

"Here I don't quite follow," he replied.

"You will see," I said, "in dogs, a second quality, which is perhaps the most remarkable thing about the animal."

"What quality?"

"If he sees anybody he does not know, he shows temper, although he has not suffered in any way; but if he sees a friend, he welcomes him, even though he may never have received any kindness from him. Hasn't that struck you?"

"Up to now," he said, "I have not got quite as far as that."

"No, but he is known to do it. And it shows that he possesses a refined philosophic nature."

And there the quotation from Plato may well stop. What greater, what finer thing could anyone, who wished to say the most he could in laudation either of men or of dogs? He compares the philosopher guardian not to a horse, or an ox, or an elephant, but to a dog. "Let a dog, being as he is of so noble a nature, guard my state. A dog has the soul of a philosopher. Wherefore let my guardian be like him in this matter."

It is not to be wondered at, then, if in ancient times those men who had the greatest reputation as philosophers amongst their contemporaries did not consider it unworthy of themselves to be called after dogs, but rather appropriated the appellation exclusively to themselves, as something indicating brilliance in a high degree, and preferred to be called cynics rather than by any other name. So we read when a stupid cad tried to raise a laugh by accusing Diogenes of being a dog. Diogenes replied with great composure that he was not concerned to deny the charge, "Dogs bite their enemies; I bite my friends in order to save them." And not only the best of mankind have been denominated dogs but also the most brilliant of the stars which shines at Midsummer. And one may add the gods too; for the Egyptians have a canine deity. And having sufficiently shown that the dog is by nature both a guardian and a philosopher, I would ask, who does not know how gentle and affectionate he is by nature also? For when his master is at home, he remains at home; and when he goes out, the dogs go out with him, and neither the length of a journey, nor rough country, nor thirst, nor storm, nor heat will deter him from following his master everywhere. And while he follows, he sometimes runs forward, and sometimes runs back to his master, and at other times plays about and wags his tail and does everything he can to sport pleasantly with him. If his master calls him, he approaches; and if he threatens him, cowers to the ground; and if he strikes him, shows no resentment. And one recalls the story of Aesop.

Aesop was told by his master Xanthus in a joking way to give certain selected slices of meat to the "well-wisher," and gave them not to his mistress but to the dog. When Xanthus returned home, and his wife began to squabble with him about this, attributing the incident to her husband's desire to insult her, and not to a prank played by Aesop, Aesop said: "Was I not right, sir, in throwing the meat before this dog, 'the well-wisher'? For even though you beat the animal or whip it, it will never remember the fact, whereas if a wife once has the idea that she has been treated insultingly, no reconciliation is possible."

One might quote a thousand cases to prove the friendliness and kindness of dogs to men, but a few salient instances out of many will suffice. There was a King Lysimachus, along with whom his dog is said to have died. And a similar story in all respects is related of Pyrrhus, a private individual. When his master was dead, it was impossible to pull him off the corpse, and after he had been placed upon the funeral pyre, the dog jumped on to it and was burned up along with him. And there was a Roman patrician, too, called Cailius, of whom we read that a dog fought

for and defended him, and would not allow him to have his head cut off until he was killed himself by his master's murderers.

When every inhabitant of Athens had actually embarked upon a naval expedition, but the dog belonging to Xanthippus, father of Pericles, had not been able to enter a ship, he jumped into the sea and, swimming alongside the ship, stuck out the whole voyage to Salamis, and expired as soon as he reached the island.

King Pyrrhus, once upon a journey, came across a dog which was mounting guard over its master's body. He took the animal and kept it until one day, when he was reviewing, the dog, who was with him, taking no notice of the others, ran forward barking and howling when he saw the murderers and assassins of his master, turning round towards the king over and over again, so as to excite suspicion against them in the mind of the king and of all who were present. The men were accordingly arrested and tortured, and confessed that they had committed the murder, and were punished, the dog in this way avenging his master's death. And a precisely similar story is told of a dog belonging to the poet Hesiod, who convicted his master's murderers of their crime. And when Titus Sabinus had been cast into prison by the Romans to await punishment, his dog could not by any amount of force be driven from the prison, and after the corpse had been thrown down the Gemonian precipice, even then he would not leave it, uttering woeful and mournful cries in the presence of many spectators, and when one of these threw him a loaf of bread, he took this and gave it to the dead man. Even when the corpse had been thrown into the Tiber, the dog bore up the body and supported its weight as best he could, with a huge crowd looking on at the spectacle in the utmost bewilderment.

Finally, that the animal is brave and warlike was proved by the King of the Albani when he sent a dog of huge size to Alexander the Great, and when the latter, being pleased with the gift, pitted a bear and a boar against it. For the dog scorned these animals and would not even look at them, as not being worth fighting, whereupon Alexander ordered the dog to be killed.

Learning of this, the Alban king sent another dog, bidding Alexander make a match not of inferior animals, but to choose a lion and an elephant, since the dog had little difficulty in subduing both of them, to the great surprise of Alexander and his courtiers. And the argument is supported by the Garamantian dogs, for two hundred dogs are said as actual combatants to have conducted the king on a triumphal march home.

One might add the Colophonian breed and that of the Castabalienses, who had regiments of dogs that fought in the Van of War, and were sturdy allies, and made a great difference to the event of the battle either way; or again the Cimbrian breed, who, when their masters had fallen in war, looked after the houses on wheels and defended them by fighting.

On the subject of dogs in general I might say a great deal more, and in particular more of this pretty little specimen, but I will stop now as I have no space for more. I wished merely to sketch out an argument in praise of the dog, and so to afford you and myself pleasure and amusement. Good-bye, and good luck.

Marmion: A Celebrated Bloodhound *by C. Hancock*

On Dogs and Introductions: A Letter

by JOHN STEINBECK

DEAR TED:*

Of course I was happy to get your dog book and flattered that you should ask me to write an introduction to it. I must refuse for two reasons.

First, I never write introductions. I have enough trouble just writing my own books.

Second, this book of yours is quite an expert job. I am no expert where dogs are concerned. It is true I have owned a number of dogs, have associated with many more and have observed myriads. But to say I am expert would be like considering a man who hung around bars and knew a lot of people an expert psychologist.

At present, I have no dog. Our house is still raw from Charley's death last spring. But Charley never considered himself a dog. He was Charley. Surely I will have another dog. Hearing that Charley had died, kind people all over the country and many in Europe have written offering to give me a dog, the best dog in the world. This is so friendly and so generous that it is hard to refuse. But I don't want to shop for a dog. My next dog will just have to happen to me and I to him. I can wait for that.

I found your book refreshing in its refutations of a number of dog myths. Dogs are remarkable enough, so that there is no reason to

*A letter to Ted Patrick explaining why he could not write an introduction for Ted Patrick's book, *The Thinking Dog's Man.* —Ed.

make up lies about them. And I was interested in what you had to say about a dog's mental processes. Is it true that there is a silly school which holds that a dog has no memory? I wonder how they arrived at that staggering generality. If they said it about me, it would be more to the point. I have also heard that a dog has no distance vision. I once had a dog who used to watch sea gulls flying almost beyond my vision. There was no question about his seeing them. His head, as well as his eyes, followed their progress. On the other hand, I once had a dog who saw things that were not there, or if they were, neither I nor my family or friends could see them. He was a large and dreamy English setter named Toby, the White Flower of the Mountain. Sometimes, when the moon was full, he would stand and bark monotonously at an oak tree for an hour at a time. Again, lying in front of an open fire, he would awaken, look at the front door and with his eyes and nose follow something across the room, sometimes watching it exit through another door and sometimes move to a chair. Toby thumped his tail in greeting to some of these things he saw, while he greeted others with a low growl of dislike. All right, Ted, so he was crazy, but he was so convinced he saw things that we could almost see them too. Toby had other odd qualities too, but I won't go into those.

Now that's another reason for not writing an

introduction. I might trap myself into telling dog stories.

But how about a man story! In Pacific Grove, I had a friend—an artist—gentle soul—a man of peace and quiet. There was no anger nor violence in him, nor for that matter was there any tendency toward crime either against persons or property. Then, how would you account for the attested fact that all dogs hated him and bit him on sight and without warning? He liked dogs and tried to make friends with them, but no dog ever accepted him. Of course, my friend was poor, but no poorer than the rest of us. And if he set off anthropophobia in dogs, he had an equally unfortunate effect on policemen. It was rare for him to go out without being picked up and questioned by the police. It went even farther. If he tried to cash a check, bank tellers told him to wait, while they subjected his paper to extreme scrutiny. And in this case, both dogs and cops were wrong. How do you explain that? If you ascribe it to a subtle odor beyond the olfactory range of man, you would have to credit policemen with bloodhound virtues they do not have.

I have always disliked people who talk baby talk to dogs, but my feeling is nothing to what dogs feel. I have watched the cold contempt in a dog's eyes when he was being addressed as "itty bitty, sweety foo!"

On the other hand, I distrust people who believe that dogs are better than we are. Dogs are not better. They are just different from us. Surely they can do some things better, but I have yet to see a dog balance a checkbook, or make an omelette or compose a sonnet.

I believe that a smart man is probably superior to a smart dog. A case in point was told me by one of the leaders of the Danish underground during the German occupation. The Danish fishing boats had to go out for food supply, and yet the Germans knew those same boats were smuggling refugees to Sweden. So the Gestapo devised a plan. Before each boat sailed, all hands were ordered ashore. Then highly efficient tracking dogs were sent aboard to smell out any secret hiding place or hidden stowaway. The dogs never found anyone.

"It was very simple," my informant told me.

"I'm surprised the Germans never figured it out. You see, we issued salt shakers of crystal cocaine to the boatman. They sprinkled it on the gangplanks. And by the time the dogs had sniffed their way aboard, their noses were so numb they couldn't have smelled an antisocial skunk." Then he sighed. "I'm afraid some of those dogs came out of the war cocaine addicts."

You know, Ted, the human—imperfect and deeply aware of his frailties—is prone to find the virtues he wishes he had in other species—courage in the lion, memory in the elephant, gentleness in the lamb and oddly enough, both loyalty and honesty in the dog. These are myths, which have little basis in fact. It is my belief that a dog in virtue at least is little better than we are. Once I was neighbor to a cynical old homosexual aunty of a dog, an unkempt long-haired rascally sex deviate who introduced pederasty to every young and gallant male on the block. I don't know how he attracted them. Perhaps his deviation was so glandular as to inflame the randy and random impulses of all the young and ignorant dogs of our neighborhood.

I have know glutton dogs, swinish dogs, dogs of incredible vanity. And then, there are fools—just plain, clumsy, stupid fools. And as for dishonesty, how about a dog I once knew in Truckee? He was an Airedale, if you will pardon the expression, Ted, and he lived at a gambling house called the Silver Mirror. I don't know how he learned his hustle, but he not only mastered it, but worked it to the limit. It is well known that when a man makes a killing at gambling, he must give something to the first bum who puts the bee on him. Well, at the Silver Mirror, that first bum was Omar, the Airedale. Maybe he learned to detect the exultant tone of voice of a winner, but with twenty tables working, let one man make a decent win at craps or blackjack and there was Omar beside him, sitting up with a wet-eyed look of utter starvation. And Omar invariably got a steak. On a good night, Omar made as many as six or seven sirloins. He operated for several years, and died of overeating, but I swear even in his obese old age, when Omar put the arm on a winner, you'd swear he hadn't eaten for a week —a born, blowed-in-the-glass hustler he was.

Believe me, Ted, I am not running dogs down. I just want to put them in their proper perspective. If all dogs were the noble beasts we pretend, how would we know a real hero when we see one? And real hero dogs there are.

There are real rules of conduct among dogs also. You have said that male dogs practically never fight females. Have you noticed another rule?

Let's say there's a fight and one dog gets the worst of it and wants to call it quits. Well, if he turns his back, it usually works and if he puts his head in a corner, it always works. No dog will bite another in the rear, unless the other dog is running away; no dog, that is, except one. I won't even mention his breed, because you and I have always been friends—well, hell, I might as well admit it—he was an Airedale, and he was mine and he wasn't as good a fighter as he thought he was. Maybe I am guilty of irreverence, or *lèse majesté*, but this Airedale was a bit of a coward. I was living in the mountains, and once a week I walked about six miles to a little combination grocery and post office for supplies and mail. The boss dog of that place was a no-good shepherd, setter, coyote-looking thing, but he knew his way around. Every week, my dog fought this grisly creature and every week, he got licked. He showed he was licked by putting his head in a corner. Then, he was safe—licked, but safe. Came a day when something went haywire with the boss dog. Maybe he'd been out all night or had a hangover, or perhaps he was overconfident from having won too many fights. Anyway, my dog beat the tar out of him, really licked him until the boss dog yelled "uncle" and turned his back and put his head in the loser's corner. Perhaps my dog was smarting from too many beatings, or it's possible he just wasn't a gentleman. But I ask you to believe that he bit the boss dog twice on the behind and then clamped down on his testicles. When we pried him loose, the boss dog was retired both as a fighter and as a stud. So you see, Ted, there can be dogs without honor, too, even as with us.

When I read your book, I was afraid I might get to reminiscing. But I won't allow myself that luxury. However, I do recall one strange happening.

Living alone, a man gets to using his dog or dogs as extra senses. They tell him when someone is coming, and sometimes they can even forecast weather. I had one experience where the absence of a dog reaction gave me a really nasty scare. Again, it was in the mountains, and the winter had come and it was deep snow. I had two dogs: an A---d--e and an Irish terrier. They were a comfort to me—gave me someone to talk to. You get lonely and sometimes, alone, you get scared for no reason. There wasn't any danger there, except breaking a leg and freezing to death for lack of help.

There were a few timber wolves in the country, but they had too much game to be dangerous to men. Now and then, I heard them howling at night and then the dogs would raise hell. I think they were scared of the wolves and were protesting too much. And once in the snow, I came on a trampled place where a young deer had got cornered and pulled down and eaten. The record was all there in the snow to see. The dogs barked stupidly and pretended to find tracks, but they didn't go far from me and my rifle.

Well, one week there came a whizzer of a blizzard, hard dry snow spouting along parallel to the ground and drifting up against anything in its way. It was so cold it stung your face like gritty sand. The wind whooped and gusted and threshed around in the firs and pines and tamaracks. It was a real wild one that continued for three days.

For me, it was a lovely time. My little house was warm. I had plenty of cut wood and canned and dried food and kerosene. I loved to sit warm, hearing the gusts and the ping of the driven sleet on the windows. Outside, my wood pile and wheelbarrow were great big mounds of drifted snow. The trees were all aproned on one side with drift.

Night came down early. I cooked a good dinner and fed the dogs and let them out and then they came in and went to sleep. The kerosene lamps looked pretty and comfortable and actually kept the cabin warm; it was that small and tight. I washed up and tossed my garbage out the door to pick up later. Besides, it sometimes attracted coons and both the dogs and I liked a young roast coon. The old ones were too tough.

It was pitch-black outside in the raging, gusting wind. I was just drying the last dishes when I heard a sound from outside that raised the hair on my head. If you can imagine the scream of a baritone woman being strangled—well, it was half that and half mountain-lion scream, which I heard once in my life—a horrible, thick, gurgling screech. Then silence.

I put the dish down and stepped to the rack for my rifle—an old heavy Winchester 38–56 that carried a slug half as long as your little finger. I had the gun in my hand when that scream came again. I glanced at the dogs and *they were sound asleep!*

I don't know, Ted, whether you've ever felt that panic that makes you suddenly wet all over and sick to your stomach. I remember sitting on my bed with a big old rifle in my lap, levered down to throw a shell into the chamber. And I remember thinking, "If the dogs didn't hear it, it isn't outside; it's in my head. I'm going nuts."

And then, the scream came again. I thought,

I can't sit here; I'll go over the edge. I have to go outside.

I remember it in slow motion. I got my flashlight, bounced the dogs awake and pulled on the inward opening door. The wind howled into the house and brought the piled snow with it. The dogs went pumping through the deep drift, each one about his business. I flashed my light around. Nothing.

And then, in a roar of wind, it came again—that horrid low scream. And do you know what it was? A three-pound coffee can upright on a snowdrift. I'd thrown it out and the wind was mouthing it like a mountain man playing a jug.

Do you see what I mean? If the dogs had reacted, I might have killed me a coffee can. As it was, I was sick all over with fear.

So you see, Ted—I can't write an introduction for your dog book. If I did—what would it be, nothing but some observations and some dog stories. I like your book fine, but let's forget the introduction, shall we?

Yours,
John

January 9, 1964

Too Hot *by Sir Edwin Landseer*

For I Will Consider Your Dog Molly

by DAVID LEHMAN

For it was the first day of Rosh Ha'shanah, New Year's Day, day of remembrance, of ancient sacrifices and averted calamities.

For I started the day by eating an apple dipped in honey, as ritual required.

For I went to the local synagogue to listen to the ram's horn blown.

For I asked Our Father, Our King, to save us for his sake if not for ours, for the sake of his abundant mercies, for the sake of his right hand, for the sake of those who went through fire and water for the sanctification of his name.

For despite the use of a microphone and other gross violations of ceremony, I gave myself up gladly to the synagogue's sensual insatiable vast womb.

For what right have I to feel offended?

For I communed with my dead father, and a conspicuous tear rolled down my right cheek, and there was loud crying inside me.

For I understood how that tear could become an orb.

For the Hebrew melodies comforted me.

For I lost my voice.

For I met a friend who asked "Is this a day of high seriousness" and when I said yes he said "It has taken your voice away."

For he was right, for I felt the strong lashes of the wind lashing me by the throat.

For I thought there shall come a day that the watchmen upon the hills of Ephraim shall cry, Arise and let us go up to Zion unto the Lord our God.

For the virgin shall rejoice in the dance, and the young and old in each other's arms, and their soul shall be as a watered garden, and neither shall they learn war any more.

For God shall lower the price of bread and corn and wine and oil, he shall let our cry come up to him.

For it is customary on the first day of Rosh Ha'shanah to cast a stone into the depths of the sea, to weep and pray to weep no more.

For the stone represents all the sins of the people.

For I asked you and Molly to accompany me to Cascadilla Creek, there being no ocean nearby.

For we talked about the Psalms of David along the way, and the story of Hannah, mother of Samuel, who sought the most robust bard to remedy her barrenness.

For Isaac said "I see the fire and the wood, but where is the lamb for the offering?"

For as soon as I saw the stone, white flat oblong and heavy, I knew that it had summoned me.

For I heard the voice locked inside that stone, for

I pictured a dry wilderness in which, with a wave of my staff, I could command sweet waters to flow forth from that stone.

For I cast the stone into the stream and watched it sink to the bottom where dozens of smaller stones, all of them black, gathered around it.

For the waterfall performed the function of the chorus.

For after the moment of solemnity dissolved, you playfully tossed Molly into the stream.

For you tossed her three times, and three times she swam back for her life.

For she shook the water off her body, refreshed.

For you removed the leash from her neck and let her roam freely.

For she darted off into the brush and speared a small gray moving thing in the neck.

For this was the work of an instant.

For we looked and behold! the small gray thing was a rat.

For Molly had killed the rat with a single efficient bite, in conformance with Jewish law.

For I took the rat and cast him into the stream, and both of us congratulated Molly.

For now she resumed her noble gait.

For she does not lie awake in the dark and weep for her sins, and whine about her condition, and discuss her duty to God.

For I'd as lief pray with your dog Molly as with any man.

For she knows that God is her savior.

Pointer *by A. Cooper*

Rab and His Friends

by DR. JOHN BROWN

FOUR-AND-THIRTY years ago, Bob Ainslie and I were coming up Infirmary Street from the High School, our heads together, and our arms intertwisted, as only lovers and boys know how, or why.

When we got to the top of the street, and turned north, we espied a crowd at the Tron Church. "A dog-fight!" shouted Bob, and was off; and so was I, both of us all but praying that it might not be over before we got up! And is not this boy-nature? And human nature too? And don't we all wish a house on fire not to be out before we see it? Dogs like fighting; old Isaac says they "delight" in it, and for the best of all reasons; and boys are not cruel because they like to see the fight. They see three of the great cardinal virtues of dog or man—courage, endurance and skill—in intense action. This is very different from a love of making dogs fight, and enjoying, and aggravating and making gain by their pluck. A boy—be he ever so fond himself of fighting, if he be a good boy, hates and despises all this, but he would have run off with Bob and me fast enough: it is a natural, and a not wicked interest, that all boys and men have in witnessing intense energy in action.

Does any curious and finely-ignorant woman wish to know how Bob's eye at a glance announced a dog-fight to his brain? He did not, he could not see the dogs fighting; it was a flash of an inference, a rapid induction. The crowd round a couple of dogs fighting, is a crowd masculine mainly, with an occasional active, compassionate woman, fluttering wildly round the outside, and using her tongue and her hands freely upon the men, as so many "brutes," it is a crowd annular, compact and mobile; a crowd centripetal, having its eyes and its heads all bent downwards and inwards, to one common focus.

Well, Bob and I are up, and find it is not over: a small thoroughbred, white bull terrier, is busy throttling a large shepherd's dog, unaccustomed to war, but not to be trifled with. They are hard at it; the scientific little fellow doing his work in great style, his pastoral enemy fighting wildly, but with the sharpest of teeth and a great courage. Science and breeding, however, soon had their own; the Game Chicken, as the premature Bob called him, working his way up, took his final grip of poor Yarrow's throat—and he lay gasping and done for. His master, a brown, handsome, big young shepherd from Tweedsmuir, would have liked to have knocked down any man, would "drink up Esil, or eat a crocodile," for that part, if he had a chance: it was no use kicking the little dog; that would only make him hold the closer. Many were the means shouted out in mouthfuls, of the best possible ways of ending it. "Water!" but there was none near, and many cried for it who might have got it from the well at Blackfriar's Wynd. "Bite the tail!" and a large, vague, benevolent, middle-aged man, more desirous than wise, with some struggle got the bushy end of Yarrow's tail into his ample mouth, and bit it with all his might. This was more than enough for the much-enduring, much-perspiring shepherd, who, with a gleam of joy over his broad visage, delivered a terrific facer upon our large, vague, benevolent, middle-aged friend—who went down like a shot.

Still the Chicken holds; death not far off. "Snuff! A pinch of snuff!" observed a calm, highly-dressed young buck, with an eye-glass in his eye. "Snuff, indeed!" growled the angry crowd, affronted and glaring. "Snuff! A pinch of snuff!" again observes the buck, but with more urgency; whereon were produced several open boxes, and from a mull which may have been at Culloden, he took a pinch, knelt down, and presented it to the nose of the Chicken. The laws of physiology and of snuff take their course; the Chicken sneezes, and Yarrow is free!

The young pastoral giant stalks off with Yarrow in his arms—comforting him.

But the bull terrier's blood is up, and his soul unsatisfied; he grips the first dog he meets, and discovering she is not a dog, in Homeric phrase, he makes a brief sort of *amende,* and is off. The boys, with Bob and me at their head, are after him: down Niddry Street he goes, bent on mischief; up the Cowgate like an arrow—Bob and I, and our small men, panting behind.

There, under the single arch of the South Bridge, is a huge mastiff, sauntering down the middle of the causeway, as if with his hands in his pockets: he is old, gray, brindled, as big as a little Highland bull, and has the Shakespearian dewlaps shaking as he goes.

The Chicken makes straight at him, and fastens on his throat. To our astonishment, the great creature does nothing but stand still, hold himself up, and roar—yes, roar; a long, serious, remonstrative roar. How is this? Bob and I are up to them. *He is muzzled!* The bailies had proclaimed a general muzzling, and his master, studying strength and economy mainly, had encompassed his huge jaws in a homemade apparatus, constructed out of the leather of some ancient *breechin.* His mouth was open as far as it

could; his lips curled up in rage—a sort of terrible grin; his teeth gleaming, ready, from out the darkness; the strap across his mouth tense as a bowstring; his whole frame stiff with indignation and surprise; his roar asking us all round, "Did you ever see the like of this?" He looked a statue of anger and astonishment, done in Aberdeen granite.

We soon had a crowd: the Chicken held on. "A knife!" cried Bob; and a cobbler gave him his knife: you know the kind of knife, worn away obliquely to a point, and always keen. I put its edge to the tense leather; it ran before it; and then!—One sudden jerk of that enormous head, a sort of dirty mist about his mouth, no noise—and the bright and fierce little fellow is dropped, limp and dead. A solemn pause: this was more than any of us had bargained for. I turned the little fellow over, and saw he was quite dead: the mastiff had taken him by the small of the back like a rat, and broken it.

He looked down at his victim appeased, ashamed and amazed; snuffed him all over, stared at him and taking a sudden thought, turned round and trotted off. Bob took the dead dog up, and said, "John, we'll bury him after tea." "Yes," said I, and was off after the mastiff. He made up the Cowgate at a rapid swing; he had forgotten some engagement. He turned up the Candlemaker Row, and stopped at the Harrow Inn.

There was a carrier's cart ready to start, and a keen, thin, impatient, black-a-vised little man, his hand at his gray horse's head, looking about angrily for something. "Rab, ye thief!" said he, aiming a kick at my great friend, who drew cringing up, and avoiding the heavy shoe with more agility than dignity, and watching his master's eye, slunk dismayed under the cart—his ears down, and as much as he had of tail down too.

What a man this must be—thought I—to whom my tremendous hero turns tail! The carrier saw the muzzle hanging, cut and useless, from his neck, and I eagerly told him the story, which Bob and I always thought, and still think, Homer, or King David or Sir Walter alone were worthy to rehearse. The severe little man was mitigated, and condescended to say, "Rab, ma man, puir Rabbie,"—whereupon the stump of a tail rose up, the ears were cocked, the eyes filled, and were comforted; the two friends were reconciled. "Hupp!" and a stroke of the whip were given to Jess; and off went the three.

Bob and I buried the Game Chicken that night (we had not much of a tea) in the back-green of his house, in Melville Street, No. 17, with considerable gravity and silence; and being at the time in the *Iliad,* and, like all boys, Trojans, we of course called him Hector.

Six years have passed—a long time for a boy and a dog: Bob Ainslie is off to the wars; I am a medical student, and clerk at Minto House Hospital.

Rab I saw almost every week, on the Wednesday; and we had much pleasant intimacy. I found the way to his heart by frequent scratching of his huge head, and an occasional bone. When I did not notice him he would plant himself straight before me, and stand wagging that bud of a tail, and looking up, with his head a little to the one side. His master I occasionally saw; he used to call me "Maister John," but was laconic as any Spartan.

One fine October afternoon, I was leaving the hospital, when I saw the large gate open, and in walked Rab, with that great and easy saunter of his. He looked as if taking general possession of the place; like the Duke of Wellington entering a subdued city, satiated with victory and peace. After him came Jess, now white from age, with her cart; and in it a woman carefully wrapped up—the carrier leading the horse anxiously, and looking back. When he saw me, James (for his name was James Noble) made a curt and grotesque "boo," and said, "Maister John, this is the mistress; she's got a trouble in her breest—some kind o' an income we're thinkin'."

By this time I saw the woman's face; she was sitting on a sack filled with straw, with her husband's plaid round her, and his big-coat, with its large white metal buttons, over her feet.

I never saw a more unforgetable face—pale, serious, lonely, delicate, sweet, without being at all what we call fine. She looked sixty, and had on a mutch, white as snow, with its black ribbon; her silvery, smooth hair setting off her dark gray eyes —eyes such as one sees only twice or thrice in a lifetime, full of suffering, full also of the overcoming of it: her eyebrows black and delicate, and her mouth firm, patient and contented, which few mouths ever are.

As I have said, I never saw a more beautiful countenance, or one more subdued to settled quiet. "Ailie," said James, "this is Maister John, the young doctor; Rab's freend, ye ken. We often speak aboot you, doctor." She smiled, and made a movement, but said nothing; and prepared to come down, putting her plaid aside and rising. Had Solomon, in all his glory, been handing down the Queen of Sheba at his palace gate, he could not have done it more daintily, more tenderly, more like a gentleman, than did James the Howgate carrier, when he lifted down Ailie his wife. The contrast of his small, swarthy, weather-beaten, keen, worldly face to hers—pale, subdued and beautiful—was something wonderful. Rab looked on concerned and puzzled, but ready for anything that might turn up—were it to strangle the nurse, the porter, or even me. Ailie and he seemed great friends.

"As I was sayin', she's got a kind o' trouble in her breest, doctor; wull ye tak' a look at it?" We walked into the consulting room, all four; Rab grim and comic, willing to be happy and confidential if cause could be shown, willing also to be the reverse, on the same terms. Ailie sat down, undid her open gown and her lawn handkerchief round her neck, and, without a word, showed me her right breast. I looked at and examined it carefully—she and James watching me, and Rab eyeing all three. What could I say? There it was, that had once been so soft, so shapely, so white, so gracious and bountiful, so "full of all blessed conditions"—hard as a stone, a center of horrid pain, making that pale face, with its gray, lucid, reasonable eyes, and its sweet resolved mouth, express the full measure of suffering overcome. Why was that gentle, modest, sweet woman, clean and lovable, condemned by God to bear such a burden?

I got her away to bed. "May Rab and me bide?" said James. "*You* may; and Rab, if he will behave himself." "I'se warrant he's do that, doctor"; and in slunk the faithful beast. I wish you could have seen him. There are no such dogs now. He belonged to a lost tribe. As I have said, he was brindled, and gray like Rubislaw granite; his hair short, hard and close, like a lion's; his body thickset, like a little bull—a sort of compressed Hercules of a dog. He must have been ninety pounds' weight, at the least; he had a large blunt head; his muzzle black as night, his mouth blacker than any night, a tooth or two—being all he had—gleaming out of his jaws of darkness. His head was scarred with the records of old wounds, a sort of series of fields of battle all over it; one eye out, one ear cropped as close as was Archbishop Leighton's father's; the remaining eye had the power of two; and above it, and in constant communication with it, was a tattered rag of an ear, which was for ever unfurling itself, like an old flag; and then that bud of a tail, about one inch long, if it could in any sense be said to be long, being as broad as long—the mobility, the instantaneousness of that bud were very funny and surprising, and its expressive twinklings and winkings, the intercommunications between the eye, the ear and it, were of the oddest and swiftest.

Rab had the dignity and simplicity of great size; and having fought his way all along the road to absolute supremacy, he was as mighty in his own line as Julius Caesar or the Duke of Wellington, and had the gravity[1] of all great fighters.

You must have often observed the likeness of certain men to certain animals, and of certain dogs to men. Now, I never looked at Rab without thinking of the greatest Baptist preacher, Andrew Fuller.[2] The same large, heavy, menacing,

[1] A Highland game-keeper, when asked why a certain terrier, of singular pluck, was so much more solemn than the other dogs, said, "Oh, Sir, life's full o' sariousness to him—he just never can get eneuch o' fetchin'."

[2] Fuller was, in early life, when a farmer lad at Soham, famous as a boxer; not quarrelsome, but not without "the stern delight" a man of strength and courage feels in their exercise. Dr. Charles Stewart of Dunearn, whose rare gifts and graces as a physician, a divine, a scholar, and a gentleman, live only in the memory of those few who knew and survive him, liked to tell how Mr. Fuller used to say, that when he was in the pulpit, and saw a *buirdly* man come along the passage, he would instinctively draw himself up, measure his imaginary antagonist, and forecast how he would deal with him, his

combative, somber, honest countenance, the same deep inevitable eye, the same look, as of thunder asleep, but ready—neither a dog nor a man to be trifled with.

Next day, my master, the surgeon, examined Ailie. There was no doubt it must kill her, and soon. It could be removed—it might never return—it would give her speedy relief—she should have it done. She curtsied, looked at James, and said, "When?" "Tomorrow," said the kind surgeon—a man of few words. She and James and Rab and I retired. I noticed that he and she spoke little, but seemed to anticipate everything in each other. The following day, at noon, the students came in, hurrying up the great stair. At the first landing-place, on a small well-known black board, was a bit of paper fastened by wafers, and many remains of old wafers beside it. On the paper were the words, "An operation today.—J. B. *Clerk.*"

Up ran the youths, eager to secure good places: in they crowded, full of interest and talk. "What's the case?" "Which side is it?"

Don't think them heartless; they are neither better nor worse than you or I: they get over their professional horrors, and into their proper work; and in them pity as an *emotion* ending in itself or at best in tears and a long-drawn breath, lessens—while pity as a *motive* is quickened, and gains power and purpose. It is well for poor human nature that it is so.

The operating theater is crowded; much talk and fun, and all the cordiality and stir of youth. The surgeon with his staff of assistants is there. In comes Ailie: one look at her quiets and abates the eager students. That beautiful old woman is too much for them; they sit down, and are dumb, and gaze at her. These rough boys feel the power of her presence. She walks in quickly, but without haste; dressed in her mutch, her neckerchief, her white dimity short-gown, her black bombazeen petticoat, showing her white worsted stockings and her carpet shoes. Behind her was James with Rab. James sat down in the distance, and took that huge and noble head between his knees. Rab

hands meanwhile condensing into fists, and tending to "square." He must have been a hard hitter if he boxed as he preached—what "The Fancy" would call "an ugly customer."

looked perplexed and dangerous; forever cocking his ear and dropping it as fast.

Ailie stepped up on a seat, and laid herself on the table, as her friend the surgeon told her; arranged herself, gave a rapid look at James, shut her eyes, rested herself on me, and took my hand. The operation was at once begun; it was necessarily slow; and chloroform—one of God's best gifts to his suffering children—was then unknown. The surgeon did his work. The pale face showed its pain, but was still and silent. Rab's soul was working within him; he saw that something strange was going on—blood flowing from his mistress, and she suffering; his ragged ear was up, and importunate; he growled and gave now and then a sharp impatient yelp; he would have liked to have done something to that man. But James had him firm, and gave him a glower from time to time, and an intimation of a possible kick—all the better for James, it kept his eye and his mind off Ailie.

It is over: she is dressed, steps gently and decently down from the table, looks for James; then turning to the surgeon and the students, she curtsies—and in a low, clear voice, begs their pardon if she has behaved ill. The students—all of us—wept like children; the surgeon happed her up carefully, and, resting on James and me, Ailie went to her room, Rab following. We put her to bed. James took off his heavy shoes, crammed with tackets, heel-capped and toe-capped, and put them carefully under the table, saying, "Maister John, I'm for nane o' yer strynge nurse bodies for Ailie. I'll be her nurse, and I'll gang aboot on my stockin' soles as canny as pussy." And so he did; and handy and clever, and swift and tender as any woman, was that horny-handed, snell, peremptory little man. Everything she got he gave her: he seldom slept; and often I saw his small shrewd eyes out of the darkness, fixed on her. As before, they spoke little.

Rab behaved well, never moving, showing us how meek and gentle he could be, and occasionally, in his sleep, letting us know that he was demolishing some adversary. He took a walk with me every day, generally to the Candlemaker Row; but he was somber and mild; declined doing battle, though some fit cases offered, and indeed submitted to sundry indignities; and was always very ready to turn, and came faster back, and trotted up the stair with much lightness, and went straight to that door.

Jess, the mare, had been sent, with her weather-worn cart, to Howgate, and had doubtless her own dim and placid meditations and confusions, on the absence of her master and Rab, and her unnatural freedom from the road and her cart.

For some days Ailie did well. The wound healed "by the first intention"; for as James said, "Oor Ailie's skin's ower clean to beil." The students came in quiet and anxious, and surrounded her bed. She said she liked to see their young, honest faces. The surgeon dressed her, and spoke to her in his own short kind way, pitying her through his eyes, Rab and James outside the circle—Rab being now reconciled, and even cordial, and having made up his mind that as yet nobody required worrying, but, as you may suppose, *semper paratus*.

So far well: but, four days after the operation, my patient had a sudden and long shivering, a "groosin," as she called it. I saw her soon after; her eyes were too bright, her cheek colored; she was restless, and ashamed of being so; the balance was lost; mischief had begun. On looking at the wound, a blush of red told the secret; her pulse was rapid, her breathing anxious and quick, she wasn't herself, as she said, and was vexed at her restlessness. We tried what we could. James did everything, was everywhere; never in the way, never out of it; Rab subsided under the table into a dark place, and was motionless, all but his eye, which followed every one. Ailie got worse; began to wander in her mind, gently; was more demonstrative in her ways to James, rapid in her questions, and sharp at times. He was vexed, and said, "She was never that way afore, no, never." For a time she knew her head was wrong, and was always asking our pardon—the dear gentle old woman: then delirium set in strong, without pause. Her brain gave way, and then came that terrible spectacle:

*The intellectual power, through words and
    things,
Went sounding on, a dim and perilous way;*

she sang bits of old songs and Psalms, stopping suddenly, mingling the Psalms of David, and the diviner words of his Son and Lord, with homely odds and ends and scraps of ballads.

Nothing more touching, or in a sense more strangely beautiful, did I ever witness. Her tremulous, rapid, affectionate, eager, Scotch voice—the swift, aimless, bewildered mind, the baffled utterance, the bright and perilous eye; some wild words, some household cares, something for James, the names of the dead, Rab called rapidly and in a "fremyt" voice, and he starting up, surprised, and slinking off as if he were to blame somehow, or had been dreaming he heard. Many eager questions and beseechings which James and I could make nothing of, and on which she seemed to set her all, and then sink back ununderstood. It was very sad, but better than many things that are not called sad. James hovered about, put out and miserable, but active and exact as ever; read to her, when there was a lull, short bits from the Psalms, prose and meter, chanting the latter in his own rude and serious way, showing great knowledge of the fit words, bearing up like a man, and doting over her as his "ain Ailie." "Ailie, ma woman!" "Ma ain bonnie wee dawtie!"

The end was drawing on: the golden bowl was breaking; the silver cord was fast being loosed—that *animula, blandula, vagula, hospes, comesque,* was about to flee. The body and the soul —companions for sixty years—were being sundered, and taking leave. She was walking, alone, through the valley of that shadow, into which one day we must all enter—and yet she was not alone, for we know whose rod and staff were comforting her.

One night she had fallen quiet, and as we hoped, asleep; her eyes were shut. We put down the gas, and sat watching her. Suddenly she sat up in bed, and taking a bed-gown which was lying on it rolled up, she held it eagerly to her breast—to the right side. We could see her eyes bright with a surprising tenderness and joy, bending over this bundle of clothes. She held it as a woman holds her sucking child; opening out her nightgown impatiently, and holding it close, and brooding over it, and murmuring foolish little words, as over one whom his mother comforteth, and who sucks and is satisfied. It was pitiful and strange to see her wasted dying look, keen and yet vague—her immense love.

"Preserve me!" groaned James, giving way. And then she rocked back and forward, as if to make it sleep, hushing it and wasting on it her infinite fondness. "Wae's me, doctor; I declare she's thinkin' it's that bairn." "What bairn?" "The only bairn we ever had; our wee Mysie, and she's in the Kingdom forty years and mair." It was plainly true: the pain in the breast, telling its urgent story to a bewildered, ruined brain, was misread and mistaken; it suggested to her the uneasiness of a breast full of milk, and then the child; and so again once more they were together, and she had her ain wee Mysie in her bosom.

This was the close. She sank rapidly: the delirium left her; but, as she whispered, she was "clean silly"; it was the lightening before the final darkness. After having for some time lain still—her eyes shut, she said, "James!" He came close to her, and lifting up her calm, clear, beautiful eyes, she gave him a long look, turned to me kindly but shortly, looked for Rab but could not see him, then turned to her husband again, as if she would never leave off looking, shut her eyes and composed herself. She lay for some time breathing quick, and passed away so gently, that when we thought she was gone, James, in his old-fashioned way, held the mirror to her face. After a long pause, one small spot of dimness was breathed out; it vanished away, and never returned, leaving the blank clear darkness without a stain. "What is our life? it is even a vapor, which appeareth for a little time, and then vanisheth away."

Rab all this time had been full awake and motionless: he came forward beside us: Ailie's hand, which James had held, was hanging down; it was soaked with his tears; Rab licked it all over carefully, looked at her and returned to his place under the table.

James and I sat, I don't know how long, but for some time, saying nothing; he started up abruptly, and with some noise went to the table, and putting his right fore and middle fingers each into a shoe, pulled them out, and put them on, breaking one of the leather latchets, and muttering in anger, "I never did the like o' that afore!"

I believe he never did; nor after either. "Rab!" he said roughly, and pointing with his thumb to the bottom of the bed. Rab leapt up, and settled himself; his head and eye to the dead face. "Maister John, ye'll wait for me," said the carrier; and disappeared in the darkness, thundering downstairs in his heavy shoes. I ran to a front window: there he was, already round the house, and out at the gate, fleeing like a shadow.

I was afraid about him, and yet not afraid; so I sat down beside Rab, and being wearied, fell asleep. I awoke from a sudden noise outside. It was November, and there had been a heavy fall of snow. Rab was *in statu quo;* he heard the noise too, and plainly knew it, but never moved. I looked out; and there, at the gate, in the dim morning—for the sun was not up, was Jess and the cart—a cloud of steam rising from the old mare. I did not see James; he was already at the door, and came up the stairs and met me. It was less than three hours since he left, and he must have posted out—who knows how?—to Howgate, full nine miles off; yoked Jess, and driven her astonished into town. He had an armful of blankets, and was streaming with perspiration. He nodded to me, spread out on the floor two pairs of clean old blankets having at their corners, "A. G., 1794," in large letters in red worsted. These were the initials of Alison Graeme and James may have looked in at her from without—himself unseen but not unthought of—when he was "wat, wat, and weary," and after having walked many a mile over the hills, may have seen her sitting, while "a' the lave were sleepin'," and by the firelight working her name on the blankets, for her ain James's bed.

He motioned Rab down, and taking his wife in his arms, laid her in the blankets and happed her carefully and firmly up, leaving the face uncovered; and then lifting her, he nodded again sharply to me, and with a resolved but utterly miserable face, strode along the passage, and downstairs, followed by Rab. I followed with a light; but he didn't need it. I went out, holding stupidly the candle in my hand in the calm frosty air; we were soon at the gate. I could have helped him, but I saw he was not to be meddled with, and he was strong, and did not need it. He laid her down as tenderly, as safely, as he had lifted her out ten days before—as tenderly as when he had her first in his arms when she was only "A. G."—sorted her, leaving that beautiful sealed face open to the heavens; and then taking Jess by the head, he moved away. He did not notice me; neither did Rab, who presided behind the cart.

I stood till they passed through the long shadow of the college, and turned up Nicolson Street. I heard the solitary cart sound through the streets, and die away and come again; and I returned, thinking of that company going up Libberton Brae, then along Roslin Muir, the morning light touching the Pentlands, and making them like on-looking ghosts; then down the hill through Auchindinny Woods, past "haunted Woodhouselee"; and as daybreak came sweeping up the bleak Lammermuirs and fell on his own door, the company would stop, and James would take the key and lift Ailie up again, laying her on her own bed, and, having put Jess up, would return with Rab and shut the door.

James buried his wife with his neighbors mourning, Rab watching the proceedings from a distance. It was snow, and that black ragged hole would look strange in the midst of the swelling spotless cushion of white. James looked after everything; then rather suddenly fell ill, and took to bed; was insensible when the doctor came, and soon died. A sort of low fever was prevailing in the village, and his want of sleep, his exhaustion and his misery made him apt to take it. The grave was not difficult to reopen. A fresh fall of snow had again made all things white and smooth; Rab once more looked on, and slunk home to the stable.

And what of Rab? I asked for him next week at the new carrier who got the goodwill of James's business, and was now master of Jess and her cart. "How's Rab?" He put me off, and said rather rudely, "What's *your* business wi' the dowg?" I was not to be so put off. "Where's Rab?" He, getting confused and red, and intermeddling with his hair, said, "'Deed, sir, Rab's deid." "Dead! What did he die of?" "Weel, sir," said he, getting redder, "he didna exactly dee; he was killed. I had to brain him wi' a rack-pin; there was nae doin' wi' him. He lay in the treviss wi' the mear, and wadna come oot. I tempit him wi' kail and meat, but he wad tak naething, and keepit me frae feedin' the beast, and he was aye gur gurrin', and grup gruppin' me by the legs. I was laith to mak' awa wi' the auld dowg, his like wasna atween this and Thornhill—but, 'deed, sir, I could do naething else." I believed him. Fit end for Rab, quick and complete. His teeth and his friends gone, why should he keep the peace and be civil?

He was buried in the braeface, near the burn, the children of the village, his companions, who used to make very free with him and sit on his ample stomach as he lay half asleep at the door in the sun, watching the solemnity.

Mastiff *by W. Smith*

Huskies

by **ROBERT DOVERS**

THE sealer *Tottan* stood against the sea ice off Port Martin, the French base on Adélie Coast, Antarctica, waiting to relieve the scientists who had passed the year there. So far the only contact with these men had been by radio, but now we saw black dots coming out over the featureless frozen sea—a sledge pulled by a team of huskies. Of all on board I was naturally the most interested, for these dogs were to be my charges. I had been posted as Australian observer with this French Antarctic Expedition of 1952, which was to spend a year on the polar ice charting the coast, recording meteorological observations and studying the penguins. Even now, at the ship's side, there was a group of Adélie penguins, the funny, inquisitive little folk, about fourteen inches tall, that are found all along the thousands of miles of Antarctica's coastline.

When the sledge reached the ship, a steel pin was driven into the ice to moor it and two bearded men in travel-stained windproofs clambered aboard. The dogs flopped down on the ice and, with tongues hanging out, looked about in lazy interest. I was not greatly impressed with them at this stage. Although most of them were big dogs, they seemed a rather nondescript lot.

The penguins lost no time in waddling up to examine the new arrivals. Apart from pricking their ears and watching intently, the huskies showed no signs of excitement as the birds approached. The leading penguin was a yard away when it happened. The huskies suddenly sprang, there was a mass of snapping and snarling dogs, a pitiful, strangled squawk, and all that was left of the little black-and-white creature was an ugly red stain on the snow and a few bedraggled feathers. It had occurred so quickly that no one could have saved the bird.

But did this slaughter send the other penguins scuttling to safety? Not a bit of it. They continued to advance, no longer friendly, but with flippers outspread, neck feathers fluffed up in anger and uttering shrill sounds of rage. The huskies flattened down against the snow and waited. Only the intervention of a sailor, who took the penguins, one by one, by the scruff of their necks and threw them into the nearby water, saved them from being massacred.

This was my introduction to the huskies. Later Georges Schwartz, who had been looking after them for the past year, showed me all the camp's dogs—twenty-odd in three teams, each group chained to a long line.

The first team, comprising mainly three-year-olds and thus at its best age for work, was lead by Bjorn, a powerful but not overintelligent dog. He bullied the other huskies unmercifully, particularly his second-in-command, Fram. If the driver threw a morsel of meat to one of the others, Bjorn would drop on the dog like a thunderbolt, so that all of them were terrified to touch anything while he was looking on. As for patting one of the other dogs, it was quite out of the question—Bjorn would move in, fangs bared and a deep, growling rumble like a lion's issuing from his formidable jaws. No amount of beating will ever break a leader of this habit; he will brook no interference in his rights over his team.

The second team, six young dogs all about a year old, was presided over by Boss, a grizzled warrior of eight years. There was something indomitable about Boss that took your heart immediately. On a sledge trip, having once been set off in the right direction, he needed no further commands. The cut of the sledge runners behind was straight without the slightest deviation. But at eight he was long past his prime and was beginning to fail from sheer age. His gallant spirit spurred him on, but the blood no longer coursed so freely to warm him in bitter cold, and the once tireless muscles had stiffened. The last team was the one which had met us at the boat. It was composed of old dogs and was led by Pickles, a great, handsome husky with the same characteristics as Bjorn. He was most fanatically attached to Judy, the bitch of the team.

The next feeding day—the dogs were not fed every day—I watched and helped as I could while Schwartz took a sledge down to the dump of frozen seal carcasses, loaded on a complete carcass and dragged it back to the first dog line. The moment the dogs scented this meat they began to howl like wolves. As we hacked the seal into four-pound lumps, their excitement rose to a crescendo and fights broke out all over the dog lines. Then, as each husky was thrown a chunk, he dragged it to the farthest limit of his chain to protect it, and fell on it ravenously, tearing great mouthfuls loose and gulping them down, pausing only to bare his fangs momentarily at his neighbors. Watching them feed dispelled any idea that these were normal, friendly dogs, such as we know in civilization.

I chose Bjorn's team for my first try at driving the huskies. The job involved was simple. The seals killed during the voyage had been tossed ashore where the ship had berthed, and I now had to haul them on the sledge, two carcasses at a time, to the food dump near the dog lines, a distance of some five hundred yards. When I appeared with the harnesses, pandemonium broke out—every husky leaped to the end of his chain clamoring to be taken. Going out with a sledge was not considered work, and each dog hoped his team would be chosen. Every husky, that is, except one. Fram, lieutenant of Bjorn's team, was so incurably lazy that he resented interrupting his slumbers even for a jaunt with a sledge.

The first precaution was always to tie the sledge to something solid before harnessing any dog. Otherwise, while I was getting the last dogs from the lines, I would hear an excited howling, and sledge and huskies would whip past at a gallop for a joyous, unattended tour of the bay ice.

I harnessed Bjorn first—the leader always claims this right—and then the beautiful, intelligent and gentle bitch, Ifaut. The bitch was always the nucleus about which our teams were built, the relationship of leader and bitch being a near man-and-wife arrangement. Bjorn never showed the least interest in any other female, nor Ifaut in any dog but Bjorn. Fram was then harnessed, and never wasted any time before falling on his stomach and licking Bjorn's lips as a token of submission; but this Bjorn always reinforced with a few heavy growls and a snap or two just to be sure that Fram realized his place. Fram would wait until the next dog was brought up. This was usually Maru, a great, shambling, friendly husky who was to be only too well-known to us later as the Terror of the Penguins. Fram would immediately attack him. Bjorn, excited by the noise, would then attack Fram. When this was over, Maru would be found at the end of his trace gazing at the distant penguins with hungry eyes. Finally, the other dogs could be harnessed up, though Bjorn found it necessary, as do all husky leaders, to subjugate each one in turn.

That first day, I succeeded in harnessing the team with no more than the ordinary number of fights, but it seemed to me that I would never get the snapping and snarling beasts straightened out. Finally I was able to loose the tie rope and call out, "*Ee, ee, les chiens!*" And as I clung grimly to the steering handles, away we went like the wind, the dogs wild with excitement and for the moment quite uncontrollable. The commands were simple: "*Ee, ee!*" for "go"; "*Heely!*" for "right"; "*Yuck!*" for "left"; and "*Whoa!*" for "stop." To emphasize them, I was supplied with a twenty-foot rawhide whip, which none but a circus performer could possibly use. My efforts with this infernal weapon often resulted in my wrapping the thong about my own neck—no doubt a source of amusement for the dogs.

This time they headed gleefully for one group of penguins after another, and I suppose I must have covered most of the bay. Finally, with much blasphemy and screaming of "*Yuck!*" I managed to steer the team toward the carcass dump. Since there was a twenty-foot ice cliff just beyond it, with freezing water beneath, I could not help wondering how I would stop them. I need not have worried; a food dump was much too interesting to be passed by and, without any command from me, the team pulled up against it and began squabbling over the nearest carcass. Bjorn, the leader, immediately fell upon Fram, not because Fram had done anything, but just as a matter of principle. After Fram had taken his beating like a good lieutenant, he and Bjorn fell upon the other huskies. Ifaut, the gentle lady, avoided all this male squabbling and profited from the diversion by steadily gulping down seal meat.

With two seal carcasses strapped on the sledge, I began the return trip. I had just reached the level snow at the top of the slope and was breathing a sigh of relief, when the dogs took charge, whisked the sledge out of my hands and bounded off toward camp in high glee. There is nothing more humiliating for a would-be dog driver than to be seen running after his team, some hundred yards behind, panting and desperately croaking, "*Whoa!*" while the huskies bound gaily ahead. I finally found the silly beasts with the sledge jammed against a pile of ice, lying down in their harness, with their great tongues lolling out in happy smiles. They were, no doubt, very pleased with their efforts in breaking in their new guardian. I could almost hear Bjorn remark-

ing to Fram, "Of course, he's young and inexperienced, but with a little more training we may be able to do something with him."

We gradually took over the duties of the men we were relieving and prepared to settle in for our year at Port Martin. The *Tottan*, which had taken three of our new party fifty miles west to Pointe Géologie so that they could study the emperor penguins, now returned to take the old party of scientists home. But before the ship could berth —it was held offshore by rough weather—a disaster occurred which changed all our plans.

At 3 A.M. I was awakened by the night-duty man rushing through the sleeping quarters crying, "*Incendie!*" Although my French was not then very good, I had no trouble deciding what he meant. Slipping on a pair of trousers and a jersey, I seized a fire extinguisher and hurried down the passageway. It was hopeless. One entire room was an inferno, and the fifty-mile blizzard blowing outside was fanning it beyond control. The main hut was engulfed as we watched. And in less than half an hour Port Martin had virtually ceased to exist as an Antarctic base. We saved only the scientific records, the weasels (our two-and-one-half-ton Caterpillar tractors), the dogs, a small emergency hut, a few supply dumps, instrument shelters and odds and ends of personal belongings.

Everyone huddled into the tiny emergency hut to escape the cold, and after some radio discussion with the *Tottan*—fortunately our radio sets were in the weasels and thus untouched— the decision was taken to abandon the base and return to France immediately. When the ship was able to berth, we loaded the dogs aboard, with such gear as we could salvage in a few hours, and sailed for Pointe Géologie to pick up the three men there. With the main base gone, we assumed that Pointe Géologie would also be abandoned. But Mario Marret, who had charge of that outpost, felt that since the place teemed with seals it would be possible to survive despite the loss of Port Martin. He decided to stay on for the full year, and when he offered me a post, I accepted.

The *Tottan* did not stay long; the season was well advanced, and she had to leave before the sea froze over. It took only four hours to land our few remaining supplies. Then the seven of us—Marret, Prévost, Rivolier, Duhamel, Vincent, Lépineux and I—watched the ship steam away, leaving us to our own devices for the coming year. We felt very small indeed in the frozen vastness of the Antarctic.

The base at Pointe Géologie consisted of only one small hut and three polar tents, but it afforded one of the finest views in the world. Our camp was on an island surrounded by a stretch of unbroken ice. Beyond was a bay studded with icebergs of fantastic shapes, the water showing indigo blue under the light of the midnight sun. A huge glacier jutted out from shore, its crevasses glowing with emerald green, its white snow-field tinged with pink. Save for a few rocky outcrops, everything else was perpetual ice. A two-hundred-foot ice cliff marked the coastline; behind it the undulating and featureless ice plateau extended in blank, unchanging whiteness to the Pole. This deep ice mantle shrouds the whole Antarctic continent, which is larger than North America; its thickness is generally believed to be between ten thousand and twelve thousand feet. The surface is polished smooth by the everpresent wind, for Adélie Coast is the windiest place in the world.

The blizzards, sweeping down from the Antarctic plateau accompanied by far-below-zero temperatures, are experiences to be remembered with a shudder. When the wind beats up above the seventy-mile-an-hour mark and visibility is reduced to a yard, then one considers it a blizzard. Anything else is merely drifting snow. Marret, who had spent a previous year there, saw snow falling vertically only once; at all other times it was sheeting by horizontally. To know the blizzard is to know Adélie Coast; everything else becomes insignificant. Such were the conditions in which my friends the huskies worked willingly and happily.

The first problem with the dogs was to secure them so they would not destroy the penguins. It sounds easy enough to chain a dog so that he cannot escape, but the ingenuity of the whole seven of us was severely taxed for the rest of the year without our ever achieving absolute certainty that no husky could get loose. The new dog lines took a day to complete, and I was quite sure they would hold. The base was a half-inch wire cable anchored at each end to steel pickets drilled into solid rock. The individual chains were knotted on the cable at intervals, and each dog was fastened to his chain with a heavy clip.

But the huskies had been on the new lines only a day when Maru slipped his collar and made for an Adélie penguin rookery just behind the camp. I followed in hot pursuit with a whip. There was already a trail of dead penguins through the rookery, and at the head of it Maru was killing with savage speed, not to eat but from sheer blood lust. He was horribly efficient—one quick sideways bite and a penguin lay quivering. He would barely release one bird before closing his jaws on another.

When he saw me, Maru began to play hide-and-seek in the rookery, pausing every few seconds to seize a penguin by the throat. He could easily have escaped the cuts of my whip by taking to flight; but he merely quickened his pace enough to keep just ahead of me. When I finally recaptured him, one hundred fifty Adélie penguins lay dead as the result of a few minutes' work. Maru thus achieved the first rating as a public enemy but, alas, he was to be joined by many others before the year was out.

In harness Maru was reasonably satisfactory. He had no great enthusiasm for pulling, but he minded his own business and was always so interested in the passing penguins that he never gave trouble. Watching penguins, he was a caricature of Walt Disney's big bad wolf looking at the fat little pigs. His eyes would follow the birds' every move, his great tongue rolling in an ecstasy of anticipation, his eyes alight with dreamy reminiscence. Strangely enough, despite his record as a penguin killer, he became a great favorite of Prévost, the biologist.

Since Bjorn's team, of which Maru was a member, was the best we had, we used it most frequently for camp chores. Although Bjorn had made himself undisputed king of all the other huskies, he was sadly lacking in intellectual capacity. His only interest in life was pulling a sledge, and from the moment he was put in harness until he was taken out, he pulled. Though he tried his utmost to understand what was wanted, mental problems, such as what to do on the command "left," were often too much for him. When the command to turn one way or the other was given, the rest of the team would usually veer off in the correct direction; seeing their leader heading in the opposite one, they would swing around and follow him. At this I would scream with rage, and Bjorn would realize that he was not doing what was required. He would stop to consider the problem, only to be bumped by Fram, his lieutenant, swinging in behind. This gave him an opportunity to save face as he fell on Fram and beat him up for heading wrong.

Fram then turned on the other dogs and gave them a small beating by way of passing on the reproof. Ifaut, the intelligent and beautiful bitch, would be standing at the end of her trace apart from the others, facing in the required direction all the time, throwing a glance of contempt at her blundering menfolk. On seeing her, a wave of understanding would dawn on Bjorn; finally realizing what direction he should take, he would bound off, throwing a sideways nip at Fram in passing, as if to say, "Now follow me, and don't get me into trouble again."

In that early period, a half-grown puppy named Roald became rather my pet. Being too young to work, he was tied at the end of the dog lines with a six-month-old bitch, Yacka, and they became devoted playmates. Later, we allowed Roald to run loose. The other dogs regarded his carefree liberty as unfair favoritism and took great pleasure in nipping him whenever he came within reach. There would be a scuffle, some startled yelps, and Roald would streak for our hut, his tail between his legs, while the aggressor yawned complacently. It was a severe shock for Roald when his little playmate, Yacka, first became strangely beautiful to the other dogs. The grizzled old warrior Boss, who never wasted such an opportunity, lost no time in breaking his chain and joining Yacka. Roald, seeing her and Boss

apparently playing together, raced over to join in the fun. He bounded round and round the two, barking and prancing, but to his annoyance neither Boss nor Yacka took the least notice of him. Feeling peeved, he gave Boss a nip on the back leg.

Perhaps it would be kindest to draw a veil over what followed. Boss turned round with a look of stunned astonishment and fell on Roald like a flash of lightning. Yacka too, vexed by the interference, joined Boss in the attack. Pieces of Roald flew in all directions, and he barely saved himself, by fleetness of foot, from complete destruction. He spent several days under the hut afterward, trying to understand what change had come over his little friend Yacka. After all, he had only wanted to play.

As the weeks slipped by and the sun at midday became lower in the sky, bringing even colder temperatures with its retreat northward, we began to expand our little hut. Originally twelve-by-eighteen feet, it was tight against snow and wind, and its coal-burning stove was a pulsing heart of warmth-giving life amid the frozen wastes. But as seven of us lived, cooked and worked in the building, the only privacy was in sleep, and even that was apt to be violated by the foot of the man in the bunk above. So, by tearing down one wall and using packing cases for building material, we finally achieved two rooms, a porch and a garage, all securely tied down with wire cables.

Packing cases also came in handy when puppies were due to arrive. The first expectant mother was Judy, the bitch of Pickles' team. I fixed her a maternity hospital just behind the hut by lining and curtaining a packing case with coal sacks, and putting rocks over it to hold it down in the wind. When I brought her in from the dog lines, Judy, an old husky who had been through this before, headed straight for her new quarters and after a brief inspection crawled inside and made herself comfortable.

It was blowing a minor blizzard when the pups found their way into the world. There were three of them to begin with, but Judy soon reduced the number by eating one. Several hours later the second pup was found frozen stiff just outside the kennel. Now, however, Judy began to take care of the third. She tucked him between her back legs, curled her tail around him, pushed her head against him to keep him warm. In that little niche of warm fur and flesh he was safely protected from the fifty-below-zero cold.

For the grown huskies, this sort of weather was normal, of course. When the wind rose and the drift snow began to sheet past, they just curled up, backs to the wind, with their paws tucked about their sensitive nose tips, and went comfortably to sleep. After a few hours in a blizzard not a dog could be seen; all would be buried and would remain so until the weather improved. You could always tell when a blizzard was over: the huskies would emerge and start shaking the ice from their fur. Ice was a problem for the dogs in a blizzard. If they remained snowed in too long their fur froze to the ice beneath, so that they could release themselves only by losing some hair. The more experienced huskies, aware of this danger, got up and shook themselves every three hours or so. For the others, we toured the dog lines regularly, giving all a gentle kick to be sure they did not become iced in.

Paton, Judy's surviving pup, thrived in the warmth and overfeeding of his mother's care. And being the sole pup in the camp, he was soon outrageously spoiled. As a result, he became little more than a round distended stomach propped up on four inadequate legs. Fortunately, Ifaut provided competition for him in a few weeks by producing four beautiful pups. She proved to be an ideal mother, making her kennel a warm haven for the little bundles of fur nestled against her stomach.

Boss, the grizzled old leader and victor of a thousand bloody battles, had to fight yet another, this time with Astro, a large white wolflike dog, the most serious threat to his leadership in the team. Wise in the ways of the pack, Boss knew he could not afford even the semblance of defeat, or the whole team would fall on him together. Boss's

strength was failing now, however, and his teeth were bad from years of chewing rock-hard frozen seal meat. He had only one of the big fang teeth in usable condition, and it is with lightning slashes of the fangs that a husky does most damage. Boss had to bite at an extraordinary angle to get results. And so the old veteran fought less and less now and to a great extent held his position as leader by pure bluff.

Normally, battles between dogs are a mere test of brute strength and savagery. The Astro–Boss battle was different. Astro was heavier and taller than Boss and at his prime, a year and a half old. He was strength and savagery personified. Against him was the old champion, lighter and smaller and minus half his teeth, but past master of every slash and parry of the game. Brute force versus science. Astro, the challenger, with nothing to lose and everything to gain. Boss, desperate, his leadership at stake.

It started over a piece of frozen seal meat lying near Boss. Astro sneaked toward it to steal it, and Boss, seeing him, growled deeply. Astro growled back and continued to advance. Boss leaped at him with one of his usual furious, bluffing rushes. But instead of recoiling as he should have done, Astro struck back, slashing down across Boss's shoulder, drawing blood.

A less experienced dog would have tried to pull free and thus had his shoulder laid open. But Boss yielded with the blow, falling heavily to the ground on his back. Astro instantly shifted his grip to Boss's throat. These holding tactics are always the weakness of young dogs, for in the thick fur of the husky they do little damage. The more experienced husky concentrates on swift, punishing slashes that tear through fur and flesh alike. Boss slowly moved his head across one of Astro's forefeet and seized the other just on the ankle joint where the flesh is thin. Then, with a quick levering of his head against Astro's free leg, he sent the big white husky flying through the air. Before Astro could recover, Boss jumped astride and with swift, raking bites attacked his tender underside. Astro snarled and snapped at Boss's grizzled forehead. One of Boss's ears, already torn and tattered, was laid open, and both huskies were now bleeding freely.

Astro shifted his grip to Boss's foreleg, and as his powerful jaws closed I could hear the bones crunch. Boss was badly hurt and rolled away to ease the pressure, still raking Astro with swift, slashing bites. As Astro once more went for Boss's throat, the two huskies met in midair. Astro reeled back, then came leaping in again with his head low. This was the move Boss had been waiting for. Incredibly swiftly, he swung his body aside, and as the snarling head of the big white husky came level with his shoulder, struck down across the muzzle. His fang tooth cut into Astro's nose and ripped up toward his eyes. It was the end of the fight.

There was no use putting Boss back in the lines for a while now; he would just get involved in another fight. So, putting his wounded leg in a plaster cast, we installed the old warrior in a private kennel behind our hut, as we had done with the expectant mothers, Judy and Ifaut. Temporarily, Boss seemed delighted with his new quarters. Soon, however, he took stock of his companions. His eyes lighted on Judy and her little pup. He seemed puzzled. Then he saw Ifaut. He thought for a few minutes. Then he must have realized what this was—a maternity ward! Jumping to his feet, Boss began to howl indignantly. Nothing so humiliating had ever happened to him before!

In early March, when winter began in earnest and the sea started to freeze up, the first emperor penguins arrived. We were glad to see them, for we were enduring the rigors of Pointe Géologie mainly to study these birds. A reasonable man might well ask to study them under more clement conditions, but the emperor penguin is not a reasonable bird. It practically never sets foot on land. It lives and feeds in the ocean and spends the summer on pack ice. And in the Antarctic winter it sites its rookeries on the frozen-over sea and raises its young under the cruelest conditions in the world.

There were soon to be twelve thousand of them on the sea ice just off Pointe Géologie, and Prévost, our biologist, would be the first man to observe them through an entire breeding season. The emperor is the largest of penguins. He stands three feet six inches high and can weigh up to eighty-five pounds. His severe coloring of black back and white front is relieved by a gorget of gold on either side of the throat. Several startled emperors were soon wandering about the rookery with large red identification numbers painted on their backs—markings so ludicrously out of place in our isolated surroundings as to seem indecent.

By the end of March, courting couples were everywhere. In mid-May the emperors' eggs were laid. At this stage the males were fat with accumulated blubber, the females extremely thin. The female lays only one large egg and immediately passes it over to the male, leaving him to guard it while she goes away to sea to feed. Probably she says to her husband, "Would you mind Junior for a few minutes while I get something to eat?" Then she disappears to the north, and he does not see her again until the end of July. Although we investigated the sea ice by weasel, we were never able to come to the end of it; but we estimated that open water, which the female had to reach to feed, must have been a hundred miles away.

Unable to leave the rookery on account of his charge, the male waits the better part of three months, living on his stored-up blubber. Toward the end he grows very thin and sometimes uses up his reserves of blubber before the egg hatches. Thus from time to time we would see a male, complete with egg—which he carries on the upper side of his feet and covers with his stomach by leaning forward—shuffling his way northward from the rookery in search of food.

From the moment it hatches until it reaches maturity and can fend for itself, the chick faces a grim struggle for survival. There is an enormous mortality rate. But when one considers the truly frightful midwinter in the Antarctic—intense cold, high winds and the nearest source of food, the open sea, scores of miles away at best—the wonder is that any of the chicks survive.

Another public enemy was soon marked down, along with Maru, as a three-star penguin killer.

This was Helen, the black bitch on Boss's team, and we learned to keep the closest kind of watch on her. Helen was one of our most remarkable huskies, but so small that she seemed quite out of place in a team of sledge dogs. I was at first shocked to find this poor little female among them when she seemed so much more suited to life as a pet in a suburban home. But her small body was a mass of steel sinew that was completely tireless. Even at the end of a hard journey when all the other huskies were content to drop in their tracks from fatigue, Helen would still be on her feet, snapping at this dog or that, trying to stir up trouble. She was never so happy as when blood and fur were flying, and she was so startlingly savage that no dog dared put fangs to her, even amid the excitement of a general brawl.

And now Helen began to show signs of needing a lodging in our packing-case maternity ward. She objected strongly to being removed from her team. Unlike Judy and Ifaut, she treated her new kennel with contempt, preferring to sleep outside in the snow. And what made it difficult for me was that she objected vocally, making her loudest protests at night, when she sustained particularly piercing howls for eight hours without a break. But her howling finally stopped—at 4 A.M. one night during a blizzard. I struggled into my windproofs, pulled on fur boots and gloves and went out to investigate. I found Helen nosing six newborn pups in a puzzled manner, but making no attempt to protect them. All were outside the kennel. I installed Helen in the kennel and then pushed the newborn pups into the softness of her stomach. With her back to the opening and the pups underneath her legs, all seemed to be well, so I returned to my warm bed.

About four hours later, when I made a further inspection, I found six little bodies lying outside the kennel frozen as hard as rocks and Helen happily asleep. I decided to put her back in her team at once. She left the kennel without a backward glance at her dead puppies. The trouble with Helen seemed to be that she had no softer side. Perhaps this had started at the time of her first litter two years before when, because of a shortage of dogs, she had had to be taken on a sledging journey with her pups almost due. She

had pulled her way with the team until the last moment, then produced the pups on the ice. The new puppies had frozen to death at once, and Helen was harnessed up and went on pulling. A husky's life is not altogether an easy one.

A new drama was soon being enacted in the dog lines. It began when Helen was mated with Astro. Old Boss, whose whole authority rested on his ancient prestige, felt the situation keenly. There was dejected shame in his attitude. His young and high-spirited team seemed delighted with this unpunished transgression. It could have passed had not the young Labrador cross, Pomme, sensing Boss's dejection, begun a series of tentative attacks. Finding Boss's defense half-hearted, he swung in on him in full battle. Waking from his mood of helplessness, Boss returned the offensive, and a real fight began. The other members of the team were beside themselves with excitement.

Backward and forward rolled the two combatants. Boss was swift and sure, slashing and cutting, each quick movement drawing blood; Pomme was blundering and heavy, but tireless in the flush of his youth. Though Boss was undoubtedly winning on points, he was unable to hurt the big Labrador cross seriously through his matted fur. And every now and then Pomme, for all his ungainliness a very powerful dog, was able to sink his fangs into Boss. What was worst for Boss was that he was physically incapable of a long fight. He needed a swift, decisive battle to win, and every minute the combat continued, his hope of victory diminished. In the breaks he stood gasping, with blood dripping from his wounds. Then, as soon as he recovered his breath, he would launch his tired old body against Pomme once more.

It was in such a breathing space that the tragedy occurred. The concerted leaping of all the excited dogs against their chains broke out a pin at one end of the center trace, and the whole team of blood-mad huskies closed in on the two fighters. I caught just a glimpse of Boss's expression as the eight powerful young huskies fell on him while I raced across to try to stop the inevitable. I had only an inkling of what must follow, but Boss knew.

He sank down, belly to the ground, to protect his soft underside, and with his lips drawn back over his broken teeth prepared to defend himself. Then he was hidden by a mass of snarling and snapping huskies, each determined to repay the old leader for past beatings. They had no fear of him now. It was the end of Boss. Had I left him there a few minutes longer they would certainly have killed him. Perhaps it would have been as well that way, because what I succeeded in pulling clear of the cruel fangs was no longer Boss but a poor tattered remnant in spirit and body of the grand old husky we had all known so well.

As seven of us were now living on stores meant for three, Marret decided to search the burnt-out base of Port Martin for further supplies. The plan was to go there in the one weasel we had, dig out and start the three weasels abandoned there, and use the four machines to tow back sledges filled with whatever food and equipment we could find which had escaped the fire. Because we were short of gas for the journey, we would have to go the shortest possible way, which was over the frozen sea. The snout of a glacier which projected far out from the coast lay across this route and presented a continuous wall of ice cliffs two hundred feet high. But by making daily scouting trips with the dogs, Vincent and I finally discovered a passage through which we could get to Port Martin.

There was now nothing to delay our departure—except the date, June 21, which is traditionally celebrated in the Antarctic as midwinter day. Our hut seemed hardly the setting for the party of the year, but we festooned it with the red pennants used as trail markers, masked the bare wood ceiling by hanging a white tent lining from the rafters and concealed the bunks with a roll of green canvas. Dipping recklessly into our stores, Lépineux and Rivolier, our best cooks, produced a fitting meal; and each of us dug deep into his poor supply of clothing to produce his gayest and cleanest garments for the occasion.

It was warm and merry in the hut, though the wind and snow whistled past outside. As we sat down to the groaning table, the seven gayest men in that sector of the Antarctic were determined to do justice to the wine and fine food— the four of us who were facing the long and hazardous weasel trip being perhaps the most determined. In the center of the table stood our greatest treasure—our sole bottle of champagne. Amid the mounting festivity there was a moment of shocked silence as Marret accidentally spilled his one allotted glass. But he carried it off. "Anyone can have champagne to drink," he remarked. "True luxury is having champagne to waste."

Then someone suggested that the small puppies be brought in to share our festivities. Soon they were squabbling under the table, stuffed with food and having a wonderful time. A little later a wandering emperor penguin was invited inside. He stood solemnly at the end of the table and viewed the proceedings with a disapproving eye. To cheer him up, we offered him a spoonful of brandy and two vitamin C pills. The effect was startling. The previously dignified and no doubt teetotaling bird began to behave in a manner that made his condition unmistakable. A fighting drunk if ever I saw one. With raucous cries he chased the pups about the floor, and when all pups were hiding, trembling with fear, he turned his aggression on the men. Regretfully, we were obliged to show our new friend the door.

Six hours later, Marret, Duhamel, Vincent and I set off for Port Martin in the weasel. The journey, which took upward of a month, proved to be as difficult as we had feared. As we traveled over the sea ice, always conscious that the water was only a yard below us, we frequently came to open leads which we had to bridge with timbers. Once the head of a seal popped up in our headlights from the apparently solid ice just ahead. This led us to the somber reflection that where a seal can come up a weasel can go down.

At Port Martin, we chipped out and salvaged from the ice two of the abandoned weasels. Even our invincibly competent mechanic, Roger Vincent, was not equal to starting the third. Despite almost constant blizzard we also unearthed gasoline, food and gear from the buried supply dumps. When we somehow got back over the same peril-strewn route—with *three* weasels now, each dragging a well-filled sledge—it was incredibly good to have the frigid journey behind us. And as we drifted off to sleep in the warm bunks of our hut (we had forgotten what temperatures above freezing felt like), the howling of the dogs sounded like music.

The salvaged supplies transformed the whole future of our group. We now had ample food for the rest of the year and, in fact, everything we needed to make us a normal expedition. The weasels were particularly useful for long-range explorations. But I could never feel for them what I did for the unpredictable, warm-blooded dogs. Since Boss's defeat and demoralization, his team had had no leader. We had to find a dog to take over the team, but the question was, which? A leader should not only be intelligent; he should also possess the fighting ability to control his team by fear. The two qualities do not necessarily go together.

But one rather significant thing had happened recently. Fram, the lazy lieutenant in Bjorn's team, had broken his chain and made a bloody tour of the dog lines, in which he had attacked and beaten every husky in the lines save one, his own leader Bjorn, with whom he still lived in a state of cringing fear. This showed his ability as a fighter, and there was little doubt about his intelligence—if a marked skill at avoiding work could be classed as such. Every one of us had had experience with Fram's sly cunning, when driving Bjorn's team. Every trace would be taut, but the sledge would not be advancing as it should. If a finger was hooked over Fram's trace he could be pulled back a yard before he realized his laziness had been detected. He could travel for miles with just enough strain on his trace to give the impression he was pulling. So it seemed just possible that Fram was smart enough to be the new leader we needed.

Physically, he was a magnificent specimen: a big husky of about a hundred pounds, with a deep chest and heavy thighs mounted on short, sturdy legs. His forehead was broad, his eyes sharp and inquisitive. He was, of all our dogs, the most typical of the popular conception of a husky. For want of a better candidate, Fram got his chance.

Before his first journey as leader, we put Fram in harness at the sledge alone, then brought over the members of his team, one by one, for mutual introduction. This was accomplished much more speedily than we had anticipated, and comparatively painlessly. A brief scrimmage ensued as each husky was attacked and beaten; then he formally acknowledged his new leader by fawning and licking Fram's jaws. Astro, the big white husky, offered no resistance at all. He saw in Fram a much tougher proposition than he could hope to handle, so immediately acknowledged Fram's leadership in the approved fashion and elected himself as Fram's lieutenant. Fram also wasted no time in claiming another perquisite of his new office—the attentions of the bitch, Helen.

As we traveled, I took stock of the team and felt confident that it would be a good one. Each day, Fram emerged more and more as a distinct individual. With his team he was stern authority, bullying, punishing and meeting the least infringement of his rule with swift attack. With me he displayed a tremendous dignity that was unassailable by a mere man; one could get so close to Fram but no closer. "You have your place in the team, and I have mine," his attitude said quite clearly. "There is no reason to attempt familiarity."

Moreover, he had an amiable obstinacy of purpose that I found impossible to combat. The behavior of the team when we went seal hunting was a case in point. I had long established the conduct of the teams about a seal carcass while the driver was skinning the beast. Severe discipline was always necessary then, for the sight and smell of fresh blood titillated the dogs' ravenous appetites to a point of frenzy, and unless the driver kept them under control, there would be a sudden stampede. So, when the team arrived about fifty yards from the seal, they would be halted, while I went ahead on foot to shoot the quarry. When the blubber was stripped off, I would call up the huskies. They would drag up the sledge, then sit round in a half circle, tongues hanging out, watching each slash of the knife avidly. From time to time I would throw each husky, in turn, a chunk of meat.

Fram did not agree with this procedure. He considered that there was no point in waiting for my call; the gunshot was sufficient advice that there was now no chance of frightening the seal. So, as soon as the shot rang out, he brought the sledge up. His gang of young toughs, encouraged by this, came rushing in with jaws agape. I was prepared to withstand boarders when suddenly Fram turned about and gave a few quick snaps. In a moment the team was sitting in the usual half circle facing Fram, who had planted himself, facing them, between the dogs and the seal.

I offered the big dog a chunk of seal meat by way of reward. He spurned it, leaving it untouched where it had fallen. He then got up and made a close inspection of the seal. Selecting a choice piece, he tore it off and gulped it down, watching my reactions as he did so. At the same time, the other huskies had all been eyeing the first morsel that I had thrown to Fram. It became too much for them, and there was a concerted rush. Fram's lazy insolence dropped away, and he sprang into action. Immediately the team recoiled into a half circle with Fram watching over them, growling. I then tried to give each husky a piece of seal, as was my usual custom. Fram objected strongly, falling on each dog as the meat was thrown to him, so that the meat lay where it had fallen, with the dog cringing on his belly.

This was a bit thick! The time had come for me to assert my waning authority. Fram was telling me I could not feed his team without his approval. So I took the whip off the sledge and advanced on Fram. As the whip fell, the dog in front of Fram took advantage of the diversion to edge toward his piece of meat. But even as the whip cut Fram, a deep-throated growl from him stopped the other dog, who whined in submission and remained still. Fram was determined not to surrender his opinion, so for the rest of the day he accepted beating after beating, but

still exercised his authority over the team. Not one of those dogs ate a morsel. In the end I had to confess I was beaten. And this was the thin edge of a very long wedge. Fram won point after point in a similar manner. I was gradually made to feel that I was a very minor piece of equipment of the sledge; all I had to do was to leave the management up to him.

One of our main undertakings for the year was a journey westward to map and survey the coast. Four of us were to go—Marret, Vincent, Rivolier and myself—and as the project would take almost two months, we planned it with much thought. We packed only the most concentrated rations and for transport decided to take two weasels and eleven dogs. We exercised great care in the selection of the dogs. The time had long passed when all the huskies looked alike to us; now we knew each one as a distinct personality. In fact, we probably knew the characters of the huskies better than we knew each other's. We finally chose Fram's team and elements of Bjorn's. The plan was that a strong team of eight dogs headed by Fram would pull a loaded sledge, while three reserve dogs would be attached to a weasel sledge and run free of load so they would always be fresh. Fram's team consisted of Astro, Helen, Roald, Maru, Pomme, Seismo and Wild. Bjorn and two younger huskies, Milk and Tiki, made the reserve.

On November 5, Marret, Vincent and Rivolier clambered into the weasels, and the procession moved off. The lead weasel, towing a heavily laden barge, was followed by the second machine towing an even more heavily laden barge and a sledge carrying a ton of gas. The three reserve dogs were attached to this gas sledge, and I brought up the rear with Fram's team, pulling their own loaded sledge. Down the slope from the hut the convoy moved, out over the sea ice and across the frozen bay toward the polar sun. The roaring of the weasel motors broke the cold Antarctic silence, and now and then as the dogs settled down to pulling, one of them whimpered. The sledge runners made a soft swishing, and, walking alongside, I pulled on my gloves and parka hood, for the wind chilled bare flesh to the bone.

The long journey was filled with trying difficulties for the weasels. In the zone of crevasses, which we struck on the second day out, they sometimes broke through deceptively solid-looking snow bridges and were barely saved from plummeting to the lethal depths below. Frequently they shed their tracks and sometimes slipped and fell over on their sides and had to be jacked upright again. And before a quarter of the journey was done we had smashed a mainspring and used our only spare to replace it.

Accidents were not limited to the machines. Once when we were ten miles inland from the coast Seismo had a shock that he no doubt remembered for a long time. We were crossing a zone of blue ice when we encountered a strip of snow. If Seismo had asked the other dogs or me, he would have been informed that this was a thin snow bridge over a crevasse. As it was, all the other dogs leaped the danger, landing on the firm ice on the other side. Seismo jumped only halfway, the snow dissolved under his feet and he went hurtling into the abyss. Standing on the sledge, I shot safely across, catching a momentary glimpse of Seismo dangling ten feet down in his harness, much too startled even to yelp. The next second he came shooting out of the crevasse like a jack-in-the-box as the onward movement of the other dogs dragged him back to safety. Before he could collect his wits, he was back in his place in the team, pulling and wearing a most puzzled expression.

Never was Bjorn's lack of intelligence more clearly demonstrated than on this journey. He was chained to a weasel sledge carrying a ton of gas. The general idea was that he could run alongside it or, if he wished, he could jump aboard and ride. But poor Bjorn had been brought up as a well-trained husky. The first lesson he had ever been taught was that the job of a husky when attached to a sledge is to pull. So, when he found himself attached to that sledge weighing a ton, he pulled as hard as he could, nonstop. Somewhere in the fuzzy recesses of his brain he had come to associate the whir of the weasel starter with the command to mush. So

each time he heard the starter he would jump down from the sledge, put his back into it and pull. In those hundred weary miles poor Bjorn never realized it was the weasel and not he that dragged that massive load. And this despite the fact that alongside him were Milk and Tiki, sitting on the weasel sledge with pleased smiles on their faces!

It was on this trip that the battle for kingship of the huskies took place. For months we had been expecting it. Until recently Bjorn had been secure in his position of king dog, the undisputed master in battle of every dog in the lines. But Fram, since his promotion to team leader, had demonstrated that he too could handle any other dog. The final combat was inevitable, for there must always be a king dog.

It was difficult to estimate who would win. If Bjorn had forced the issue when Fram first became a leader, there would have been no doubt about the outcome. The long years that Fram had spent in submission to him would have won the day for Bjorn. But Bjorn was uncertain and hesitated. In hesitating, he gave Fram confidence, while the wily Fram avoided battle and undermined Bjorn's bullying self-assurance. Thus it was two months before the heavyweight championship was settled.

We did not see the fight when it occurred, and afterward we could only deduce what had happened. Fram, as was customary, was roaming free, and Astro, his big white lieutenant, had broken loose and was with him. The two of them, prowling about, had evidently found themselves on an ice shelf ten feet above the sleeping and unprepared Bjorn. The first intimation Bjorn had of battle must have been when two hundred pounds of husky in two snarling lumps dropped out of the heavens above him.

We pictured Bjorn suddenly awakened to find the most decisive battle of his life already in progress, not against one husky but against two who, through past training, moved as though directed by one mind. Perhaps, if it had started with preliminary skirmishes, Bjorn might yet have won, for he was enormously powerful and almost impervious to punishment. But the battle was half lost to him before he knew it had commenced.

Bjorn probably attempted to concentrate on Astro, trying with a swift attack to put the lesser enemy out of action first. But Fram must have been too cunning for that, pressing the attack until Bjorn lay exhausted and whimpering on the ground. Thus Fram won the husky kingship of our polar world.

On our return trip, Pomme distinguished himself at one overnight camp by eating my fifteen-foot sealskin whip. I came out of the tent in the morning to find him at the final stage of this repast. He had managed most of his fifteen-foot meal, and he stood there with a dreamy expression in his eyes, masticating gently, with the butt of the whip still hanging sadly out of his mouth. Otherwise, the return was almost without event. Fram proved to be at his very best in the broken terrain that we encountered. He continually looked back, so that, when the sledge lurched on a dangerous ice slope, without a word from his driver he would bring his team to one side to save it from slipping to disaster. When running along narrow snow cornices, with a drop of a hundred feet on either side, there was no need to shout directions to him; before I could decide what should be done, Fram would take the necessary action and avert the danger. More and more on that trip, I realized that the fewer orders I gave Fram, the less trouble we had.

When we got back to the hut, there was a touching reunion between Bjorn and Ifaut, separated by the journey. It was like husband and wife coming together after a long absence. Bjorn showed her his half-healed wounds, and she licked them sympathetically, baring her teeth at Fram, who was chained nearby. After a few days near Ifaut, Bjorn recovered most of his old spirit.

All that remained for us now was to fill in the little time left until the arrival of the *Tottan*. We had come through our year on the ice unscathed. But over the dog lines was the shadow of death: The directors of the expedition in Paris had radioed us that arrangements could not be made to

bring them back to France. All must be shot.

There are no rewards for the husky. All his adult life he lives on a chain, in the open, racked by the wind and snow and bitter cold. He suffers the stern discipline of the driver and the even sterner discipline of his leader. He is fed meat frozen so hard that an ax can hardly cut it. Water he never knows: he slakes his thirst with dry, cold snow. His only relief from boredom is battle with other huskies. Every day he works, his team is expected to pull a heavily laden sledge from twenty to thirty miles, and when he is no longer capable, there is no leisured old age—only execution. Thus the average husky's lot is not a happy one. But ours, owing to circumstance, were not even to live out their normal span. We found this hard to accept, for we had become extremely fond of our dogs despite their savagery.

We often speculated as to whether they would turn on a badly injured driver if he were on his own—a question, fortunately, that was never resolved. I do not think they would, since from puppyhood they have been taught that the one unforgivable sin is to bite a man. During the whole year with this group I was bitten only once, by mistake. I was leading another dog across Fram when he leaped, but misjudged his stroke. Immediately he cowered back, struck by the enormity of his crime. Any one of us could wade into a snarling, seething mass of huskies, all engaged in a desperate free-for-all, and cuff the blood-mad brutes without risk of being bitten.

It was sad, now, to walk past our canine comrades, each of whom followed our progress with trusting and friendly eyes, and to think that soon we must be their executioners. To say that we were not looking forward to this massacre would be a masterpiece of understatement. Yet each man volunteered to do away with his own favorite husky. Each of us wanted to be sure that the dog would know nothing. The thought of taking old Boss on his last walk was a melancholy one. As for Fram . . .

Then one day Marret shouted from the wireless set, "Our dogs are saved!" A message had just come through from Paris saying that

Esquimaux Dogs *by W. Smith*

satisfactory arrangements had been made for taking the huskies to France, and that all dogs, including even the useless veterans like Boss, were to go back.

Seven days after Christmas the high crow's nest of the *Tottan* appeared over the horizon. The motor launch was an interminably long time in being lowered and in covering the few miles to shore. After a year that seemed to have passed away almost unnoticed, this last hour was endless.

Without regret we closed the door of the hut for the last time, then trooped down to the landing. The huskies were driven to the water's edge, their traces were cut, and one by one they were lowered, still in harness, into the waiting launch. A little later I stood on the *Tottan*'s afterdeck looking back. In the far distance I could see the bright light of the midnight sun showing reddish on the polar plateau. Then that too was gone, and our horizon was the boundless sea.

I took leave of my fellow adventurers sadly —men and dogs—at the ship's side in Australia.

When I gave a final pat to Fram, who left a gap in my life no other dog will ever fill, it was like saying farewell for the last time to an old and dear friend. Fram and his team were soon pulling a sledge at Chamonix; most of the others were scattered in the Alps. Boss, who had known the full gamut of a husky's life, who had been born among the Eskimos in Greenland, served as a team member, fought his way to leadership and finally had been deposed after years of unremitting service, who in the normal way of things would have been eased to a well-earned rest with a bullet in his skull, found a closing chapter to his years so just that I hesitate to record it, for fear of being accused of romancing.

Each morning, inside the wall surrounding a certain gracious home not far from Paris, a servant would approach a spacious kennel with a bowl of chocolate. A grizzled, scarred old dog would emerge from the kennel to receive it. He would then be taken to the center of the garden, to a tree where he would lie most of the day, warming his old bones under a friendly sun, interrupted only at midday when a bowl of soup would be brought to him. Accustomed to such attentions, he would not even get to his feet; he would merely lean his head over the bowl and lap up the soup while lying on his side. Yes, Boss lazed out his last years in the sunshine near Paris, visited frequently by his human friends and idolized by the lady who volunteered to provide a home for him. No one who knew the grand old husky could dispute his claim.

Dog Days

by **KONRAD LORENZ**

Knowing me in my soul the very same—
One who would die to spare you touch of ill!—
Will you not grant to old affection's claim
The hand of friendship down Life's
          sunless hill?

                              Thomas Hardy

I once possessed a fascinating little book of crazy tales called *Snowshoe Al's Bedtime Stories.* It concealed behind a mask of ridiculous nonsense that penetrating and somewhat cruel satire which is one of the characteristic features of American humor, and which is not always easily intelligible to many Europeans. In one of these stories Snowshoe Al relates with romantic sentimentality the heroic deeds of his best friend. Incidents of incredible courage, exaggerated manliness and complete altruism are piled up in a comical parody of Western American romanticism culminating in the touching scenes where the hero saves his friend's life from wolves, grizzly bears, hunger, cold and all the manifold dangers which beset him. The story ends with the laconic statement, "In so doing, his feet became so badly frozen that I unfortunately had to shoot him."

If I ask a man who has just been boasting of the prowess and other wonderful properties of one of his dogs, I always ask him whether he has still got the animal. The answer, then, is all too often strongly reminiscent of Snowshoe Al's story, "No, I had to get rid of him—I moved to another town—or into a smaller house—I got another job and it was awkward for me to keep a dog," or some other similar excuse. It is to me amazing that many people who are otherwise morally sound feel no disgrace in admitting such an action. They do not realize that there is no difference between their behavior and that of the satirized egoist in the story. The animal is deprived of rights, not only by the letter of the law, but also by many people's insensitivity.

The fidelity of a dog is a precious gift demanding no less binding moral responsibilities than the friendship of a human being. The bond with a true dog is as lasting as the ties of this earth can ever be, a fact which should be noted by anyone who decides to acquire a canine friend. It may of course happen that the love of a dog is thrust upon one involuntarily, a circumstance which occurred to me when I met the Hanoverian Schweisshund, "Hirschmann," on a skiing tour. He was at the time about a year old and a typical masterless dog; for his owner the head forester only loved his old Deutscher Rauhaar (German pointer) and had no time for the clumsy stripling which showed few signs of ever becoming a gun-dog. Hirschmann was soft and sensitive and a little shy of his master, a fact which did not speak highly for the training ability of the forester. On the other hand I did not think any the better of the dog for coming out with us as early as the second day of our stay. I took him for a sycophant, quite wrongly as it turned out, for he was following not us but me alone. When one morning I found him sleeping outside my bedroom door, I began to reconsider my first opinion and to suspect that a great canine love was germinating. I realized it too late: the oath of allegiance had been sworn, nor would the dog recant on the day of my departure. I tried to catch him in order to shut him up and prevent him from following us, but he refused to come near me. Quivering with consternation and with his tail between his legs he stood at a safe distance saying with his eyes, "I'll do anything at all for you—except leave you!" I capitulated. "Forester, what's the price of your dog?" The forester, from whose point of view the dog's conduct was sheer desertion, replied without a moment's consideration, "Ten shillings." It sounded like an expletive and was meant as such. Before he could think of a better one, the ten shillings were in his hand and two pairs of skis and two pairs of dog's paws were under way. I knew that Hirschmann would follow us but surmised erroneously that, plagued by his conscience, he would slink after us at a distance, thinking that he was not allowed to come with us. What really did happen was entirely unexpected. The full weight of the huge dog hit me broadside on like a cannon ball and I was precipitated hip foremost on to the icy road. A skier's equilibrium is not proof against the impact of an enormous dog, hurled in a delirium of excitement against him. I had quite underestimated his grasp of the situation. As for Hirschmann, he danced for joy over my extended corpse.

I have always taken very seriously the responsibility imposed by a dog's fidelity, and I am proud that I once risked my life, though inadvertently, to save a dog which had fallen into the Danube at a temperature of $-28°$ C. My Alsatian, Bingo, was running along the frozen edge of the river when he slipped and fell into the water. His claws were unable to grip the sides of the ice so he could not get out. Dogs become exhausted very quickly when attempting to get up too steep a bank. They get into an awkward, more and more upright swimming position until they are soon in imminent danger of drowning. I therefore ran a few yards ahead of the dog which was being swept downstream; then I lay down and, in order to distribute my weight, crept on my belly to the edge of the ice. As Bingo came within my reach, I seized him by the scruff of the neck and pulled him with a jerk towards me on to the ice, but our joint weight was too much for it—it broke, and I slid silently, head first into the freezing cold water. The dog, which, unlike myself, had its head shorewards, managed to reach firmer ice. Now the situation was reversed; Bingo ran apprehensively along the ice and I floated downstream in the current. Finally, because the human hand is better adapted than the paw of the dog for gripping a smooth surface, I managed to escape disaster by my own efforts. I felt ground beneath my feet and threw my upper half upon the ice.

We judge the moral worth of two human friends according to which of them is ready to make the greater sacrifice without thought of recompense. Nietzsche who, unlike most people, wore brutality only as a mask to hide true warmness of heart, said the beautiful words, "Let it be your aim always to love more than the other, never to be the second." With human beings, I am sometimes able to fulfil this commandment, but in my relations with a faithful dog, I am always the second. What a strange and unique social relationship! Have you ever thought how extraordinary it all is? Man, endowed with reason and a highly developed sense of moral responsibility, whose finest and noblest belief is the religion of brotherly love, in this very respect falls short of the carnivores. In saying this I am not indulging in sentimental anthropomorphization. Even the noblest human love arises, not from reason and the specifically human, rational moral sense, but from the much deeper age-old layers of instinctive feeling. The highest and most selfless moral behavior loses all value in our estimation when it arises not from such sources but from the reason. Elizabeth Browning said:

If thou must love me, let it be for nought
Except for love's sake only.

Even today man's heart is still the same as that of the higher social animals, no matter how far the achievements of his reason and his rational moral sense transcend theirs. The plain fact that my dog loves me more than I love him is undeniable and always fills me with a certain feeling of shame. The dog is ever ready to lay down his life for me. If a lion or a tiger threatened me, Ali, Bully, Tito, Stasi, and all the others would, without a moment's hesitation, have plunged into the hopeless fight to protect my life if only for a few seconds. And I?

The brilliant smell of water,
The brave smell of a stone.
      G. K. CHESTERTON, *Quoodle's Song*

I do not know how the dog days got their name. I believe from Sirius the dog star, but the etymological origin of the North German synonym, the "Sauregurkenzeit" (sour cucumber time), seems much more appropriate. But for me personally, the dog days could not be better named, because I make a habit of spending them in the exclusive company of my dog. When I am fed to the teeth with brain work, when clever talk and politeness nearly drive me distracted, when the very sight of a typewriter fills me with revulsion, all of which sentiments generally overtake me at the end of a normal summer term, then I decide to "go to the dogs." I retire from human society and seek that of animals—and for this reason: I know almost no human being who is lazy enough to keep me company in such a mood, for I possess the priceless gift of being able, when in a state of great contentment, to shut off my higher thinking powers completely, and this is the essential condition for perfect peace of mind. When, on a hot summer day, I swim across the Danube and lie in a dreamy backwater of the great river, like a crocodile in the mud, amongst scenery that shows not the slightest sign of the existence of human civilization, then I sometimes achieve that miraculous state which is the highest goal of oriental sages. Without going to sleep, my higher centers dissolve into a strange at-oneness with surrounding nature; my thoughts stand still, time ceases to mean anything and, when the sun begins to sink and the cool of the evening warns me that I have still another three and a half miles to swim home, I do not know whether seconds or years have passed since I crawled out on to the muddy bank.

This animal nirvana is an unequaled panacea for mental strain, true balm for the mind of hurried, worried, modern man, which has been rubbed sore in so many places. I do not always succeed in achieving this healing return to the thoughtless happiness of prehuman paradise but I am most likely to do so in the company of an animal which is still a rightful participant of it. Thus there are very definite and deep-rooted reasons why I need a dog which accompanies me faithfully but which has retained a wild exterior and thus does not spoil the landscape by its civilized appearance.

Yesterday morning at dawn, it was already so hot that work—mental work—seemed hopeless—a heaven-sent Danube day! I left my room armed with fishing net and glass jar, in order to catch and carry the live food which I always bring home for my fishes from every Danube excursion. As always, this is an unmistakable sign for Susi that a dog day, a happy dog day is pending. She is quite convinced that I undertake these expeditions for her exclusive benefit and perhaps she is not altogether wrong. She knows that I not only allow her to go with me but that I set the greatest store by her company; nevertheless, to be quite sure of not being left behind, she presses close to my legs all the way to the yard gate. Then, with proudly raised bushy tail, she trots down the village street before me, her dancing, elastic gait showing all the village dogs that she is afraid of none of them, even when Wolf II is not with her. With the horribly ugly mongrel belonging to the village grocer—I hope he will never read this book—she usually has a short flirtation. To the deep disgust of Wolf II, she loves this checkered creature more than any other dog, but today she has no time for him, and when he attempts to play with her she wrinkles her nose and bares her gleaming teeth at him before trotting on to growl, according to her custom, at her various enemies behind their different garden fences.

The village street is still in the shade and its hard ground is cold beneath my bare feet, but beyond the railway bridge the deep dust of the path to the river presses itself, caressingly warm, between my toes, and above the footprints of the dog trotting in front of me it rises in little clouds in the still air. Crickets and cicada chirp merrily and, on the nearby river bank, a golden oriole and a black-cap are singing. Thank goodness that they are still singing—that summer is still young enough. Our way leads over a freshly mown meadow and Susi leaves the path, for this is a special "mousing" meadow. Her trot becomes a curious, stiff-legged slink, she carries her head very high, her whole expression betraying her excitement, and her tail sinks low, stretched out behind, close above the ground. Altogether she resembles a rather too fat blue Arctic fox. Suddenly, as though released by a spring, she shoots in a semicircle about a yard high and two yards forwards. Landing on her forepaws close together and stiffly outstretched, she bites several times, quick as lightning, into the short grass. With loud snorts she bores her pointed nose into the ground, then, raising her head, she looks questioningly in my direction, her tail wagging all the time: the mouse has gone. She certainly feels ashamed when her tremendous mouse jump misses its mark, and she is equally proud if she catches her prey. Now she slinks further on and four further leaps fall short of their goal—voles are amazingly quick and agile. But now the little Chow bitch flies through the air like a rubber ball and as her paws touch the ground there follows a high-pitched, painfully sharp squeak. She bites again, then, with a hurried shaking movement, drops what she was biting, and a small, gray body flies in a semicircle through the air with Susi, in a larger semicircle, after it. Snapping several times, with retracted lips, she seizes, with her incisors only, something squeaking and struggling in the grass. Then she turns to me and shows me the big, fat, distorted fieldmouse that she is holding in her jaws. I praise her roundly and declare that she is a most terrifying, awe-inspiring animal for whom one must have the greatest respect. I am sorry for the vole but I did not know it personally, and Susi is my bosom friend whose triumphs I feel bound to share. Nevertheless, my conscience is easier when she eats it, thereby vindicating herself by the only action that can ever justify killing. First she gingerly chews it with her incisors only to a formless but still intact mass, then she takes it far back into her mouth and begins to gobble it up and swallow it. And now for the time being she has had enough of mousing and suggests to me that we should proceed.

Our path leads to the river, where I undress and hide my clothes and fishing tackle. From here the track goes upstream, following the old tow-path where in former times horses used to pull the barges up the river. But now the path is so overgrown that only a narrow strip remains which leads through a thick forest of golden rod, mixed unpleasantly with solitary nettles and blackberry bushes, so that one needs both arms to keep the stinging pricking vegetation from one's body. The damp heat in this plant wilderness is truly unbearable and Susi walks panting at my heels, quite indifferent to any hunting prospects that the undergrowth may hold. I can understand her apathy because I am dripping with sweat, and I pity her in her thick fur coat. At last we reach the place where I wish to cross the river. At the present low level of the river a wide shingle bank stretches far out into the current and, as I pick my way somewhat painfully over the stones, Susi runs ahead joyfully and plunges breast high into the water where she lies down till only her head remains visible: a queer little angular outline against the vast expanse of the river.

As I wade out into the current, the dog presses close behind me and whines softly. She has never yet crossed the Danube and its width fills her with misgiving. I speak reassuringly to her and wade in further, but she is obliged to start swimming when the water reaches barely to my knees and she is carried rapidly downstream. In order to keep up with her, I begin to swim too, although it is far too shallow for me, but the fact that I am now traveling as swiftly as she is reassures her and she swims steadily by my side. A dog that will swim alongside its master shows particular intelligence: many dogs can never realize the fact that in the water a man is not upright as it is used to seeing him, with the unpleasant result that, in an attempt to keep close behind the head on the surface of the water, it scratches its master's back horribly with its wildly paddling paws.

But Susi has immediately grasped the fact that a man swims horizontally and she carefully avoids coming too near to me from behind. She is nervous in the broad, sweeping river and keeps as close beside me as possible. Now her anxiety reaches such a pitch that she rears up out of the water and looks back at the bank we have left behind us. I am afraid that she may turn back altogether but she settles down again, swimming quietly at my side. Soon another difficulty arises: in her excitement and in the effort to cross the great, wide current as quickly as possible, she strikes out at a speed which I cannot indefinitely maintain. Panting, I strain to keep up with her, but she outstrips me again and again, only to turn round and swim back to me every time she finds herself a few yards ahead. There is always the danger that, on sighting our home shore, she will leave me and return to it, since for an animal in a state of apprehension the direction of home exerts a much stronger pull than any other. In any case, dogs find it hard to alter course while swimming, so that I am relieved when I have persuaded her to turn again in the right direction and, swimming with all my might to keep close behind her, to send her on again each time she tries to come back. The fact that she understands my encouragement and is influenced by it is fresh proof to me that her intelligence is well above the average.

We land on a sandbank which is steeper than the one we have just left. Susi is some yards in front of me, and as she climbs out of the water and makes her first few steps on dry land I see that she sways noticeably to and fro. This slight disturbance of balance, which passes in a few seconds and which I myself often experience after a longer swim, is known to many swimmers, who have confirmed my observation. But I can find no satisfactory physiological explanation for it. Although I have repeatedly noticed it in dogs, I have never seen it in such a marked degree as Susi showed on this occasion. The condition has nothing to do with exhaustion, which fact Susi at once makes clear to me by expressing in no uncertain measure her joy at having conquered the stream. She bursts forth in an ecstasy of joy, races in small circles round my legs and finally fetches a stick for me to throw for her, a game into which I willingly enter. When she grows tired of it, she rushes off at top speed after a wagtail which is sitting on the shore some fifty yards away: not that she naïvely expects to catch the bird, for she knows quite well that wagtails like to fly along the river bank and that, when they have gained a few dozen yards, they sit down again, thus making excellent pacemakers for a short hunt.

I am glad that my little friend is in such a happy mood, for it means much to me that she should often come on these swimming expeditions across the Danube. For this reason, I wish to reward her amply for her first crossing of the river, and there is no better way of doing this than by taking her for a long walk through the delightful virgin wilderness flanking the shores of the river. One can learn a lot when wandering through this wilderness with an animal friend, particularly if one lets oneself be guided by its tastes and interests.

First we walk upstream along the river's edge, then we follow the course of a little backwater which, at its lower end, is clear and deep; further on, it breaks up into a chain of little pools, which become shallower and shallower as we proceed. A strangely tropical effect is produced by these backwaters. The banks descend in wild luxuriance, steeply, almost vertically, to the water, and are begirt by a regular botanical garden of high willows, poplars and oaks between which hang dense strands of lush wood vine, like lianas; kingfishers and golden orioles, also typical denizens of this landscape, both belong to groups of birds, the majority of whose members are tropical dwellers. In the water grows thick swamp vegetation. Tropical too is the damp heat which hangs over this wonderful jungle landscape, which can only be borne with comfort and dignity by a naked man who spends more time in the water than out of it; and finally let us not deny that malaria mosquitoes and numerous gadflies play their part in enhancing the tropical impression.

In the broad band of mud that frames the backwater the tracks of many riverside dwellers can be seen, as though cast in plaster, and their visiting cards are printed in the hard-baked clay until the next rainfall or high water. Who says that there are no more stags left in the Danube swamps? Judging by the hoof-prints, there must still be many large ones, although they are scarcely ever heard at rutting time, so furtive have they become since the perils of the last war whose final, terrible phases took place in these very woods. Foxes and deer, muskrats and smaller rodents, countless common sandpipers, wood sandpipers and little ringed plovers, have decorated the mud with the interwoven chains of their footsteps. And if these tracks are full of interest for my eyes, how much more so must they be for the nose of my little Chow bitch! She revels in scent orgies of which we poor noseless ones can have no conception, for "Goodness only knowses the noselessness of man." The tracks of stags and large deer do not interest her, for, thank heaven, Susi is no big game hunter, being far too obsessed with her passion for mousing.

But the scent of a muskrat is a different thing: slinking tremulously, her nose close to the ground and her tail stretched obliquely upwards and backwards, she follows these rodents to the very entrance of their burrows which owing to the present low water are above instead of below the water line. She applies her nose to the holes, greedily inhaling the delicious smell of game, and she even begins the hopeless task of digging up the burrow, which pleasure I do not deny her. I lie flat on my stomach, in the shallow, lukewarm water, letting the sun burn down on my back and I am in no hurry to move on. At last Susi turns towards me a face plastered with earth; wagging her tail, she walks panting towards me and, with a deep sigh, lies down beside me in the water. So we remain for nearly an hour, at the end of which time she gets up and begs me to go on. We

pursue the ever drier course of the backwater upstream, and now we turn a bend and beside another pool, quite unconscious of our presence, for the wind is against us, is a huge muskrat: the apotheosis of all Susi's dreams, a gigantic, a godlike rat, a rat of unprecedented dimensions. The dog freezes to a statue and I do likewise. Then, slowly as a chameleon, step by step, she begins to stalk the wonder beast. She gets amazingly far, covering almost half the distance which separates us from the rat; and it is tremendously thrilling for there is always the chance that, in its first bewilderment, it may jump into the pool which has shrunk away into its stony bed and has no outlet. The creature's burrow must be at least some yards away from the spot, on the level of the normal waterline. But I have underestimated the intelligence of the rat. All of a sudden he sees the dog and streaks like lightning across the mud in the direction of the bank, Susi after him like a shot from a gun. She is clever enough not to pursue him in a straight line but to try to cut him off at a tangent, on his way to cover. Simultaneously she lets out a passionate cry such as I have rarely heard from a dog. Perhaps if she had not given tongue and had instead applied her whole energy to the chase she might have got him, for she is but half a yard behind as he disappears into safety.

Expecting Susi to dig for ages at the mouth of the earth, I lie down in the mud of the pool, but she only sniffs longingly at the entrance, then turns away disappointedly and rejoins me in the water. We both feel that the day has reached its climax: golden orioles sing, frogs croak, and great dragonflies, with a dry whirr of their glossy wings, chase the gadflies which are tormenting us. Good luck to their hunting! So we lie nearly all afternoon and I succeed in being more animal than any animal or at any rate much lazier than my dog, in fact as lazy as any crocodile. This bores Susi and, having nothing better to do, she begins to chase the frogs which, made bold by our long inertia, have resumed their activities. She stalks the nearest one, trying out her mouse-jump technique in the attempt to kill this new prey. But her paws land with a splash in the water and the frog dives away unhurt. Shaking the water from her eyes, she looks around to see where the frog has got to. She sees it, or thinks she does, in the middle of the pool where the rounded shoots of a water mint appear, to the imperfect eyesight of a dog, not unlike the head of a squatting frog. Susi eyes the object, holding her head first on the left side then on the right, then slowly, very slowly, she wades into the water, swims up to the plant and bites at it. Looking round with a long-suffering air to see if I am laughing at her absurd mistake, she turns about and finally swims back to the bank and lies down beside me. I ask, "Shall we go home?" and Susi springs up, answering "Yes" with all her available means of expression. We push our way through the jungle, straight ahead to the river. We are a long way upstream from Altenberg but the current carries us at the rate of nearly twelve miles an hour. Susi shows no more fear of the great expanse of water, and she swims quietly beside me, letting the stream carry her along. We land close by my clothes and fishing tackle and hastily I catch a delicious supper for the fish in my aquaria. Then in the dusk, satisfied and happy, we return home the same way as we came. In the mousing meadow, Susi has better luck, for she catches no less than three fat voles in succession—a compensation for her failure with the muskrat and the frog.

Today I must go to Vienna, although the heat forecasts another "dog day." I must take this chapter to the publisher. No, Susi, you cannot come with me, you can see I've got long trousers on. But tomorrow, tomorrow, Susi, we'll swim the Danube again and, if we try very hard, perhaps we'll even catch that muskrat.

*This thought is as a death, which cannot choose
But weep to have that which it fears to lose.*
SHAKESPEARE, *Sonnets*

When God created the world, He evidently did not foresee the future bond of friendship between man and the dog, or perhaps He had definite and, to us, inexplicable reasons for assigning to the dog a span of life five times shorter than that of his master. In human life there is enough suffering—of which everybody gets his share—

when we come to take leave of someone we love, and when we see the end approaching, inevitably predestined by the fact that he was born a few decades earlier than ourselves, we may well ask ourselves whether we do right to hang our hearts on a creature which will be overtaken by senility and death before a human being, born on exactly the same day, has even passed his childhood; for it is a sad reminder of the transience of earthly life when the dog, which a few years ago—and it seems but a few months—was a clumsy cuddlesome pup, begins to show unmistakable signs of age and we know that his end must be expected in some two or three years. I must admit that the aging of a dearly loved dog has always depressed me and at times considerably enhanced the gloom which occasionally afflicts every man when he thinks of griefs to come. Then there is the severe mental conflict which every master has to undergo when his dog is finally stricken in old age with some incurable disease, and the fatal question arises whether and when one should have him painlessly destroyed. Strangely enough fate has so far spared me this decision, since, with one exception, all my dogs have died a sudden and painless death at a ripe old age and without any intervention on my part. But one cannot count on this and I do not altogether blame sensitive people who shrink from acquiring a dog in view of the final inevitable parting. Not altogether blame them? Well, actually, I suppose I do. In human life all pleasures must be paid for by sorrow, for, as Burns says,

*Pleasures are like poppies spread,
You seize the flower, its bloom is shed;
Or like the snow falls in the river
A moment white—then melts for ever;*

and fundamentally I consider the man a shirker who renounces the few permissible and ethically irreproachable pleasures of life for fear of having to pay the bill with which, sooner or later, fate will present him. He who is miserly with the coin of suffering had better retire to some spinsterly attic and there gradually desiccate like a sterile bulb which bears no blossoms. Certainly the death of a faithful dog which has accompanied its master for some fifteen years of his life's walk brings with it much suffering, nearly as much as the death of a beloved person. But in one essential detail the former is easier to bear: the place which the human friend filled in your life remains for ever empty; that of your dog can be filled with a substitute. Dogs are indeed individuals, personalities in the truest sense of the words and I should be the last to deny this fact, but they are much more like each other than are human beings. The individual differences between living creatures are in direct proportion to their mental development: two fishes of one species are, in all their actions and reactions, practically the same; but, for a person familiar with their behavior, two golden hamsters or jackdaws show noticeable diversities; two hooded crows or two gray-lag geese are sometimes quite separate individuals.

In dogs this holds good to a still greater extent, since they, as domestic animals, exhibit in their behavior an immeasurably greater amount of individual variation than those other non-domesticated species. But, conversely, in the depths of their soul, in those deep instinctive feelings which are responsible for their special relationship with man, dogs resemble each other closely, and if on the death of one's dog one immediately adopts a puppy of the same breed, one will generally find that he refills those spaces in one's heart and one's life which the departure of an old friend has left desolate. Under certain conditions the consolation thus afforded can be so thorough that one feels almost ashamed of one's unfaithfulness to one's former dog. Here again, the dog is more faithful than his master, for had the master died the dog would scarcely have found a substitute within the space of half a year. These considerations will perhaps seem absurd to people who will not admit of any moral responsibility towards an animal but they have prompted me to an unusual course of action.

When one day I found my old Bully lying dead of a stroke on his old accustomed barking beat, I at once regretted deeply that he had left no successor to take his place. I was then seventeen years old and this was the first time I had lost a dog; I am unable to express how much I missed him. He had been my inseparable companion for years and the limping rhythm of his trot when he ran behind me—he was lame from a badly healed broken foreleg—had become so much the sound of my own footsteps that I no longer heard his rather weighty tread and the snuffling that accompanied it. I only noticed it when it was no longer there. In the weeks that immediately followed Bully's death, I really began to understand what it is that makes naïve people believe in the ghosts of their dead. The constant sound throughout years of the dog trotting at my heels had left such a lasting impression on my brain—psychologists call this an "eioletic" phenomenon—that for weeks afterwards, as if with my own ears, I heard him pattering after me.

On quiet Danube paths this reached the pitch of an almost sinister hallucination. If I listened consciously the trotting and snuffling ceased at once, but as soon as my thoughts began to wander again I seemed to hear it once more. It was only when Tito, at that time still a wobbly half-grown puppy, began to run behind me that the specter of Bully, the limping ghost dog, was finally banished.

Tito too died long ago, and how long ago! But her spirit still trots sniffing at my heels. I have taken good care that it should do so, by resorting to a peculiar course of action: when Tito lay dead before me, just as unexpectedly as Bully had done, I realized that another dog would take her place just as she had taken Bully's, and, feeling ashamed of my own faithlessness, I swore a strange pledge to her memory: henceforward only Tito's descendants should accompany me through life. A man cannot keep faith with an individual dog for obvious biological reasons, but he can remain true to the breed. The dog is much nearer than man to nature, whose relentlessness Tennyson so aptly sums up with the words,

> *So careful of the type she seems,*
> *So careless of the single life.*

Even in mankind, with our exaggerated individualities, the type is preserved in a remarkable

High Life *by Sir Edwin Landseer*

way by heredity. When my little daughter, in a moment of embarrassment, throws back her head with the peculiarly arrogant movement which was typical of my mother, whom the child has never seen; when she and likewise her brother under stress of deep thought wrinkle their brows just as my wife's father used to do, what is this but "reincarnation" in the most literal sense of the word? I have always had a particularly sharp eye for expressive movements and it is this faculty which has destined me for the work of animal observation. Owing to these acute powers of mine, I am always deeply moved by those expressive movements of my children which, years before their birth, I had noticed in their grandparents. These movements are, after all, the outward and visible signs of deeply rooted, immutable properties of soul, good and bad, desirable and dangerous. I often find it uncanny—as the ghosts of the dead are to the living —when I observe how, in one of my children, the character traits of all four grandparents crop up one after the other, or sometimes all at once. If I had known their great-grandparents, I should probably see them too in my children and might even discover them strangely jumbled and divided amongst my children's children.

I am constantly stimulated to such reflections on death and immortality by the apparently innocent and uncomplicated personality of my little bitch Susi, nearly all of whose forebears I knew, since in our stud a certain amount of unavoidable and permissible inbreeding was practiced. Just as the personal character traits of a dog are incomparably simpler than those of a man and are thus correspondingly more obvious when encountered in combination in an individ-

ual descendant, so every reappearance of the character traits of their progenitors is immeasurably more patent than in man. In animals, where the inherited is much less overshadowed by the individually acquired than in man, the spirit of their ancestors takes more immediate possession of the living, where the character propensities of the dead find more unmistakable living expression.

When, hypocritically, I assure a guest who interrupts my work that he is welcome, and Susi, not in the least deceived by my words, growls and barks implacably at the intruder (when she is a little older she will certainly bite him gently), then the little dog is not only revealing the remarkable capacity to read my inmost thoughts which is the heritage of Tito, but she *is* Tito, the very personification of Tito! When in a dry meadow she hunts mice, and dashes along in a series of exaggerated leaps like so many mice-hunting beasts of prey, exhibiting thereby the exaggerated passion for this activity of her Chow ancestor, Pygi, then she *is* Pygi. When, during her training to "lie down" which we have been practicing for some time, she finds exactly the same hollow excuses for getting up again which her great-grandmother Stasi invented eleven years ago, and when, like the latter, she wallows ecstatically in every puddle, and afterwards, coated in mud and slime, walks innocently into the house, then she *is* Stasi, Stasi rediviva. And when, along quiet riverside ways, dusty roads or city streets, she follows in my footsteps, straining every sense not to lose me, then she is every dog, every dog that ever followed its master since the first jackal began: an immeasurable sum of love and fidelity.

My Last Five

by ELIZABETH OF THE GERMAN GARDEN

I would like, to begin with, to say that though parents, husbands, children, lovers and friends are all very well, they are not dogs. In my day and turn having been each of the above—except that instead of husbands I was wives—I know what I am talking about, and am well acquainted with the ups and downs, the daily ups and downs, the sometimes almost hourly ones in the thin-skinned, which seem inevitably to accompany human loves.

Dogs are free from these fluctuations. Once they love, they love steadily, unchangingly, till their last breath.

That is how I like to be loved.

Therefore I will write of dogs.

Up to now I have had fourteen, but they weren't spread over my life equally, and for years and years at a time I had none. This, when first I began considering my dogs, astonished me; I mean, that for years and years I had none. What was I about, I wondered, to allow myself to be dogless? How was it that there were such long periods during which I wasn't making some good dog happy?

Lately, in order to answer these questions, I have been casting about a good deal in the past, and in its remoter portions found that the answer to them was my father. There have been other answers of more recent date, as I shall presently explain, but he was the first one. He didn't like dogs. A just but irritable man, with far too few skins really for comfort, noise easily exasperated him, and dogs do often make a noise. Therefore he wouldn't suffer them nearer than out in the backyard, watching, poor sad beasts, on a chain for the burglar who never came; and if a visitor chanced to bring his dog with him, and it did what perhaps it oughtn't to have done, such as gnaw the rug, or jump up and bark, or, worst of all, omit to remain self-contained, my father, determined that nothing should shake him out of politeness, would stand applauding its behavior so sardonically, beating his hands gently together, and saying at intervals with so awful a mildness, Good dog, Fine little chap, Splendid fellow, that the visit was never repeated.

My mother, too, didn't care about them—or rather, being far too sweet-natured and sunnily pleased with everything to have a feeling so negative as not caring, was simply unaware, I think, of their existence. She didn't seem to know that they too were in the world, breathing the same air, pattering along on their little feet, even as she was, inevitably from birth to death, and I doubt if she had ever stooped and stroked one in her life.

The fact was she was too pretty, too busy with her admirers, to have any time left over for noticing such of her fellow-pilgrims as had more than two legs. A happy, adorable little creature, she went singing through the years, always crowded round by friends and admirers, and never within measurable distance of that secret loneliness, that need for something more than human beings can give, that longing for greater loyalty, deeper devotion, which finds its comfort in dogs. They were nothing to her. Where they were concerned, her imagination, lively enough about other things, became a blank; and since our parents were for us children the supreme authority, the final word, and we reverenced and feared my father, and worshiped my mother, their attitude in all things was our attitude, and what they thought we not merely thought, but passionately upheld.

Therefore dogs were ruled out of the category of possessions we might otherwise have liked to have ... My father, very luckily, was one of your cat men, so that at least there was always something living about the place which didn't mind, and indeed liked, being stroked and gently tickled. I was the youngest, and alone now at home, handed over to a Mademoiselle whose duty it was to educate me and see that I washed my ears. You can't tickle a Mademoiselle. You can't expect her to turn over and let you stroke her tummy. Besides, I didn't want to stroke it. Therefore these cats came in useful, and I concentrated on them.

But it is a bleak business really, concentrating on cats. One likes response, and there is very little of that to be got out of them. Lofty and aloof, forever wrapped in remote, mysterious meditation, they allow themselves to be adored, and give hardly anything back. Except purrs. I admit purrs are enchanting, and I used to long to have one myself, but just purrs don't nourish the hungry human heart in search of something to fill its emptiness; and being to all intents and purposes by this time an only child, and my parents absorbed in their particular interests, and my Mademoiselle on the other side of a barrier of French, I did very often feel extraordinarily empty. Besides, how chilling, how snubbing, to be merely looked at when one calls. No blandishments could make those cats stir if they weren't

in the mood, and one does want whatever one is calling to *come*. More, one wants it to come enthusiastically, ready for any lark going. One wants, that is, a playfellow, a companion, a friend. One wants, in fact, a dog. . . .

Anxious to make what amends I could, I never let anyone do anything for him or take him out except myself, and he grew extremely devoted to me, poor Pincher,* and if I was out at a party would sit immovable, however long it went on, just inside the door of the flat, waiting for me to come in.

Touching little dog. But being touched doesn't make one love. I am sorry to say I had left off loving Pincher. He had too many just claims on my affection, and affection won't be bounced. Nor it is easy for the wronger to love the wronged. And who, again, can be fond of a reproach that is ever present and never uttered? Poor Pincher couldn't have uttered, even if he had wanted to, but he didn't want to. Written all over him was a gross contentment. He was stupefied with contentment and food. And his being so much pleased with everything afflicted me more than any amount of bad temper, for did I not, if he had only known it, deserve the worst that he could do to me?

No, I didn't love Pincher. Apart from his wrongs and claims, he had become—my fault too —a most dull dog, and a very odd, unattractive one to look at. But if I couldn't love him I could pretend I did, and he was no longer quick enough to notice it was only pretending. I patted and stroked him a great deal, and often, to please him, would take my hat off again when I had been going out, and stay at home with him instead— just so that he should know I was there, and feel he might stretch out and snore comfortably by the fire, and not have to go, urged by his devotion, into the cold hall and wait for me in a draught.

"Poor old Pincher—poor, poor little dog," I would whisper softly to him, full of remorse and

*A small, originally feisty, hellraising dog who pursued forest game and farm poultry, and whom the author, on the advice of a gamekeeper, had castrated.—Ed.

pity, sitting on the floor beside him and taking his head in my lap; and it made things no better that he hadn't an idea I had ever been anything but an angel to him.

The friend whose present he was, puzzled by his torpor and increasing bulk—I was dumb as a fish about what had happened—began once more carefully to observe, and, having observed, opined that there was something wrong with the dog.

Such bulk, the friend explained, while I sat uneasily by, was unnatural, and must be due to the torpor, and the torpor was due to his being, so to speak, an only child. Give him a playmate, said the friend, and I would soon see a difference.

Too well did I know I wouldn't; but, not wishing to embark on explanations, I merely threw cold water on the playmate. More than one dog in a London flat would be impossible, I said; and anyhow the management wouldn't allow it.

"Try," said the friend, looking thoughtfully at Pincher's broad body and small, almost disappearing head; adding that, though he wasn't much more than a year old, he might easily, from his appearance and behavior, be taken for ten.

Such remarks made me feel very bad. Only too well did I know that Pincher's age, through my fault, was indeed the equivalent of ten. And a poor ten, too; ten, already nearly senile. Still, there it was, and no playmate would ever change it; so I stood out obstinately against the suggestion, even going so far as to declare that all it would do to the dog would be to plunge him into acute fits of jealousy.

Acute fits! The contented, passive little lump on the rug didn't look much like acute fits of anything. He was past that. He was definitely *jenseits des Guten und Bösen*. But I wasn't going to say so and provoke questions difficult to answer, and stooping down to pat my poor dog very gently, very apologetically, I murmured that we were perfectly content, he and I, to have only each other.

There is no stopping friends, however, when once they are bent on doing what they imagine will be a kindness, and the playmate arrived next day. Without either further argument or by your leaves, it was sent round in a basket.

I thought the basket had violets in it. It was March, and everywhere in London were violets. The shops were full of them; the street corners were massed with them; and I called my maid to bring a bowl and water, while I cut the string and opened the lid.

But this wasn't violets. Curled up snugly, its head between its paws, and looking at me with great gravity out of the corner of one lifted eye, was a little smooth white creature, with a card tied round its neck on which was written: *I am Knobbie. A young lady three months old. Try me on Pincher.*

We looked at each other. She lay motionless, merely keeping that lifted eye on me. Pincher, indifferent before the fire, didn't even trouble to raise his head, nor did she take any notice of him, though she must have smelt him because, since I had had him seen to, even if one weren't a dog one easily smelt poor Pincher.

In his direction, however, she didn't so much as twitch a nostril. It was on me that her attention was concentrated, and I wouldn't have supposed a single eye could hold so much in it of grave appraisement. What she saw I cannot say, for who shall guess how we appear to dogs? But what I saw was a baby fox terrier, snow white except for her ears, which were—and are; she is sitting beside me as I write—a lovely glossy chestnut, divided from each other by a straight, broad band of more white.

Perfect and spotless, as though that very morning she had had her bath and breakfast in Paradise, she lay completely unembarrassed, waiting for what I would do next, and merely looked at me with that lifted eye. "Knobbie," I said, almost with a bow, as though introducing her to myself; and almost it seemed as if she bowed back, as if she made a small, polite movement of her head. I have known dogs do more surprising things than that. Winkie, for instance, once, when he was going to be sick—

But I haven't got to Winkie yet.

"Would you like me to lift you out of your basket, Knobbie?" I asked, very politely, for she somehow brought out politeness in others.

Apparently she had no objection, and taking her in my two hands—she was like satin to touch, and as smooth as plumpness could make her—I put her carefully down on the floor, and was enchanted to find that the first thing she did was not to wet the carpet . . . she was a lady. I now know that ladies, in the dog world, wouldn't dream of doing such a thing, once it has been pointed out to them as undesirable. They are most elegantly clean and particular, and will wait almost any time to be put out of doors, rather than behave as they shouldn't. Of this, though, I was then unaware, and not wishing to take any risks, besides being anxious that so bright a beginning should remain undimmed, I took her up in my arms, and a second time was enchanted, for she snuggled.

There was no doubt about it: she did snuggle, and she was the first of my dogs to do so. Great Danes, in the nature of things, can't snuggle, and all the others—except Bijou, who doesn't count—had been grown up. Of course I was enchanted. Of course my heart glowed, as the little thing pressed against me and tucked her head confidently beneath my chin. All good women, and most good men, go on having maternal instincts to the very end, and adore it when something small and helpless is so obliging as to show its trust by snuggling—especially, I think, women in my then situation, whose husbands, for one cause or another, aren't there, and whose children are married and living in faraway countries. Such women, however haughtily they may say, "I don't want anybody to love me," do in fact often want, in a vague, uneasy sort of way, everybody to love them, and should this wish narrow down, as it occasionally does, from everybody to somebody, there may be trouble.

It is then that dogs come in. It was then that Knobbie came in. Not that I would suggest I myself had been in the condition just described, but the truth is that life, as it proceeds, does become a good deal pruned of its simpler joys, which are mostly connected with the love and

rearing of one's young. These certainly had now been pruned from me. My days of rearing children were done. My love could follow them only in spirit. So that there was an outward bareness, a seeming emptiness about my life at that time, which was apparently noticeable, since my friend had observed it and had tried to clothe and fill it with Pincher.

Here he had failed, for reasons, he was never told; but, trying again with Knobbie, he succeeded, for if Pincher's arrival had set me off recovering some of the balance I had lost, Knobbie's arrival completed my cure.

An odd effect for a single small puppy to produce; but not more odd than the effect a single lilac-bush, flowering in the sun one May morning, produced on a woman I know. She had meant, being more full of griefs than she felt she could conveniently hold, to finish with life that day, but, taking a turn in the garden first, she saw this bush, and having seen it thought that perhaps she had better wait a little. For, she argued, a world that can produce such beauty shouldn't lightly be left; and I too, holding the snuggly little warm Knobbie in my arms, perceived again, after a space of years, that the world had many most admirable sides, and that the best thing I could do was once more to seek and ensue them.

And there sighed through my mind the word *resolut,* as if the old vow were turning in its sleep.

Im Wahren, Guten, Schönen resolut zu leben . . .

Why, not, I asked myself, my cheek on Knobbie's soft ears, have another try?

But it is no use having tries at things like that in London. At least, it was no use for me. I found I couldn't be *resolut* in company. At a party, I simply forgot the *Wahr* and *Gut* and *Schön.* Such gatherings had much the same effect on me as telephones—they deflected me from that which I like to believe is my true self. With concern and shame, I noted that my ear at them was basely cocked for flattery, and all my thoughts were finicking. No wonder when, after one of them, I at last got home to the simple Pincher, waiting up for me so patiently on the doormat, and the guileless Knobbie sweetly sleeping in her basket, and at sight of these two innocents regained some, at least, of my scattered self-possession, no wonder I would then ask myself whether parties were really worthwhile.

They weren't. They never have been, for me. Friends, too, though delightful, seemed, at those moments of weariness, only delightful if properly spaced, and how is one to space anybody or anything in London? Of everything there, there appeared to be too much. And I would sit despondent on the edge of the bed, and fall to remembering the roomy years in Pomerania, when only every six months did we go to, or give, a party, and the glorious times I had had in Switzerland between the visits of guests, when Coco* and I were alone with mountains.

From these meditations it did finally appear that I wasn't suited to crowds, and Knobbie, judging by her behavior when I took her out for exercise in the park, was evidently not suited to them either. The noise of the traffic, as I carried her across Whitehall, terrified her. That composure which so charmed me when we were in the flat disappeared entirely out of doors, and the mere sight of another dog approaching in the distance was enough to make her almost faint. Plainly, conventual life was best for my thin-skinned, inexperienced young lady, and it appeared best for me too, if I seriously meant to do anything about being *resolut*. There remained Pincher to be considered, but Pincher was content wherever he was as long as it included me and dinner, so one fine day, with him waddling at my heels, and Knobbie tucked under my arm, I turned my back on London, and went again to live in the country.

Very different were my feelings now from the ones I had had when I fled into the New Forest, to hide and forget. It wasn't only, I believe, that time had been at its usual work of healing, of glossing over—it was also that I was accompanied by dogs. There had been no dog with me during the lamentable years which included Coco's death and ended with the arrival of Pincher; if there had been, I might sooner have got mended. Now, with two of them, even

*An earlier dog—*Ed.*

if one was more a burden than a joy, I went off confidently, sure it was the best thing for a person who was still, I suppose, what my aunts Charl and Jessie called peculiar, while as for Knobbie, I felt it would save her reason.

Really I was very much obliged to Knobbie, whose nerves gave me the necessary push-off. Without her, I might have lingered on in London indefinitely, becoming permanently convivial.

Pincher took me to London, and Knobbie brought me away. It looked as if I were beginning to be led about by dogs.

My relations, indeed, pointed this out, and expressed regret. They used the word infatuation, and said infatuation was always a pity. But I paid no heed, for he who heeds relations won't get anywhere, not even into the country, and on getting into the country I was absolutely bent.

This time, though, I didn't go farther than twenty miles out, so that I would still be able easily to visit friends for a few hours, should I have a relapse into gregariousness; yet, although so near London, the effect of being in pure country was complete, because the house, standing alone, faced golf links, and on its other three sides was surrounded by woods.

In these woods were endless safe paths for Knobbie, where she would never meet a soul, while for Pincher there was a roomy garden in which he could lie and pant comfortably, with ancient trees to shade him should he be inconvenienced by the sun. The day we took possession there was no sun, but since sun, sooner or later, is bound to shine, its absence didn't at the moment disturb me, and we settled in in high good humor—at least, Knobbie and I did, and I think Pincher too must have been in some sort of good spirits beneath his outer apathy, for the first thing he got was an extra big dinner.

I thought it a very charming little house. It breathed peace and silence. The woods, dressed for autumn, brooded close over it at the back, and in front stretched the golf course, empty that day because of fog. Outside the sitting-room window was a dovecote, filled by the same friend who had given me my dogs with doves whose cooings were to soothe me while I worked; and on the hearth-rug, also a present from this same —ought I not now to call him zoological?— friend, sat a coal-black cat for luck, which at once took to Knobbie, and began diligently tidying and washing her ears.

Tea was brought; curtains were drawn; the firelight danced; the urn hissed. We might have been a picture in a romance, when the pen, swerving a moment aside from high life, pauses on a simple cottage interior. And while I ate muffins—things I had never been able even to look at in London, but now swallowed with complacence—and Pincher sat in front of me watching every mouthful, just as though he hadn't had an enormous dinner a few minutes before, and the cat, finished with Knobbie's ears, deftly turned her over and began tidying her stomach, I did feel that my feet were set once more in the path of peace, and that all I had to do was to continue steadily along it.

So did I enter upon a fresh lap of that solitude decorated with dogs which, each time it had been my portion, had given me such contentment.

It was Knobbie, of course, who decorated, growing every day more charming now that she was freed from fear, for Pincher, since I had had him seen to, couldn't any longer be called an ornament. Yet he had been a personable little dog when first he came. That he should have become odd-looking enough for no small boy to be able to pass him in silence was entirely my fault, and I regarded the comments he roused during his daily exercise on the Embankment, while I lived in London, as part of my just punishment.

I was glad to get away from these comments into the quiet country, for they used to force me to walk with my head unnaturally high, pretending I heard nothing or, if I heard, that I didn't care—especially during those trying moments, familiar to all who take their dogs on leads, when I had to stand still and wait.

What could I do, faced by derision, except hold my head high and pretend to be deaf? I found it very difficult, though, because often

what I heard made me want to laugh. "See that there dawg?" a tram-conductor called one day to anybody who would listen, his tram having happened to pause just where I, too, was being obliged to pause by Pincher, "I know 'is pedigree, I do. 'Is mother was a 'edge 'og, and 'is father a blinking fool."

Always I was thankful when it was time to go back to the cover of the flat; but now, in the spacious garden round the cottage, everything was easy, and my poor hedgehog—he really did look rather like one—could be turned loose, and needn't be taken for walks. It was a great relief, I think, to him, and certainly it was a relief to me who, apart from not enjoying rousing the mirth of passersby, would any day rather run with Knobbie than waddle with Pincher. But unfortunately, just as he used to wait on the doormat of the flat until I came home, so did he wait at the gate, however cold or wet it might be, for me to reappear, and I was always being dragged back from my walks long before Knobbie, who had developed the swiftness and grace of a greyhound, had had enough, by the vision of that patient little image sitting there stolidly, and determined not to budge till he got me again.

And when he had got me again, what did he do? He went to sleep. It was all he wanted—to go to sleep knowing I was there. Indeed, that was all Pincher ever wanted, besides his dinner: that I should stay by his side while he snored. Which annoyed me, for after all he wasn't a husband.

I have a photograph of Knobbie the following summer, grown by that time into a great girl, and turning her head away from Pincher.

He isn't in the picture, because just as I was taking it he waddled away, caring as little for Knobbie's company as she for his. From first to last she turned her head away from him, while he, for his part, didn't give a rap for her. But then, of course, the poor dog hadn't any raps, whatever they may be, to give, and if it hadn't been for the cat, Knobbie might have spent a lonely, play-starved childhood. The cat, however, did what it could, and they had a good deal of fun together till Chunkie, yet another present from the same friend, joined our party; whereupon Knobbie, staring at the unexpected apparition of a brand-new puppy marching so confidently into the room as though it were his room and she and the cat and Pincher belonged to him too, forever forgot such things as cats, and fell head over ears in love.

It was a *coup de foudre*. I had heard of *coups de foudre*, but never either experienced one or witnessed one being administered. With my own eyes I now beheld *foudre* hurtling down on Knobbie. Chunkie, a semi-Sealyham puppy ten weeks old, incredibly small and cocky and game, had only to swagger in, look insolently round, give a loud bark or two which said as plainly as words that he was ready to take on the lot of us, for her instantly to become his slave.

Chunkie was, and is, a charmer of the first order. He is curled up in my lap as I write, and the paper is propped on his sleeping back.

In a picture when he was four months old, the funny markings on his face, like raised eyebrows, to which everyone at once succumbed, give him an air of permanent astonishment.

But I wish I had been able to take a photograph of him the day the door of the sitting room opened and he appeared, alone and unannounced. The chauffeur who brought him discreetly didn't show himself, leaving him to make his own impression, and never could I have believed anything so small could be so fearless, or anything, plunged into the middle of complete strangers, all much bigger than himself, be so cocky.

His tail, proud symbol of an unconquerable spirit, stuck up gaily, and has stuck up ever since. Not once have I seen it lowered during the whole five years I have had him, not even when, outraged by his behavior, which is often reprehensible—he is a great lover, and will run miles and stay away hours, risking being stolen, run over or shot, if there is any lovemaking to be done—when, I say, outraged by such behavior I raise an indignant hand against him, his tail, instead of drooping, wags, and his eyes, fixed on my face, are the eyes of one who knows he has done wrong, but thinks it was well worth it. At once smug, ingratiating and defiant, he looks me boldly in the face, and my hand falls nerveless at my side. After all, I can't help being glad he has enjoyed himself, and anyhow I am deeply thankful to have got him safe home again.

That friend who is now becoming monotonous as a giver, in giving me Chunkie added him to what my relations were beginning to speak of as a menagerie, and he added him because, when the second winter at the cottage loomed close, he thought he saw signs of restiveness in me, of a tendency to walk to the window and scowl at the weather, of a desire that seemed to him excessive, to whom such things meant nothing, for more sunshine than England provided; and having observed these signs for a time in silence, opined that what I needed was another dog. To steady me. To hold me down in the place I was in already. For if, he reckoned, a woman could easily go abroad with one dog, and not so easily with two, with three it would be so difficult that she wouldn't attempt it, and, loving all three, she would be quite unable to leave them, would stay where she was, and her friends could continue to come down and have tea with her.

Such were his simple calculations, which up to a point were correct. Where they went wrong was in taking for granted, after Chunkie's arrival, that I loved three dogs. I didn't; I only loved two. In regard to Pincher, all I felt was self-reproachful responsibility, and at any time since I had had him seen to would gladly have parted from him, if I could have found him a good home. But naturally I never told my friend this, whose gift he was, and for all his observing he hadn't noticed that Pincher wasn't in my heart.

For all his observing, too, he didn't find out the reason why I dreaded another winter in the cottage. Ours was a friendship based on, and chiefly nourished by, dogs; that is how I, at least, saw it, keeping myself otherwise a good deal to myself. Opine as he might, he at no time really *knew*, and the last things I would ever have talked to him about would have been my secret disappointments and shames.

There he would sit, the days he came to call, quietly having tea surrounded by his four-legged gifts, and he hadn't an idea that a few hours before, during the heavy, hopeless rain of the morning, I had been gnawing my knuckles because of my inability, increasing with each wet day, to be *resolut* in bad weather.

No doubt one has often sat thus at tea among people sleek with muffins, imperturbable of aspect, and in conversation calm, who weren't at all like that inside—people who, perhaps, too that very morning had been gnawing their knuckles over some secret trouble. How can one tell from outsides? For all I knew my zoological friend might be actually gnawing his in spirit at that very minute, while he sat so apparently placid by the fire; but I don't think so, because he was a man of one idea, which was to give me dogs, and to have one idea only does tend to promote that inner tidiness which is peace.

But I, after ten weeks of almost constant cold downpours, was making the shameful discovery that those plans for living resolutely, which had brought me away from London and lodged me in a noble solitude, came to nothing if it rained. In other words, though I wanted as much as ever to seek and ensue the *Wahr* and *Gut* and *Schön,* I could only do so, with any real zest, if the sun shone.

No wonder I gnawed my knuckles. The disconcerting discovery took all the wind out of my sails. I was ashamed to death. But there it was, and being ashamed didn't stop the cold rain, and the cold rain gave me chilblains, and chilblains upset everything. Especially upsetting was it to remember that I hadn't been and felt like this in my mountain home, where the wind roared and the rain dashed against the windows for weeks on end, without quenching a single spark of my inner glow. Probably I had had chilblains there too, but they had so little affected my spirit that I couldn't even be sure. Was it that I was older now? Was this perhaps the way, the trivial, contemptible way, age was going to manifest itself— in ups and downs, in dependence on warmth, and in an extreme distaste for clouds that didn't go away?

Age. I had never till then thought about it, except for other people. Now, for the first time, the idea that I too perhaps might soon get old,

was, perhaps, already beginning to, entered my head; and I was much struck by it.

There was another friend of mine—a woman this time—who was living beautifully in the sun. In Provence she lived, and on one of her visits to London she came down to see me, bringing into the room with her that dark afternoon, I thought, all the radiance of the south. The light and warmth of a more blessed climate seemed still to linger round her, she seemed still to reflect the sunshine she had left, and whenever she moved I fancied there was delicately shaken into the air a fragrance of sweet flowers, such as jasmine.

"Why not come and live near me?" she said. "I know a little house among olive trees. In November"—it was then November—"the grass round it is thick with those long-stalked, pink-and-white daisies."

Strange how few words are needed to alter one's whole life. I didn't then know those long-stalked, pink-and-white daisies, but I know them now, and it is in that little house, expanded at each end to a greater roominess and turned the color of honeysuckle, that I am at this moment writing—changed from a shivering creature brittle with cold, who tries, by blowing on her fingers, to be able after breakfast to hold a pen, into one who no longer has to hope it may be fine tomorrow, because it invariably is; or, if not quite invariably tomorrow, certainly the day after.

I cannot tell how other people feel, but to me this makes the entire difference between praising God for my creation, preservation and all the blessings of my life, and remaining ominously silent. If only I had come here straight from Pomerania—concentrated, from the very beginning of that freedom to choose where to live which characterizes widows, on light, heat, color and fragrance—how good it would have been for my disposition! Instead of becoming mellow merely by dint of growing older, I would have mellowed young; instead of having moments of despair, I would have been unshakably serene. Impossible not to catch some, at least, of the serenity, the urbanity, of the skies under which one lives. When beauty is all round one it is bound to get into one's spirit and stay there. I walk in beauty—not like Byron's lady who walked in her own, but in the beauty of light, heat, color and fragrance. Easy enough to be *resolut* here. It is child's play. It is one's normal condition. And if it weren't that dogs are what I am writing about, I would pause a moment to set down the many reasons I have for blessing the friend who brought me to this place.

Knobbie and Chunkie came with me to Provence, but Pincher, during the year we had to wait in the cottage on the golf course for the honeysuckle-house to be added to and got ready, grew so old, so heavy, so almost entirely immovable, that it seemed it would be a kindness, rather than leave him with anyone I wasn't quite sure of, to have him put to sleep.

I did all I could to find a home for him, for still he loved his dinner, and the thought that he would never have another at a word from me was distressing. But nobody I could trust wanted poor Pincher. Whoever I offered him to, invariably answered he would be pleased to take Chunkie. Even the friend who gave him to me declined to have him back, on the ground that he wasn't the dog he used to be—didn't I know it? —and that although he was now only three years old, he might well have been thirty.

"For each year in a normal dog's life," said my friend, thoughtfully observing him, "this dog seems to advance ten."

And since thirty is no age for a dog, and it wasn't to be supposed that forty would be any better, and no one wanted him, and I couldn't take him with me, everything pointed to his being put to sleep.

But it is a terrible thing actually to give the order that launches a living creature into the eternal cold of death. Here was Pincher today, warm and content, still able to lie by the fire and snore, still adoring his dinner; how could I bring myself to stop him from having a tomorrow? I couldn't. I didn't. I put it off and off, and he kept on having tomorrows, and dinners of an increasing, solicitous lavishness.

Poor little Pincher. Not till our very last day at the cottage, when it had become inevitable, did the vet, who had taken care of that which my relations now called Whipsnade, come over, and after the poor dog had had a final dinner—a banquet, really, of all the things he liked best— put him gently and comfortably to sleep.

He was buried in the garden. I wish my end may be as easy. But even now, five years afterwards, I never can think of Pincher without remorse.

If this weren't a book about dogs only, I might here dwell on a great-grandfather I had, and his daughter my great-aunt, who both died like Pincher, after an extra good dinner. No vet was needed in their case; the dinner did it. Warned, my great-grandfather defied; and tradition insists that his last words were that he didn't care what anybody said, duck and green peas were worth any amount of dying. My great-aunt, of the same dogged, indomitable blood, in her turn made similar statements, it is said, though what she died of was, more ignobly I think, cod. But since I am not here writing of my ancestry but about Chunkie and Knobbie, let me get back to them, whose children were born in the honeysuckle-colored house—a house already scrambled over, almost to its roof, by the eager roses of the south.

Chunkie, once he was grown up, was not the dog to put off getting married, and having been frequently thwarted in this wish by my interference and by the fact that he was lower on the ground than Knobbie, became artful, watched his opportunity, found it when she was going downstairs one day in front of him, seized it, and nine weeks later the pledges of their loves were born on my bedroom sofa.

I could have wished she had chosen a different place. I never expected the *accouchement* to happen in my house, and had made all arrangements for her to go to a nursing home well ahead, as I thought, of the time. But my calculations were a week out, and one night while I was quietly reading, and she was lying at my feet apparently asleep, she suddenly got up, turned round, sat down straight in front of me and stared.

She stared so hard that it pierced through the covers of my book, and putting it down I asked her if she wanted to go out.

She didn't move—merely went on staring; and I, inexperienced in such occasions, began to read again. But I couldn't fix my attention. Those eyes on the other side of the book bored through it, and presently I got up and went to the door and encouraged her to go out into the garden. Instead, she hurried up to my bedroom, jumped on the sofa and began having puppies.

The house immediately woke to activity. My maid, who was tidying the room, dropped everything and came running down, announcing with loud cries what was going on on the sofa. I flew upstairs; bells rang; feet scuttled; the chauffeur rushed away to fetch the vet; and only Knobbie, among the lot of us, was calm.

To see the way she behaved before the vet appeared, after whose arrival she placed herself, with touching confidence, entirely in his hands, one would have imagined it to be her tenth confinement instead of her first. She knew exactly what to do with each puppy as it arrived, and did it. She was composure itself, only asking, till the vet came, to be let alone. And by the time she had done, there were six puppies—two born dead because, said the vet, of that jump on to the sofa. . . .

I think I was as proud of them as Knobbie was. I know she couldn't have loved them more than I did.

One consequence, though, of her motherhood, and I thought it very odd, was that she took a deep dislike to Chunkie. It wasn't as if she hadn't had a perfectly easy confinement; she owed him no grudge on account of agony. Yet there she was, evidently disliking him very much, making the most dreadful faces at him whenever he sauntered past, and if he dared so much as cock an eye in the direction of his offspring her growls were frightening.

My gentle Knobbie, transformed to savagery by precisely the experience which is supposed to soften a lady out of all knowledge! I watched her in astonishment, remembering the extreme devotion she used to show Chunkie, how she couldn't bear him out of her sight, coaxing him to play with her, flattering him by laughing with eager diligence at what I presume were his jokes—and if there are still people who say dogs don't laugh, let them look at a picture I have of Knobbie doing it: Is she not laughing? And has not Chunkie something of the air of the skilled *raconteur*, who has made his point and is resting gravely on his laurels, while the audience gives way to the expected mirth?

Dogs are forever reminding me of myself. I know I must often have looked like this picture of Knobbie when, before I married them, I laughed at the good stories of those who became my husbands. Naturally I couldn't laugh quite so wholeheartedly later on, when marriage had made me familiar with the stories, but repetition does have the advantage of enabling the listener to know the exact right moment to throw back his or her head, like Knobbie, and begin to roar.

When this picture was taken, though, she was in the days of her carefree girlhood. After that, she laughed no more. From the birth of her puppies on, nothing that Chunkie could do, no joke, however amusing, that he might communicate to her in the mysterious way dogs do communicate, would get a smile out of her. Less courteous—or shall I say less abject?—and more honest than myself, she simply didn't bother to laugh. Her thoughts were only for her children. The nuzzling little creatures took up her whole attention; and they took up the whole of mine too, I found, because four puppies, once they begin to crawl about, need a great deal of looking after.

For a long while I tried to believe that I would be able to keep them all, so equally enchanting did they seem, but as they grew bigger this belief faded, it became more and more difficult to cope with so many, and at last I was obliged, with the greatest reluctance and most sorrowfully, to give two away to friends.

For all that, I still had four dogs, and my relations, getting wind of it, wrote and said it was a pity. "You are becoming," they wrote, "all dog," and really I sometimes felt that way myself, so much absorbed had I to be, of necessity, in the four, if they were to have their just dues as regards runs, grooming, food and, where the puppies were concerned, training in those ways of cleanliness which alone would bring them peace.

Four dogs not only seem, but are, a great many, and I wasn't surprised by my relations' comments. What, though, they didn't know was the excessive pleasure, amusement and exercise I got out of them. True the exercise sometimes appeared to be a little much, and when I was tired I was inclined to think that perhaps I ought to have started on this sort of thing younger; but anyhow the eighteen months during which all four were with me were much the gayest and liveliest, if also the most breathless, of my life.

I would recommend those persons who are inclined to stagnate, whose blood is beginning to thicken sluggishly in their veins, to try keeping four dogs, two of which are puppies. Not leaving them to servants; really keeping them.

The two I finally picked out to keep were Woosie and Winkie. As to Winkie, I never had a doubt that he was my dog, so evident, quite early, was his intelligence and sensitivity. Pure white, except the right side of his face, which was black, and except for one big black spot in the middle of his left ear, he quickly stood out from the rest by his affectionateness and devotion to me. He was a one-man dog, and I, as soon as he was old enough to know his own mind, was his man.

Over Woosie I hesitated, weighing him up a good while against the merits of the other two, and finally deciding on him because he seemed, of the litter, to be the only one like Chunkie.

Seemed. No reality, as it turned out, could have had a greater discrepancy with its appearance. Chunkie was a very adorable dog, and Woosie wasn't. Their coats were the same, but not their characters. Afterwards, when it was too late and I had given the other two away, I was surprised at my blindness in being taken in by such a superficial resemblance. Except for the coat, by the time Woosie was two months old there wasn't a shred of likeness to his enchanting father. His head had none of the generous width of Chunkie's, but was a narrow, oddly bumpy

affair, and his eyes, which almost had a cast in them, were without a spark of the easy good-nature, the kindly live-and-let-live expression, that shone so attractively in Chunkie's. If I had been more experienced, the shape of his head and the almost crookedness of his eyes would have warned me, but on the strength of his curly coat I chose him, and the minute he was old enough to get really going, he revealed himself as a thorough-paced little devil.

How the saintly Knobbie could have produced such a child, I can't think; how two such delightful parents could have had a son like that is a mystery. For a long while I didn't believe his snaps and growls were in earnest, but supposed they were just fun. They were, anyhow, diminutive, matching his diminutive size; but as he grew bigger so did they, and it was a shock one day to realise that if Winkie hadn't happened to be bigger still, there wouldn't have been much of him left. Even as it was, he got torn about sometimes. That white ear with the black spot in its middle, which was my special pride, was in constant danger of being rent asunder, and very soon I was obliged to interfere in what I had so long supposed were games, and face the fact that Woosie was a bad little dog, whose playing was really nothing but bitter strife.

It was especially upsetting if he started quarreling in the car. It was my practice, when they were old enough, to drive them out with their parents every afternoon at three o'clock—before, that is, the hour at which I was liable to get caught in the wash of social merriment which convulses the Côte d'Azur from five in the afternoon till an hour, deep in the night, which I have never investigated. I drove them to woods and fields, far enough from main roads for them to be able to run in safety. Directly the car came round, the four of them leapt into it, three on the back seat and Knobbie in front beside me, and alarmingly often, instead of sitting all good and quiet like the others, Woosie would begin to fight.

It is highly unpleasant to drive a car in which dogs are fighting. I know of nothing more difficult and frightening. If you stop and tumble them out into the road, they risk being run over. If you stop and don't tumble them out, you are more or less certain to come out torn and bleeding yourself. But on the whole it was safer to stop, and I used to draw up by the side of the road with as little wobble as I could manage under the circumstances, and then, safe at least from collisions with other cars, leaned over and did my best, by grabs and minatory exhortations, to separate the struggling mass at the back.

Knobbie never fought, but when a fight was going on withdrew into her corner as far as she could, and looked pained. Chunkie never began a quarrel, but once it had started couldn't resist having a go at it too. Flinging himself into the fray, he fought with a thoroughness and gusto that scared me, because his little belly was very round and tightly stretched, and a stray jab from one or other of his infuriated sons' teeth might have punctured it. However, it never did get punctured, nor were any of us ever seriously wounded, though from the noise and violence one would have supposed nobody could come out of that car alive, let alone whole; and at least going home there was peace, and we arrived in some sort of order, because by that time they had had their run and were exercised into quiet.

But what a lot of exercise they needed before they reached this state! Surely of all races the terrier race is the most lively. Every day our walks seemed to have to be longer, to keep pace with their growing strength, and it was no use trying to evade my share of the exercise by sitting down on a tree trunk while they chased each other, for if I did they instantly left off doing whatever they had been doing and sat down too —fidgeting, whining, quivering with impatience to be off again, but not stirring till I got up and went on.

It was extremely wearing. They had been born on All Saints' Day, which, as every choirboy knows, is November 1, and by the time they were old enough to be tireless the warmths of April and May had begun. Not so easy, I found, for me to be violently active in a southern spring. It didn't affect them, though, and headed by the fleet and graceful Knobbie, and tailed by the shortlegged but indomitable Chunkie, they would stream across the fields as though no such thing as heat existed, while I, far behind, labored along, thankful if I didn't lose sight of the four little white bodies.

For me, the only really pleasant moment of our outings was when we got back to the car. Then, having safely shut them in, with a sigh of relief I could sink into the driving seat and praise God that I needn't, at least for that day, walk any farther. Yet, really, great was my reward for those daily exertions. They did stretch me, and lighten me, and prevent the sorts of curves collecting which nobody cares to have, they did stave off the moment, which I suppose easily arrives for those who accumulate rather than shed, of being short of breath and extended of outline; and certainly till then I had never known the sheer deliciousness of sitting still.

"We are told," wrote my relations, "that you are growing thin. Scragginess is never becoming. It is, of course, all those dogs."

In a picture I have, all those dogs are waiting to be let out of the car on getting home from one of our outings. Knobbie is on the left, then Chunkie, then Winkie, and then Woosie.

I can't help thinking that, even in this moment of calm, Woosie looks a bad little dog, alert for opportunities of evil.

Nevertheless, when he died I grieved. A gifted friend who stayed with me that summer, one who broke out easily into noble verse, wrote thus of my house and its then contents:

> *This is the home of Graces and of Muses.*
> *It's also Knobbie's, Chunkie's, Winkie's,*
> > *Woosie's.*

Alas, it didn't stay Woosie's long. Hardly was the ink dry on that couplet than it ceased to apply to the poor dog, for he was cruelly snatched away by death; and it made it no less distressing that it should have been his own fault, his own defiant disobedience, which hurried him off to his doom.

Early in his career it was apparent that Woosie had no intention of ever obeying anybody. I might whistle till breath failed, call, threaten, beseech, cajole, and he would still continue unheedingly to do whatever happened at the moment to be interesting him. If, having finally got him back by the ignominious method of fetching him, I proposed to spank him, he, for his part, at once proposed to bite, and sometimes did; if, in order to prevent further departures, I put him on a lead, he sat down and refused, unless actually dragged, to stir. I couldn't bring myself to drag him, therefore he didn't stir; and presently, defeated, I would take the lead off, pick him up, and ignoring his furious snappings and struggles carry him a while—just to show that, positively, he had to come along with the rest of us, and not go rushing off so dangerously on his own account.

But what was the good of that? The minute I put him down—and I soon had to, for nobody can carry a struggling dog very far—off he darted again, sometimes luring Winkie who, left to himself, was exquisitely obedient, to dart off after him. Winkie, however, I easily persuaded back. At all times he was only happy if he knew I was near, and though he would stream off with the others in the first excitement of being let out of the car, he alone of the pack would stop every now and then, and look round to see if I were coming. So that he was as safe as his more experienced parents crossing roads—waiting, on arriving at one, till I reached it too, and then hurrying across it with me at the word of command.

But Woosie never dreamed of either waiting for me or, when we crossed it, hurrying. The only occasions on which he seemed to be at leisure were in the middle of a road. There he would loiter, he who never loitered, and sniff in absorbed examination of any objects of interest, behaving as if such things as cars swooping round corners and bearing down on him with relentless French impetuosity didn't exist.

It was his death. A day came when the others and I had, as usual, hurried across a road which seemed quite quiet, and he, as usual, stayed loitering in the middle. Arrived on the other side, I called and whistled as usual, and as usual no notice was taken. It was only a secondary country road, on which I had never yet seen any traffic, so that I didn't at once go back and catch hold of him, as I would have if it had been a *route nationale*, but walked on a few paces through the

scrub of sage and rock-roses, exhorting him, over my shoulder, to be a good dog and come along; and those few paces were enough to make it impossible to get to him in time to save him when a car came rushing round the corner.

On him before I could even begin to run, it continued its way in complete indifference to what it had left behind in the road. He was still alive but unconscious when I reached him, and picking him up I drove frantically to the nearest vet, with the other three dogs huddled, appalled, in the back.

On the way the poor mangled thing came to, and then began horror. I had to slow down for fear of adding to his agony, and it seemed as if we would never get to the vet's. Suppose, too, the vet should be out when we did get there? Oh, I have been thankful often in my life, deeply thankful, but never more deeply than when I found that man was in.

Together we carried my unhappy little dog to the operating table, where, quieter by then, he lay as he was put, his eyes fixed on me to whom, strong and well, he had paid so little head. In this last dreadful moment I was his only hope—and what a hope! Somebody who could do nothing for him except stroke his poor head and whisper, desperate for the vet to be quick and end such sufferings, "You'll soon be better, darling—soon be better . . ."

He seemed, though, to understand and believe. He never took his eyes off my face till the blessed sleep the vet was giving him gradually dimmed them. He couldn't have lived. He was most grievously damaged. And what, I asked the vet when it was over, about the people in the car, who knew what they had done—for I saw them, while I was still struggling through the bushes, looking out of the back window—and yet drove on indifferently? Did he suppose that in all the wide world there could be forgiveness for such people?

He shrugged his shoulders. *"Après tout, madame,"* he said, *"ce n'est qu'un chien."*

It seemed to me as I drove home, with Woosie wrapped in a cloth I had begged of the vet, at my feet—Woosie so quiet now, who had never yet been quiet, so forever acquiescent—it seemed to me as if I saw for the first time, in their just proportions, the cruelty and suffering which are life, and the sure release, the one real consolation, which is death. From having thought highly of being alive—for, with a few stretches of misery, I have been a fortunate and a happy person —I began to think highly of being dead. Out of it all. Done with torment. Safe from further piteous woes. My mind, that is, during the drive, ran in directions which the comfortable would call morbid; it ran, in other words, in the direction of stark truth. And I don't see how it could do anything else with a little dead thing, a thing so lately of my intimate acquaintance, which an hour before had been almost fiercely alive and furiously enjoying itself, lying at my feet in the awful meekness of death. Finished, Woosie was; and the manner of his ending left me with a great desire, if only it were possible, to beg his pardon, and the pardon of all poor helpless creatures, for the tragic unkindness of human beings.

I passed a donkey on the way—a small beast, plodding stoutly along, doing his best for the enormous man sitting on a pile of household goods who was driving him. But doing his best didn't save him from being hit. He was hit hard and often. And looking at the man's face, I thought that to an overworked donkey, to a kicked dog, to a pelted cat, it may well seem that this is a world of devils.

Yet there, when I got home, was the familiar heavenly peace of a summer evening in the south. Devils? Such a word was an outrage. The sky was still limpid after a sunset of pure gold. The jagged line of the Esterels, delicate and dark against it, stretched into a sea the color of pearls. Cypresses, very black and still, stood like solemn witnesses, it might easily be imagined, to the glory of God; and a hush so holy lay over the countryside that it seemed as if the entire world must be at its goodnight prayers. It wasn't, of course. Those people in the car who had killed Woosie must have got by that time to Monte Carlo, and were probably at anything rather than prayers; and in the peasants' houses, in whose windows lights were beginning to twinkle, there

were, from their point of view, few reasons for sending up blessings.

But what *sort* of a world was it, then? I asked myself, looking round at these things in great perplexity and perturbation of spirit. Was its loveliness merely mockery? Was it nothing but a bad joke played off on its helpless children? Was it just a blanket of beauty drawn across horror, and if a corner were lifted something so terrible would be seen, such suffering and cruelty, that nobody could ever be at peace again?

The gardener helped me bury Woosie. In complete silence we buried him. No questions were asked, and no explanations offered. By the time we had done, the brief southern twilight was over, and the stars were out—

Plainness and clearness without shadow of stain . . .

These poets.

Another photograph shows me and my three remaining dogs the following winter—Chunkie in my right arm, Knobbie in my left, Winkie standing, holding on to my knee, and all of them uneasily interested in what the man with the camera was doing.

The had now become almost painfully precious to me. Not that I had any fear of their fate being like Woosie's, for both Knobbie and Winkie were perfectly obedient, and Chunkie, if he didn't react to orders quite so instantly, yet was very clever and handy with roads; but after Woosie's death we seemed to draw closer together, in a more undistracted affection. Fights were things of the past. Admonishments grew rusty for want of use. No hand had ever to be lifted. And so greatly did Winkie's intelligence and quickness develop in this atmosphere of peace, that he grew to be really a most remarkable dog.

For instance, what could be more remarkable than his way of dealing, one night, with a highly unpleasant and difficult situation? I was woken up by his getting out of his basket and beginning those heavings which are preliminary to being sick, and at once losing my head, for I had just bought a new carpet, I could think of nothing better to do than to run hither and thither in the room like a distracted hen, first to the door leading on to the balcony, then to the door leading into the passage, unable to decide which would be the best for him to go out of, but very conscious that he must at once go out of something. And he, deeply engaged though he was, yet found time, between two heaves, to turn his head and look at me, exactly as if he were saying, "Don't fuss—this is my affair," and then proceeded, heaving but clear-headed, to my bathroom, where, having placed himself in front of the lavatory, he carefully, skilfully, and deliberately was sick into it.

I hold that it isn't possible not to feel that such a dog is almost painfully precious. And besides his sapience and self-control, he had the added charm of adoring me exclusively. It is a great thing to be adored exclusively. Whenever it has happened in my life, I have liked it very much. And with Winkie it lasted, too; he really did carry out the injunctions of the marriage service, and forsaking all others keep only to me.

Rarely did he take his beautiful, kind eyes off me. When he went to sleep and was obliged to shut them, he still had the thought of me vivid in his heart, for at my faintest small movement he instantly opened them, and looked at me inquiringly, as if asking whether there was anything I wanted and he could do; and wherever I went there he would be too, and wherever I sat he would jump up and sit beside me—close, protecting me, his head on my knee.

A most dear dog. Of all my dogs, not excluding Coco, he was the one I loved best. And I say was, and I put my love into the past tense, because he is dead.

Fuit. Amavi.

This story, like life, as it goes on is becoming dotted with graves. It would seem that the more you care for a dog, and the more care you take of him, the more, as it were, he dies. My milkman's dog, who never gets a kind word and is chained up and half starved doesn't die; during the whole five years I have been here, an old Alsatian has lain about in the most dangerous places and hasn't been run over; and a hoary *chien de chasse* belonging to the postman, so long past his work that he is hardly able to crawl, still goes on living. Only Winkie dies—Winkie, watched over, guarded, loved and in the heyday of his youth; only he, of all the dogs scattered about everywhere, falls into the clutches of the one tick, among millions of ticks waiting on grass and bushes to fasten onto passing dogs, which is death to catch. And to this story, and to my life, there is added another grave.

Yet, deeply unhappy as his death made me, and for a time quite extraordinarily forlorn, I didn't feel the peculiar distress and horror that swept over me when Woosie died. There was no cruelty, hideous because conscious, behind this death. It isn't possible to be indignant with a tick. Like the rest of us, ticks must live, and nature, having arranged that they shall do so most conveniently to themselves attached to a dog, what is there to be done except try, intelligently and untiringly, to defeat nature? When it comes to ticks, there is no end to my understanding and resignation, nor, after the lesson I have had, is there any end to the skill and patience with which I search for them on my surviving dogs. Unresentfully, but also completely unrelentingly, I track them down, with a zeal so unflagging that it would be a clever tick indeed who should, in future, escape my tweezers.

But this doesn't give me back Winkie, and it is heartbreaking to know that I might have saved him if I had been as skilled, as patient and as much alive to the danger before he died as I have since become. Through those perilous hot months, April to October, I ought never to have left my dogs; but, supposing all was well with them, for they ate and slept and played as usual, and if Winkie didn't rush about quite as much as the others I merely thought it sensible of him, in such heat—supposing, then, that all was as well as it seemed, I did leave them once during the summer, and went for a jaunt to Corsica.

Why I, who never jaunt, on this occasion did so, was because it was August, and in August I have a birthday, and birthdays, my Pomeranian training taught, are of the utmost importance, and on no account to be ignored. So firm a hold has this teaching got on me that I couldn't ignore it now if I tried. Years pass, yet still, as the day comes round, I feel a stir in me of excitement, of expectation, of an urge to celebrate, of an impulse to do something spectacular; for this, Pomerania insisted and I cannot forget, is the day of days in one's life, a day on which it is a duty, as well as a privilege, to let oneself go.

Accordingly each year I look about me with earnest attentiveness in search of a direction the letting-go can take. But, after a while, there are few directions left which appear sufficiently seemly; and the problem's difficulty is much increased by the fact that I am alone, with no children or husbands to egg me on by setting the day about with candles, and decorating it with cake. I spent my penultimate birthday, so impossible did it seem to find a form of festive activity which should be at the same time reckless and respectable, sulking in bed; and when, on my last one, some young blades of my acquaintance who were at Calvi—female blades, but blades, I take it, can be of either sex—wrote inviting me to join them in what they described as the most perfect bathing in the world, I jumped at the suggestion as a God-sent solution of my troubles, and without an instant's hesitation let myself go to Corsica.

Corsica is only six hours from Nice by calm sea—by sea which is not calm, considerably more —Nice is only one hour's drive from me, and off I went, lightheartedly to join other persons of light hearts, and was away a week. A single week, one would think, is not a very long time to leave one's dogs and one's duties, but it had been too long for Winkie, and when I got home he was already past saving.

Still thinking, in my ignorance, that his extreme languor was because of the heat, I asked the vet to give me a tonic for him; but the vet, when he saw him, at once looked at his gums and his tongue, and in a dismay that struck my heart cold said, *"Mais c'est effrayant."*

It was indeed *effrayant*. Winkie's gums and tongue, I now for the first time saw, were almost snow-white, and the vet explained that he had got the fatal tick-disease, the disease more feared than any other in these parts, whose effect is that its victims bleed, internally, to death. Slowly. Each day growing weaker, colder, less able to stand.

I will not go into the details of Winkie's dying; it is still too close.

Yesterday, looking out of the window at the darkening garden, where the unaccustomed rain was dripping on yellow leaves, I found my eyes resting on the very place we spent our last few hours together—he lying on a chair, his eyes, grown curiously wise and sad, gazing at the fields he was never to run in again, I sitting on the grass beside him, my hand holding his cold paw, so cold because so bloodless, waiting for the vet, who was coming at six o'clock to put him to sleep; and counting up the weeks, I found there were ten of them since then, and that yesterday was the exact day, ten weeks ago, that he died. So that it is still very close, and cannot easily be thought of.

My comfort is that I was able to prevent the suffering of the last stages of this dreadful disease by cutting it short, and I can think of him as never having known real pain. Always, till the very end, when his eyes grew so strangely wise and sad, Winkie had been happy. Nobody ever scolded him. From first to last he heard nothing but words of kindness and of love. His short life was filled with everything a good dog deserves, and its end was quite painless: just a lying down, when I told him to—his final obedience—with his head on my lap, where he had so often laid it; and then sleep. Before he knew anything different, deep sleep.

And now I have got to the end of my fourteenth dog, and with him this record finishes. At the beginning I explained that I have had, altogether, fourteen dogs, and having seen the fourteenth through his brief life, from the day he was born on my bedroom sofa to the day he died on my lap, there is no more to be said.

His bereft parents watched for him, unable to make out why he didn't come back.

The Highland Keeper's Daughter *by R. Ansdell*

Every morning, for the first few days after his death, directly they were let out they jumped onto his stool in the garden, from which they could get a better view of the various paths he might come home by. On it they sat patiently together for hours, Knobbie watching one side and Chunkie the other, and hardly to be persuaded to get off it for meals.

And in a final picture a little later, Chunkie is alone with me—but alone only for three weeks, because Knobbie, most unfortunately just when we most needed the comfort of each other's company, had to go away on her biannual visit to the friend who, at such times, keeps her safe from Chunkie's attentions.

In the picture it can be seen that Chunkie is feeling cheerful again. At first, when Knobbie too left him, he was greatly depressed and bewildered, and to console him for his different trials I took him, each afternoon, down to the sea,

knowing that he loves bathing and digging holes in the sand; and after a few days of this treatment I observed, with pleasure, that air of never-say-die, which I have always so much admired in him, reappearing.

Chunkie certainly, whatever I may be, is *resolut*. He, certainly, is ready, after any setback, to face life again as soon as possible in the proper spirit.

And what is the proper spirit?

Chunkie's, I think—keeping one's end up, and the flag of one's tail briskly flying to the last.

Wise and sensible dog; making the most of what he has, rather than worrying over what he hasn't. And ruminating on the rocks during those afternoons by the sea, it occurred to me that it would be very shameful if I were less sensible, less wholesome and less sturdy of refusal to go down before blows, than Chunkie.

So I made another vow.

The Turnspit

by EDWARD JESSE

How well do I recollect, in the days of my youth, watching the operations of a turnspit at the house of a worthy old Welsh clergyman in Worcestershire, who taught me to read. He was a good man, wore a bushy wig, black worsted stockings and large plated buckles in his shoes. As he had several boarders, as well as day-scholars, his two turnspits had plenty to do. They were long-bodied, crooked-legged and ugly dogs, with a suspicious, unhappy look about them, as if they were weary of the task they had to do and expected every moment to be seized upon to perform it. Cooks in those days, as they are said to be at present, were very cross, and if the poor animal, wearied with having a larger joint than usual to turn, stopped for a moment, the voice of the cook might be heard rating him in no very gentle terms. When we consider that a large solid piece of beef would take at least three hours before it was properly roasted, we may form some idea of the task a dog had to perform in turning a wheel during that time. A pointer has pleasure in finding game, the terrier worries rats with considerable glee, the greyhound pursues hares with eagerness and delight, and the bulldog even attacks bulls with the greatest energy, while the poor turnspit performs his task by compulsion, like a culprit on a treadwheel, subject to scolding or beating if he stops a moment to rest his weary limbs, and is then kicked about the kitchen when the task is over. There is a story (it is an old one) of the Bath turnspits, who were in the habit of collecting together in the abbey church of that town during divine service. It is said, but I will not vouch for the truth of the story, that hearing one day the word "spit," which occurred in the lesson for the day, they all ran out of the church in the greatest hurry, evidently associating the word with the task they had to perform.

These dogs are still used in Germany, and Her Majesty has two or three of them amongst her collection of these quadrupeds. They are extremely bandy-legged, so as to appear almost incapable of running, with long bodies and rather large heads. They are very strong in the jaws, and are what are called hardbitten. It is a peculiarity in these dogs that they generally have the iris of one eye black and the other white. Their color varies, but the usual one is a bluish gray, spotted with black. The tail is generally curled on the back.

As two turnspits were generally kept to do the roasting work of a family, each dog knew his own day, and it was not an easy task to make one work two days running. Even on his regular day a dog would frequently hide himself, so cordially did he hate his prescribed duties. A story is said to have been related to a gentleman by the duke de Liancourt, of two turnspits employed in his

217

kitchen, who had to take their turns every other day to get into the wheel. One of them, in a fit of laziness, hid himself on the day he should have worked, so that his companion was forced to mount the wheel in his stead, who, when his employment was over, began crying and wagging his tail and making signs for those in attendance to follow him. This was done, and the dog conducted them into a garret, where he dislodged his idle companion and killed him immediately.

The following circumstance is said to have taken place in the Jesuits' College at La Flèche.

After the cook had prepared his meat for roasting, he looked for the dog whose turn it was to work the spit, but not being able to find him, he attempted to employ for this service another that happened to be in the kitchen. The dog, however, resisted, and having bitten the cook, ran away. The man, with whom the dog was a particular favorite, was much astonished at his ferocity. The wound he had received was a severe one and bled profusely, so that it was necessary to dress it. While this was doing, the dog, which had run into the garden and found out the one whose turn it was to work the spit, came driving him before him into the kitchen, when the latter immediately went of his own accord into the wheel.

Buffon calls the turnspit the *Basset à jambes torses*, but some of the breed are said to have straight legs. Short as they are, the body is extremely strong and heavy in proportion to the height of the dog, and this weight must facilitate the turning of the wheel.

The Intruder *by Sir Edwin Landseer*

Country Matters

by VANCE BOURJAILY

ONE of the strongest of the several minority hunting opinions I hold is that a bird dog's place is in the home. Perhaps the most depressing thing related to this opinion is precisely that it should be a minority one, nor will I pretend to be anything but self-righteous about the matter: since I admit no possibility that I am wrong, it must follow that in my view the majority of American sporting men are about as sorry a collection of dog handlers as could readily be imagined.

The basic tenet of this majority, and it is always advanced as if it were a fact, is that hunting dogs are ruined if they are allowed to become pets. Advocates of this fact are apt to know for sure such other facts as that dogs must be penned or tied outdoors, regardless of how hot or cold it is; that dogs benefit from being hauled to and from the hunting field in airless car trunks; that the more harshly they are spoken to or punished, the more eagerly they respond; and that, in a general way, any impulse of consideration, let alone affection, for the animal must be stoutly fought down. This indicator of the handler's infinite virility is for the dog's own good.

The basic tenet of the minority is one I shall advance as a fact, without any expectation of provoking much agreement: every really good hunting dog I've ever known has been the pet of the man he hunted with. The rest are an army of lost dogs.

Let me cite the revolting case of Eddie-Joe X., whose dialogue in the following should be read in a mean, midsouthern accent:

A mutual, nonhunting friend whom I am visiting has arranged for Eddie-Joe to take me out for quail; we are driving in Eddie-Joe's car. His dogs, two wan pointers called Jake and Birdie, are, of course, in the trunk; my dog, thank heavens, is five hundred miles away. I have protested, as we got in, that there's no need to shut the dogs away on my account, hell, I don't mind them climbing on me. Eddie-Joe's reply has been a sour look, which conveyed considerable doubt that he and I were going to get along.

Now, as we drive, perhaps considering his obligation to the friend who arranged this hunt, Eddie-Joe decides to be ingratiating:

"That son-of-a-bitching Jake dog, back there. I got him right at the end of last season. He's a real dog, but he's a stubborn bastard if you let him get by with it. He'll chase fur, and there's only one cure for that."

"This looks like bird country all right," I say, hoping to be spared the particulars of Eddie-Joe's prescription.

"Let him get on a rabbit in the brush, maybe forty, fifty yards out and shoot him in the ass with birdshot."

"You've done that?" I ask. I have heard other rabid pharmacists prescribe corrective shooting, but never met one who'd say he'd actually administered the dose.

"Hell, yes, I let go a blast at him," Eddie-Joe says. "We were hunting through the woods, hunting singles, and I don't think any of the shot got to him. But he came back in right now."

"How was he afterwards?" I ask.

"You won't see him chase fur," Eddie-Joe says.

He is absolutely right. No one will ever see old Jake chase anything again. He slinks along, not always in front of us, tail down, looking over at us from time to time, not so much (I fancy) in the shy hope of being approved of as simply to keep the fount of correction located at all times.

Yet there is something of the bird dog he once was left in Jake. When he scents quail in the air, he does quicken, and his tail comes up. He leads us into a rather steep draw, false points, moves forward stiff-legged, points, moves—this is the behavior, if I am any judge, of a dog working an unalarmed covey which is strung out, feeding, walking along. Birdie, the other dog, who has less experience but more training, stiffens into a point, backing Jake.

As I am about to observe that these must be moving birds, two of them rise, whir away; then another; then half a dozen from various points in the draw. Eddie-Joe and I both fire, late and disconcerted, missing what seem easy enough shots but are actually the most unlikely kind—the shots one takes without being quite set for them. In the serene, philosophical moment which follows such a display of skill, Eddie-Joe screams:

"Did you see him blink that point?" And runs at Jake with the intention of kicking him. Jake, who has been kicked before, apparently, and has some curious objection to it, crawls under a bush, and Birdie, the other dog, gets knocked off balance as surrogate, by Eddie-Joe swiping side-footed.

Eddie-Joe has had Birdie just two weeks, he tells me, and right now's the time to stop her from picking up any bad habits. She's a young dog, and quite well trained; she makes the next point for us, half an hour later, and this time the birds are properly coveyed up. Old Jake, I notice, doesn't back her. He just lies down, panting,

while Eddie-Joe and I walk in. The covey goes up and this time Eddie-Joe shows me how to shoot, dropping two birds neatly. I make my customary covey rise score, a hit and a miss, so we have three quail in front of us now, lying out in the grass.

Birdie, steady to wing and shot, is still holding her point, and is praised for the achievement with the soothing words, "Hunt dead, goddamnit!"—as if her waiting for the command were a fault rather than a virtue some trainer has spent many weeks of patience (and, perhaps, love) to develop. By now Jake has slipped by, is out hunting dead, and retrieves one of the birds for us. He brings it to me instead of Eddie-Joe, and I risk patting him for it. He goes out to resume searching; Birdie has found a quail, and holds it in her mouth, looking over at us, a bit uncertain just what's wanted.

Eddie-Joe informs her: "FETCH!" loud enough to make *me* jump. "What the hell's the matter with you? FEH-ETCH!"

When I jumped, Jake scurried away. As for Birdie, she sees Eddie-Joe running at her, and a good bit before he arrives she puts the bird down and backs away from it.

He picks it up. "Hunt dead," he commands. "Come on, you dogs, there's another bird out here."

I hand him the one Jake brought me. "Here's your other one," I say.

"Didn't you get a bird?"

"No. No, I missed."

"Could've sworn you got one," Eddie-Joe says, and we move towards the next field, where the singles are scattered. The dogs seem happy to be leaving.

By the time we have shot a single or two, and chanced onto another covey while looking for more, the hunt has gone on for just over an hour, covering about a two-mile circle around the car. Birdie, who is still eager, has probably run six or eight miles as Eddie-Joe and I walked the two, and Jake, in spite of his moping, must have covered four. Birdie, eager though she may feel, is beginning to look exhausted, and Jake is pretty much dragging himself along. I understand that their thinness is from underfeeding, not exercise. These dogs don't get out of the pen from

Country Matters • 221

the end of one hunting season till the beginning of the next.

"Dogs are starting to settle down and work careful now," Eddie-Joe says, throwing a clod of dirt at Jake to get him moving.

"I wish I could say the same," I say, angling us towards the car. "Guess I'm out of condition."

"The hell you are."

Actually, I feel great. I love this country and I love these birds. It's the first real quail shoot for me in a long while, and I've carefully arranged to keep the whole day clear for it.

"Want to rest a while?" Eddie-Joe says.

"I'm sorry, Eddie-Joe," I say. "Guess I just can't take it. I'd like to go back to town."

"Well, I'll be go-to-hell," Eddie-Joe says, and tries to cajole me, but I insist I've had enough.

In the disgruntled silence on the way back to town, I ask the one question which could induce Eddie-Joe ever to speak a civil word to me again. It's not that I feel any great civility towards him, but I want to confirm a hunch.

"What'll you take for Birdie?"

"Hell, you want a dog you better buy Jake. You can't keep up with her."

"That's my business. Is she for sale?"

"Any dog's for sale," Eddie-Joe says. "Last week it would've cost you five hundred for her, but you saw how she was about retrieving. I don't know. What'll you give? See, I know a man's got some year-old setters. . . ."

I can't really buy the two exhausted dogs lying in the trunk, though I wish I could. Well, it'll protect one of those setter pups from what happens when an Eddie-Joe ventures into trying an untrained dog—the pup's allowed to hunt once, makes a few zealous mistakes and after that is tied in the yard where he learns to bark. But I've learned what I wanted to know, which is that Eddie-Joe's a shopper and a swapper, who will go through several dogs a season, ruining each in turn. Eddie-Joe is a composite, too, of course, of some number of men that I've encountered—but every characteristic and attitude with which I've endowed my composite is prevalent, and often stoutly defended as correct.

There is all too much resemblance to all too many people, living and dead, in my composite,

and that is really why I can't buy poor old Jake and young Birdie—if we rescued them all, at a dollar a dog, it would still run up around a million.

One can err, I guess, in the other direction, and I suppose I have. I've hunted the same dog for ten years now. He is my old Weimaraner, Moon, of indifferent conformation and average breeding. He is a house dog, and because of it he knows me well enough to know precisely what he can get away with as far as obedience goes.

On the other hand, he has never been out of condition; a dog whining in the kennel can be ignored, but one living in the house, bugging you to exercise him, cannot. You find that you are making time, somehow (or your wife is), to give the dog his daily run, and I cannot see that the daily walk you must take after him does you anything but good.

Though Moon was beautifully trained at one time by Chet Cummings, an absolutely first-rate professional up in Litchfield, Connecticut, I have been too soft-headed to keep him properly in hand. He is still reasonably steady to wing, but at the sound of a shot he charges off like a berserk locomotive, and I no longer try to control this. Instead of a pattern of precise control, what Moon and I have worked out is a high degree of compatibility, based on our mutual pleasure in what we are doing—he knows his part of it, rough though it may be around the edges. And it can be said that very few of the men who have hunted with Moon and me more than a time or two have failed to inquire if there weren't some way to get one of Moon's pups. Since this can't come from admiration for a polished performance, it must come from seeing how much Moon and I are enjoying one another—and this enjoyment, I am convinced, comes from nothing more than the fact that Moon has been a pet, played with and catered to, since the time he was a pup.

Admittedly, this can get to be a bother. Moon sleeps on beds, is often reluctant to yield a favorite sofa corner to a guest and must be figured on like two extra persons when we are calculating the seating capacity of the car. He is, in his resting behavior at home, particularly fond of goose down; we own four goose-down pillows, and Moon can generally manage to pre-empt one, particularly if forestalled from settling onto the goose-down comforter with which my wife keeps warm; I have often speculated on whether, if I should sometime manage to shoot a goose while hunting with Moon, he would try to retrieve it or run over and lie down on it.

Let me acknowledge that there are occasional private dog owners who operate like professional trainers and handlers—that is, they provide well-kept, thermally sound kennels, feed intelligently and keep their dogs in training and in condition in hunting season and out. Such a hobbyist, assuming him to be a reasonably gifted trainer with time to work at it, would certainly produce a more finished hunting field performance than I get from Moon. Whether this perfectionist would get as much pleasure out of hunting his dogs may well be a matter of temperament—some prefer hunting with a close friend, some with an absolutely efficient guide.

Some say, "I love to watch the dogs work"; others like to go hunting with their dogs.

The sort of devoted and successful amateur I've described—a briefer and more abstract composite—may argue that good hunting dogs are ruined if allowed to become pets, then, but he and I will be talking about different things. As for all the others, who support his view without following his practices, I can only say that it seems to me that we have the whole licensing thing backwards. It isn't dogs who need licenses, it's owners, and if I were your commissioner, there'd be damned few issued.

EDITOR'S NOTE: The following is an excerpt from a letter to an imaginary correspondent whom Mr. Bourjaily calls Ophelia.

The dog in question is a Springer spaniel. We allowed our son, then in fifth grade, to name him, and the child said, "Pottowattomie."
The dog is four years old now and we still call him Pup. We try not to let Pup know that we like his sire, Bix, whom we have owned for a long time, a little better.
Choose your dog Ophelia as we chose Bix.

Let me assume though that you won't do anything as dumb as to pick one of the breeds that have no function—you weren't going to, were you? In the country animals without function are neglected, like old farm machines rusting in tall grass. It will be a sporting, working, watch or guard dog then—they all crave affection and give amusement, in their plainer way, as much as any Sealyham or Afghan.

Now, since you know nothing, do not go to a kennel, or a pet shop, or confuse yourself with books; dog-book writers are the most simple-minded of advocates. Go to a friend you really like, who has a dog you really like.

Our friends the Lardners had a Springer bitch, a four-legged sofa cushion whose hunting instincts were mostly evident in dreams. But four Lardner children grew up mauling and lolling on this incredibly good-tempered dog, with never a curled lip out of her; she just didn't acknowledge abuse. In the field she'd sniff curiously around, sometimes an ancestral tingle would communicate itself to her at the scent of game, be evident in lazy movement at the base of her tail, and she'd look up and smile. If I liked to shoot birds over a dog, I also had small children.

Here is some more general instruction about dogs: breed means everything to show and field competitors, to trainers, handlers, kennel clubs—but to you, once you have decided on a group of breeds (hunting, working, guard, etc.), particular breed means nothing at all. This is because there are by now, within every breed, various strains selectively and often disastrously bred for certain stupid characteristics.

Among the hunting breeds this has reached a point of absurdity. There is a show strain, bred for appearance; a field trial strain, bred for speed; a gun dog strain, bred from discards from the first two, for service. The first category is useless, the second brainless, both too high-strung to be borne with unless you feel compelled to artificial competition; in the third there will be some good individual dogs, and a lot of bad ones. So your only chance is to find an individual dog you really like, and your only way of forming that attachment is for a dog belonging to a friend.

Wait the friend out. Eventually he will do what all dog owners do who cherish their dogs—breed a bitch, put a male to stud. The drive to promote reproduction in our pets and favored animals is a human urge Freud could have had some fun with. Big Sig. (I wonder if he knew this Mexican scene: it takes place at a *ganaderia*, where fighting cattle are raised. The virgin heifers are tested, one by one, for courage—will she charge a horse? Will she charge a man? If she does, she is sent out of the ring through a door above and beside which the ranch owner stands. As she goes by, he holds his arm, palm down, an inch or two above her, so that the whole length of her body passes just under his hand. If she is thought unworthy of being bred, he signals that she is to go out a different door. Spanish country matters.)

What you are aiming to get, probably not free, is the pick of a certain litter, or at least an early choice. Now you are looking at a basket full of pups that have inherited very specific traits you like from at least one parent. There is a good chance, by the way, that an early choice is as good as first pick, because most people are going to look with misty eyes at the little squealers and pick for cuteness, color, nostalgic resemblance to a past dog or, worst, because that poor little one there is always getting pushed aside.

You want the pup that does the pushing.

"You did pick the boss of the litter?" my wife asked, when I described my visit to the Lardners to mark the pup we'd like to have.

"First to climb out of the basket and commit a nuisance," I said. "And look around for something to chew up."

You can cut down aggressiveness and adventurousness by training; you can't impart either one.

Men often project wishes in the names of their dogs. My friend Richie Lyons always names dogs Pete, because he wished that had been his nickname as a boy. Bix the Springer pup was named for the legendary trumpeter Bix Beiderbecke, one of my personal heroes; oddly enough there was a real connection, too. The Lardners had bred their sofa cushion to a fine gun dog named Major, who belonged to Lou Black. Lou had been the banjo player in the Original New Orleans Rhythm Kings, was thus one of the men from whom Bix Beiderbecke learned music, listening to them as a boy.

Lou Black, Dek Lardner and I used to hunt together, fish sometimes. Lou was an extraordinary wing shot and tackle handler, a function of the same dexterity and concentration which made him a great banjo player, I suppose. We used to talk endlessly about jazz and sporting dogs, and he approved my choice of Bix:

"That's my favorite of all the pups Major's sired," Lou would say.

Bix was, still is, built like a cinder block. He is one of those nice, genial, somewhat slow-witted creatures, without the brain-size to conceive dishonest or malicious thoughts. I know people like that, and treasure them, too.

Intelligence is an overrated thing, Ophelia. Don't get smart. Bixie never has, and his meals always come on time.

He has never gotten over the cinder-block look. Seeing him, people think him overweight. Responding to his frank, dopey cheerfulness, they pat him and feel, under the soft hair, a muscularity so hard you can hurt your hand on it. As a gun dog he is diligent and good-humored, rather than slick or fast. His pace suits me. Once I had a splendid pointing dog, and I miss the elegance of that. But the Springer way, which is simply to find and flush game at close range and then retrieve, is good enough for pheasant country like this.

When Bix was a couple of years old, Lou Black found a bitch to buy. He'd been corresponding with kennels and private breeders all over the country, looking at bloodlines and photographs, and talked the matter over so often with us and the Lardners that we all felt we'd participated in the search which brought Meg to Lou from California.

Meg was a charmer.

She was that special dog that turns up in a businesslike kennel which the operating family can't resist and so, against their principles, take into the house. She had the silky, curly hair Lou wanted (Bixie's is straight and coarse), not just on her ears but all over, and she had eyelashes like the flirtatious cartoon thoroughbred to which the alley mongrel foolishly offers his blue-ribbon bone.

Lou was dippy about her.

"I just hope Major's not too old," said old Lou. He had located Meg to keep a line going: he'd owned Major's sire.

And I inherited a jazz banjo player's dream of a dog, for Major was too old. A season or two went by and Lou phoned me; I agreed that Bix should serve as stud in his sire's place.

We are not in a hurry out here. Sometimes I guess we ought to be. Another season passed, and before Meg was ready again to be bred, Lou died. We went to the funeral and came back with Meg. Natalie Black and the children wanted us to complete Lou's scheme.

Whatever it was my wife liked in girlhood when I won her, she now quite distinctly prefers character to charm in animals and humans both. In a situation in which her devotion is divided among her family, thirty Angus cows and a bull, five horses, a pony, forty-two sheep and two rams, a couple of dozen chickens, a pair of peacocks, the dogs, occasional pigs, the steers and lambs being fed for slaughter and whatever cats happen to be stopping off, she does not take much to individual creatures whose central wish is that she indicate preference. She has preferences; they go unindicated, being for the independent, the consistent, even the mischievous animal—not the dependent and temperamental, no matter how fine their coats and winning their ways. Winning ways rather put my wife off.

So poor Meg didn't get along too well during her time with us. When she ran around crazy, it wasn't considered cute—it was called neurotic. When she pressed against the human leg she probably got an absentminded pat, but it was found to be as much cloying as it was lovable. And when she walked away winsomely from a pan of dog food, ogling the refrigerator, the dog-food pan just got picked up behind her. Sorry, Meg.

In the field that fall she showed enormous hunting instinct and energy—she was as busy a dog as I've ever tried to shoot over, and I like a dog that keeps buzzing. But she was uncontrolla-

ble, and she thought retrieving was nasty, something low-class dogs might do, nice ones never.

In the spring, hoping to combine good qualities, aware we might not discard bad ones, we bred her to Bix. Rather, the vet did. Meg would flirt, but wouldn't stand, and the job finally had to be done by artificial insemination. If you can see, in terms of my invocation of Big Sig not long ago, some grounds for male disaffection on his dog's behalf at this indignity, consider, Ophelia, whether, like my wife, you would have found the business made a lady yet less fond of Meg.

Country matters. What Hamlet meant by his improper remark ("Shall I lie in your lap?" "No, my lord." "I meant my head in your lap." "Yes, my lord." "Do you think I meant country matters?") was just that. Not sex. Sex is a city word for a city hang-up. There is not the time nor the smog nor the density out here for sex—only coupling; romping; ragging; harvest moon sentimentalizing; passion, sometimes leading to violent attempts; not much adulterous opportunity, though a farmer will take him a six-pack of beer and go round to see can he help out a widow woman by ploughing her garden for her . . . what the farm wife and the hired man might do if the farmer were away on a fishing trip and there weren't so many children around, I can't be sure. But there is much boy-and-girl excitement, pregnancies, mistakes, marriages; hard work making a fellow physically tired at night; boozy weekends to make up for it; driving around in pickup trucks to country dances; frustration often, release sometimes; dark things sometimes, of course; all the secret things and practices, I suppose, mostly between consenting partners; sometimes the consent a little one-sided, but rarely without provocation thereunto . . . all of it, anyway, light and dark, carrying with it awareness of the obvious: there maybe are lines to be drawn between human and animal behavior, but the reproductive urge, its fulfillment and consequences, is not the place to draw one. No one who lives in the country would buy a book called *How to Be the Sensuous Woman,* or man, or pig, or horse, or cow or caterpillar.

Rather, we exchange wisdom: some

neighbors came by to talk about buying a couple of Red Angus from us. The conversation turned from the artificial insemination of dogs, as with Bix and Meg, to the more ordinary sort—the artificial insemination of cows with semen from very expensive, faraway, prize-winning, pure-bred bulls.

My wife asked: "How do you know exactly when?" That is, in a particular three-week period, at just what hour to catch up the cow in the head-chute and use the syringe you've been keeping in the refrigerator up to now.

"Some say take her temperature," the neighbor said. "Most just leave her in the herd and watch for her to start bulling."

"I wouldn't always have the time and help to cut her out and bring her down without notice," my wife said. "The stuff's expensive and perishable, isn't it?"

"I know. I think the best way's to keep her out of the herd where she'll be handy. And set a fifteen-year-old girl to watch her. She'll let you know when the cow's ready."

Meg had a big litter, and our son violated all our hardhearted pup-choosing rules in picking a male: he liked the one with the darkest markings. We argued briefly, but honored his choice.

Since I'd already trained Bix in a way that satisfied me, I didn't have much hesitation about working in my eclectic way with Pup. In training I use bits picked up in various ways: from a conversation with a professional, that one way to insure against gun-shyness is to call a pup to supper with a cap pistol. From a book: never help him over a fence—let him learn to climb or run around until he finds a way through. As a result all explosions delight Pottowattomie, and he can climb anything including the side of an eight-foot, cyclone-fence dog pen. But most of the first year's training was no more than what you'd do with that Sealyham or Afghan—housebreak him, teach him to come without hesitation, to stop on command, sit and stay. In the field, and I'm not sure where I picked this suggestion up but it surely works, Pup was allowed to spend his first hunting season skylarking. He ran up a lot of

birds out of range for me, admittedly, but he got me a few shots and he had a marvelous time. As a result, hunting is both the purpose and the joy of his life; there's nothing at which he has a better time.

In the second spring and summer, we began working birds, pigeons which I'd catch in the barn at night, climbing up over baled hay with flashlight and gunny sack.

Theoretically, what you do is tuck the bird's head under its wing, rock it back and forth a couple of times, and then plant it in long grass where it should stay until the dog is about to find it, flying up just as he does. I never got very good at pigeon rocking, though; my birds were either still alert enough to fly away the moment I set them down, or so dopey that Pup would catch them before they got started, perhaps bringing them in but not without injury. As often as not when the sequence did work right, I'd spoil it by being so distracted watching that I'd shoot in haste when the bird did fly, and miss it.

I'd thought my wife might help, you see; she's a good natural shot, and has a nice touch with animals—but she found she wanted to give up hunting just about the summer Pup was trained. I settled for getting my boy—he was ten then—to release the birds for me by hand, one by one, at the edge of the farm pond. They'd fly out over the pond, I'd shoot and drop them in the water (most of the time), and then Pup would retrieve on command. The only difficulty with the procedure was that pigeons didn't smell or taste or feel right to him, and though he'd get them in to shore his inclination was then either to spit them out or chew them up, rather than bring them to me.

In the same season, I taught my boy to shoot. We did pistol, rifle and shotgun, and like his mother (unlike his father) he was naturally good—even with the shotgun, which, while not as difficult as pistol shooting, is more athletic in that it involves not just pointing but swinging and follow through, in about the same way you'd follow a moving subject with a movie camera.

The boy shot a .410, first at balloons moving along in the wind, then at croquet balls rolled

Spanish Pointer *by P. Reinagle*

downhill at some speed, finally at clay birds from a hand-trap. He could hit them fine.

The first Monday after Labor Day, with the opening of dove season in Illinois, which is sixty miles from here and to which Dek Lardner had invited me, I took Pup; I would have to say that my training paid off. I was sitting under a medium-sized pine tree, waiting for pass shots, and the dog had been told to sit and stay behind me. I didn't hear him leave, but after a moment, when I looked around, he was gone. It was hard to believe; in fact, I could hear him pant. It was a puzzled minute or two before it occurred to me to look up. There, balanced fairly comfortably on a branch six feet up, was the dog who had learned to climb anything, and at that moment doves appeared out front. I shot quickly and luckily, a dove fell and I told Pup to fetch—his

first real hunting-season retrieve. So out he leapt, rather than climbing down, using my head as a springboard, found the bird without difficulty, sat down and ate it. I guess gunfire still suggested mealtime to him.

We finally did work out that he wasn't to eat doves—though they were apparently too much like pigeons in scent and feathering to be handled seriously, and he never brought one all the way in. With pheasant, quail and ducks, later in the fall, to my great relief, he did and does the proper thing.

He is, in fact, better than Bixie in the field— a smarter dog, inheriting it from his mother, faster, trimmer, prettier to watch, less dependable and more eager to please. That last, another inheritance perhaps, is, oddly enough, a defect. Unlike Bix, who seems secure in the conviction that no one could possibly be displeased by him, Pup does the equivalent of Meg's nervous cuddling and running around. He makes up to people unnecessarily. He seems to need reassurance that he is liked and approved of.

But it is also possible—there is no way of being sure of this with a dog—that he is often in some degree of pain. He has poor teeth, and a low resistance to infection in places like his ears, so it may be that the reassurance that he needs is something more like being promised things are going to be okay.

That is the dog, then; not so much a perfect as an interesting dog.

The pointing dog which came before Bix and Pup was Moon, of course. I didn't train Moon; he trained me.

When we had had him for eleven years—in Connecticut, Uruguay, Chile, California and finally here—he began to fail. He ate hardly anything, and what little he did eat didn't seem to nourish him. We tried every way we could to help —even (did you know such things exist?) a special formula of dog food for senile dogs, like pabulum for old men and infants.

He became incontinent; being almost catlike about cleanliness, he hated that as much as you would. He went from eighty pounds down to thirty-five, and I knew he'd have to be put down.

I took him to the vet. He'd known Moon for close to eleven years, too, had shot over him with me, sewed Moon up more than once when he'd ripped open his stomach leaping barbed wire, done surgery on him.

"How do you do it, Jim?" I asked. "Is it chloroform, or what?"

"These days just an injection."

"Fast?"

"Instantaneous. No pain. Just goes like that."

"Okay."

"Leave him with me."

"No," I said. I couldn't believe Moon wouldn't know why I was leaving him. He was so damn sensitive to me. He'd have felt and disapproved my cowardice, if I'd left the room.

So I lifted my old dog onto the operating table; he was too weak to climb up by himself. Stroked him. Talked to him. Told him he was a good dog. Moon was looking at me when Dr. Jim Lowe found the vein.

Country matters, girl.

To the Man Who Killed My Dog

by RICHARD JOSEPH

I hope you were going some place important when you drove so fast down Cross Highway across Bayberry Lane, Tuesday night.

I hope that when you got there the time you saved by speeding meant something to you or somebody else.

Maybe we'd feel better if we could imagine that you were a doctor rushing somewhere to deliver a baby or ease somebody's pain. The life of our dog to shorten someone's suffering—that mightn't have been so bad.

But even though all we saw of you was the black shadow of your car and its jumping red taillights as you roared down the road, we know too much about you to believe it.

You saw the dog, you stepped on your brakes, you felt a thump, you heard a yelp and then my wife's scream. Your reflexes are better than your heart and stronger than your courage —we know that—because you jumped on the gas again and got out of there as fast as your car could carry you.

Whoever you are, mister, and whatever you do for a living, we know you are a killer.

And in your hands, driving the way you drove Tuesday night, your car is a murder weapon.

You didn't bother to look, so I'll tell you what the thump and the yelp were. They were Vicky, a six-month-old Basset puppy; white, with brown and black markings. An aristocrat, with twelve champions among her forebears; but she clowned and she chased, and she loved people and kids and other dogs as much as any mongrel on earth.

I'm sorry you didn't stick around to see the job you did, though a dog dying by the side of the road isn't a very pretty sight. In less than two seconds you and that car of yours transformed a living being that had been beautiful, warm, clean, soft and loving into something dirty, ugly, broken and bloody. A poor, shocked and mad thing that tried to sink its teeth into the hand it had nuzzled and licked all its life.

I hope to God that when you hit my dog you had for a moment the sick, dead feeling in the throat and down to the stomach that we have known ever since. And that you feel it whenever you think about speeding down a winding country road again.

Because the next time some eight-year-old boy might be wobbling along on his first bicycle. Or a very little one might wander out past the gate and into the road in the moment it takes his father to bend down to pull a weed out of the driveway, the way my puppy got away from me.

Or maybe you'll be real lucky again, and only kill another dog, and break the heart of another family.

The Story of Two Dogs

by **DORIS LESSING**

GETTING a new dog turned out to be more difficult than we thought, and for reasons rooted deep in the nature of our family. For what, on the face of it, could have been easier to find than a puppy once it had been decided: "Jock needs a companion, otherwise he'll spend his time with those dirty Kaffir dogs in the compound"? All the farms in the district had dogs who bred puppies of the most desirable sort. All the farm compounds owned miserable beasts kept hungry so that they would be good hunters for their meat-starved masters; though often enough puppies born to the cage-ribbed bitches from this world of mud huts were reared in white houses and turned out well. Jacob our builder heard we wanted another dog, and came up with a lively puppy on the end of a bit of rope. But we tactfully refused. The thin flea-bitten little object was not good enough for Jock, my mother said; though we children were only too ready to take it in.

Jock was a mongrel himself, a mixture of Alsatian, Rhodesian ridgeback, and some other breed—terrier?—that gave him ears too cocky and small above a long melancholy face. In short, he was nothing to boast of, outwardly: his qualities were all intrinsic or bestowed on him by my mother who had given this animal her heart when my brother went off to boarding school.

In theory Jock was my brother's dog. Yet why give a dog to a boy at that moment when he departs for school and will be away from home two-thirds of the year? In fact my brother's dog was his substitute; and my poor mother, whose children were always away being educated, because we were farmers, and farmers' children had no choice but to go to the cities for their schooling—my poor mother caressed Jock's too-small intelligent ears and crooned: "There, Jock! There, old boy! There, good dog, yes, you're a *good* dog, Jock, you're such a *good* dog. . . ." While my father said, uncomfortably: "For goodness sake, old girl, you'll ruin him, that isn't a house pet, he's not a lapdog, he's a farm dog." To which my mother said nothing, but her face put on a most familiar look of misunderstood suffering, and she bent it down close so that the flickering red tongue just touched her cheeks, and sang to him: "Poor old Jock then, yes, you're a poor old dog, you're not a rough farm dog, you're a good dog, and you're not strong, no you're delicate."

At this last word my brother protested; my father protested; and so did I. All of us, in our different ways, had refused to be "delicate"—had escaped from being "delicate"—and we wished to rescue a perfectly strong and healthy young dog from being forced into invalidism, as we all, at different times, had been. Also of course we all (and we knew it and felt guilty about it) were secretly pleased that Jock was now absorbing the force of my mother's pathetic need for something "delicate" to nurse and protect.

Yet there was something in the whole business that was a reproach to us. When my mother bent her sad face over the animal, stroking him with her beautiful white hands on which the rings had grown too large, and said: "There, good dog, yes Jock, you're such a gentleman—" well, there was something in all this that made us, my father, my brother and myself, need to explode with fury, or to take Jock away and make him run over the farm like the tough young brute he was, or go away ourselves forever so that we didn't have to hear the awful yearning intensity in her voice. Because it was entirely our fault that note was in her voice at all; if we had allowed ourselves to be delicate, and good, or even gentlemen or ladies, there would have been no need for Jock to sit between my mother's knees, his loyal noble head on her lap, while she caressed and yearned and suffered.

It was my father who decided there must be another dog, and for the expressed reason that otherwise Jock would be turned into a "sissy." (At this word, reminder of a hundred earlier battles, my brother flushed, looked sulky and went right out of the room.) My mother would not hear of another dog until her Jock took to sneaking off to the farm compound to play with the Kaffir dogs. "Oh you bad dog, Jock," she said sorrowfully, "playing with those nasty dirty dogs, how could you, Jock!" And he would playfully, but in an agony of remorse, snap and lick at her face, while she bent the whole force of her inevitably betrayed self over him, crooning: "How could you, oh how could you, Jock?"

So there must be a new puppy. And since Jock was (at heart, despite his temporary lapse) noble and generous and above all well-bred, his companion must also possess these qualities. And which dog, where in the world, could possibly be good enough? My mother turned down a dozen puppies; but Jock was still going off to the compound, slinking back to gaze soulfully into my mother's eyes. This new puppy was to be my dog. I decided this: if my brother owned a dog,

then it was only fair that I should. But my lack of force in claiming this puppy was because I was in the grip of abstract justice only. The fact was I didn't want a good noble and well-bred dog. I didn't know what I did want, but the idea of such a dog bored me. So I was content to let my mother turn down puppies, provided she kept her terrible maternal energy on Jock, and away from me.

Then the family went off for one of our long visits in another part of the country, driving from farm to farm to stop a night, or a day, or a meal, with friends. To the last place we were invited for the weekend. A distant cousin of my father, "a Norfolk man" (my father was from Essex), had married a woman who had nursed in the war (First World War) with my mother. They now lived in a small brick and iron house surrounded by granite *kopjes* that erupted everywhere from thick bush. They were as isolated as any people I've known, eighty miles from the nearest railway station. As my father said, they were "not suited," for they quarreled or sent each other to Coventry all the weekend. However, it was not until much later that I thought about the pathos of these two people, living alone on a minute pension in the middle of the bush, and "not suited"; for that weekend I was in love.

It was night when we arrived, about eight in the evening, and an almost full moon floated heavy and yellow above a stark granite-bouldered *kopje*. The bush around was black and low and silent, except that the crickets made a small incessant din. The car drew up outside a small boxlike structure whose iron roof glinted off moonlight. As the engine stopped, the sound of crickets swelled up, the moonlight's cold came in a breath of fragrance to our faces; and there was the sound of a mad wild yapping. Behold, around the corner of the house came a small black wriggling object that hurled itself towards the car, changed course almost on touching it and hurtled off again, yapping in a high delirious yammering which, while it faded behind the house, continued faintly, our ears, or at least mine, straining after it.

"Take no notice of that puppy," said our host, the man from Norfolk. "It's been stark staring mad with the moon every night this last week."

We went into the house, were fed, were looked after; I was put to bed so that the grown-ups could talk freely. All the time came the mad high yapping. In my tiny bedroom I looked out onto a space of flat white sand that reflected the moon between the house and the farm buildings, and there hurtled a mad wild puppy, crazy with joy of life, or moonlight, weaving back and forth, round and round, snapping at its own black shadow and tripping over its own clumsy feet—like a drunken moth around a candle flame, or like . . . like nothing I've ever seen or heard of since.

The moon, large and remote and soft, stood up over the trees, the empty white sand, the house which had unhappy human beings in it; and a mad little dog yapping and beating its course of drunken joyous delirium. That, of course, was my puppy; and when Mr. Barnes came out from the house saying: "Now, now, come now, you lunatic animal . . ." finally almost throwing himself on the crazy creature, to lift it in his arms still yapping and wriggling and flapping around like a fish, so that he could carry it to the packing case that was its kennel, I was already saying, as anguished as a mother watching a stranger handle her child: Careful now, careful, that's my dog.

Next day, after breakfast, I visited the packing case. Its white wood oozed out resin that smelled tangy in hot sunlight, and its front was open and spilling out soft yellow straw. On the straw a large beautiful black dog lay with her head on outstretched forepaws. Beside her a brindled pup lay on its fat back, its four paws sprawled every which way, its eyes rolled up, as ecstatic with heat and food and laziness as it had been the night before from the joy of movement. A crust of mealie porridge was drying on its shining black lips that were drawn slightly back to show perfect milk teeth. His mother kept her eyes on him, but her pride was dimmed with sleep and heat.

I went inside to announce my spiritual ownership of the puppy. They were all around the breakfast table. The man from Norfolk was swapping boyhood reminiscences (shared in space, not time) with my father. His wife, her eyes still red from the weeping that had followed a night quarrel, was gossiping with my mother about the various London hospitals where they had ministered to the wounded of the war they had (apparently so enjoyably) shared.

My mother at once said: "Oh my dear, no, not that puppy, didn't you see him last night? We'll never train him."

The man from Norfolk said I could have him with pleasure.

My father said he didn't see what was wrong with the dog, if a dog was healthy that was all that mattered: my mother dropped her eyes forlornly, and sat silent.

The man from Norfolk's wife said she couldn't bear to part with the silly little thing, goodness knows there was little enough pleasure in her life.

The atmosphere of people at loggerheads being familiar to me, it was not necessary for me to know *why* they disagreed, or in what ways or what criticisms they were going to make about my puppy. I only knew that inner logics would in due course work themselves out and the puppy would be mine. I left the four people to talk about their differences through a small puppy, and went to worship the animal, who was now sitting in a patch of shade beside the sweet-wood-smelling packing case, its dark brindled coat glistening, with dark wet patches on it from its mother's ministering tongue. His own pink tongue absurdly stuck out between white teeth, as if he had been too careless or lazy to withdraw it into its proper place under his equally pink wet palate. His brown buttony beautiful eyes . . . but enough, he was an ordinary mongrelly puppy.

Later I went back to the house to find out how the battle balanced: my mother had obviously won my father over, for he said he thought it was wiser not to have that puppy: "Bad blood tells, you know."

The bad blood was from the father, whose history delighted my fourteen-year-old imagination. This district being wild, scarcely populated, full of wild animals, even leopards and lions, the four policemen at the police station had a tougher task than in places nearer town; and they had bought half a dozen large dogs to (a) terrorize possible burglars around the police station itself and (b) surround themselves with an aura of controlled animal savagery. For the dogs were trained to kill if necessary. One of these dogs, a big ridgeback, had "gone wild." He had slipped his tether at the station and taken to the bush, living by himself on small buck, hares, birds, even stealing farmers' chickens. This dog, whose proud lonely shape had been a familiar one to farmers for years, on moonlit nights, or in gray dawns and dusks, standing aloof from human warmth and friendship, had taken Stella, my puppy's mother, off with him for a week of sport and hunting. She simply went away with him one morning; the Barneses had seen her go; had called after her; she had not even looked back. A week later she returned home at dawn and gave a low whine outside their bedroom window, saying: I'm home; and they woke to see their errant Stella standing erect in the paling moonlight, her nose pointed outwards and away from them towards a great powerful dog who seemed to signal to her with his slightly moving tail before fading into the bush. Mr. Barnes fired some futile shots into the bush after him. Then they both scolded Stella who in due time produced seven puppies, in all combinations of black, brown and gold. She was no purebred herself, though of course her owners thought she was, or ought to be, being their dog. The night the puppies were born, the man from Norfolk and his wife heard a sad wail or cry, and arose from their beds to see the wild police dog bending his head in at the packing-case door. All the bush was flooded with a pinkish-gold dawn light, and the dog looked as if he had an aureole of gold around him. Stella was half wailing, half growling her welcome, or protest or fear at his great powerful reappearance and his thrusting muzzle so close to her seven helpless pups. They called out, and he turned his outlaw's head to the window where they stood side by side in striped pajamas and embroidered pink silk. He put back his head and howled, he howled, a mad wild sound that gave them gooseflesh, so they said; but I did not understand that until years later when Bill the

puppy "went wild" and I saw him that day on the antheap howling his pain of longing to an empty listening world.

The father of her puppies did not come near Stella again; but a month later he was shot dead at another farm, fifty miles away, coming out of a chicken run with a fine white Leghorn in his mouth; and by that time she had only one pup left, they had drowned the rest. It was bad blood, they said, no point in preserving it, they had only left her that one pup out of pity.

I said not a word as they told this cautionary tale, merely preserved the obstinate calm of someone who knows she will get her own way. Was right on my side? It was. Was I owed a dog? I was. Should anybody but myself choose my dog? No, but . . . very well then, I had chosen. I chose this dog. I chose it. Too late, I *had* chosen it.

Three days and three nights we spent at the Barneses' place. The days were hot and slow and full of sluggish emotions; and the two dogs slept in the packing case. At nights, the four people stayed in the living room, a small brick place heated unendurably by the paraffin lamp whose oily yellow glow attracted moths and beetles in a perpetual whirling halo of small moving bodies. They talked, and I listened for the mad far yapping, and then I crept out into the cold moonlight. On the last night of our stay the moon was full, a great perfect white ball, its history marked on a face that seemed close enough to touch as it floated over the dark cricket-singing bush. And there on the white sand yapped and danced the crazy puppy, while his mother, the big beautiful animal, sat and watched, her intelligent yellow eyes slightly anxious as her muzzle followed the erratic movements of her child, the child of her dead mate from the bush. I crept up beside Stella, sat on the still-warm cement beside her, put my arm around her soft furry neck, and my head beside her alert moving head. I adjusted my breathing so that my rib cage moved up and down beside hers, so as to be closer to the warmth of her barrelly furry chest, and together we turned our eyes from the great staring floating moon to the tiny black hurtling puppy who shot in circles from near us, so near he all but crashed into us, to two hundred yards away where he just missed the wheels of the farm wagon. We watched, and I felt the chill of moonlight deepen on Stella's fur, and on my own silk skin, while our ribs moved gently up and down together, and we waited until the man from Norfolk came to first shout, then yell, then fling himself on the mad little dog and shut him up in the wooden box where yellow bars of moonlight fell into black dog-smelling shadow. "There now, Stella girl, you go in with your puppy," said the man, bending to pat her head as she obediently went inside. She used her soft nose to push her puppy over. He was so exhausted that he fell and lay, his four legs stretched out and quivering like a shot dog, his breath squeezed in and out of him in small regular wheezy pants like whines. And so I left them, Stella and her puppy, to go to my bed in the little brick house which seemed literally crammed with hateful emotions. I went to sleep, thinking of the hurtling little dog, now at last asleep with exhaustion, his nose pushed against his mother's breathing black side, the slits of yellow moonlight moving over him through the boards of fragrant wood.

We took him away next morning, having first locked Stella in a room so that she could not see us go.

It was a three-hundred-mile drive, and all the way Bill yapped and panted and yawned and wriggled idiotically on his back on the lap of whoever held him, his eyes rolled up, his big paws lolling. He was a full-time charge for myself and my mother, and, after the city, my brother, whose holidays were starting. He, at first sight of the second dog, reverted to the role of Jock's master, and dismissed my animal as altogether less valuable material. My mother, by now Bill's slave, agreed with him, but invited him to admire the adorable wrinkles on the puppy's forehead. My father demanded irritably that both dogs should be "thoroughly trained."

Meanwhile, as the nightmare journey proceeded, it was noticeable that my mother talked more and more about Jock, guiltily, as if she had betrayed him. "Poor little Jock, what will he say?"

Jock was in fact a handsome young dog. More Alsatian than anything, he was a low-standing, thick-coated animal of a warm gold color, with a vestigial "ridge" along his spine, rather wolflike, or foxlike, if one looked at him frontways, with his sharp cocked ears. And he was definitely not "little." There was something dignified about him from the moment he was out of puppyhood, even when he was being scolded by my mother for his visits to the compound.

The meeting, prepared for by us all with trepidation, went off in a way which was a credit to everyone, but particularly Jock, who regained my mother's heart at a stroke. The puppy was released from the car and carried to where Jock sat, noble and restrained as usual, waiting for us to greet him. Bill at once began weaving and yapping around the rocky space in front of the house. Then he saw Jock, bounded up to him, stopped a couple of feet away, sat down on his fat backside and yelped excitedly. Jock began a yawning, snapping movement of his head, making it go from side to side in half-snarling, half-laughing protest, while the puppy crept closer, right up, jumping at the older dog's lifted wrinkling muzzle. Jock did not move away; he forced himself to remain still, because he could see us all watching. At last he lifted up his paw, pushed Bill over with it, pinned him down, examined him, then sniffed and licked him. He had accepted him, and Bill had found a substitute for his mother who was presumably mourning his loss. We were able to leave the child (as my mother kept calling him) in Jock's infinitely patient care. "You are such a good dog, Jock," she said, overcome by this scene, and the other touching scenes that followed, all marked by Jock's extraordinary forbearance for what was, and even I had to admit it, an intolerably destructive little dog.

Training became urgent. But this was not at all easy, due, like the business of getting a new puppy, to the inner nature of the family.

To take only one difficulty: dogs must be trained by their masters, they must owe allegiance to one person. And who was Jock to obey? And Bill: I was his master, in theory. In practice, Jock was. Was I to take over from Jock? But even to state it is to expose its absurdity: what I adored was the graceless puppy, and what did I want with a well-trained dog? Trained for *what*?

A watchdog? But all our dogs were watchdogs. "Natives"—such was the article of faith—were by nature scared of dogs. Yet everyone repeated stories about thieves poisoning fierce dogs, or making friends with them. So apparently no one really believed that watchdogs were any use. Yet every farm had its watchdog.

Throughout my childhood I used to lie in bed, the bush not fifty yards away all around the house, listening to the cry of the nightjar, the owls, the frogs and the crickets; to the tom-toms from the compound; to the mysterious rustling in the thatch over my head, or the long grass it had been cut from down the hill; to all the thousand noises of the night on the veld; and every one of these noises was marked also by the house dogs, who would bark and sniff and investigate and growl at all these; and also at starlight on the polished surface of a leaf, at the moon lifting itself over the mountains, at a branch cracking behind the house, at the first rim of hot red showing above the horizon—in short at anything and everything. Watchdogs, in my experience, were never asleep; but they were not so much a guard against thieves (we never had any thieves that I can remember) as a kind of instrument designed to measure or record the rustlings and movements of the African night that seemed to have an enormous life of its own, but a collective life, so that the falling of a stone, or a star shooting through the Milky Way, the grunt of a wild pig and the wind rustling in the mealie field were all evidences and aspects of the same truth.

How did one "train" a watchdog? Presumably to respond only to the slinking approach of a human, black or white. What use is a watchdog otherwise? But even now, the most powerful memory of my childhood is of lying awake listening to the sobbing howl of a dog at the inexplicable appearance of the yellow face of the moon; of creeping to the window to see the long muzzle of a dog pointed black against a great bowl of stars. We needed no moon calendar with those dogs, who were like traffic in London: to sleep at all, one had to learn not to hear them. And if one did not hear them, one would not hear the stiff warning growl that (presumably) would greet a marauder.

At first Jock and Bill were locked up in the dining room at night. But there were so many stirrings and yappings and rushings from window to window after the rising sun or moon, or the black shadows which moved across whitewashed walls from the branches of the trees in the garden, that soon we could no longer stand the lack of sleep, and they were turned out on to the verandah. With many hopeful injunctions from my mother that they were to be "good dogs": which meant that they should ignore their real natures and sleep from sundown to sunup. Even then, when Bill was just out of puppyhood, they might be missing altogether in the early mornings. They would come guiltily up the road from the lands at breakfast-time, their coats full of grass seeds, and we knew they had rushed down into the bush after an owl, or a grazing animal, and, finding themselves farther from home than they had expected in a strange nocturnal world, had begun nosing and sniffing and exploring in practice for their days of wildness soon to come.

So they weren't watchdogs. Hunting dogs perhaps? My brother undertook to train them, and we went through a long and absurd period of "Down, Jock," "To heel, Bill," while sticks of barley sugar balanced on noses, and paws were offered to be shaken by human hands, etc., etc. Through all this Jock suffered, bravely, but saying so clearly with every part of him that he would do anything to please my mother—he would send her glances half proud and half apologetic all the time my brother drilled him, that after an hour of training my brother would retreat, muttering that it was too hot, and Jock bounded off to lay his head on my mother's lap. As for Bill he never achieved anything. Never did he sit still with the golden lumps on his nose, he ate them at once. Never did he stay to heel. Never did he remember what he was supposed to do with his paw when one of us offered him a hand. The truth was, I understood then, watching the training sessions, that Bill was stupid. I pretended of course that he despised being trained, he found it humiliating; and that Jock's readiness to go through with the silly business showed his lack of spirit. But alas, there was no getting around it, Bill simply wasn't very bright.

Meanwhile he had ceased to be a fat charmer; he had become a lean young dog, good-looking, with his dark brindled coat, and his big head that had a touch of Newfoundland. He had a look of puppy about him still. For just as Jock seemed born elderly, had respectable white hairs on his chin from the start; so Bill kept something young in him; he was a young dog until he died.

The training sessions did not last long. Now my brother said the dogs would be trained on the job: this to pacify my father, who kept saying that they were a disgrace and "not worth their salt."

There began a new regime, my brother, myself, and the two dogs. We set forth each morning, first, my brother, earnest with responsibility, his rifle swinging in his hand, at his heels the two dogs. Behind this time-honored unit, myself, the girl, with no useful part to play in the serious masculine business, but necessary to provide admiration. This was a very old role for me indeed: to walk away on one side of the scene, a small fierce girl, hungry to be part of it, but knowing she never would be, above all because the heart that had been put to pump away all her life under her ribs was not only critical and intransigent, but one which longed so bitterly to melt into loving acceptance. An uncomfortable combination, as she knew even then—yet I could not remove the sulky smile from my face. And it *was* absurd: there was my brother, so intent and serious, with Jock the good dog just behind him; and there was Bill the bad dog intermittently behind him, but more often than not sneaking off to enjoy some side path. And there was myself, unwillingly following, my weight shifting from hip to hip, bored and showing it.

I knew the route too well. Before we reached the sullen thickets of the bush where game and birds were to be found, there was a long walk up the back of the *kopje* through a luxuriant pawpaw grove, then through sweet potato vines that tangled our ankles, and tripped us, then past a rubbish heap whose sweet rotten smell was expressed in a heave of glittering black flies, then

the bush itself. Here it was all dull green stunted trees, miles and miles of the smallish, flattish, msasa trees in their second growth: they had all been cut for mine furnaces at some time. And over the flat ugly bush a large overbearing blue sky.

We were on our way to get food. So we kept saying. Whatever we shot would be eaten by "the house," or by the house's servants, or by "the compound." But we were hunting according to a newer law than the need for food, and we knew it and that was why we were always a bit apologetic about these expeditions, and why we so often chose to return empty-handed. We were hunting because my brother had been given a new and efficient rifle that would bring down (infallibly, if my brother shot) birds, large and small; and small animals, and very often large game like koodoo and sable. We were hunting because we owned a gun. And because we owned a gun, we should have hunting dogs, it made the business less ugly for some reason.

We were on our way to the Great Vlei, as distinct from the Big Vlei, which was five miles in the other direction. The Big Vlei was burnt out and eroded, and the waterholes usually dried up early. We did not like going there. But to reach the Great Vlei, which was beautiful, we had to go through the ugly bush "at the back of the *kopje*." These ritual names for parts of the farm seemed rather to be names for regions in our minds. "Going to the Great Vlei" had a fairy-tale quality about it, because of having to pass through the region of sour ugly frightening bush first. For it did frighten us, always, and without reason: we felt it was hostile to us and we walked through it quickly, knowing that we were earning by this danger the water-running peace of the Great Vlei. It was only partly on our farm; the boundary between it and the next farm ran invisibly down its center, drawn by the eye from this outcrop to that big tree to that pothole to that antheap. It was a grassy valley with trees standing tall and spreading on either side of the watercourse which was a half-mile width of intense greenness broken by sky-reflecting brown pools. This was old bush, these trees had never been cut: the Great Vlei had the inevitable look of natural bush—that no branch, no shrub, no patch of thorn, no outcrop could have been in any other place or stood at any other angle.

The potholes here were always full. The water was stained clear brown, and the mud bottom had a small movement of creatures, while over the brown ripples skimmed blue jays and hummingbirds and all kinds of vivid flashing birds we did not know the names of. Along the lush verges lolled pink and white water lilies on their water-gemmed leaves.

This paradise was where the dogs were to be trained.

During the first holidays, long ones of six weeks, my brother was indefatigable, and we set off every morning after breakfast. In the Great Vlei I sat on a pool's edge under a thorn tree, and daydreamed to the tune of the ripples my swinging feet set moving across the water, while my brother, armed with the rifle, various sizes of stick, and lumps of sugar and biltong, put the two dogs through their paces. Sometimes, roused perhaps because the sun that fell through the green lace of the thorn was burning my shoulders, I turned to watch the three creatures, hard at work a hundred yards off on an empty patch of sand. Jock, more often than not, would be a dead dog, or his nose would be on his paws while his attentive eyes were on my brother's face. Or he would be sitting up, a dog statue, a golden dog, admirably obedient. Bill, on the other hand, was probably balancing on his spine, all four paws in the air, his throat back so that he was flat from nose to tailtip, receiving the hot sun equally over his brindled fur. I would hear, through my own lazy thoughts: "Good dog, Jock, yes good dog. Idiot Bill, fool dog, why don't you work like Jock?" And my brother, his face reddened and sweaty, would come over to flop beside me, saying: "It's all Bill's fault, he's a bad example. And of course Jock doesn't see why he should work hard when Bill just plays all the time." Well, it probably was my fault that the training failed. If my earnest and undivided attention had been given, as I knew quite well was being demanded of me, to this business of the boy and the two dogs, perhaps we would have ended up with a brace of efficient and obedient animals, ever ready to die, to go to heel and to fetch it. Perhaps.

By next holidays, moral disintegration had set in. My father complained the dogs obeyed nobody, and demanded training, serious and unremitting. My brother and I watched our mother petting Jock and scolding Bill, and came to an unspoken agreement. We set off for the Great Vlei but once there we loafed up and down the waterholes, while the dogs did as they liked, learning the joys of freedom.

The uses of water, for instance. Jock, cautious as usual, would test a pool with his paw, before moving in to stand chest deep, his muzzle just above the ripples, licking at them with small yaps of greeting or excitement. Then he walked gently in and swam up and down and around the brown pool in the green shade of the thorn trees. Meanwhile Bill would have found a shallow pool and be at his favorite game. Starting twenty yards from the rim of a pool he would hurl himself, barking shrilly, across the grass, then across the pool, not so much swimming across it as bouncing across it. Out the other side, up the side of the vlei, around in a big loop, then back, and around again . . . and again and again and again. Great sheets of brown water went up into the sky above him, crashing back into the pool while he barked his exultation.

That was one game. Or they chased each other up and down the four-mile-long valley like enemies, and when one caught the other there was a growling and a snarling and a fighting that sounded genuine enough. Sometimes we went to separate them, an interference they suffered; and the moment we let them go one or another would be off, his hind quarters pistoning, with the other in pursuit, fierce and silent. They might race a mile, two miles, before one leaped at the other's throat and brought him down. This game too, over and over again, so that when they did go wild, we knew how they killed the wild pig and the buck they lived on.

On frivolous mornings they chased butterflies, while my brother and I dangled our feet in a pool and watched. Once, very solemnly, as it were in parody of the ridiculous business (now over, thank goodness) of "fetch it" and "to heel," Jock brought us in his jaws a big orange and black butterfly, the delicate wings all broken, and the orange bloom smearing his furry lips. He laid it in front of us, held the still fluttering creature flat with a paw, then lay down, his nose pointing at it. His brown eyes rolled up, wickedly hypocritical, as if to say: "Look, a butterfly, I'm a *good* dog." Meanwhile, Bill leaped and barked, a small brown dog hurling himself up into the great blue sky after floating colored wings. He had taken no notice at all of Jock's captive. But we both felt that Bill was much more likely than Jock to make such a seditious comment, and in fact my brother said: "Bill's corrupted Jock. I'm sure Jock would never go wild like this unless Bill was showing him. It's the blood coming out." But alas, we had no idea yet of what "going wild" could mean. For a couple of years yet it still meant small indisciplines, and mostly Bill's.

For instance, there was the time Bill forced himself through a loose plank in the door of the store hut, and there ate and ate, eggs, cake, bread, a joint of beef, a ripening guinea fowl, half a ham. Then he couldn't get out. In the morning he was a swollen dog, rolling on the floor and whining with the agony of his overindulgence. "Stupid dog, Bill, Jock would never do a thing like that, he'd be too intelligent not to know he'd swell up if he ate so much."

Then he ate eggs out of the nest, a crime for which on a farm a dog gets shot. Very close was Bill to this fate. He had actually been seen sneaking out of the chicken run, feathers on his nose, egg smear on his muzzle. And there was a mess of oozing yellow and white slime over the straw of the nests. The fowls cackled and raised their feathers whenever Bill came near. First, he was beaten, by the cook, until his howls shook the farm. Then my mother blew eggs and filled them with a solution of mustard and left them in the nests. Sure enough, next morning, a hell of wild howls and shrieks: the beatings had taught him nothing. We went out to see a brown dog running and racing in agonized circles with his tongue hanging out, while the sun came up red over black mountains—a splendid backdrop to a disgraceful scene. My mother took the poor inflamed jaws and washed them in warm water and

said: "Well now Bill, you'd better learn, or it's the firing squad for you."

He learned, but not easily. More than once my brother and I, having arisen early for the hunt, stood in front of the house in the dawn hush, the sky a high far gray above us, the edge of the mountains just reddening, the great spaces of silent bush full of the dark of the night. We sniffed at the small sharpness of the dew, and the heavy somnolent night-smell off the bush, felt the cold heavy air on our cheeks. We stood, whistling very low, so that the dogs would come from wherever they had chosen to sleep. Soon Jock would appear, yawning and sweeping his tail back and forth. No Bill—then we saw him, sitting on his haunches just outside the chicken run, his nose resting in a loop of the wire, his eyes closed in yearning for the warm delicious ooze of fresh egg. And we would clap our hands over our mouths and double up with heartless laughter that had to be muffled so as not to disturb our parents.

On the mornings when we went hunting, and took the dogs, we knew that before we'd gone half a mile either Jock or Bill would dash off barking into the bush; the one left would look up from his own nosing and sniffing and rush away too. We would hear the wild double barking fade away with the crash and the rush of the two bodies, and, often enough, the subsidiary rushings away of other animals who had been asleep or resting and just waiting until we had gone away. Now we could look for something to shoot which probably we would never have seen at all had the dogs been there. We could settle down for long patient stalks, circling around a grazing koodoo, or a couple of duikers. Often enough we would lie watching them for hours, afraid only that Jock and Bill would come back, putting an end to this particular pleasure. I remember once we caught a glimpse of a duiker grazing on the edge of a farmland that was still half dark. We got onto our stomachs and wriggled through the long grass, not able to see if the duiker was still there. Slowly the field opened up in front of us, a heaving mass of big black clods. We carefully raised our heads, and there, at the edge of the clod sea, a couple of arm's lengths away, were three little duikers, their heads turned away from us to where the sun was about to rise. They were three black, quite motionless silhouettes. Away over the other side of the field, big clods became tinged with reddish gold. The earth turned so fast towards the sun that the light came running from the tip of one clod to the next across the field like flames leaping along the tops of long grasses in front of a strong wind. The light reached the duikers and outlined them with warm gold. They were three glittering little beasts on the edge of an imminent sunlight. They then began to butt each other, lifting their hind quarters and bringing down their hind feet in clicking leaps like dancers. They tossed their sharp little horns and made short half-angry rushes at each other. The sun was up. Three little buck danced on the edge of the deep green bush where we lay hidden, and there was a weak sunlight warming their gold hides. The sun separated itself from the line of the hills, and became calm and big and yellow; a warm yellow color filled the world, the little buck stopped dancing and walked slowly off, frisking their white tails and tossing their pretty heads, into the bush.

We would never have seen them at all, if the dogs hadn't been miles away.

In fact, all they were good for was their indiscipline. If we wanted to be sure of something to eat, we tied ropes to the dogs' collars until we actually heard the small clink-clink-clink of guinea fowl running through the bush. Then we untied them. The dogs were at once off after the birds who rose clumsily into the air, looking like flying shawls that sailed along, just above grass level, with the dogs' jaws snapping underneath them. All they wanted was to land unobserved in the long grass, but they were always forced to rise painfully into the trees, on their weak wings. Sometimes, if it was a large flock, a dozen trees might be dotted with the small black shapes of guinea fowl outlined against dawn or evening skies. They watched the barking dogs, took no notice of us. My brother or I—for even I could hardly miss in such conditions—planted our feet wide for balance, took aim at a chosen bird and shot. The carcas fell into the worrying jaws be-

neath. Meanwhile a second bird would be chosen and shot. With the two birds tied together by their feet, the rifle, justified by utility, proudly swinging, we would saunter back to the house through the sun-scented bush of our enchanted childhood. The dogs, for politeness' sake, escorted us part of the way home, then went off hunting on their own. Guinea fowl were very tame sport for them, by then.

It had come to this, that if we actually wished to shoot something, or to watch animals, or even to take a walk through bush where every animal for miles had not been scared away, we had to lock up the dogs before we left, ignoring their whines and their howls. Even so, if let out too soon, they would follow. Once, after we had walked six miles or so, a leisurely morning's trek towards the mountains, the dogs arrived, panting, happy, their pink wet tongues hot on our knees and forearms, saying how delighted they were to have found us. They licked and wagged for a few moments—then off they went, they vanished, and did not come home until evening. We were worried. We had not known that they went so far from the farm by themselves. We spoke of how bad it would be if they took to frequenting other farms—perhaps other chicken runs? But it was all too late. They were too old to train. Either they had to be kept permanently on leashes, tied to trees outside the house, and for dogs like these it was not much better than being dead—either that, or they must run free and take their chances.

We got news of the dogs in letters from home and it was increasingly bad. My brother and I, at our respective boarding schools where we were supposed to be learning discipline, order and sound characters, read: "The dogs went away a whole night, they only came back at lunchtime." "Jock and Bill have been three days and nights in the bush. They've just come home, worn out." "The dogs must have made a kill this time and stayed beside it like wild animals, because they came home too gorged to eat, they just drank a lot of water and fell off to sleep like babies. . . ." "Mr. Daly rang up yesterday to say he saw Jock and Bill hunting along the hill behind his house. They've been chasing his oxen. We've got to beat them when they get home because if they don't learn they'll get themselves shot one of these dark nights. . . ."

They weren't there at all when we went home for the holidays. They had already been gone for nearly a week. But, or so we flattered ourselves, they sensed our return, for back they came, trotting gently side by side up the hill in the moonlight, two low black shapes moving above the accompanying black shapes of their shadows, their eyes gleaming red as the shafts of lamplight struck them. They greeted us, my brother and me, affectionately enough, but at once went off to sleep. We told ourselves that they saw us as creatures like them, who went off on long exciting hunts: but we knew it was sentimental nonsense, designed to take the edge off the hurt we felt because our animals, *our* dogs, cared so little about us. They went away again that night, or rather, in the first dawnlight. A week later they came home. They smelled foul, they must have been chasing a skunk or a wildcat. Their fur was matted with grass seeds and their skin lumpy with ticks. They drank water heavily, but refused food: their breath was fetid with the smell of meat.

They lay down to sleep and remained limp while we, each taking an animal, its sleeping head heavy in our laps, removed ticks, grass seeds, blackjacks. On Bill's forepaw was a hard ridge which I thought was an old scar. He sleep-whimpered when I touched it. It was a noose of plaited grass, used by Africans to snare birds. Luckily it had snapped off. "Yes," said my father, "that's how they'll end, both of them, they'll die in a trap, and serve them both right, they won't get any sympathy from me!"

We were frightened into locking them up for a day; but we could not stand their misery, and let them out again.

We were always springing gametraps of all kinds. For the big buck, the sable, the eland, the koodoo, the Africans bent a sapling across a path, held it by light string, and fixed on it a noose of heavy wire cut from a fence. For the smaller buck there were low traps with nooses of

fine baling wire or plaited tree fiber. And at the corners of the cultivated fields or at the edges of waterholes, where the birds and hares came down to feed, were always a myriad tiny tracks under the grass, and often across every track hung a small noose of plaited grass. Sometimes we spent whole days destroying these snares.

In order to keep the dogs amused, we took to walking miles every day. We were exhausted, but they were not, and simply went off at night as well. Then we rode bicycles as fast as we could along the rough farm tracks, with the dogs bounding easily beside us. We wore ourselves out, trying to please Jock and Bill, who, we imagined, knew what we were doing and were trying to humor us. But we stuck at it. Once, at the end of a glade, we saw the skeleton of a large animal hanging from a noose. Some African had forgotten to visit his traps. We showed the skeleton to Jock and Bill, and talked and warned and threatened, almost in tears, because human speech was not dogs' speech. They sniffed around the bones, yapped a few times up into our faces—out of politeness, we felt; and were off again into the bush.

At school we heard that they were almost completely wild. Sometimes they came home for a meal, or a day's sleep, "treating the house," my mother complained, "like a hotel."

Then fate struck, in the shape of a bucktrap.

One night, very late, we heard whining, and went out to greet them. They were crawling towards the front door, almost on their bellies. Their ribs stuck out, their coats stared, their eyes shone unhealthily. They fell on the food we gave them; they were starved. Then on Jock's neck, which was bent over the food bowl, showed the explanation: a thick strand of wire. It was not solid wire, but made of a dozen twisted strands, and had been chewed through, near the collar. We examined Bill's mouth: chewing the wire through must have taken a long time, days perhaps: his gums and lips were scarred and bleeding, and his teeth were worn down to stumps, like an old dog's teeth. If the wire had not been stranded, Jock would have died in the trap. As it was, he fell ill, his lungs were strained, since he had been half strangled with the wire. And Bill could no longer chew properly, he ate uncomfortably, like an old person. They stayed at home for weeks, reformed dogs, barked around the house at night, and ate regular meals.

Then they went off again, but came home more often than they had. Jock's lungs weren't right: he would lie out in the sun, gasping and wheezing, as if trying to rest them. As for Bill, he could only eat soft food. How, then, did they manage when they were hunting?

One afternoon we were shooting, miles from home, and we saw them. First we heard the familiar excited yapping coming towards us, about two miles off. We were in a large vlei, full of tall whitish grass which swayed and bent along a fast regular line: a shape showed, it was a duiker, hard to see until it was close because it was reddish brown in color, and the vlei had plenty of the pinkish feathery grass that turns a soft intense red in strong light. Being near sunset, the pale grass was on the verge of being invisible, like wires of white light; and the pink grass flamed and glowed; and the fur of the little buck shone red. It swerved suddenly. Had it seen us? No, it was because of Jock who had made a quick maneuvering turn from where he had been lying in the pink grass, to watch the buck, and behind it, Bill, pistoning along like a machine. Jock, who could no longer run fast, had turned the buck into Bill's jaws. We saw Bill bound at the little creature's throat, bring it down and hold it until Jock came in to kill it: his own teeth were useless now.

We walked over to greet them, but with restraint, for these two growling snarling creatures seemed not to know us, they raised eyes glazed with savagery, as they tore at the dead buck. Or rather, as Jock tore at it. Before we went away we saw Jock pushing over lumps of hot steaming meat towards Bill, who otherwise would have gone hungry.

They were really a team now; neither could function without the other. So we thought.

But soon Jock took to coming home from the hunting trips early, after one or two days, and Bill might stay out for a week or more. Jock lay watching the bush, and when Bill came, he licked his ears and face as if he had reverted to the role of Bill's mother.

Once I heard Bill barking and went to see. The telephone line ran through a vlei near the house to the farm over the hill. The wires hummed and sang and twanged. Bill was underneath the wires, which were a good fifteen feet over his head, jumping and barking at them: he was playing, out of exuberance, as he had done when a small puppy. But now it made me sad, seeing the strong dog playing all alone, while his friend lay quiet in the sun, wheezing from damaged lungs.

And what did Bill live on, in the bush? Rats, bird's eggs, lizards, anything *soft* enough? That was painful too, thinking of the powerful hunters in the days of their glory.

Soon we got telephone calls from neighbors: Bill dropped in, he finished off the food in our dog's bowl. . . . Bill seemed hungry, so we fed him. . . . Your dog Bill is looking very thin, isn't he? . . . Bill was around our chicken run—I'm sorry, but if he goes for the eggs, then . . .

Bill had puppies with a pedigreed bitch fifteen miles off: her owners were annoyed: Bill was not good enough for them, and besides there was the question of his "bad blood." All the puppies were destroyed. He was hanging around the house all the time, although he had been beaten, and they had even fired shots into the air to scare him off. Was there anything we could do to keep him at home? they asked; for they were tired of having to keep their bitch tied up.

No, there was nothing we could do. Rather, there was nothing we *would* do; for when Bill came trotting up from the bush to drink deeply out of Jock's bowl, and to lie for a while nose to nose with Jock, well, we could have caught him and tied him up, but we did not. "He won't last long anyway," said my father. And my mother told Jock that he was a sensible and intelligent dog; for she again sang praises of his nature and character just as if he had never spent so many glorious years in the bush.

I went to visit the neighbor who owned Bill's mate. She was tied to a post on the verandah. All night we were disturbed by a wild sad howling

Old English Hounds *by Sydenham Edwardes*

from the bush, and she whimpered and strained at her rope. In the morning I walked out into the hot silence of the bush, and called to him: Bill, Bill, it's me. Nothing, no sound. I sat on the slope of an antheap in the shade, and waited. Soon Bill came into view, trotting between the trees. He was very thin. He looked gaunt, stiff, wary—an old outlaw, afraid of traps. He saw me, but stopped about twenty yards off. He climbed halfway up another anthill and sat there in full sunlight, so I could see the harsh patches on his coat. We sat in silence, looking at each other. Then he lifted his head and howled, like the howl dogs give to the full moon, long, terrible, lonely. But it was morning, the sun calm and clear, and the bush without mystery. He sat and howled his heart out, his muzzle pointed away towards where his mate was chained. We could hear the faint whimperings she made, and the clink of her metal dish as she moved about. I couldn't stand

it. It made my flesh cold, and I could see the hairs standing up on my forearm. I went over to him and sat by him and put my arm around his neck as once, so many years ago, I had put my arm around his mother that moonlit night before I stole her puppy away from her. He put his muzzle on my forearm and whimpered, or rather cried. Then he lifted it and howled. . . . "Oh my God, Bill, don't do that, please don't, it's not the slightest use, please, dear Bill. . . ." But he went on, until suddenly he leaped up in the middle of a howl, as if his pain were too strong to contain in sitting, and he sniffed at me, as if to say: That's you, is it, well, good-bye—then he turned his wild head to the bush and trotted away.

Very soon he was shot, coming out of a chicken run early one morning with an egg in his mouth.

Jock was quite alone now. He spent his old age lying in the sun, his nose pointed out over the miles and miles of bush between our house and the mountains where he had hunted all those years with Bill. He was really an old dog, his legs were stiff, and his coat was rough, and he wheezed and gasped. Sometimes, at night, when the moon was up, he went out to howl at it, and we would say: He's missing Bill. He would come back to sit at my mother's knee, resting his head so that she could stroke it. She would say: "Poor old Jock, poor old boy, are you missing that bad dog Bill?"

Sometimes, when he lay dozing, he started up and went trotting on his stiff old legs through the house and the outhouses, sniffing everywhere and anxiously whining. Then he stood, upright, one paw raised, as he used to do when he was young, and gazed over the bush and softly whined. And we would say: "He must have been dreaming he was out hunting with Bill."

He got ill. He could hardly breathe. We carried him in our arms down the hill into the bush, and my mother stroked and patted him while my father put the gun barrel to the back of his head and shot him.

Variously, On Dogs

by JOHN BURROUGHS

Walking

YOU will generally fare better to take your dog than to invite your neighbor. Your cur-dog is a true pedestrian, and your neighbor is very likely a small politician. The dog enters thoroughly into the spirit of the enterprise; he is not indifferent or preoccupied; he is constantly sniffing adventure, laps at every spring, looks upon every field and wood as a new world to be explored, is ever on some fresh trail, knows something important will happen a little farther on, gazes with the true wonder-seeing eyes, whatever the spot or whatever the road, finds it good to be there—in short, is just that happy, delicious, excursive vagabond that touches one at so many points, and whose human prototype in a companion robs miles and leagues of half their power to fatigue.

Lark and I went on a long walk through the woods—found the nests of a robin, a kingbird, a bush sparrow, a hawk and a gray squirrel, and started a rabbit from her form. Besides, Lark had a tussle with a mink, and the mink got away. I first saw it coming up the creek on the rocks and stones. I sat down and waited for him to come up, but within a few rods of me he saw or smelled me and ran under some large stones. Then I poked him with my cane and he came boldly out in Lark's face. Lark caught him, but dropped him in a hurry, both dog and mink crying out; and then he escaped as quickly as if he had dropped into the earth. Where he went to, I have no idea.

A long walk to the woods through knee-deep snow, carried Lark on my shoulder a part of the way. No one had yet been to the woods, only a big dog whose track we saw. We started up several partridges over in cedar lane.

Considering the gulf that separates man from the lower orders, I often wonder how, for instance, we can have such a sense of companionship with a dog. What is it in the dog that so appeals to us? It is probably his quick responsiveness to our attention. He meets us halfway. He gives caress for caress. Then he is that lighthearted, irresponsible vagabond that so many of us half-consciously long to be if we could and dared. To a dog, a walk is the best of good fortunes; he sniffs adventure at every turn, is sure something thrilling will happen around the next bend in the path. How much he gets out of it that escapes me!—The excitement of all the different odors that my sense is too dull to take in. The ground to him is written over with the scent of game of some sort, the air is full of the lure of wild adventure. How human he is at such times!

He is out on a lark. In his spirit of hilarity he will chase hens, pigs, sheep, cows, which ordinarily he would give no heed to, just as boys abroad in the fields and woods will commit depredations that they would be ashamed of at home.

Some Specific Dogs

I knew a farmer in New York State who had a very large bob-tailed churn-dog by the name of Cuff. The farmer kept a large dairy and made a great deal of butter, and it was the business of Cuff to spend nearly half of each summer day treading the endless round of the churning-machine. During the remainder of the day he had plenty of time to rest and sleep, and sit on his hips and survey the landscape. One day, sitting thus, he discovered a woodchuck about forty rods from the house, on a steep side hill, feeding about near his hole, which was beneath a large rock. The old dog, forgetting his stiffness, and remembering the fun he had had with woodchucks in his earlier days, started off at his highest speed, vainly hoping to catch this one before he could get to his hole. But the woodchuck seeing the dog come laboring up the hill, sprang to the mouth of his den, and, when his pursuer was only a few rods off, whistled tauntingly and went in. This occurred several times, the old dog marching up the hill, and then marching down again, having had his labor for his pains. I suspect that he revolved the subject in his mind while he revolved the great wheel of the churning-machine, and that some turn or other brought him a happy thought, for, the next time, he showed himself a strategist. Instead of giving chase to the woodchuck when first discovered, he crouched down to the ground, and, resting his head on his paws, watched him. The woodchuck kept working away from his hole, lured by the tender clover, but, not unmindful of his safety, lifted himself upon his haunches every few moments, and surveyed the approaches. Presently, after the woodchuck had let himself down from one of these attitudes of observation and resumed his feeding, Cuff started swiftly but stealthily up the hill, precisely in the attitude of a cat when she is stalking a bird.

When the woodchuck rose up again, Cuff was perfectly motionless and half hid by the grass. When he again resumed his clover, Cuff sped up the hill as before, this time crossing a fence, but in a low place, and so nimbly that he was not discovered. Again the woodchuck was on the outlook, again Cuff was motionless and hugging the ground. As the dog neared his victim he was partially hidden by a swell in the earth, but still the woodchuck from his outlook reported "All right," when Cuff, having not twice as far to run as the woodchuck, threw all stealthiness aside and rushed directly for the hole. At that moment the woodchuck discovered his danger, and, seeing that it was a race for life, leaped as I never saw a marmot leap before. But he was two seconds too late, his retreat was cut off, and the powerful jaws of the old dog closed upon him.

The next season Cuff tried the same tactics again with like success, but when the third woodchuck had taken up his abode at the fatal hole, the old churner's wits and strength had begun to fail him, and he was baffled in each attempt to capture the animal.

When I go to my neighbor's house his dog of many strains, and a great crony of mine, becomes riotous with delight. He whines with joy, hops upon my lap, caresses me, then springs to the door, and with wagging tail and speaking looks and actions says, "Come on, let's off!" I open the door and say, "Go if you want to." He leaps back upon my lap and says, "No, no, not without you." Then to the door again with his eloquent pantomime, till I finally follow him forth into the street. Then he tears up the road to the woods, saying so plainly, "Better one hour of Slabsides than a week of humdrum at home." At such times, if we chance to meet his master or his mistress on the road, he heeds them not, and is absolutely deaf to their calls.

We expect every hour will be his [Rab's] last. It is almost like losing a child. Indeed, half the people do not mourn so much over the death of their children as we do over Rab. He is a homely cur, but you can hardly imagine how much he has been to us. He has been the life and light of the place for a year . . .

Rab is dead, and it seems as if a chapter in my life had closed. We buried him this morning by the rock near the path to the spring, where we shall pass and repass in all our farm work, and where the poor dog can hear the footfalls of the horse he loved so well.

I may live to be an old man, but I shall not live long enough to forget Rab. There was nothing between my heart and his; he was wholly within the circle of my most private affection; he touched me warm and close. I do not know in what way I should have loved a child differently —more deeply, perhaps, but not more genuinely. If my love for Rab was not the precious gold of the heart, it certainly was the silver. In my younger days I should have thought less of him, but, next to the members of my own family, Death could not have singled out an object half so precious and necessary to me. So great is my need of a comrade, an untalking companion, on my walks, or boating, or about the farm; and, next to one's bosom friend, what companion like a dog? Your thought is his thought, your wish is his wish, and where you desire to go, that place of all others is preferable to him. It was bliss enough for Rab to be with me, and it was a never-failing source of pleasure for me to be with Rab. Why should my grief be so acute? Only a dog. My neighbor, or my friend, dies, or my man-servant, or maid-servant, who has served me long, and my grief is far less poignant. My dog is a part of myself. He has no separate or independent existence; he lives wholly in and for me. But my friend, or my neighbor, revolves in an orbit of his own. He has his own schemes and purposes, and touches me only casually, or not closely at all. My dog is interested in everything I do. Then he represents the spirit of holiday, of fun, of adventure. The world is full of wonders to him, and in a journey of a mile he has many adventures. Every journey is an excursion, a sally into an unknown land, teeming with curiosities. A dog lives only ten or fifteen years, but think how much he crowds into that space, how much energy and vitality he lives up!

Hounds

It is amusing when the hunter starts out of a winter morning, to see the hound probe the old tracks to determine how recent they are. He sinks his nose down deep in the snow so as to exclude the air from above, then draws a long full breath, giving sometimes an audible snort. If there remains the least effluvium of the fox, the hound will detect it. If it be very slight, it only sets his tail wagging; if it be strong, it unloosens his tongue.

A fox cannot trip along the top of a stone wall so lightly but that he will leave enough of himself to betray his course to the hound for hours afterward. . . . The fox baffles the hound most upon a hard crust of frozen snow: the scent will not hold to the smooth, beadlike granules.

Judged by the eye alone, the fox is the lightest and most buoyant creature that runs. His soft wrapping of fur conceals the muscular play and effort that are so obvious in the hound that pursues him, and he comes bounding along precisely as if blown by a gentle wind. His massive tail is carried as if it floated upon the air by its own lightness.

The hound is not remarkable for his fleetness, but how he will hang!—often running until late into the night, and sometimes till morning, from ridge to ridge, from peak to peak; now on the mountain, now crossing the valley, now playing about a large slope of uplying pasture fields. . . .

The hound is a most interesting dog. How solemn and long-visaged he is—how peaceful and well disposed! He is the Quaker among dogs. All the viciousness and currishness seem to have been weeded out of him: he seldom quarrels, or fights, or plays, like other dogs. Two strange hounds, meeting for the first time, behave as civilly toward each other as two men. I know a hound ["Singer"] that has an ancient, wrinkled, human, faraway look that reminds one of the bust of Homer among the Elgin marbles. He looks like the mountains toward which his heart yearns so much.

The hound is a great puzzle to the farm dog; the latter, attracted by his baying, comes barking and snarling through the fields, bent on picking a quarrel; he intercepts the hound, snubs and insults and annoys him in every way possible, but the hound heeds him not. If the dog attacks him, he gets away as best he can and goes on with the trail; the cur bristles and barks and struts about for a while, then goes back to the house, evidently thinking the hound a lunatic, which he is, for the time being—a monomaniac—the slave and victim of one idea. I saw the master of a hound one day arrest him in full course, to give one of the hunters time to get to a certain runway; the dog cried and struggled to free himself, and would listen neither to threats nor caresses. Knowing he must be hungry, I offered him my lunch, but he would not touch it. I put it in his mouth, but he threw it contemptuously from him. We coaxed and petted and reassured him, but he was under a spell; he was bereft of all thought or desire but the one passion to pursue that trail.

One marked difference between the greyhound and all other hounds and dogs is that it can pick up its game while running at full speed, a feat that no other dog can do. The foxhound, or farm dog, will run over a fox or a rabbit many times without being able to seize it.

They & We and They

One's pleasure with a dog is unmixed. There are no setbacks. They make no demands upon you, as does a child; no care, no interruption, no intrusion. If you are busy, or want to sleep, or read, or be with your friend, they are as if they were not. When you want them, they are at your elbow, and ready for any enterprise. And the measure of your love they always return, heaped up.

. . . A dog loves to play at the game of hunting the ball or the stone which you throw, because this act is in line with his instincts, and he never tires of the fun. Of course a dog can be trained to do almost anything, but to enlighten his mind about the whys and the wherefores of the thing is quite another matter. You can train an animal to act, but can you train it to think? Of course

your dog or your horse could not be trained to do its trick did it not possess certain powers that may be called mental, such as power of attention, power of imitation, power of association and the capacity to feel a stronger will. But these powers are all phases of the animal's instinctive activities, and do not presuppose judgment or reason. When we train an animal, we make, as it were, an artificial channel for its mental currents to flow in, and they flow there without conscious choice or self-direction, as water flows in the channel we make for it . . .

In many ways an animal is like a child. What comes first in a child is simple perception and memory and association of memories, and these make up the main sum of an animal's intelligence. The child goes on developing till it reaches the power of reflection and generalization—a stage of mentality that the animal never attains to.

All animal life is specialized; each animal is an expert in its own line of work—the work of its tribe. Beavers do the work of beavers, they cut down trees and build dams, and all beavers do it alike and with the same degree of untaught skill. This is instinct, or unthinking nature.

On a hot day a dog will often dig down to fresh earth to get cooler soil to lie on. Or he will go and lie in the creek. All dogs do these things. Now if a dog were seen to carry stones and sods to dam up the creek to make a deeper pool to lie in, then he would, in a measure, be imitating the beavers, and this, in the dog, could fairly be called an act of reason, because it is not a necessity of the conditions of his life; it would be of the nature of an afterthought.

Wild animals may be trained, but not educated. We multiply impressions upon them without adding to their store of knowledge, because they cannot evolve general ideas from their sense impressions. Here we reach their limitations. . . . You may train your dog so that he will bound around you when he greets you without putting his feet upon you. But do you suppose the fond creature ever comes to know why you do not want his feet upon you? If he does, then he takes the step in general knowledge to which I have referred.

In denying thought or free intelligence in animals, an exception should undoubtedly be made in favor of the dog. I have said elsewhere that the dog is almost a human product; he has been the companion of man so long, and has been so loved by him, that he has come to partake, in a measure at least, of his master's nature. If the dog does not at times think, reflect, he does something so like it that I can find no other name for it. Take so simple an incident as this, which is of common occurrence: A collie dog is going along the street in advance of his master's team. He comes to a point where the road forks; he takes, say, the road to the left and trots along it a few rods, and then, half turning, suddenly pauses and looks back at the team. Has he not been struck by the thought, "I do not know which way my master is going: I will wait and see"? If the dog in such cases does not reflect, what does he do? Can we find any other word for his act? To ask a question by word or deed involves some sort of mental process, however rudimentary. Is there any other animal that would act as the collie did under like circumstances?... The dog is often quick to resent a kick, be it from man or beast, but I have never known him to show anger at the door that slammed to and hit him. Probably if the door held him by his tail or his limb, it would quickly receive the imprint of his teeth.

The dog undoubtedly exhibits more human traits than any other animal, and this by reason of his long association with man. There are few of our ordinary emotions that the dog does not share, as joy, fun, love of adventure, jealousy, suspicion, comradeship, helpfulness, guilt, covetousness and the like—or feelings analogous to these—the dog-version of them. I am not sure but that the dog is capable of contempt. The behavior at times of a large dog toward a small, the slights he will put upon him,

is hardly capable of any other interpretation. . . .

At any rate, the dog does many things that we can name only in terms applicable to ourselves. My dog coaxes me to go for a walk, he coaxes to get upon my lap, he coaxes for the food I am eating. When I upbraid him, he looks repentant and humiliated. When I whip him, he cries. When I praise him, he bounds; when I greet him in the morning, he whines with joy. It is not the words that count with him, it is the tone of the voice.

When I start out for a walk, he waits and dances about till he sees which way I am going. It seems as if he must at such times have some sort of mental process similar to my own under like circumstances. Or, is his whole behavior automatic—his attitude of eagerness, expectancy, inquiry and all? As automatic as the wagging of his tail when he is pleased, or as his bristling up when he is angry? It evinces some sort of mental action, but the nature of it is hard to divine. When he sits looking vaguely out upon the landscape, or rests his chin upon his paws and gazes into the fire, I wish I knew if there were anything like currents of thought, or reminiscence, or anticipations passing through his mind. When I speak sternly to him and he cowers down, or throws himself upon his back, and puts up his paws pleadingly, I wish I knew just the state of his mind then. One day my dog deserted me while I was hunting, and when I returned, and before I had spoken a word to him, he came creeping up to me in the most abject way, threw himself over, and put up his pleading paws, as if begging forgiveness. Was he? We should call it that in a person. Yet I remember that I upbraided him when he first showed the inclination to desert me, and that fact may account for his subsequent behavior.

When you speak to your dog in a certain way, why does he come up to you and put out his front legs and stretch, and then stretch his hind legs, and maybe open his mouth and gape? Is it an affectation, or a little embarrassment because he does not know what you are saying? All dogs do it. The human traits of the dog are very obvious.

The Cavalier's Pets *by Sir Edwin Landseer*

The most wonderful thing about the dog is not his intelligence, but his capacity for loving. We can call it by no other name. The more you love your dog, the more your dog loves you. You can win your neighbor's dog any time by loving him more than your neighbor does. He will follow you to the ends of the earth if you love him enough. He may become so attached to you that he fairly divines your thoughts, not through his own power of thought, but through his intense sympathy and the freemasonry of love.

He is the ideal companion because he gives you a sense of companionship without disturbing your sense of solitude. Your mind is alone, but your heart has company. He is below your horizon, but something comes up from his life that mingles with your own. This friend walks with you, or sits with you, and yet he does not come between you and your book, or between you and the holiday spirit you went out to woo. He is the visible embodiment of the holiday spirit; he shows you how to leave dull care behind; he goes forth with you in the spirit of eternal youth, sure that something beautiful, or curious, or adventurous will happen at any turn of the road. He finds no places dull, he is alert with expectancy every moment.

In him you have good fellowship always on tap, as it were. Say the word and he bounds to your side, or leads the way to the woods.

My dog enjoys a walk more than I do; his nature-study is quite as real as mine is, though of a totally different kind; the sense of smell that plays such a part in his excursions plays little or none in mine; and the eye and the mind which contribute so much to my enjoyment, are almost a blank with him. He enjoys the open fire, too, and a warm, soft bed and a good dinner. All his purely animal enjoyments are as keen or keener than mine, but has he any other?

How different his interest in cats is from mine, and in dogs, and in men! He is not interested in the landscape as a whole; I doubt very much if he sees it at all; but he is interested in what the landscape holds for him—the woodchuck hole, or the squirrel's den or the fox's trail. His life is entirely the life of the senses, and on this ground we meet and are boon companions.

If he has any mind-life, any ideas, if he ever looks back over the past, or forward into the future, I see no evidence of it. When there is nothing doing, he sleeps; apparently he could sleep all the time, if there were nothing better going on.

I would not be unjust or unsympathetic toward the current tendency to exalt the lower animals to the human sphere. I would only help my reader to see things as they are, and stimulate him to love the animals as animals, and not as men. Nothing is gained by self-deception. The best discipline of life is that which prepares us to face the facts, no matter what they are. Such sweet companionship as one may have with a dog, simply because he is a dog, and does not invade your own exclusive sphere! He is, in a way, like your youth come back to you, and taking form—all instinct and joy and adventure. You can ignore him, and he is not offended; you can reprove him and he still loves you; you can hail him and he bounds with joy; you can camp and tramp and ride with him, and his interest and curiosity and adventurous spirit give to the days and the nights the true holiday atmosphere. With him you are alone and not alone; you have both companionship and solitude. Who would have him more human or less canine? He divines your thought through his love, and feels your will in the glance of your eye. He is not a rational being, yet he is a very susceptible one, and touches us at so many points that we come to look upon him with a fraternal regard.

Notes on the Authors

Unless otherwise indicated, the authors are living. Those for whom no nationality is given are American.

J. R. Ackerley (British, 1896–1967) was a memoirist, playwright, novelist, poet and editor. For many years he was the literary editor of the *Listener*, published by BBC. Among his books are *We Think the World of You, E. M. Forster: A Portrait, My Father and Myself* and *My Dog Tulip*.

An Anonymous Nineteenth-Century Sportsman (British) is the unnamed author of a letter concerning several of his dogs to Edward Jesse. The letter appears in Jesse's lengthy introduction to his *Anecdotes of Dogs*, published in 1858.

Vance Bourjaily is an essayist and novelist whose short works have appeared in such publications as Harper's, Esquire, The Saturday Evening Post, Horizon and the Atlantic Monthly. His books include *Brill Among the Ruins, The Unnatural Enemy, Country Matters* and *Now Playing at Canterbury*.

Dr. John Brown (Scottish, 1810–1882) was a physician, essayist and belletrist who wrote frequently on dogs and rural topics and published three volumes under the series title *Horae Subsecivae*.

John Burroughs (1837–1921) was a naturalist and essayist who wrote often of the Hudson Valley and the Catskills. Among his many collections are *Riverby, Ways of Nature, Field and Study* and *The Summit of the Years*. The extracts in this anthology are drawn from various of his essays, journals and letters.

Edwin H. Colbert is a scientist and author associated with several universities and scientific institutions including the American Museum of Natural History where he served, among other capacities, as Curator of Vertebrate Paleontology. He is the author of numerous scientific papers and essays. Among his books, both textbooks and those intended for a more general audience, are *Men and Dinosaurs, Evolution of the Vertebrates* and *Millions of Years Ago*.

William Cowper (British, 1731–1800) was a poet who wrote frequently on country life and natural beauty.

Phil Drabble (British) is the author of several books on dogs and rural subjects and discusses these topics regularly on British television and radio. He writes a weekly column for the *Birmingham Evening Mail* and is personally responsible for the televising of the annual sheep dog trials in Britain.

Robert Dovers (Australian) spent five years in the Antarctic on research expeditions sponsored by the French and Australian governments, and was decorated by both for his work. He had an experience with sledge dogs there, which he recounted in his book, *Huskies*.

"Elizabeth of the German Garden" (British, 1886–1941) was the Countess Mary Annette Russell. She was related to and kept company with several literary figures of her day. She wrote under the pseudonyms "Elizabeth of the German Garden" and, later, simply "Elizabeth." Among her books are *Elizabeth and Her German Garden, The Enchanted April, Mr. Skeffington* and the autobiographical *All the Dogs of My Life*.

Theodore Gaza (Greek, 1400–1475) was a scholar who fled to Italy when the Turks conquered his homeland, and there became one of the leading forces in the revival of learning in fifteenth-century Europe. He taught in major universities, participated in important religious councils, wrote widely and translated many classical Greek authors, including Aristotle, into Latin.

John Graves is a writer who has taught college English and lives in Texas on a small farm. He has written on conservation subjects for the United States Department of the Interior and the Sierra Club. His essays have appeared in such publications as American Heritage, Esquire, Holiday and the Atlantic Monthly. Many are included in his collection *From a Limestone Ledge*. He is also the author of *Goodbye to a River*.

Lars Gustafsson (Swedish) is a critic, poet and novelist who has published widely in Sweden and in other countries. Among his works that have appeared in English are *Selected Poems, Warm Rooms and Cold, Forays into Swedish Poetry* and the novel, *Death of a Beekeeper*.

James Herriot (Scottish) is a veterinarian who lives and practices in Yorkshire, England, and whose quartet of books detailing his long years of practice have won him an international readership over the last decade. The first was *All Creatures Great and Small*, the most recent *The Lord God Made Them All*.

Edward Hoagland has written novels and short stories, but has concentrated over the last several years on the essay. He has been published widely in such magazines as Harper's, Esquire, The New Yorker and The Paris Review, and his work has been collected into several volumes, including *The Courage of Turtles, Red Wolves and Black Bears* and *The Tugman's Passage*.

Richard Joseph (1910–1976) was a journalist and travel writer who published widely in magazines and is the author of several travel books as well as the memoir, *A Letter to the Man Who Killed My Dog*. The original letter, which appears in this anthology, was first printed in a local newspaper, then picked up and reprinted across the country, resulting in Mr. Joseph receiving more than fifty thousand letters in response to it.

Edward Jesse (British, 1780–1868) was an essayist and writer on natural history. Among his several books are *Gleanings in Natural History, An Angler's Rambles* and *Anecdotes of Dogs*. He also edited Izaak Walton's *The Compleat Angler*.

David Lehman's poems have appeared in Poetry, The Paris Review, Partisan Review, Shenandoah and the Times Literary Supplement. He has edited the anthology *Beyond Amazement: New Essays on John Ashbery* and is co-editor of *James Merrill: Essays in Criticism*.

Doris Lessing (British) is a novelist, playwright, essayist and short-story writer who was raised on a farm in Southern Rhodesia. She has been published widely throughout the world. She is the author of, among others, *The Golden Notebook, A Man and Two Women, Children of Violence* and, most recently, the volumes under the series title *Canopus in Argos*.

Konrad Lorenz (Austrian) is a zoologist and professor of comparative anatomy and animal psychology who has taught, among other places, at the Albertus University of Königsberg and under the auspices of the Max Planck Foundation for the Promotion of Science. He has written widely and among his books are *King Solomon's Ring, The Evolution and Modification of Behavior, On Aggression* and *Man Meets Dog*.

Donald McCaig lives in the western mountains of Virginia where he and his wife raise sheep and work border collies. He is the author of *The Butte Polka*, a novel, the forthcoming *Nop's Trials*, a novel, as well as articles for the Atlantic Monthly, Harper's and other magazines.

Maurice Maeterlinck (Belgian, 1862–1949), a Nobel laureate, was a poet, dramatist, essayist and nonfiction writer. He was a prolific author and leading figure in the Belgian and French Symbolist movements. His work of natural history, *The Life of the Bee,* remains a standard reference.

Farley Mowat (Canadian) is a wildlife biologist and the author of several nonfiction books, including *Never Cry Wolf, The Dog Who Wouldn't Be, The People of the Deer* and *A Whale for the Killing.*

John Muir (Scottish-American, 1838–1914) emigrated from Scotland to America when he was a young boy. He became an extraordinary naturalist who covered most of the American wilderness alone and on foot during his lifetime. He was instrumental in winning government protection for the Grand Canyon and Arizona's Petrified Forest, was one of the founders of the Sierra Club and its first president. He was a prolific essayist and keeper of journals. Among his collected works are *A Thousand-Mile Walk to the Gulf, The Mountains of California, The Yosemite* and *Travels in Alaska.*

Jerrold Mundis, the editor of this anthology, is a novelist, short-story and nonfiction writer whose short work has appeared in such publications as Harper's Weekly, New York and American Heritage. Among his books are the novels *Gerhardt's Children* and the forthcoming *The Retreat,* and a work of nonfiction, *The Guard Dog.* He has bred and trained German shepherds for many years and has lectured widely on dogs.

Ian Niall (British) was born in Scotland and is the author of several novels and books of nonfiction, among them *Portrait of a Country Artist,* a biography of C. F. Tunnicliffe who was widely known for his paintings of birds. Niall has also been a con-

tributing editor to Country Life, writing on outdoor subjects, for more than thirty years.

Leslie Norris (Welsh) is a poet, essayist and short-story writer whose work, often dealing with country and rural subjects, has appeared in The New Yorker, the Atlantic Monthly, Esquire and Audubon Magazine. Several of his stories have been collected into the book, *Sliding.*

H. Allen Smith (1907–1976) was a columnist, humorist, essayist and nonfiction writer. Among his books are *Low Man on a Totem Pole, Life in a Putty Knife Factory* and *Lost in the Horse Latitudes.*

John Steinbeck (1902–1968) was a novelist, short-story writer and Nobel laureate. His many books include *The Grapes of Wrath, Of Mice and Men, In Dubious Battle, East of Eden* and a nonfiction account of a journey across the United States with his dog, *Travels with Charley.*

James Thurber (1894–1961) was for many years a contributing editor to The New Yorker. He was a humorist, short-story writer, essayist and a deft and comic social commentator. His works have been collected into several books, including *My Life and Hard Times, Men, Women, and Dogs* and *The Thurber Carnival.*

Marcus Terentius Varro (Roman, 116–27 B.C.) was a brilliant polymath who wrote more than six hundred books on a vast range of subjects. *De Re Rustica,* in three volumes, is a practical guide to farming, based upon the author's experience running his Sabine estates. He began the book when he was eighty.

E. B. White is an essayist, poet and novelist who was for many years a contributing editor to The New Yorker. Among his collected works are *One Man's Meat, The Second Tree from the Corner* and *The Points of my Compass.* He is the author of two juvenile classics, *Charlotte's Web* and *Stuart Little,* and also edited and amplified for latter-day writers *The Elements of Style* with William Strunk, Jr.